Steve From

The Reincarnation
of Bennett McKinney

NONE
THE
LESS
PRESS

Lenexa, Kansas

Printed in the United States of America
Library of Congress Control Number: 2002112818
ISBN: 1-932053-06-9

Book design by Z-N

NONE
THE
LESS
PRESS

http://www.nonethelesspress.com

10   9   8   7   6   5   4   3   2   1

This book is dedicated to my parents, Jim and Mary Jo From, and to the memory of John Tomlinson...as long as we're alive, you live on in our hearts.

Contents

Chapter 1: January 1987

The door of Room 128 in the Rapid City Holiday Inn was wide open. Just inside, a few beer cans and an Old Crow bottle lay empty on the floor. All of the lights in the room were on and the *Late, Late Show* was on the TV with the volume turned down. The two big double beds against the west wall were both messed up, and a table lamp was lying on the bed to the right. A chair was tipped over by the other door leading to the swimming pool area and beside the door was a table supporting more empty beer cans and a half-full quart of Old Crow. Everything was quiet, but there had obviously either been a wild party, a drunken fight, or both.

The sound of laughter came down the hall. A drunken voice sang out and echoed off the walls, "She's wild and she's woolly, my San Antose Roan!"

The laughter got closer and louder. So did the singing, "She's wild and she's woolly, my San Antose Roan!"

"Is that the only verse you know?" asked another voice.

"Yep," said the first.

"Then why don't you sing another song?"

"You picked a fine time to leave me, Lucille!"

Through the door came a big, black cowboy hat. Under it was a little, short cowboy with black hair, wire framed glasses, a big nose, and a wide grin, singing, "You picked a fine time to leave me, Lucille!" He found an upright chair and plopped down in it as if he hadn't been off his feet for days. His name was Bennett McKinney. Like everyone with him, he had come to Rapid City to compete in the rodeo as a professional. Unlike everyone with him, he was strictly a bullrider. He had placed fourth that day in Rapid City's big indoor arena and was partying it up on the last day of January.

Next in the door stumbled T.J. Jergenson and Dave Whitney. T.J. was a tall, thin rather dumb-looking cowboy, with a dark complexion and black hair. His long neck carried his head a good way ahead of the rest of his ostrich-like body. The back brim of his gray felt hat barely covered his neck. He had a huge lower lip that stuck out as far as his nose, which was crooked from accidentally kissing a spinning bull on the head six weeks earlier. His left eye was a little messed up, too. The pupil and cornea were fine, but the white of his eye was still bright red. T.J.'s tallness wasn't at all in his body. His legs were so long he had a hard time buying jeans long enough to fit him. He was a bullrider, and on a small bull he could almost wrap his legs all the way around a bull's belly and hook his spurs underneath.

Standing next to T.J., Dave Whitney looked like a little kid. The top of his black cowboy hat wasn't even as high as T.J.'s shoulders. His curly brown hair stuck out of the bottom of his hat, covering part of his ears and the back of his neck. He was twenty-six and had the face of a cute fourteen-year-old. His eyes weren't big, but they weren't little or squinty either. His nose wasn't big and crooked or little and straight. It was just a regular good-looking nose, turned up slightly. He had no dimples, no wrinkles on the sides of his mouth. In fact, he didn't have a scar or wrinkle on his whole face. Even though he was considered good-looking, girls who knew him very well didn't like him. He never had much to say, drank way too much, and didn't give a damn what people thought about him. Dave had won a second in the saddle bronc riding that night. He was wearing a long yellow rain slicker and each arm cradled a full bottle of whiskey.

Shot Palmer dragged his lanky frame in next, stumbling over Dave's raincoat. Though not as big as T.J., Shot was rather tall and wiry, and surprisingly quick. He could be meaner than hell, and actually enjoyed pain. These qualities are the makings of a good bull-fighter, which was an understatement of Shot. Many people are loud and obnoxious when they get drunk, but Shot was loud and obnoxious anyway. These qualities are the makings of a good clown, which was also an understatement of Shot. It's rare in rodeo to find someone as gifted in both fighting bulls and entertaining the crowd all throughout the show. The only things that kept this twenty-nine-year- old comic daredevil from becoming rich were a few doctor bills, two sets of monthly alimony payments, child support payments, and a third wife who was steadily falling out of love. He seldom covered his thick, red mop-top with a hat. He had a mean-looking face, his jaw favoring the right, and his nose favoring the left. He had extra-thin protruding lips, and the bottom tip of his right ear was gone. His brother had cut it off and fed it to the cat when they were kids.

Last but not least came Randy Corey. Quiet and sober, Randy placed his brown Stetson upside down, as always, for good luck, in the overhead closet. Grinning, as always, he showed off a perfect set of bright white teeth. His medium length, bright blond hair looked almost yellow. Tall and handsome was Randy, but not dark. He had a red complexion and a quiet disposition. No alcohol or tobacco for this cowboy. Sit-ups and push-ups were a daily ritual and jogging was a priority every chance he got. When traveling to rodeos, Randy would have the driver let him out of the vehicle about five miles from the rodeo grounds when time allowed so that he could jog the rest of the way. He credited dedication and clean living for his being such a tough steer wrestler and saddle bronc rider. Although he drew a bad steer that day and didn't pick up a check in that event, he did win the bronc riding, edging out Dave Whitney by one point with a 79 score. Randy placed an overturned chair in its upright position, sat down at the table, and began playing with an ashtray, spinning it on its edge. Like a top, the ashtray made its way to the edge of the table, then jumped off onto the carpet and rolled over to Bennett McKinney's feet.

"Here now!" yelled Bennett in a playful but scolding voice. "Let's not be playing with the ashtrays! You can put an eye out that way!" He picked up the ashtray and, out of orneriness and drunkenness, flung it at Randy's face. Randy's sharp reflexes saved him from getting nailed in the forehead as he ducked under the soaring projectile, allowing it to crash into the wall.

"Thought it was gonna hit ya, didn't ya?" said Bennett, his hat pulled so far down on his head that the tops of his ears were bent over. Then he looked around and noticed the room. "My God, this place is a mess!"

"You and T.J. tore the hell out of it giving each other piggy-back rides," grinned Randy.

T.J., already stripped down to his jeans and about to go to bed, came to life when he heard the word 'piggy-back'. "Give me another piggy-back ride, Bennett!"

"No! Get away from me, Jergenson!" argued Bennett. "You'll fall and bust your head!"

Not hearing a word Bennett had said, T.J. jerked him out of the chair, stood up on it, and said, "OK, hold still!" He threw his long left leg over Bennett's shoulder. Bennett, being considerably inebriated for a task like this, found it difficult to keep his feet directly under his body. As T.J. tried to bring his other leg up, Bennett stumbled over the chair and table, knocking the lamp over with them and scattering empty beer cans across the room.

Everyone except Dave Whitney, who was already passed out on the bed, laughed long and loud.

"We better quit this," T.J. pointed out. "I could fall and bust my head!"

"Or poke an eye out!" warned Bennett as he searched around for his glasses. He flung his big, black hat across the room, put his glasses back on, and said, "We better cut this out. They're liable to kick us outta here or call the cops on us."

Shot Palmer, who had been lying on the other bed quietly watching the whole spectacle, took a big drink of whiskey, then threw his pillow, hitting Bennett in the face.

"Hey! What's that for?" asked Bennett.

"For havin' a big nose!" was Shot's reply.

Bennett started to laugh but was interrupted by a hiccup.

"Here," Shot bellowed out, "Take this, too!" He tossed the open, half-full bottle to Bennett. Bennett caught it, but a stream of whiskey splashed out and hit him in the glasses.

"Ho! Nice shot!" cheered T.J., who was back on the bed with Dave.

Bennett took off his glasses and carelessly slammed them down on the floor. "Want to see me kill the bottle?" he asked.

"Yeah!" "Kill it, McKinney!" "Do it!" came voices from all over the room.

Bennett stood up, grabbed the bottle around its neck and pretended to strangle it. Again the room reverberated with laughter. Then Bennett picked the pillow up off the floor and hit Dave Whitney with it. Whitney didn't budge.

"Sheesh. He's out cold," said Bennett, thumping him on the head with his forefinger. "Hee, hee, hee... this is kinda fun," he said as he lightly slapped Dave across the face. Then he hollered into his ear, "Hey, Stupid! Wake up!" Whitney still didn't twitch a muscle.

"Think he's dead?" asked Shot.

"We better get his clothes off and let him sleep," said Randy, not smiling as much this time.

Bennett grabbed Whitney by the collar and sat him up. As Bennett tried to take his shirt off, Dave flopped around like a rag doll. Randy worked on his boots and socks.

"Hell, he'll be alright," said T.J. as he took another swig of whiskey.

Together, Bennett and Randy got his jeans off and put him under the covers.

"Looks like a good idea," said Shot Palmer as he fumbled with the buttons on his shirt. "I'm goin' to bed, too."

"Hey, Shot, where's the little woman?" asked Bennett.

"Aw, she locked me outta the Ramada."

"What's the matter with her?" T.J. asked as he tried to suppress a belch.

"She's a little P.O.'d that I wouldn't take her to the dance tonight."

"That bitch!" said Bennett. "Well, don't worry about it, ol' buddy. Just grab a blanket and find a soft spot on the floor."

About that time Dave pushed his blankets out of the way and reached up to scratch the bridge of his nose. Then he settled back down and was still again.

Grinning mischievously, Bennett ran his finger ever so lightly across Dave's nose, jerking it back as Dave unconsciously hit himself in the face, causing more loud laughter throughout the room.

"Hoo, hoo, hoo! I got an idea!" laughed Bennett as he ran to the bathroom. Seconds later he came back with a can of shaving cream.

Whitney was sleeping on his right side with both hands in front of him. Bennett filled Whitney's right hand with lather. Everyone else sat around wondering what Bennett was doing. He took the long pheasant feather out of Whitney's hat and tickled him on the nose. Now everyone knew what was supposed to happen. Suddenly the room was full of 'awwws' of disappointment when Whitney reached up and rubbed his nose with the wrong hand. Saying nothing, Bennett filled Whitney's other hand. Again he tickled him on the nose. Whitney unconsciously reached up, scratched his nose, putting a little dab of cream on its tip. The shaving cream must have tickled his nose, because he then rubbed his whole face with both hands, turning it pure white. Drunken cowboys rolled on the floor laughing. Pretty quick, as if allergic to the shaving cream, Whitney started sneezing, causing a miniature snowstorm on his side of the bed.

Shot Palmer was caught by the surprise of his own sudden laughter as a big swig of whiskey went down the wrong pipe and back up again, sending T.J. Jergenson gagging all the way to the bathroom.

When everything had settled down, Bennett decided to do Dave a favor and wipe off his face. "Here," he chuckled as he used Dave's shirt as a washcloth, "Let me get this stuff off your face. You're a damn mess!"

Whitney, still asleep, grabbed the shirt from Bennett and wiped the cream off his face. Then he started to put the shirt on.

Bennett was laughing so hard that he could hardly stop Whitney. "Don't do that! Hee, hee, hee! You're gonna get it all over! Here... hey...

give me the shirt!" By the time Bennett got the shirt away from him, Whitney's back was smeared with lather. Bennett finally sat back in his chair and threw his hands in the air. "Aw, the hell with it!"

Randy Corey, who still had streams of laughter trickling down over his red cheeks, finally caught his breath, "Oh, I wish Dave coulda' been awake to see this!" he sighed.

They sat around and laughed a while longer and were still giggling like schoolgirls as everyone except Bennett kicked their clothes off and settled down for bed. "So," he said as he took his last drink of Old Crow and let out a little cough, "Shot, how's the married life treatin' ya?"

"Real good, Bennett," came the reply, "real good."

"Real good for you," interrupted T.J. "You treat her like a slave."

"A slave?" Shot repeated, sounding a bit surprised. "What the hell makes you think..."

"She'll do anything you tell her to," T.J. interrupted again, egging on an argument.

"So, what's wrong with that?" Bennett asked. "I could use a woman like that."

"Do this! Do that!" mocked T.J., "Bring me a beer! Drive the truck!"

"So? She ain't complainin," said Shot.

"I sure don't know why," T.J. came back again. "I treat my dog better than you treat her."

"You ain't got a dog," said Bennett.

"And I'll tell you why she don't complain," Shot stated as he sat up in bed and raised a finger. "It's because she loves me and she knows she's lucky to have me."

"I'd rather have herpes," grumbled T.J.

"Well," said Bennett thoughtfully, "she must not be too much of a slave if she locked you out of your room."

"Yeah, Jergenson," Shot agreed defiantly, "you ball blastin' butt buster!"

Bennett kicked off his cowboy boots and rubbed his toes through his socks. "Besides," he added, "you'd rather be here with us anyhow. Wouldn't you, Shot?"

"I don't know," Shot replied. "She ain't bad in bed, you know."

"No, I don't know," said T.J. "Tell me about it."

Shot grinned. "You just use your imagination."

"I don't know if I can remember what it's like," mused T.J. "It's been so since long since I've had any..."

"Oh, yeah!" interrupted Bennett.

"Tell us all about it!" hollered Shot. "How about Alice Ketchum?"

"Alice Ketchum?" T.J. blurted. "Are you kiddin'?"

"Don't act innocent, boy!" Shot shot back. "I know all about you and her at Franklin, Tennessee!"

"Hey!" argued T.J. "That was Corey!"

Randy, who had been trying to sleep with no success at all, came to life. "The hell it was!" he hollered.

"The hell it wasn't," claimed T.J.

"I think Randy was with Alice's chubby little friend," said Bennett.

"Anyway," added Shot, "all you guys are livin' in sin and I ain't."

"Oh, what's this?" hollered Bennett. "All of us are sinners. You're on your third wife, but your soul is saved?"

"I don't run around on her," said Shot.

"Well, this is the first one you ain't runnin' around on," said Randy.

"I've changed my ways, boys," Shot testified. "And you ought to think about doin' the same."

"Don't preach at me," said Bennett. "I know you too well."

"Now that you've been saved, I suppose you're goin' to church tomorrow," said T.J.

"Maybe I will," replied Shot. "What about it?"

"Yeah," agreed Randy. "Me and Shot just might go to church together."

"Aw," groaned Bennett, "are you kiddin'?"

"Hell no!" said Randy.

"I just can't see you on your knees," said Bennett.

"We don't get on our knees in my church," claimed Randy.

"What are you," T.J. snapped sarcastically, "some kind of atheist?"

"No!" Randy snapped back, "I'm Baptist."

"When I was a kid we had to kneel down," said T.J.

"You was Catholic," said Randy.

"How'd you know?" asked Bennett.

" 'Cause Catholics kneel down," replied Randy. "I think you Catholics gotta go to confession, too, don't you, T.J.?"

"I used to go all the time," said T.J. "You gotta keep the devil away."

"You guys really believe all that stuff?" asked Bennett doubtfully.

"More or less," said Shot.

"I don't believe the part about confession and Lent and stuff like that," confessed T.J. "But I sure believe in Heaven and hell... and God."

"I'm kinda like you, T.J.," said Randy. "I believe, but I'm just too busy to go to church."

"You ain't that busy," Shot argued.

"I know it," admitted Randy. "I just don't care to do my praying in a church, being told when to pray, what to believe, and how to live. Hell, I don't mind going once in a while..."

"How about you, McKinney?" asked T.J.

"I wouldn't go to church if you paid me," came his reply.

"Aw, hell," said Randy, "you'd go on Easter, wouldn't you?"

"Nope."

"Why not?" asked Shot.

"It's a bunch of bull," declared Bennett. "That's why."

"You mean you don't believe in going to church?" asked T.J.

"I believe in other people going if they want to," said Bennett.

"But you're already good," joked T.J., "so you don't have to."

"I just think it's a waste of time," explained Bennett. "Kneeling down and talking to somebody who ain't ever there."

"What?" Randy asked disbelievingly. "You mean you *are* an atheist?"

"Some people call it that."

"Well, if you don't believe in God," asked Shot, "then just who do you believe in?"

"Oh." Bennett thought for a moment. "I don't know for sure."

"Let me get this straight," said Shot. He looked Bennett right in the eye and began to question. "You don't believe in God, right?"

"That's right," answered Bennett.

"Then you don't believe in heaven and hell, right?"

Bennett ignored Shot's question. "What is this...a courtroom?"

"I just..." "Just let me ask you a few questions," coaxed Shot. "Alright?"

"I don't speak without a lawyer."

"Come on, Bennett, two more questions... that's all," urged Shot.

"Hold it...hold it!" T.J. hollered as he jumped out of bed. He ran up to Bennett and said, "Stand up, please. Raise your right hand and repeat after me."

Bennett played along.

"I," said T.J., "Bennett McKinney..."

"You ain't Bennett McKinney!" said Bennett McKinney. "I'm Bennett McKinney!"

"Alright," said T.J. "You, Bennett McKinney..."

"I, Bennett McKinney..."

"Swear to tell the truth..."

"The whole truth..."

"And nothing but the truth!"

"I don't think you guys are doing that right," said Randy.

"Objection overruled!" hollered Shot, who was now standing on the bed. "I, Judge Shot Palmer, call Defendant Bennett McKinney, to the witness chair."

"Where's the witness chair?" asked Defendant McKinney.

"You're in it," stated Judge Palmer. "O.K., Mr. Jergenson, fire away."

"Mr. McKinney," said T.J., scratching his chin, looking at the ceiling and acting important. Then he looked hard and cold into Bennett's eyes and fired his first question. "Do you believe in heaven and hell?"

"No," came the answer again.

"That means when you die you won't go to either place!"

"That's right."

T.J. thought again for a while. This time he very calmly looked at Bennett and quietly said, "Then just what do you plan on doing when you die?"

As a grin spread across Bennett's face, he said, "Oh, I suppose I'll just get a job and settle down."

That really got Randy in the funny bone. He was the only one in the room who laughed.

"Come on!" demanded T.J.

"O.K. You know what I really think?" said Bennett, "I think I'll come back as an animal."

"A what?" asked Shot.

"That's right...reincarnation," explained Bennett.

Everyone looked at each other as if to say 'Is this guy for real?' Then Randy started laughing again. "McKinney," he said, "now I know you're crazy!"

"What?" argued Bennett. "It makes as much sense as your heaven and hell!"

"Are you seriously believing this?" asked Randy, still disbelieving.

"Damn right, I believe it!" Bennett was totally serious and defensive now. "You guys have had all this Catholic and Lutheran and Baptist stuff drummed into your heads all your lives, and I think it's a bunch of shit!"

"Yeah!" boomed T.J., shaking his fist, mocking Bennett's vindication.

"So," said Shot, "Bennett McKinney's going to come back as an animal, huh?"

"What kind of an animal are you gonna be?" Randy asked jokingly.

"I'll give you three guesses."

"A skunk," said T.J.

"No, a gopher," Shot guessed enthusiastically.

"Nope," said Bennett, "you're wrong."

"A buffalo?" asked Randy.

"Hey," said Bennett as he snapped his fingers, "you're gettin' close."

"I got it!" announced T.J. "You're going to come back as a bucking bull!"

Bennett grinned.

"Yep, that's it," said T.J. "I hope you die before me, McKinney. I'd like to see you as a bull."

"Naw, you wouldn't like me as a bull," explained McKinney.

"Why not?" inquired T.J.

" 'Cause I'd buck you off!"

Shot turned to Randy. "I don't know if he's serious or just kidding."

"I'm serious," Bennett repeated. "I'm going to come back in my next life and be a big Braymer-cross bull."

"Baloney," said T.J., flat out.

"O.K. Don't believe me," Bennett responded. "But, by God, if I die first, you'll see!"

"How are we gonna know it's you?" asked Randy.

"I'll show you," said Bennett, taking off his shirt. "See this?" There on his right bicep was a simple 'BM' tattooed in black ink.

"So what?" said T.J. "That ain't nothing but a jailhouse tattoo!"

"O.K.," Bennett explained, "if you ever see a bull with a 'BM' brand on the right shoulder, you'll know it's me."

"I ain't even going to listen to this anymore," said T.J. as he headed for the bathroom.

"Get outta here, Bennett," moaned Shot.

Bennett took his shirt off the rest of the way. "Hey! I don't care if you believe me or not, but that's the way it's going to happen!"

"How do you know you'll be a Braymer-cross?" asked Randy.

"Well, I don't know for sure about that," Bennett admitted.

"That's just what kind I'd like to be." He took his jeans off and took the place in bed where T.J. had been lying.

Things got quiet for a while. Randy rolled over in bed and shut his eyes. Then he opened them again. Without looking up, he thoughtfully said, "McKinney, you're screwed in the head."

Before Randy had even finished his sentence, Bennett, not so thoughtfully, snapped back, "Randy Corey, why don't you shove it?"

"Where's the Bible?" Corey asked nobody in particular as he looked on the shelves that sat next to his bed. "I'll prove it to you."

"Prove what to me?" Bennett snapped again, "That if I'm a good boy, I can go to Heaven?"

"Yeah," Randy answered as he got out of bed, "Where's the Bible at?"

No one answered.

Randy started going through the dresser drawers. "Where do they keep the Bible?"

"I smoked the Bible," said Shot in a much lower, crusty, prospector voice.

"Boy! I couldn't live like that," said Bennett in the same mock voice.

"They keep a Bible in all hotels, don't they?" asked Randy.

"No," answered Shot, "just the Holiday."

"Oh." Randy got back into bed, then realized, "Hey! This is the Holiday!"

"I don't care about the Bible," claimed Bennett. "It don't mean nothing to me."

"Why don't you just drop it and go to sleep?" hollered T.J. from the bathroom.

"If I could find the Bible," said Randy, "I could show you in black and white."

"The Bible is a big farce!" Bennett argued again. "It was all made up! Everything in the Bible is a bunch of horse shit!"

"Randy," said Shot, "you're never going to convince him. Why don't you shut up and go to sleep?"

The toilet in the bathroom flushed. T.J. came out and looked at Bennett. "Get outta my bed, you atheistic bastard!"

Bennett sighed as he rolled over and ignored T.J.

"Well, hell," said T.J. to himself, "where am I going to sleep?"

Shot reached up above his headboard and shut off the light.

"Come on! I gotta sleep somewhere," T.J. said as he turned the light back on.

No one answered him, so he took a blanket and pillow from Dave and Bennett, went into the bathroom and bedded down in the tub.

T.J. had heard and read about people claiming that they can remember living past lives, but he always thought they were full of crap. Having gone to church almost regularly until he was out of high school, he was brought up to believe in Heaven and hell. Although he never questioned it aloud, he had often wondered, in the back of his mind, if it was true or not. In his mind, he questioned a lot of his church's beliefs, although he was told not to, because questioning the church, according to the church, means questioning God, which is a sin, and he could go to hell for that. He just couldn't help it. He wondered what really does happen when someone dies. Is hell really as bad as they say it is? Is there really a devil down there running things with a pitchfork, horns on his head, and a pointy tail? And is Heaven really as boring as they make it sound? T.J. tried to picture himself and his rodeo buddies, sitting around on a cloud, wearing those big white robes, plucking on a harp. He chuckled to himself and immediately wondered if he had just sinned. He tried not to even think of the subject anymore, but what if Bennett is right? He sure seemed awfully positive about it. T.J. began running the possibilities through his head. Maybe you do go to Heaven if you are good and hell if you are bad. So where would that leave T.J.? Maybe you are reincarnated, and start all over again. Maybe we are all a part of God, He is actually in us all, and when we die... T.J. shook his head. Nope, this is way too deep. Maybe there is no reincarnation, no Heaven, no hell, no God, and when you die, everything is over. Your body dies, your mind dies, and your soul dies. To T.J., this was the theory that made the most sense. He decided to go with the last theory. He let out a sleepy sigh, satisfied that he had it all figured out, and praying to God that he was wrong, he slowly drifted off to sleep.

Chapter 2: February 1987

When T.J. woke up in the morning, he found the water running and a foot of lukewarm water in the tub with him. With his right side dry and his left side wet, he threw the heavy soaked blankets off him. Surging out of the water like a submarine, he ran to the other room. "Alright! Who's the smart-ass?"

Bennett, Dave, and Shot lay in deep sleep and didn't even twitch a muscle. Randy Corey's spot in bed was empty.

The first person T.J. suspected was Bennett McKinney. He was going to pounce on him to wake him up, but instead he got a better idea. He found the ice bucket on the floor, took it into the bathroom, and filled it full of cold water. Then he took it back into the other room, stood above Bennett, and tipped the bucket slowly.

Bennett, who was sleeping on his left side, automatically woke up when he felt the cold water hit his face, flow down his neck and onto his pillow. He jumped up on the bed and shouted, "You son of a bitch!"

Then, just for the fun of it, T.J. threw the rest of the water on Dave Whitney, who was asleep by Bennett.

"What's going on?" grumbled Dave as he rolled out of bed.

T.J. stepped back and snickered.

Dave looked at Bennett and made a suggestion. "We're gonna drown that rat!"

As they tried to grab T.J., he bolted out the door and slammed it shut. He heard the door lock from the inside and he realized he was in the hallway wearing nothing but wet underwear. The grin across his face dropped to a worried frown as he grabbed the door handle and tried to twist it both ways. When the door wouldn't open, he started pounding on it and pleading in a panicky, quiet voice, "Open up the door now, guys... O.K., you guys can let me in, now... McKinney... Come on... Somebody's gonna see me out here... Open the door and let me in!"

"Not by the hair of my chinny-chin-chin!" came the reply from inside.

"Whitney, if you don't open up, I swear I'll kick this door down!"

"Then get after it," came Dave's voice.

"Hey Jergenson!" Bennett giggled. "Why don't you go to the office and get a key?"

"Bennett, please let me in," T.J. begged.

"Not 'til somebody walks by and sees you," Bennett replied.

T.J. thought for a few seconds and said, "Hell with you guys, then. I'm takin' the van!"

He turned around and quietly ran down the hall and around the corner where he bumped into a lady with her teenage daughter and two younger sons. "'Scuse me, ma'am," he apologized as he dashed out the door.

The frozen concrete sidewalk felt as though it was burning the soles of T.J.'s bare feet. The winter morning air put instant goosebumps on his body and caused tears to well up in his eyes, half blinding him in the early morning sunshine.

The keys were still in Bennett's red Chevy van, as Bennett never thought of taking them or locking up when he was drunk. T.J. was shaking like a leaf as he sat down in the driver's seat, slammed the door and turned on the ignition. Neglecting to even let the engine warm up, he jammed the gearshift into reverse and hit the gas, backing right in front of a black Cadillac and barely avoiding a fender bender. He was feeling wild and reckless as he darted out of the parking lot and merged onto the four-lane highway in front of a Kenworth Conventional semi. He wondered where he was going. He turned on the radio and sang along with Willie Nelson. "It's a Bloody Mary Mornin', baby left me without warnin' sometime in the night..." He was watching the traffic, the buildings, signs, and different shapes and sizes of the other vehicles, when he noticed a jogger on the left side of the road with the oncoming traffic.

"Crazy!" he thought. As he got closer to the jogger, his one good eye could make out the yellow hair and red complexion of his colorful friend, Randy Corey.

T.J. rolled down his window. He waved and yelled at Randy as he sped by. Up the road a ways and just on the other side of an underpass, he flipped a U-turn and headed back the other way.

He checked around for any cops who might have seen him break the law. Not spotting any, he turned off the radio and slowed down as he approached Randy on the shoulder of the highway.

Breathing heavily, Randy found it difficult to laugh at the sight of T.J. sitting there in nothing but his underwear.

"Wh...where's your clothes?" he panted as he opened the door and hopped in.

"Back at the hotel!" said T.J. as if he were bragging.

"What?" asked Randy, confused.

"Aw, Bennett locked me out," said T.J., "but I'm gettin' even. Let's just go to the rodeo and make them hitch a ride."

"What about our clothes?" inquired Randy.

"We can scrape up something," answered T.J., motioning to the back of the van. Among the saddles and gearbags were a couple pairs of jeans, wrinkled shirts, and an assortment of boots and socks.

"Yeah, but I gotta take a shower and stuff," argued Randy. "How come ya got locked outta the room, anyhow?"

"Oh, we got into a water fight," T.J. explained as he pulled onto the highway. "First of all, when I woke up in the bathtub this morning, the water was running!"

"Haw, haw, haw. Did ya get wet?"

"Hell, I almost drowned! Then I filled up the ice bucket and poured it on McKinney."

"Why on McKinney?" asked Randy.

" 'Cause I figured he's the one who turned on the water, see?" explained T.J.

Randy broke out into hysterical laughter.

"And then," T.J. continued, "I let him, Dave, and Shot chase me outta the room."

When Randy regained his composure, he grinned at T.J. asking, "Didn't it cross your mind that maybe I'm the one who turned on the water?"

T.J. looked at Corey with a half mad, half surprised look on his face. "You did?"

"Haw, haw, and you went and threw water on Bennett..."

"I didn't even notice you was gone!" hollered T.J.

"Well, did ya notice I was there?" laughed Randy.

Jergenson was about to answer when he looked in his rear view mirror. A city police car was directly behind him with lights flashing.

"Aw hell," moaned T.J. "You think he means me?"

"Hu...huh?" giggled Randy, unaware of what was going on.

As T.J. pulled the van onto the shoulder of the highway, Randy inquired, "What are you doin'?"

"Well, ya see that cop car back there?" T.J. asked sarcastically, "There's probably a cop in there who don't like people speedin'."

"Oh," said Randy, surprised. Then his eyes lit up and his mouth dropped open. "You're in your underwear!"

"Shut up!" whispered T.J. "Here he comes!"

A black woman in a blue police uniform approached the van. She was about thirty years old. Above her badge was a little copper name tag that read, "J.L. Griffin."

"Mornin'," greeted T.J., forcing a smile.

Not returning the greeting, the officer looked T.J. over suspiciously. "May I see your driver's license, please?"

"Sure," said T.J., reaching for his left hind pocket, which wasn't there. "Uh...I musta' left it at the hotel."

"Driving without a license," Officer Griffin stated to herself. "What's your name, sir?"

"Tim Jergenson."

"Is that your full name?"

"Timothy Joseph," T.J. said with an impatient sigh.

"And where are you from, Timothy Joseph?"

"Enid, Oklahoma, ma'am."

"Out of state with no license," said the officer as she wrote in her pad. "Not a real smart thing to do."

"The hotel's not far away..."

"Stay in the van," she interrupted. "I'll be back in a moment." And she walked back to the patrol car.

"Timothy Joseph," Randy Corey quietly said as he tried to keep a straight face, "I think you're in trouble."

"Oh?" T.J. replied sarcastically, "How do ya figure? Stupid son-of-a...was I speedin'?"

"Probably."

"Hell, I didn't see no signs! Wha'd she stop me for? I didn't do nothin'! Of all the cops in South Dakota, I gotta get a damn woman!"

"She's gonna die when she makes ya get outta the van and sees you runnin' around naked!" mentioned Randy.

"Gawdamn!" cursed T.J. as he hit his palm against the steering wheel. After a pause, he said, "I oughta take off right now."

"Maybe this'll teach ya not to speed!" Randy jokingly preached.

"Up yers!" replied T.J.

About that time, Officer Griffin reappeared at the window. "Mr. Jergenson, I'd like you to step back to my car with me, please."

"Uh...well...?...I'd...kinda rather not...if you don't mind?"

"Why not?"

"Uh...well...I don't have no pants on."

The officer thought this over for a while. "I see." She thought some more. "Mr. Jergenson?"

"Yeah?"

"Why don't you have any pants on?"

"Well...uh, ya see..." said T.J. searching for words, "...uh...somebody stole 'em!"

"Oh. I see. Would you describe the thief to me?"

T.J. took a deep nervous breath, "He was this big, black dude...No! He wasn't black! He was only big. He wasn't black though. He had a...black bag over his head!"

"And how big would you say this man is?"

"Oh, big! Big sucker, and mean lookin'!"

"I thought you couldn't see his face."

"Huh? Oh, no...no I couldn't see his face. Hell, he had a sack over it...mean lookin' sack!"

"Mr. Jergenson!"

"Ma'am?"

"Did he have a sack over his face or not?" she insisted.

"Uh...I dunno," replied T.J., "I didn't see him. See, he came in when I was sleepin.'"

"Then why did you even attempt to describe him to me if you don't know what he looks like?" Officer Griffin questioned impatiently.

"I dreamed about him!" T.J. snapped back.

"Mr. Jergenson," sighed Officer Griffin, "I am placing you under arrest for willful, reckless driving, driving without a license, and indecent exposure. Anything you say can and will be used against you in a court of law. You have the right to an attorney. If you cannot afford an attorney, one will be appointed for you. Do you understand what I have just told you?"

"Yessir," mumbled T.J.

"Now, step out of the van, please."

"Step out of the van?" T.J. protested, "What the hell for?"

"I have to frisk you!"

Chapter 3: March 1987

One of the road signs read, "Leaving Oklahoma, Come Again." The other read, "Welcome to Kansas, the Sunflower State." Neither one could be seen. It was midnight, pitch black and not a headlight in sight. Even the snow in the ditches that straddled the two-lane highway was covered by darkness.

Three miles to the south and headed toward the signs, a red Chevy custom van hummed along the blacktop. Inside, co-pilot and navigator T.J. Jergenson popped the top of a Coors Light and handed it to the driver, Bennett McKinney. T.J. and Bennett were traveling without the rest of the team on this run. They had left Randy and Dave a few hours ago in Muskogee and were heading back to Rapid City where T.J. was going to face the judge on the charges brought up on him the month before. Then it would be back to Lincoln, Nebraska, to the night rodeo where they'd meet back up with Randy and Dave and drive to Phoenix, Arizona, to join Shot Palmer who was clowning that rodeo.

It was the first leg of a long trip and the boys sometimes had strange ways of keeping themselves entertained on the road.

"Now, I, I, I...I'm Jimmy Stewart," mimicked T.J. to Bennett, "and, and, and...I just wanna say what a beautiful night it is tonight and..."

"N-no," Bennett stuttered back, "I, I'm Jimmy Stewart and, and...and I want to tell you..."

"And I just wanted to say it's a wonderful life, isn't it, Bennett? Don't you think it's just a wonderful..."

"N, n...now wait just a cotton'-pickin' minute here," interrupted Bennett again. "I, I, I...I'm the real Jimmy Stewart and I, I...I'm sick and tired of all these people doin' all these doggone imitations of me all the time!"

"But, but...but dontcha think, Bennett, that it's just..."

"My name's not Bennett, it's Jimmy Stewart, and, and this town ain't big enough for the two of us!"

"Well," said T.J., still in a mock voice, "I, I...I 'spose we're just gonna hafta move to a bigger town then."

"Ya know, ya, ya...ya know who's voice I've been workin' on but just can't quite pin down?"

"J, J...Jimmy Stewart?" asked T.J.

"No, not Jimmy Stewart. I am Jimmy Stewart. I, I was talking about the Duke."

"The Duke?" asked Jimmy, a.k.a. T.J.

"Y, yeah. I been workin' on him, but..."

"Well, would, would ya like to hear my impression of the Duke?"

"Well...well, I, I, I...I'd be proud to hear your impression of the Duke, T, T, T...T.J."

"W...w...w...well," continued Jergenson in the same voice, "I, I, I...I think he's a real...a real nice fella, at least that's my impression of him."

"That, that's not exactly what I meant by..."

"Kinda reminds me of a...of a...of a little story," T.J. rambled on, "It's...it's...it's...it's a sad story...it's a story about a dog...a three legged dog...well, this little three-legged dog, he walks into this...this saloon, ya see, and...and he says...," suddenly T.J.'s Jimmy Stewart turned into the voice of John Wayne, "Well, I'm lookin' for the man who shot my paw!"

Bennett, who was taking a big swig of beer, was caught completely off guard by the punch line. Not being able to suppress his laughter, or his beer, he spit Coors Light all over the windshield, the dash, his lap, and down the front of his shirt. Then, as he tried to regain control of himself, he lost control of the van. The van shook and rumbled as the right side tires dropped off the pavement and skipped across frozen clumps of grass. As T.J. looked up to see what the problem was, all he could make out was "Leaving Oklahoma, Come Again." Bennett swerved to the left. T.J. heard the 'thunk' of his own head hitting the passenger side window. Bennett could see they were about to go into the ditch on the other side of the road. He stomped on the accelerator and steered the van back to the right, this time not so sharply. The left tires kicked up a little snow, but he got her straightened out before they plowed nose first into the white blanket of frozen powder. Bringing all four wheels back upon the blacktop, Bennett hit the brakes, bringing the van to a screeching halt and killing the engine.

T.J. looked over at Bennett, realizing he had never stopped laughing. The lights of the dash reflected off the giggle-tears that streamed down his face as uncontrollably as his high-pitched cackling.

Trying to regain his composure, Bennett took off his glasses and wiped his eyes. After about thirty seconds, his hysteria slowed to a whimper.

T.J.'s face went from bewilderment to amusement. Again he stuttered in his old Jimmy Stewart voice. "B, b, b...boy, howdy!" sending Bennett into another fit.

"Bennett. Settle down, bud. You're gonna laugh yourself to death!" said T.J. in his own voice. "I know one thing. I ain't tellin' any more jokes to you unless this van is parked!"

Bennett, still consumed by his own laughter, didn't hear a word T.J. said. He beat his head on the steering wheel and covered his ears, wailing, "Oh...oh, God, that's funny! Oh... shut up or you're gonna kill me!"

"Can't you listen to a joke and drive at the same time?" scolded T.J.

Bennett struggled to get out the words without cracking up again. "I thought I was gonna piss my pants!"

"Piss your...hell, you might as well have. You got beer all down the front of your shirt...and all over the dash, and windshield..." T.J. shook his head in playful disgust as he opened his van door and stepped out.

"Where you goin'?" asked Bennett.

"I'm walkin' to Rapid City!"

"Get back in here!" Bennett giggled.

"Not really," hollered T.J. "I'm just gonna write my name in the snow. You'd better do the same. I might tell another joke!"

"Sounds like a hell of an idea," agreed Bennett as he fumbled for the door latch. "Hey! How do ya get outta here?"

"Well, shit, it's your van," T.J. hollered from the ditch. "You oughta' be able to..."

"I found it, I found it," said Bennett as he stepped out, "...had myself locked in. My God, it's cold out here! I don't know if I wanna do this or not. My fingers are already numb. It's so cold out here...can hardly get my belt undone. Mr. Tickle's in there sayin' 'No, please don't make me come out!' You're awful quiet over there, Jergenson. What are ya doin'? Hell, all you gotta do is make a 'T' and a 'J'. I gotta spell out 'Bennett'. B...E...N...Hey! Are there's two n's in 'Bennett'?"

T.J. walked around the van and climbed into the captain's chair. "Bennett, I ain't never seen a man have as much fun as you just takin' a leak. Dammit," he said as he raised up, "the seat's still wet."

"Get outta that chair!" Bennett barked over his shoulder.

"I'm drivin' for a while," T.J. stated. "You darn near killed us."

"Let me drive a little farther," Bennett insisted.

"No way," T.J. argued. "I wanna get to Rapid in one piece."

"Oh, yeah, like you got a real clean drivin' record. I hope the judge takes your license."

"Man! Get in here, Bennett! It's freezing out!" T.J. said as he shut his door. He then stepped down on the clutch pedal and turned on the key. The engine turned but wouldn't start. "Come on you son of a bitch," T.J. thought to himself. He tried again. Nothing.

"You want me to show you how to start that?" asked Bennett as he crawled in the passenger side.

Ignoring Bennett's question, T.J. said, "If we're gonna be stuck out here in this freezin' weather, I'm gonna be real pissed off."

"Well, turn off the headlights for one thing. Now pump the shit outta the gas...O.K., try her."

T.J. twisted the key again. The engine gave three slow moans. T.J. began to moan also. "You sorry son of a..."

"Hey! Don't you cuss at my van," Bennett broke in. "You talk nice to Maybelline and she'll start for ya."

T.J. looked around in despair. "I don't even see no yard lights from no farm houses."

"Tell Maybelline you love her," said Bennett.

"Well, hell!" shouted T.J., completely ignoring Bennett.

"Tell her you love her, T.J. I swear it. Pump the gas, tell her you love her, and let's get outta here."

T.J. looked at Bennett as he let out a disgusted sigh.

"Want me to drive?" Bennett coaxed.

T.J. answered by pumping furiously on the accelerator. "Maybelline," he pleaded, "you know that Uncle T.J. loves ya... It's cold out here and we got places to go, honey..." He bit his lip as he turned the key once again. Three dying moans.

"Don't give up T.J....keep her goin'!" Bennett coached.

T.J.'s eyes lit up as the fourth moan buzzed to new life and the engine rushed to full acceleration. After a high five and a mutual "Yee-haw", T.J. slammed her into gear and smoked the tires against the frozen pavement as they headed north from the Oklahoma/Kansas border.

"Let's have some headlights," suggested Bennett as he grabbed another beer.

"Check," said T.J. "That's better."

"I can't believe," said Bennett, "that you didn't know how to start my van."

"Did I leave my beer back there?" asked T.J.

"How many years have you been drivin' this van?" asked Bennett.

"I didn't think I took my beer outside with me..."

"Here, have this one," said Bennett handing T.J. his can, "and make it last. It's the last one."

"The last one? We bought a twelve-pack, didn't we? Well, here," T.J. said, "I don't wanna take your last one."

"No, that's O.K.," said Bennett, refusing T.J.'s offer. "I'm about beered out anyway."

"Well, thanks, buddy."

"Anyway, back to what I was askin' you. How long have you been drivin' this van?"

"Ever since you've had it," was T.J.'s answer.

"And you still don't know how to start Maybelline?"

T.J. hesitated a moment and said, "Well, I forgot."

For a mile or more, nothing but the hum of the engine could be heard as Bennett settled back in his chair, letting his memory drift over some of the miles that he and T.J. had traveled together. He thought mostly of the good miles, but treasured the not-so-good ones, too. He remembered the bad bulls, the wild women, the honky-tonks they'd raised hell in, the scars they'd accumulated along the way, the buckles they'd won, and the friends. He recalled the time he and T.J. drove the van in reverse from Durango, Colorado to Farmington, New Mexico because the front part of the muffler was loose and dragging on the ground. Then there was the time T.J. greased Bennett's clutch and brake pedal. Bennett backed right through a motel wall. One time they were running late for a rodeo in Woodstown, New Jersey, and...

"Yessir, we have put a lot of miles on the ol' van," T.J. interrupted the quiet.

"Yeah," Bennett said with a pause, "we sure have."

"I wonder how many?"

"How many what?"

"Miles."

"Oh, man," said Bennett. "I'd hate to guess. A bunch of 'em though." He went on, "But you know, it ain't the miles that are important."

"It ain't?"

"Nope. It's the stops you make that count."

T.J. smiled in agreement. Then he said, "Hey, how 'bout that time we were headed for that rodeo up in New Jersey..."

"Woodstown? I was just thinking about that!"

"Where was we comin' from, anyway?"

"Somewhere in Illinois, I think."

T.J. laughed. "By God, we made it in time for the bullridin'!"

"Grayslake, Illinois," said Bennett. "Fourteen miles from the Woodstown rodeo grounds and I got pulled over doin' ninety-seven miles an hour."

"You're saying to me, 'Act injured...act like you're hurt!'"

"You did a helluva job, too, T.J. I don't think I ever heard anybody moan as loud as you."

"Hell," T.J. chuckled, "I had to keep moanin' louder and louder just to keep from laughin'!"

"That cop sure fell for it, didn't he? 'We better get this man to the hospital!' Haw, haw!"

"What'd you tell him...that I had some busted ribs that were pokin' through a lung?"

"You did have some cracked ribs at the time," Bennett reminded his friend. "That's all I could think of right then."

"That was something else...police escort all the way to town! Lights goin', siren flashing, everybody getting the hell out of the way..."

Bennett howled hysterically as he pounded his fist on the dash. "What do you s'pose them cops thought when we went by the rodeo grounds..." He stopped and caught his breath before going on, "...and we turned out from behind them and they kept goin'!" His laughter cackled like a chicken as he thrashed about in his chair, stomping his heels on the floorboard.

"I bet...hee, hee, hee, hee...I bet they pulled up to the hospital," giggled T.J., "looked around and said, 'Wuh...where'd they go?'"

"Ohhhh, shit," howled Bennett.

"So here they come a little later...I'm s'poseta have busted bones and punctured lungs...I'm chapped up, sittin' on my bull, puttin' the rope on him!"

Again Bennett had tears streaming down his face. When he settled down enough to speak, he said, "Oh, man. You know, it was real good of them to let us ride our bulls before they hauled us to jail."

"Good thing they did, too," recalled T.J. "We won just enough between the two of us to bail ourselves out!"

"Yup," Bennett sighed. "Too bad we can't go back to that state no more."

T.J. chuckled and thought for a moment before saying, "You know, I wouldn't trade the richest man in the world for this life."

"I know what you mean, buddy," agreed Bennett. "The stuff we've been through...we're probably lucky we're still kickin'."

"I love it," said T.J., mostly to himself. Then he looked at Bennett, "How long can it last?"

"Not long enough," said Bennett without hesitation. "We've been goin' for over fifteen years now...Seems like just the other day we was practicin' on Dad's ol' herd bulls."

"Yep," said T.J. "Now there's where we're lucky to be alive. If your ol' man knew we was buckin' them bulls, he'd a' killed us."

"Aw, hell," mused Bennett, "we didn't hurt 'em none."

"No, but they put you in the hospital. You hung up to that big Hereford. He knocked you out, stomped all over me before I got you outta there. Broke your arm and gave you a concussion."

"Ha, ha! Told my mom I fell off the barn!"

After another short pause, T.J. said, "It's been me and you from the start, you know it?"

Bennett reached over and squeezed T.J.'s shoulder, and with a shake that sent T.J.'s head teetering from side to side, said, "Yeah, and it'll be you and me to the end, too." He went on to say, "I got plans for me and you, buddy. We're goin' to the National Finals and one of us is gonna win it. It may not be this year, and it may not be next year, but before we're through, we're goin'. You know, like I say, we've been ridin' bulls now for over fifteen years. Traveling and partying and chasin' girls. I've loved it all. But I'm thinkin' that maybe it's time we left our mark on rodeo. Time to get a little bit serious about it. Hell, we ain't kids no more."

T.J. listened thoughtfully as Bennett went on. "Now, I ain't sayin' we gotta quit havin' fun, raisin' hell and stuff like that. I'm just sayin' we oughta make winnin' the world our first goal and let everything else come in after that.

"T.J., I know..." Bennett stopped to search for the right words, then continued, "...when you are on...I mean, when you're ridin' to your potential, there ain't a cowboy in the country that can ride the real bad ones like you, including me. And I don't know anybody that has your style of ridin'. It's just that so often you pressure up on the really important ones...the big money rodeos."

"Yeah, I know," mumbled T.J.

"And they're bulls that shouldn't have thrown you off. I've seen you ride some double-rank, eliminating sons of bitches."

"I've seen you do the same..."

"I know it, we both have. We both know we're good enough, so why ain't we ever won the world?"

T.J. hesitated. "Just bad breaks, I guess."

"What do you mean 'bad breaks'?" Bennett scowled.

"Last year, Bennett, I couldn't draw a money bull to save my soul. You know that. The year before you were out with a busted leg."

"Minor setbacks," said Bennett.

"And it don't seem like I can ride worth a damn when you ain't around."

"You'd better quit dependin' on me so much, T.J. I ain't gonna be around forever."

"Ain't none of us gonna be around forever," T.J. said solemnly. Then a grin spread across his face, "But we're sure makin' the best of it."

Bennett smiled and held out his fist to T.J. "To the National Finals."

Taking his cue, T.J. gave Bennett's fist a brotherly punch and repeated, "To the National Finals."

Chapter 4: April 1987

"Good evening, ladies and gentlemen, and welcome to the eighteenth and final performance of the Houston Livestock Show and Rodeo!" The rodeo announcer's voice echoed through the speakers and off the walls of the Astrodome. "First of all, let me introduce myself to you..."

Meanwhile, directly under the announcer's stand, Bennett McKinney was hanging his bull rope on an iron-pipe back pen fence. Like the crowd and the bucking stock tonight, Bennett was full of electricity. It had been two weeks since he'd been on the back of a bull due to an injury in Lincoln, Nebraska. A horned bull had jerked him down on his head, which resulted in three broken ribs and some torn ligaments in his right arm. He was riding against doctor's orders.

Bennett knew which bull he had drawn, and he knew the bull well. It was a large, black Brahma-Simmental cross named Big Foot that would usually spin both directions and throw more riders than not. Bennett had watched his bull buck four previous times and was very pleased with his draw. He knew that he could ride this bull if things went right and he didn't let his injuries get him down. He also knew that if he did ride Big Foot, he would surely be in the big money. The one bull Bennett was glad he did not draw was a dark-red wide-horned Watusi-Brahma they call Genghis Khan, #000. Genghis had been ridden only once in the last three years. Considered an eliminator, he was a bad chute fighter, as powerful as he was quick, and mean, throwing his head high, trying to hook riders off his back with his horns. He paid little attention to rodeo clowns, preferring downed bullriders. For eight long seconds that night, Genghis Khan would belong to T.J. Jergenson.

T.J., appearing cool and relaxed, was enjoying the guff the other cowboys were giving him about his indecent exposure charge in Rapid City. That incident, like so many cowboy tales in the last century and a half, was carried by rumor, pushed a little farther by exaggeration, and then loaded up and hauled to town by lies. T.J. laughingly denied the story about the high-speed chase through the Black Hills that ended in a sexual interlude with a black policewoman, asking, "Where the hell did you hear that?"

"That's what Randy Corey told me," said a cowboy.

"The heck I did!" hollered Randy, who was sitting in his bronc saddle on the ground, near enough to hear.

"Corey, you're rotten...," said T.J. with a halfway grin as he shook his head.

"Whattaya got drawed tonight, Randy?" asked another bronc rider.

"Ol' Lodge Pole. You know her?"

"That little black mare over there. She won't buck unless you really run the iron to her."

It was not until two hours later that the bulls were loaded into the chutes and Bennett, with the help of T.J., hung his braided manila grass bullrope on his opponent, Big Foot. It would be a while before T.J. got on, as Genghis Khan was still in the back pens, slinging dirt behind him with his deadly front hooves and snorting at any human who dared to get too close to his pen.

So far, the team had been pretty successful that night. Randy won a fifth place on Lodge Pole. Dave Whitney, who showed up just in time to get on, won the bronc riding with a showy eighty-one point ride, while all through the rodeo, clown and bullfighter Shot Palmer had the audience, as usual, eating out of his hand.

Bennett sat right down on Big Foot and fed the braided tail of his rope through the loop where hung two brass bells. He then let the bells slide back down to Big Foot's chest. The bull stood calmly all the while Bennett adjusted and readjusted the loop in his rope.

T.J. peeked up at Bennett through the iron rails of the chute gate. "How's your ribs feel?" he asked.

"They'll be alright," Bennett answered as he tied off his rope. He grasped the rails on each side of the chute and lifted himself off the back of the bull. A wince of pain flashed across Bennett's face as he felt the sharp twinge in his unhealed rib cage.

T.J. could see that his friend was hurting. "You get good and loose, now," was his only advice.

"Well, folks, have you enjoyed the wild shenanigans of Shot Palmer tonight?" the announcer asked the audience. The crowd cheered and clapped with approval as Shot tipped his little black derby in thanks. "Because now, friends," the announcer continued, "you're going to see the serious side of this wild man. He's the bullrider's savior, and this part of his job is no laughing matter." Shot trotted around in a couple of small circles and hopped a couple of times, springing off only his ankles, getting his body and mind right and ready for his upcoming task. As the first bullrider was getting set in the chute, Shot recognized the bull. A seasoned predictable animal that usually took two jumps and to the left. He wouldn't go out of his way to hurt a cowboy, but if one was on the ground in front of him, he wouldn't waste an opportunity either.

The cowboy nodded and the gate swung wide. The beast lunged from its box; once, twice, and a hard left. The cowboy, trying to stay up over the bull's mighty shoulders, was rocked back as his feet swung forward and he was tossed off the back end. The bull, having completed his job, stopped bucking and calmly trotted off to the catch pen. "Easy money," Shot thought to himself, although he'd just as soon earn it.

The next bull set to go was new to this rodeo string, and Shot had no recollection of having dealt with him before. Shot handled most new bulls the same way; keep off his head at first to give him an opportunity to buck and spin on his own, but stay in close enough to get right in his face should he want to beeline for the other end of the arena. Shot stood back as the gateman threw open the gate. It was a rather young Brangus bull, although his horns were over a foot long each, ranging wide and curving forward. He bellowed and leapt in the air two times, looking at the far end of the arena. Shot knew it was time. He darted across in front of the bull's path, barely missing a horn by the seat of his baggy britches. Taking the cue, the 'little' bull instinctively followed Shot around in a tight circle to the right. The cowboy aboard began spurring wildly with his outside foot. Every jump, the cowboy would throw his blunt spur rowel at the bull's thick hide. The bull barely felt a thing. At the sound of the eight second whistle, the cowboy grabbed the tail of his bullrope with his free hand and jerked it loose from his riding hand, while at the same time throwing his left leg over the shoulders of the animal, launching himself free to land safely on his feet and run to the fence. As soon as Shot knew that the cowboy was a safe distance away, he cut the other direction, and the riderless bull bucked down the arena looking for an open gate.

Shot was smiling now. Few things in life made him happier than turning back a good bull in front of an enthusiastic audience.

"How about a hand for our rodeo clown and bullfighter, folks? Isn't he doing a great job?" coaxed the announcer. "We've got the scores on this bullrider coming to us right now...listen to this, folks...a seventy-six! Unofficially fourth place so far, but we've got a lot of good bullriders and bulls coming up. Speaking of good bullriders, if you follow the sport of rodeo, you'll no doubt recognize this next young man's name. He's Bennett McKinney, and he's currently ranked number four in the world standings. He has drawn the great bull from the Stingin' B Rodeo Company, Big Foot. Now, to win this rodeo, Bennett must ride this bull and score at least an eighty-four, set last night. If you weren't here to witness it, I'll tell you it was quite a ride! As Bennett gets set in the chute, I'd like to introduce, or reintroduce that is, our chuteboss and the owner of the Stingin' B Rodeo Company, Sonny Joe Barker."

While the crowd applauded their approval, the man they were clapping for, dressed like the rest of the cowboys but also wearing a suit jacket and tie, did not respond to their show of appreciation. He was busy giving Bennett advice. "Don't be too long in there, Bennett, or he'll get to leanin' on ya," he warned in his usual gruff sandpaper voice. "Be quick, now!" Sonny Joe Barker owns every bucking horse and bull in this string, considered by many to be one of the best in the world. He knows each animal by name and number; each one's dispositions and habits. He's the man who feeds them every morning and night and doctors them back to health when they're ailing. Sonny Joe has a respect for his animals, and it shows. They, in turn, have a respect for him. "Cock your hammer, cowboy!" were the last words of encouragement Sonny had for Bennett as he stood back to watch the excitement.

Inside the chute, Sonny's seasoned bull waited patiently for Bennett to take his wrap and slide up to the bullrope. Bennett's heart was pumping fast. Adrenaline had chased the pain in his rib cage and arm out of his body. His ears no longer heard the announcer's voice blaring through the loudspeaker, the rumble of the crowd, or the words of encouragement from Dave Whitney and Randy Corey, who gathered around to cheer him on, or Shot Palmer, or T.J., who wanted Bennett to win almost as badly as himself. Bennett's mind had blacked out the entire world with the exception of this bull, Big Foot, which was right then the most important ride of his life. Right there was where it boiled down. Bennett wasn't doing this for the money, the glory, his world standings, or even for his love of the sport. All of that would come later. Right then, he was doing it because it had to be done, and he had to do it. The veins turned purple on Bennett's neck, his face reddened as his rage reached its boiling point, and with tucked chin and clenched teeth, he nodded for the gate.

The chute gate moved only six inches when Big Foot thrust his mighty head into it, sending it wide open. In the same instant, he gathered his hind feet under him and bailed high in the air with violent agility. Bennett saw the bull's head turn out to the arena, and he felt the bull blast off right underneath him. He lifted on his bullrope and squeezed with his legs as Big Foot uncoiled and snapped back toward the ground kicking his hooves high behind him. He felt the jolt as the bull's front hooves collided with the arena floor and sprang back up into the air again. Naturally reacting to Big Foot's every move, Bennett instinctively began spinning to the left, right into his riding hand. He could feel his right foot lose its grip and slide back behind the bullrope. He jammed his spur up to the bull's shoulder. Another vigorous lunge, and Bennett felt his spur let loose again and again... He jammed it back to its proper place...and again...and again. Suddenly the bull switched the direction of the spin, catching Bennett off guard as his right spur was only halfway to its destination, and clinging to nothing. This caused Bennett to slide away from his rope a little, farther toward the bull's hips. With all his might, Bennett threw his right spur into the bull's twisting, turning body, reached his free hand out over the bull's head and with the momentum of the bull's actions, threw his own body back to home base–the handhold of his bullrope. As Big Foot continued to kick and spin to the right, Bennett let go with his left foot, this time on purpose, relentlessly jabbing the bull's thick hide with his dull spur, time and time again.

It was as if a morning alarm went off and awakened Bennett from a dream he wasn't ready to part with when he heard the sound of the eight second buzzer. But with this alarm, you don't waste any time getting out of bed. You throw back the covers and bail out. Bennett hit the ground running and didn't stop until he was on the chute gate where it had all started. Suddenly he could hear again, and the music of the ecstatic crowd embraced him like an old friend. T.J. reached across the chute and embraced him like a true, genuine friend. Having done what had to be done, Bennett's teeth were no longer clenched. It was time to savor the glory, count the money, check the standings, and love his sport as he loved his life. Even the pain in Bennett's ribs was back, and yes, it was a good pain.

"Ladies and gentlemen! What do you think of Bennett McKinney and the great bull, Big Foot?"

The crowd needed no encouragement from the announcer to applaud, nor could they even hear him over the sounds of their own rapture.

Sonny Joe Barker grabbed Bennett's hand and shook it firmly. He nearly had to yell to be heard above the crowd as he looked Bennett in the eyes. "You rode like a champ."

There's not a higher compliment a cowboy can receive from a

stock contractor. "Thank you, Sonny," Bennett said in sincere modesty, "I 'preciate it."

Bennett watched Big Foot as the bull trotted to the other end of the arena and back again toward the catch pen gate. All bullriders have a respect for these great animals, but for Bennett, it was much more; an admiration, an envy, even. His glory was put on hold for the moment as he took in the rugged beauty of the majestic creature. The smoothness of his easy gait. The dewlap hanging from his neck flopped from side to side with every step. The muscle tone bulging from beneath his dirty black hide. The massive hump carried upon his brawny shoulders for no apparent reason but raw fascination. The wide up-turned horns worn like a crown as he held his head high with pride even though he had lost this round. And the last thing seen as he exited the arena, big ol' testicles hanging halfway to the ground. Yes, envy played a part in Bennett's feelings for this, and other great bulls. Awesome is a word people throw around nowadays without thinking about its true meaning, but to Bennett, this bull was truly awesome. Bennett thanked Big Foot in his mind.

The announcer's voice broke over the loudspeakers again. "Folks, the judges have tallied up the score of that last ride and I think you're going to like what you hear...45 on one side and 44 on the other for a total of 89 points! We have a new leader!"

Again the crowd went crazy.

Bennett stepped down off the chute gate and walked back into the arena where he was met by Shot Palmer.

"Not bad for a rookie!" Shot called out, smiling through his painted-on smile. He grabbed Bennett by the shoulder with one hand, the back of the neck with the other and forcefully jerked Bennett into a big bear hug. "Helluva ride, pard."

Bennett couldn't find, nor did he search for, words of thanks for his compadre. None were needed. He did, however, interrupt Shot's hug with the painful, high-pitched sound of, "My ribs..."

Shot let go immediately. "Oh, shit, I'm sorry."

Lips tight and forehead wrinkled in agony, Bennett said in the same hoarse, breathless voice, " 'S alright."

As Bennett picked up his bullrope, tipped his hat to the crowd and left the arena, Shot couldn't help but chuckle at what he'd just done and the look on Bennett's face.

By now, Genghis Khan was in the narrow alleyway leading to the bucking chutes. T.J. was breathing deep, doing stretching exercises, running and re-running his riding moves through his mind. On most bulls, he would be putting his rope on by now, but given the disposition of Genghis Khan, he opted to wait until the bull was in its chute. The less time you spend with a bull like this, the better off you are. T.J. imagined himself sitting on the bull, lifting with his left arm, squeezing with his legs, digging with his spurs. In his mind's eye, the bull spins to the left, and T.J. physically throws his body into a spin, right hand slashing through the air. Suddenly, his mind spins the bull in the other direction, and T.J. whirls to the right, furiously pumping his right arm over his head. A woman in the stands near enough to see mentioned to her neighbor that the tall cowboy, flailing about behind the chutes, brought to mind a chicken with its head cut off. Not all riders prepared themselves in this manner, but it worked for T.J. As he went through his ritual, he whispered to himself, "Feet! Feet! Lift! Hustle! Charge!" Then he settled down, relaxed a little bit, staying loose. Keeping his long legs straight and stiff, he bent at the waist and grabbed his ankles, slowly pulling his chest to his knees and causing his leg muscles to stretch to their full extent. Pulled groins are hell.

A bullrider was bucked down. The slidegates were pulled opened and the bulls moved forward one position. Two more riders and Genghis would be in his chute.

T.J. knew that he'd better not tilt his upper body forward on this particular bull and chance catching a horn in the face. However, if he sat back very far at all, the bull could use his eighteen hundred pounds of momentum to jerk T.J. down on his head, and then there'd be a wreck.

He looked through the iron slats at his bull and was caught off guard. The bull was already staring at T.J. Two dozen or so cowboys behind the chutes and old Triple Zeroes, Genghis Khan, was staring directly at T.J. "He knows," thought T.J. to himself. "He knows."

Another bull and rider battled. Again the bulls in the chutes moved forward.

T.J. gathered his bullrope from the fence where he'd had it hanging, and, it being the main tool of his trade, coiled it up with meticulous caution and care. He walked over beside Genghis and patiently waited for their turn.

Genghis slid a horn between the steel slats of the fence and lashed it at T.J., barely grazing his arm. T.J. backed off a step.

Dave Whitney, with a beer in his hand, and Randy Corey made their way through the sparse crowd of cowboys toward T.J. to give him their support. Dave did not utter a word. He punched T.J. on the shoulder and winked. His eyes said, "You can do it, buddy."

T.J. nodded. He knew he could do it.

Randy, although considerably taller than Dave, had to reach up to put his arm across T.J.'s shoulder. "You be runnin' when you hit the ground, now," he said.

T.J. nodded again, even though this was useless advice to him. He always ran when he hit the ground. It was as instinctive as breathing.

Another cowboy nodded for his bull and another bucking chute was empty. As soon as the gateman closed the chute gate, a cowboy pulled the slidegate to allow the bull in the next chute back to walk forward and shut the slidegate behind him. And so on and so on until Genghis Khan had a bucking chute of his own. T.J. arrived at the chute when the bull did. He did not sit on the bull or even straddle the rails above him like he would on an average non-chute-fighting bull. He stepped up onto the three-foot-high wooden plank that ran along the back side of the chutes, and there he stood as he dangled the bells and loop of his bullrope down the right side of his animal. Already Genghis was raising hell. Reaching back with his right horn, he hooked the bullrope and nearly jerked it out of T.J.'s hand. Both front and back slidegates clanked and clattered as the bull wallowed about in the chute, lunging and kicking. T.J. yanked his bullrope back and hung it down beside the bull again.

On the opposite side of the chute from T.J. stood Bennett, waiting to help his friend. "He's fired up tonight," Bennett said to himself, but loud enough for T.J. to hear. Bennett, still wearing his spurs, had packed away his chaps, glove, and bullrope in his gearbag. He put his own ride behind him for the moment, and his only interest right now was helping T.J. win this rodeo. In Bennett's hand was a four foot iron rod with one end bent back around as a hook. Bennett slid the hook between the rails of the chute and fished it underneath Genghis' belly, catching the loop of T.J.'s rope and pulling it to himself. Ordinarily, Bennett would reach through the rails with his hand to slip the rope from the hook, but with a miserable brute like Genghis, that's an easy way to lose fingers. Instead, Bennett pulled the rope partway through the rails to take the hook out. He handed the hook up to T.J., who, in turn, reached it down inside the chute, hooked the loop, took it from Bennett and pulled the rope up to himself. T.J. fed the tail of his bullrope through the loop and, after several attempts, secured it on the back of his bull as the beast continued to thrash around.

As T.J. pulled his rawhide glove onto his riding hand, he heard Sonny Joe Barker call out from the arena, "You'll be next, T.J."

T.J. swung a long leg over the top rail of the chute and was about to climb in when Sonny warned, "I wouldn't even get over him 'til this last bull is out of the arena. And be quick in there! Don't sit down on him 'til you're ready for the gate. He's gonna fight you all the way."

Then in a quieter, less forceful voice, Sonny Joe said to T.J., "This sum'bitch needs rode, Tom. You be the one to do it."

Randy Corey slapped T.J.'s back. "Ride up, cowboy!"

The previous bull had exited the arena. It was time.

T.J. pounded his chest one time. He let out a small growl and for a split second, he bared his teeth like a dog as the red lines in his one good eye grew thicker, larger and even more red. He took two deep settling breaths and crawled over the chute above his bull.

As T.J. slowly and gently lowered his body toward the bull, Bennett carefully climbed up the outside of the chute as to not disturb Genghis, who was, for once, standing still.

"Careful not to touch him with your spurs," Bennett cautioned, "or he'll blow up!"

T.J. reached down, grabbed the tail of his bullrope and handed it to Bennett.

Without warning, Genghis Khan lunged into the air throwing his head back while twisting his neck to one side, smacking T.J. hard in the upper lip with his blunted left horn.

Randy Corey, who was on the chute opposite Bennett, grabbed T.J. around his waist and steadied him above his still grappling bull.

T.J. blinked a couple of times and shook his head as blood flowed freely from both the front of his lip where Genghis' horn hit, and the back of his lip, which was cut wide open from his own teeth.

"You O.K., T.J.?" asked Randy.

"Yeah," muttered T.J.

Randy looked at Bennett. "Is he?"

Dave Whitney peered through the rails of the chute at T.J. He looked past the throbbing, swollen, purple lip and the blood dripping off T.J.'s chin, soaking into his rodeo shirt, and saw an intense determination and grit in his eye, "Hell yes, he's O.K.," barked Dave. "If he don't get out now, he never will!"

T.J. stuck his hand into the braided handhold of his bullrope. "Pull," he told Bennett. Bennett tugged quickly on the tail of T.J.'s rope. When the rope was good and snug around the bull's belly, T.J. said, "That's good." Bennett handed the tail back to T.J. Still straddling the rails above the bull, T.J. laid the rope across the palm of his riding hand

and handhold as Genghis continued to bounce around in the chute. With Randy holding him steady, T.J. then wrapped the rope around the back of his hand and across his palm once again. He squeezed the rope with all his might and cocked his thumb over his forefinger when Genghis ducked his head and lunged forward with such intensity that T.J. was jerked from Randy's arms and found himself lying face down on the bull. Fortunately, the bullrope had not been jerked from T.J.'s hand. Thinking quickly, he dropped his legs down both sides of the bull, sat up, slid up to the rope, and nodded for the gate to open. The man in charge of opening the chute gate was caught off guard by T.J.'s swiftness on such a bad chute-fighter. He fumbled with the latch. Genghis pointed his nose to the roof and reared up on his hind legs. He knocked Bennett off the chute gate with a left horn to the chest. Bennett landed with a thud, square on his back on the arena floor a good six feet from the chute.

"Get up, Bennett!" screamed Shot Palmer.

The chute gate swung wide. The bull's front feet were still in the air. T.J. was planted firmly in the middle of the bull's back. Bennett rolled to his stomach. Shot ran toward Bennett. Before the bull's front end even came down, he saw Bennett scrambling on the ground, and he zeroed in on him. From the corner of his eye, Bennett could see Genghis, like a locomotive, bearing down on him. Bennett kicked dirt behind him as he helplessly struggled to get to his feet. He felt as if he was moving in slow motion, and he knew it was too late. Genghis, not even worried about shedding his rider, took a run at Bennett. Nose to the ground, Genghis was less than two feet from his prey when Shot appeared from the left, leaping over Bennett in full view of the bull. The bull paid the clown no mind whatsoever. He stuck a horn under Bennett's belly, and with a flick of his neck, flung him upside down another eight feet into the arena, and charged him again. Shot was now uselessly behind the bull. He knew he had to get right in the bull's face if he were to do any good at all. He tried frantically to catch up as he roared, "Hey bull!   Heeeeey...!" T.J. spurred the bull in the shoulders and, grabbing his own cowboy hat with his free hand, began slapping the bull madly on the head. Anything to distract the bull...anything. Bennett lifted his face from the dirt to realize that he'd been flipped around and was facing Genghis Khan. He had time to do nothing, and that's what he did.

Right before the impact of the collision, Bennett saw into one of Genghis' fervent black eyes. There was no look of fright in his eye, no look of bitterness. It was the look of sheer exuberance. Violent, aggressive exhilaration. The same look that comes from a wild dog as it mercilessly slaughters a lamb just to leave it lie and go on to slaughter more. The same look that came from Bennett's own eye not ten minutes ago.

Their heads met.

A flutter of white light appeared before Bennett's eyes. A steady whistle-like buzz filled his ears. He was comfortable now. Comfortable and relaxed. Comfortable in every aspect, except for that glaring white light. As the buzz got quieter, the light got brighter. Then a thin line slowly appeared in the center of the light from one side to the other, and the line became a horizon. Miles and miles of sand... nothing else. Sand and hazy sun, as far as could be seen. He felt familiar here... like he'd been here before. The light began to fade, and a soft breeze caressed him from no particular direction.

"Get off him!" T.J. had jumped off his bull before the eight second buzzer and was tugging on his left horn. Shot tried to lay his own body over Bennett's, but with a horn to the belly was tossed out of the way, and Genghis continued to gore Bennett's limp body. Shot landed on his head and shoulders, rolled to his feet, and charged into battle again. This time he put his chest to the bull's head, both arms over the horns, and locked his hands together with all of his might. By now, Randy Corey had arrived and Dave Whitney was on his way. Randy grabbed Genghis' right horn. Genghis swung his head and sent him sailing. T.J. still had a hold on the left horn, and Shot had a tight fix on the head. Genghis shook his head back and forth. T.J.'s grip loosened a little. Genghis leaned into T.J. and pinned him to the ground. Had the points of the bull's deadly horns not been tipped back to half-dollar size blunt ends, he surely would have rammed one through T.J.'s chest like a saber. T.J. let go and gasped for air as the dull stump pressed hard on his right rib cage, his bones giving way to the pressure. With Shot still clinging tight, the bull finally loped slowly away from the downed cowboys, flinging his head from side to side.

Several cowboys now rushed into the arena to get Bennett and T.J. out of there before Genghis came back to do more damage. Others followed the bull and clown, not knowing what they'd do if they caught up.

Dave Whitney knelt beside T.J. "Come on, buddy. I'm getting you outta here."

T.J. was still fighting to get air to his lungs. He let Dave help him to his feet but would not leave Bennett. "Help him!" he grunted. Dave obeyed his orders.

Dave, Randy and Sonny Joe rolled Bennett onto his back. His open eyes stared sightlessly at the rafters. Blood trickled from his nose, his mouth and one ear.

Tears welled up in T.J.'s eyes. He made short, hoarse, grunting sounds as he wept for Bennett while struggling for his own breath. He pulled at his own blood soaked shirt. He began to get dizzy. His long legs collapsed beneath him, and he fell unconscious to the ground.

They were both carried from the arena.

Genghis was getting tired and Shot knew it. The bull slung his head back and forth much slower now and with much more effort. He was breathing hard and carrying his head low. So low, in fact, that Shot's heels drug in the dirt as he clung to the bull's head. Shot tried to back step, but couldn't keep up. His own legs were getting stepped on by the bull's front hooves. He could see five or more willing cowboys chasing after him hoping to somehow be there for the rescue. He was about to holler at them to get on the fence, save their own lives, when Genghis' big hoof landed squarely in the middle of the bullfighter's kneecap, dragging him from the bull's face and trampling the entire length of him. As the bull ran over Shot, he also stomped on his shoulder with a right hind hoof and grazed his cheek with the left, peeling the outer layer of skin back to his ear. The pain Shot felt in his face and shoulder was nothing compared to the agony of his shattered kneecap.

As he lay writhing in the dirt, he prayed that the bull was through, that he would just give up and go away. Shot looked up. Genghis had turned around and faced him. "Be still," Shot thought to himself. "Play dead. He'll go after someone else if I don't move." The pain was excruciating. His leg twitched. "Don't move," he thought. It twitched again. "Stop it!"

Genghis snorted and raked dirt with a deadly front hoof, daring Shot to make a move. Again Shot's leg twitched... and again... harder this time and more often. The harder Shot tried to control the spasms, the worse it got. Some well-meaning cowboys could have caught up, but they had stopped short when the bull had turned around to challenge them. One wave of his mighty horns sent them scrambling over the fence. It took all Shot had to keep from moaning. He bit his lip and told himself, "He's played out...he's too tired...he don't want me...if I could just...hold...still!" Genghis lowered his head and charged at a helpless and convulsing Shot Palmer. Shot rolled his back to the bull, closed his eyes, and braced himself for the crash. "This is it...this is..." With one horn under Shot's neck, another to his crotch, and the forehead against the middle of his back, Genghis launched him eight feet into the air. As Shot opened his eyes, he could see the arena fence underneath him. He hit the fence with his hip, bounced over, and landed hard on the concrete floor below.

Shot lay still where he landed on his back. From the corner of his eye, he could see Genghis on the other side of the fence watching him, pawing at the ground, daring him to try again. No thanks. He could no longer feel the pain. He could see the crowd gather around him. He heard one man ask, "You OK?" He could not answer. He could not move.

He could hear the rodeo announcer, "How about a big hand for our bullfighter, once again, Shot Palmer!" He heard the applause. He didn't care.

He heard a lady. "Well, he should've known better..."

The announcer. "You know, nobody wants to see a cowboy get hurt, but nobody wants to miss it when he does!"

A man. "Is he alright?"

A kid. "He's just pretending, isn't he, mom?"

"Bennett! How's Bennett? Where's T.J...where's the paramedics..."

Chapter 5: May 1987

T.J. Jergenson lay in his hospital bed and flipped through the TV channels with the remote control. It was early afternoon and there was nothing good on. Just soaps, game shows and talk shows. After five days of lying there in the Texas Medical Center, he was pretty much burnt out on TV anyway. He could sit up on his own if he wanted to and would, in fact, rather be sitting, but it wasn't worth the pain he had to go through to do it. He set the remote down and fumbled for the control to raise his bed to the upright position. Even the movement of the raising bed sent a dull ache through his ribs and chest. He raised it to its full extent. Still not comfortable. Why in the hell was the place where the bed bends halfway up his back instead of under his butt where it belonged? Must be the nurse's fault. Dammit. He lowered the bed halfway. That still wasn't right. He grabbed the side rails of the bed with his hands, pushed with his feet, lifted his butt, and winced in misery as he scooted his body up on the bed where he wanted it. The pressure from his broken collarbone and broken ribs all moving against one another each time he moved his body told him to hold still for a while.

But then his pillow wasn't right.

Heck with it. He'd rather be uncomfortable for the next thirty minutes than to suffer this merciless agony for the next ten seconds. He let out a quiet, dismal moan as his body tried to relax. Again, he picked up the remote and flipped through the channels as he tried to forget about the constant pain.

"T.J., if you can't find nothin' to watch, then why don't ya turn the son of a bitch off?" It was Shot Palmer in the next bed. The right half of Shot's face was not even remotely recognizable. It looked like nothing more than a big, red, puffed-up scab with a narrow slit for an eye to peek out. His left leg was in a sling and elevated above the rest of his body. It was operated on the night of the wreck, but the infection caused it to swell to twice its normal size, and he had been miserably sick ever since. That was five days earlier.

"What's the matter with you?" T.J. had to ask slowly and deliberately. The swelling in his upper lip had gone down considerably, but he still needed to be careful of the stitches across the inside and outside of his lip.

"You been flippin' through them damn channels ever since they moved you in here," snapped Shot, "and I'm gettin' sick of it!"

T.J., uncomfortable, in pain, and not feeling very congenial, ignored Shot's request and continued to press the channel button.

"You son of a bitch," Shot scowled quietly.

T.J. heard him, ignored him, and continued.

Shot's jaws tightened as he glared at T.J. "That dirty little bastard," he thought to himself. He felt the anger churning in his guts. He wanted to jerk him out of bed. He wanted to shove him in the ribs, shake him by the shoulder. He wanted to at least get that goddamn remote out of his grubby little hands!

T.J. could feel Shot's cold eyes upon him. He began switching channels faster now, and he turned up the volume just a little.

"He's tryin' to drive me nuts," Shot thought to himself again. "The only reason he's doin' it is because he knows I can't do a damn thing about it. If I could get outta this bed, I'd...I'd..." Shot looked at the pitcher of water on his bed table. "I bet I could throw that at him from here and hit him. That'd fix him." He eyed the pitcher for a moment and looked back at T.J. He imagined himself swinging the pitcher toward T.J., letting the cold water slap him in the face. He imagined the vengeance he would feel after seeing the look of surprise and anger on T.J.'s face. He imagined T.J. cursing and throwing the remote at him, missing him, and then he imagined himself laughing at T.J....

The channels continued to click...

"Should I do it?" Again in his mind's eye he picked up the pitcher. He let it sail at T.J., this time in slow motion. The water flowing through the air and ricocheting in every direction off T.J.'s sorry, arrogant, overbearing face. He replayed it in his mind until...

"Hey! What's goin' on?" came an old familiar voice from the hallway.

Shot's evil thoughts disappeared and a smile spread across his face as Dave Whitney and Randy Corey entered the room.

"How we doin', boys?" greeted Randy.

T.J. turned the TV off. He wanted to shout and holler, but when he raised his voice and said, "Hey!" his ribs felt as though they were being pushed out from the inside and the short, "Hey!" was as far as he got.

"It's about time you guys got here," welcomed Shot. "Pull up a chair!"

"No, thanks. We've been on the road for damn near eleven hours," said Randy as he shook Shot's hand and then T.J.'s.

"Damn, guys," said Dave as he extended a hand to T.J., "I'd hug ya, but I'm afraid I'd hurtcha."

"Don't even think about huggin' me," warned T.J. as he weakly squeezed Dave's hand. "Just the thought of it makes me hurt."

"I know the feeling," agreed Dave.

"Well, I'm a little sore but you ain't gonna hurt me!" spoke Shot as he sat up in bed.

Dave came to Shot, bent down and they embraced each other. "I love ya, buddy," said Dave. "Hell, I love all you guys."

T.J.'s fat lips formed a smile.

Randy suddenly felt awkward standing there. He loved them all, too, as much if not more than Dave. He just didn't talk that way. He found a chair and sat in it.

Dave let go of Shot and stood up straight. He said, to no one in particular, "I guess we don't realize just how much we do love somebody until..." His vision became blurry as his eyes began to well up, "...boy, you ain't lookin' too good, Shot."

"Well," said Shot as he lay back in the bed, "I may be down, but I ain't out."

"Alright," said Dave with much approval. "How long do they think you're gonna be down?"

"They say it'll probably be at least a year and a half before I can do any bullfighting. I guess they had to completely reconstruct my knee. According to the doctor, it'll be a good nine months before I can even walk on it."

"Where's your wife, Shot?" asked Randy.

"I've only talked to her once on the phone since it happened," said Shot. "I think she's through with me for good this time."

"Damn," whispered Dave to himself.

"Well, at least I didn't have no kids with this one," said Shot, trying to convince his friends, and himself, that it was no big deal.

The room fell quiet for a while as everyone tried too hard to think of something to talk about.

"So, where are you guys goin' from here?" asked T.J.

"We got three rodeos in California, then we're headin' over to Fort Smith, Arkansas," said Randy. "We'll stop through if you're still here."

"Yeah," said T.J. and after a pause, "Well, ride up."

"You know it," replied Dave. "So what do you guys do all day?"

"Ain't much we can do," T.J. answered. "Watch a little TV."

Shot cut in, "He never puts down that channel flipper. I swear he's gonna wear it out. Flips through them things like he's never gonna see a TV again in his life. This is the first time it's been off in three days."

"Aw, the heck it is," said T.J. to Shot. Then he said to Dave, "Watched Andy and Barney at noon."

"Yeah?" smiled Dave.

"Yeah," T.J. repeated, "Goober says 'Hey.'"

"Yeah," Dave said again, " 'Hey' to Goob."

"Well, T.J.," Randy spoke up, "Your face looks pretty rough but at least your eye's startin' to look better."

"That's good," said T.J., "Nothin' like a new injury to drive away an old one."

"What'd the doctors say about you?" Randy asked.

"Punctured lungs, broke ribs, bruised kidney. They said I'm really pretty lucky to be alive."

"How was the funeral?"

"Well, as far as funerals go," said Randy, "I guess it was about the worst one I ever been to." His guts tightened up and he chewed on his lip and looked at the floor as he fought off the urge that had been pestering him for the last five days. The urge to cry. Only twice since Bennett's death had Randy given in to the urge. Once when they lowered Bennett's casket into the ground, and another time when he was all alone. He didn't cry when he, Dave and Sonny Joe Barker carried Bennett's body from the arena that night, and he couldn't figure out why. He felt like he should be crying, but couldn't. Dave cried. T.J. cried right up until he passed out. Even Sonny Joe, who fought it off harder than anybody, sobbed that night and again at the funeral. Randy ought to just let loose and cry right now, but he couldn't.

"I hated to miss it," Shot said solemnly. "Me and T.J. just didn't have no choice."

Again there was a long, miserable pause.

"How's his folks?" T.J. finally asked.

"Seems like his mom took it better than his dad," said Dave. "I think when Bennett first started ridin' bulls she made herself realize this could happen any time...and when it happened, she was ready."

Shot looked surprised. "Really?"

"Well, maybe not 'ready,'" Dave searched for the right words, "but 'prepared'...in a way."

"How about his dad?" asked Shot.

"Boy, he didn't take it good at all," said Randy.

"Bennett was a part of that ol' man," Dave added. "Sure hated to see ol' Bill cry like that."

"They were real close," said Shot.

T.J. had forgotten about his own pain. He let out a deep long sigh that would have hurt bad only moments ago, and said, "Bennett used to call him every week just to tell him how he was doin', no matter where we were. They'd shoot the shit for an hour, sometimes more." And he smiled a little.

A faraway look engulfed his eyes as they looked past the walls of the hospital room and through the walls of time. "I'd always get on the line and talk to him for a few minutes, if I was around. He'd always ask me, 'You takin' good care of my boy?' I'd say, 'We're takin' pretty good care of each other.'" He chuckled once and held his ribs. The smile faded from his lips and his eyes came back to here and now. He looked at Dave. "I guess I let him down."

"Aw, now..." were the only words of consolation Dave could find.

"We'll hafta give ol' Bill a call from time to time," Randy suggested.

There was another long silence, but not one of those awkward, strained pauses where everyone is trying to think of something to say. They were all relaxing in their own thoughts, basically all thinking the same thought. Nothing else needed to be said.

Chapter 6: June 1987

As the dawn slowly unfolded into the morning, six cowboys loped their horses across the short buffalo grass that sparsely covered the high country flatland. Behind them was a grove of pine trees standing protecting a house, barn, corrals, tractor shed, and bunkhouse from the harsh northwest winds. In front of them were the Rocky Mountains. It would take a day of hard riding to reach the foothills. However, these cowboys would be at their destination in less than half an hour.

Steam puffed from the noses of horses and riders alike, disappearing into the chill of the Wyoming air. Clad in high heeled, high topped cowboy boots, shotgun chaps or chinks, layers of clothing under big coats or dusters, big bandannas, and weather-beaten old cowboy hats, a few straw, mostly felt, and some with stampede strings, it was easy to see that these were working cowboys, not rodeo. These boys only heard about the glory and romance of the rodeo cowboy. They could have gotten in on it if they'd wanted to. A good number of them could rope and ride with the best of them. They just didn't want to. They preferred the comfort of a familiar bunk every night, and the convenience of a home-cooked meal every morning, noon, and night. They still got to be out in the open spaces, the open air, the elements of freezing cold, blistering heat, forty mile an hour winds, and blinding snow. They got the wide variety of jobs, the menial jobs such as building fence, repairing windmills, digging out stock tanks, busting ice, grinding feed, and the more exciting and satisfying jobs such as breaking a colt and making a good horse out of him, or the ultimate good feeling job, helping a cow give birth to a healthy calf.

This day, the cowboys were headed for a job they looked forward to all year long; it was branding time at the Wheeler Ranch. To most of them, this meant hot, dusty, sweaty work, but it was also a social event of sorts. It was a time when all the neighboring ranchers showed up to lend a hand, and brought with them their hired hands and sons to rope and wrestle calves, their wives to serve the food and, hopefully for some of the young cowboys, their daughters.

Young Jake Wheeler was riding a little bit ahead of the pack. His father, Walt, and his grandfather, Morgan, ran the Wheeler Ranch. Jake, the only child of the only child, had big plans of taking over soon for his grandfather. Jake was twenty-three years old, fresh out of college with a degree in agriculture. He knew the business end of ranching well. He knew when to buy cattle, when to sell, he knew all about feed intake and grazing, and he could spot a sick critter a half mile away. But he was hard on horses and hired hands, unhandy with a rope, didn't like to fix fence and refused to work on machinery. Grandpa Morgan said he was as worthless as tits on a boar.

The billowy clouds above were turning an impressive pink as the snowcaps on the mountains before them glowed with anticipation of the day to come. A meadowlark could be heard, not seen, and somewhere a lone red fox studied the band of humans and horseflesh as they slowed to a stop at a barbed wire fence.

Although Jake was the first to get there, he didn't dismount to open the gate. "Open 'er up, Shorty," he ordered.

Shorty Abbott was the youngest and littlest cowboy of the bunch. He was sixteen and looked three or four years younger. Being that way, he was forced to take a lot of flack from the other cowboys. This was the second summer he'd come to work for the Wheeler outfit, and he was old Morgan's favorite. Morgan claimed it's the small cowboy that's got the big heart. Pushing his glasses up to the bridge of his nose, Shorty rode his little red roan mare up to the gate, got off and opened it. The others filed through and Jake said without a smile, "A real cowboy wouldn't of had to get off his horse to open the gate."

Shorty said nothing. He shut the gate and climbed back onto his horse, Little Red.

"O.K.," announced Jake, "Wade, you and Jay ride south along the fence to the corner and push any cattle west. Josh and Nathan, you ride that gully 'til it comes out at the dam and don't let nothin' by ya. Shorty, you come with me." With that, he jabbed his spurs into the ribs of his big bay gelding and rode up and over the hill.

Shorty leaned forward in the saddle and gave his horse the reins. Taking her cue, she raced up the hill after the leader. As they loped down the other side of the hill and to the flats, Shorty wondered why Jake always had to run his horse everywhere. He also thought about that last crack about 'a real cowboy' and wished he'd have said something back. Then again, what could he have said? Jake was right...but he was still a jerk.

They hadn't ridden a half mile when they came upon a herd of about seventy head of Black Angus cows and their Hereford-crossed calves. The cows were sporting a simple 'W' brand on their right shoulders. Those that were grazing stopped and watched as Jake and Shorty approached them, slowing to a walk. The ones that were lying down got to their feet. The calves, fat and sassy, three months old and close to two hundred pounds, some black, some red, some with white faces, were fearless and carefree so far. Some stood and watched along with their mamas. Others darted about, tails high in the air. A few jumped high in the air, twisting, turning, and kicking at imaginary predators. One walked a little way toward the riders, stopped, and lowered his head, challenging them to come closer. They did, and he scampered back to his mama.

"Heeya!" hollered one cowboy as he approached the herd.

"Hey, cows! Hey cows!" the other called out.

The cows are familiar with this routine. Mooing for their calves, they turned around and slowly began to drift westward.

"O.K., Shorty," yelled Jake over the noise of the now bellowing herd, "take 'em due west 'til you see the big catch pen. There'll be a few pickups and horse trailers down there and some of Dad's hands'll be there to help ya. Bring along any strays you see, and don't let nothin' get by you or you'll answer to me! I'm gonna go up and take the north end of the pasture."

Shorty waved him on.

Jake rode away from the herd, his mind fixed on the upcoming task, to ride the rimrocks of what the hired hands jokingly called 'The Ridge from Hell'. It was a mile and a half long and a half mile wide, with several gulches winding to the far end, steep canyon walls, giant boulders, and thick brush only where the rocks allowed it to grow. It was beautiful country, but he'd have to ride across it at least three times to make damn sure there were no stragglers left behind. Even then, it wouldn't be at all hard for a cow and calf to slip by in these canyons. Dad would sure be mad if they missed a calf and it was Jake's fault. Besides, there were snakes in there.

Jake stopped his horse, jerked him around, and ran him back to the herd.

"Shorty! he hollered. "Shorty!"

Shorty pulled up.

"Hey," said Jake as he trotted up beside him, "I better take this bunch so I can get a count when the rest of 'em come in. You go up the ridge."

"O.K.," said Shorty with the squeak of a voice that doesn't know if it belongs to a boy or a man. As he rode toward the ridge, he could hear Jake going on and on about, "...you better not leave none or I'll..." He ignored him and kept riding.

It was nearly three hours later when Shorty rode out of the ravine that exited the 'Ridge From Hell'. He had seen some markings but they were at least two days old. He enjoyed the ride through the canyon, seeing plenty of wildlife, too. He'd scattered a herd of antelope on his way to the ridge, saw three young coyotes' heads poking out from their den at the foot of the canyon wall, an owl that hadn't turned in yet from a night of hunting, ground squirrels, hawks, and, as the sun climbed higher, a few rattlesnakes stretched out on flat rocks to soak in the warmth. They would shake their tails in warning if he accidentally wandered too close, but they were still too frigid and slow to do any damage. The first times, his little mare, just two-and-a-half years old, darted sideways, taking Shorty by surprise and nearly dumping him.

Now, with the sun halfway up the eastern sky, Shorty let his horse walk along the sandy draw as he took off his denim coat and tied it to the back of his saddle.

He looked back at the canyon, confident that he left nothing behind. He looked straight above. A lone golden eagle circled the cloudless Wyoming sky. He looked to the south. Close to two miles away, dust rose into the air from the hooves of Jake's growing herd along with the two dozen or so pair brought in by Wade and Jay from the far end of the pasture. Ahead, the draw widened and the clay walls shrank. Not a cow in sight. To the north, rolling hills. Chances were there were cows all over up there.

Shorty pointed his horse uphill and loped him to the top of the first knoll. He was right. Black specs dotted the tops of the distant hills. This was going to be quite a job for one man, Shorty realized. And a lot of miles to be put on Little Red.

Instead of heading out right away, he sat there for a moment and studied the scene. It appeared they were already heading west. Great. They must have been heading in for water. He could just pick them up at the windmill.

He watched and listened some more. They were mooing a lot. He turned his head a little and stuck one ear closer to the herd. Little Red's ears perked up. She heard it, too...it was getting clearer..."Heeyah, heeyah cattle, get movin'!" It was barely audible. "Come on calves, heeup, heeup!" Yep, that's what it was. Somebody else was already bringing them. Must have been Walt and the hands from the main ranch.

The thought no more than crossed his mind when he saw a horse and rider top one of the many hills.

This'd work out fine. He could ride this edge of the hills and still keep an eye on the several draws, just in case.

He hadn't ridden two hundred yards when from somewhere in the draw, he heard something. But what? He stopped his horse and listened again. There was no breeze to interfere, but the only sound to be heard was the far-off cattle herd. Maybe he hadn't heard anything. He listened some more. Nothing. If he hadn't heard anything, he no doubt sensed something down there. He walked Little Red down the hill.

The clay banks that straddled the sandy draw were about fifteen feet high and straight down at the spot where Shorty rode his horse up to the edge, or tried to. His mount, trusting though she was, didn't want to get so close that they could look straight down over the edge.

"Come on, Red," Shorty coaxed as he nudged her in the ribs.

Five feet was as close as she'd get. She stammered around, left and right, trying to turn completely around, head and ears held high, rear end low with a slight hump in her back.

"Alright," Shorty gave in. He dismounted and walked to the edge of the drop off, still holding on tight to the reins. He looked down and, sure enough, a little mouse-gray calf was nursing on a big black cow. The cow, too dumb to look up, but knowing something was around, peered over her back for any predators that might bring harm to her baby. Shorty couldn't tell for sure from where he stood, but the calf looked much smaller than all the rest he'd seen today. It couldn't have been more than two months old. All the rest had been born in February and early March. The calf stopped suckling for a moment and looked around. "My God, look at the big ears on that little sucker!" Shorty thought to himself. "He doesn't look like any Hereford-cross calf. Way too skinny. And with ears like that he must be a Brahma..."

Suddenly, the ground gave out below Shorty's feet. He let the reins slip from his fingers as he fell to the sandy floor below. As he descended, he could see the little Brahma calf dart under its mother's belly and out into the draw. The old cow wasn't quick enough. The dirt hit her in the side and sent her rolling. In less than a second, Shorty was sitting in the dirt at the bottom of the wall without a scratch or bruise on him. His first thought was his horse. Evidently she didn't fall, so she must be all right. He just hoped she wouldn't run off. His second thought was of the mad cow running straight at him with her head down! Having no time to get up and run, Shorty rolled to his side and covered his head with his arms and waited for the first hit. She'd stopped short and stood at his feet. He could feel the gusts of hot breath on his legs. Though he dared not look up, his mind pictured her in a fighting stance, daring him to make a move. Why doesn't she just run away? As young as the calf is, she must think she's protecting it. If it were as old as the other calves, she wouldn't even care. Shorty ran the whole situation through his mind. There he was, helpless, in front of a protective mother cow, and his horse was probably headed back to the ranch already. Should he just lie there? If only there were a piece of driftwood nearby, he'd have grabbed it and whacked her on the nose. Of course that might have been a mistake. It might have really put her on the fight. How much longer was she going to stand there? He slowly moved an arm. She snorted at him. He froze. He could see her out of the corner of his eye. She was pawing dirt. He waited.

Five minutes. This was dumb. Maybe he could scramble up the bank before she gets to him. But what if he couldn't? What if the bank was too steep and there was nothing to grab on to? She surely couldn't do much damage, could she? She didn't even have horns.

Another five minutes passed. Shorty was torn between boredom and fright. He didn't even feel the fright anymore, but about the time boredom told him to run, fear or perhaps just common sense told him to wait.

"Shorty, you O.K.?"

It took a moment for Shorty to recognize the voice. It was Walt Wheeler. "You O.K. down there, Shorty?"

Shorty did not know how to answer. Any noise or movement might cause the cow to charge. He nodded his head just a little. So little, in fact, that Walt could not make it out.

"You hurt?"

The cow slung her head from side to side, snorting up at Walt.

"Shorty, I'm gonna throw you my rope," said Walt. "Grab the end and I'll pull you up."

With that, Walt, who was mounted on a big sorrel gelding, tossed the end of his lariat down to Shorty and wrapped the other end around his saddle horn. "The rope's right by your head, Shorty. When I say 'now,' you grab it." He turned his horse away from the hill. "Now!" he commanded as he spurred his horse into action.

Shorty latched onto the rope and was instantly jerked from the ground into the solid dirt wall. He looked over his shoulder to see the mad cow right behind him running at full speed. When she was about two feet away, she ducked her head with all her might, slammed it into the wall, barely missing Shorty as he was elevated up the side.

Walt stopped Shorty a couple of feet short of the top, jumped off his horse, and ran to the edge. On hands and knees, he reached over, grabbed Shorty by the arm and lifted him to safety.

Below, the old cow seemed completely calm now. She trotted back to her calf, satisfied that it was out of danger, and the two of them headed west down the draw.

"Are you alright?" Walt asked again.

"Yeah," Shorty answered as he dusted himself off.

"Did she hit ya?"

Walt towered above little Shorty, doubling him in weight. Shorty did not lift his head to look his boss in the eyes. He was embarrassed. "No, she never touched me."

"What were ya doin' down there without your horse?"

Shorty told him about the ground breaking away underneath him and how he laid still until help arrived.

"Well, I reckon' you done the right thing," said Walt. He turned and walked back to his horse. His foot found the stirrup as he swung his heavy frame into the saddle. As he coiled his rope, he said, "Seen your pony headin' down the trail or else I'da' never come a-lookin' for ya. I'll go get 'im." As he loped off he yelled over his shoulder, "Ain't you never taught him to ground tie?"

Shorty stood there alone, thinking about what the boss had said. He was right, too. Shorty had broken and trained Little Red, his first ever, and the one thing he'd neglected to teach her was to stay put when her rider dismounted and dropped the reins to the ground. Of course, if the horse hadn't wandered off, Shorty would still be lying in front of that mad old cow.

Ten minutes later, Walt came trotting his horse back up the trail, leading the little mare behind. Shorty wondered what Walt was thinking of him now. Did he think he was a little screw up for what just happened? Shorty knew that Walt's dad, Morgan, liked him because he'd just come out and say so. Frankly, he didn't care what Jake thought of him but it would sure have been nice to know how he stood with Walt.

Walt handed him the reins. He mounted, saying nothing.

"The boys got everything wrangled and they'll be comin' together at the creek. I reckon the only thing we got to tend to is that ol' cow and her calf, and they're headin' the right direction," said Walt. "We'll just ride along this draw here. I believe there's a place we can get in behind 'em, down yonder."

"Yessir," replied Shorty as he coaxed Little Red into a trot.

"Slow down," commanded Walt as he eased his horse into a walk, "We'll get there in due time."

Shorty pulled up and waited for Walt to catch up.

Walt tipped his gray, sweat-stained felt hat back on his head as he rode along, letting the bright summer sun caress his smooth pale forehead. What was left of his thinning hair was a graying blond. He pulled a pouch of loose tobacco from a shirt pocket, along with some papers, and began to leisurely roll himself a cigarette. His eyes were little more than slits hiding under bushy gray eyebrows. His cheeks were red and extremely coarse from battling frost bitten winters. A thick gray mustache covered his mouth. Shorty figured him to be about fifty-three, fifty-four years old. Walt laid the reins over the neck of his horse while he rolled and lit his cigarette. "Coulda' been a helluva wreck if you'da' been sittin' on your pony when that wall gave out."

"Yessir," said Shorty, "I tried to ride her right up to the edge, but she wouldn't go."

Walt took a drag and let the smoke billow from his nose before he spoke. "Sometimes they know more about it than we do."

Both herds could be seen now, up ahead a ways. Jake and his bunch trailing them northwest, and Walt's crew just spilling them out of the hills heading southwest. There was still a good mile or so between the two.

The old cow in the draw was trotting along at a pretty good pace, her calf right behind her. She couldn't possibly see the cattle herd from down there. Shorty wondered how she knew they were there. Maybe she could hear them. Shorty could if he listened real hard. Perhaps she could just sense that the rest of the cows were moving and her instincts were leading her to them. Then again, maybe she just wanted to get away from Walt and Shorty. Shorty thought he and Walt ought to go a little faster to keep up with the pair, but Walt just eased along nonchalantly. If it were Jake instead of his dad, they'd have been right behind the old cow, whipping and spurring, pushing her every step of the way. Shorty came to the conclusion that Walt's way was better.

The little calf was starting to tire, its head hanging a little lower than before. Shorty wondered why it was so little and didn't look like the rest of the calves. He'd have asked Walt, but he didn't want to seem dumb. There's nothing worse than feeling dumb in front of your boss, and he was still feeling a little dumb from the boss having to not only pull him up out of the sand draw, but having to go fetch his horse for him afterwards. That was enough humiliation for one morning. Then Shorty thought of what old Morgan had told him once, "The only real asinine question is the one that wasn't asked." Meaning that it's a lot better to ask a dumb question now that to make a dumb mistake later.

"How come that calf's so much littler than the others?" Shorty asked.

Walt didn't answer right away. He seldom did. "He's younger than the others."

Shorty thought for a moment, "Well, how come he's younger?"

Walt seldom gave a straight answer when a smart one would do. "He's born later."

A lot of help that was. To heck with him then. "If he thinks I'm so dumb and is going to treat me like I'm dumb, then I ain't gonna talk to him anymore. No wonder Jake's like he is," thought Shorty.

Walt took one last drag off his cigarette and flicked it over the bank. "The only thing that's got me confused is..." He pulled his hat back down over his forehead and rested his arm on the saddle horn, "...why that little son of a bitch is a Braymer and not a Hereford?"

As they rode along, the walls that cradled the sand in the gulch shrank until they were nonexistent. The cow and calf could see the two herds closing together now, and as much as they wanted to be a part of those herds, they had begun to tire under the hot sun and slowed to a brisk walk.

"The closest Braymer bulls around here are a good ten miles north a' here," Walt said as he rubbed his jaw. "That'd be John Franklin's place. I heard he had a fence jumper, but I'll be damned, you'd think I'da' heard about it if he'da' ended up on my place...unless he'da' just bred her an' kept a-movin'...but another thing I can't figure out is why in the hell she wasn't already bred at the time...all the rest of 'em were...hell, all the rest of 'em were a ...month, month and a half along."

Walt's sudden inclination to talk surprised Shorty a little. He had never heard Walt talk this much at one time, unless he was giving orders.

Walt went on, "Why, it was the last parta' April when she had him. I was there. I had to pull the little bastard. His two front feet were stickin' out, but he had his head cocked around backwards...ignorant little shit...I pushed his feet back in her and reached in to pull his nose around and the first thing I got ahold of was one of them big Braymer ears and I thought, 'What the sam-hell is goin' on...closest Braymers are ten miles from here, now how in the hell could that happen?'"

Shorty thought Walt would never shut up.

"I got his head turned around and his nose out the hole, and shit, he squirted outta there like gas through a nozzle. Damn calf was slingin' his head around so hard, I had a helluva time clearin' his nose so he could breathe. An' then don't you think that ol' mama cow didn't get on the fight! If I hadn't had a damn good horse on the other end a' my rope, we'da' been in one helluva mess." Walt paused for awhile. His story was done, but he continued to think aloud. "I just can't figure out how in the hell she got herself bred to a Braymer bull..."

Soon the two herds came together and formed one. Shortly after, the mama cow and the Brahma calf caught up and buried themselves in the middle of three hundred other bawling calves and their bellowing mothers. Walt had to yell to be heard above the noise, "How'd we get stuck ridin' drag?" Referring to the fact that he and Shorty were directly behind the herd crowding them on, and consequently, breathing, eating, and wearing the fine Wyoming dust that hung behind these large herds. "The boss ain't supposed to hafta ride drag!" Although this was true, Walt said it in jest. He pulled his bandanna up over his nose, and Shorty did the same.

"Hyah!" Shorty called out from time to time at the slower moving critters that were lagging behind.

A huge, fat Hereford bull trudged along behind his harem. He was reddish brown with a white face and neck, horns straight out from both sides of his head and curling forward. Walt whacked him on the rump with his lariat and jokingly yelled at the beast, "Get up, there, ya worthless son of a bitch! If you'da' been doin' your job, I wouldn't be stuck with a Braymer calf!"

The herd moved along smoothly and had very little trouble crossing the creek. In less than an hour, they were to the branding pen.

The branding pen sat a quarter of a mile from the west end of the pasture, out in the flats. It was thirty yards square, with three sides consisting of mesh wire and hedge post, while one side was completely open. After the herd was driven into the pen, neighboring ranchers lined their pickup trucks and trailers across the open end to keep the cows and calves corralled until after the noon meal.

To the south of the pen, women began to set up the folding tables. From the backs of their pickups and trunks of their cars, they produced broilers of hot roast beef, kettles of beans, bowls of fruit and potato salad, coolers full of lemonade, iced tea, and to top it all off, pies and desserts of every kind. Children too young to help were generally raising a ruckus and having the time of their lives, playing with friends they hadn't seen since the day their country school let out for the summer and would not see again until the Fourth of July rodeo.

When the cattle were secure in the pen, Shorty rode over to the windmill and stock tank to give his horse a much needed and deserved drink. A few of the other cowboys were already there. Among them was Jake.

"How'd it go for you, Shorty?" Jake asked.

"Alright," said Shorty, not wanting to discuss the little incident at the sand draw.

"You didn't miss no calves up there, did ya?"

"No," said Shorty as he climbed down from the saddle.

"If you did," warned Jake as he rode off, "your ass is grass!"

As Little Red got a long, cool drink, Shorty loosened the cinch on his saddle a little. The horse had put in a good morning, and it was time for her to relax a little.

Shorty took his glasses off and placed them on the seat of his saddle before splashing stock tank water on his hot, dusty face. It felt so good that he went ahead and stuck his whole head in the water beside his trusty horse. He lifted his face from the water and let out a long, contented sigh, "Ahhhhh."

Little Red, her thirst quenched, raised her head. Shorty stood up, leaned on his horse's shoulder and patted her on the neck because she was his friend. The next evening, Little Red would begin to learn to ground tie.

Shorty put his glasses back on, led his horse to the branding pen fence, and tied the reins to a hedge post. "See ya later, buddy," he said, as he walked away toward the serving tables.

Dinner wasn't ready yet, and Shorty wasn't all that hungry anyway. He was looking for Morgan. He didn't have anything to tell or ask the old man, he just liked being around him.

Shorty spotted him at the far end of the branding pen, sitting in a green and white Ford pickup in front of the long red gooseneck stock trailer. Morgan grinned when he saw Shorty coming. Shorty walked past the corner of the pen, behind the other horses tied there, between the pickups and cars, past the women busy loading up the serving tables. He even walked by pretty little Mary Ann Garner and didn't notice her.

"Hello, Mister Wheeler!" Shorty greeted the old man as he approached the pickup.

"Well, if it ain't the young Abbott boy!" hailed Morgan, "How are you, Shorty?"

"Real good," said Shorty as he reached in the window and shook the old cowboy's hand. Although Shorty worked for Morgan, he seldom got to see him. Morgan was on the main ranch, and Shorty's bunkhouse was thirty miles away by road at what they call the Busted Spoke Ranch, which was run by Jake. "How you doin'?" asked Shorty.

"Oh, can't complain," said Morgan, "Wouldn't do me a damn bit of good if I did. How's your folks?"

"Alright, I guess. Ain't seen 'em since school got out."

"Better give 'em a call... let 'em know we ain't killed ya off yet."

"Yeah, I'm gonna," said Shorty.

"How'd it go for ya this mornin'?" asked Morgan.

Shorty's eyes shifted from Morgan's face to the ground as he muttered, "Went purdy good." Time to change the subject. "You still got that old pistol?"

Without looking, Morgan picked up his Colt 45 revolver from beside him on the pickup seat. "Got it right here," he said, handing the gun to Shorty.

Shorty took it, closed one eye and sighted down the barrel into nowhere. "How come you carry this thing?"

"Shoot Indians," Morgan said without hesitation. Morgan never smiled when he was joking, but Shorty could always tell.

"Yeah, right," he said, handing the gun back to its owner, "Now tell me the truth."

Morgan looked him in the eye, "How'd it go for you this mornin'?"

Shorty knew he'd been busted. He stammered around a little before telling about the ground giving out from under him and the cow holding him hostage until help arrived.

"Well, that ain't nothin' to be ashamed of," Morgan said as he put the pistol back on the seat. "That's what any smart man woulda' done."

Shorty looked up from the ground again and forced a smile. "Is that what you'da' done?"

"Maybe it is," stated Morgan, "and maybe it ain't."

"So how come you carry that gun?" Shorty asked again.

"Shoot Indians," Morgan answered again.

Shorty laughed.

The lines in Morgan's face were deep and many. They portrayed the life of a man who had lived through more than most eighty-year-olds are allowed. Shorty could see a story in every wrinkle, and he wanted to hear them all.

"Shot a coyote with it yesterday mornin'," said Morgan.

"Ya did?"

"Third one this month," he boasted. Before Shorty could respond, Morgan asked, "See little Mary Ann Garner over there?"

Shorty looked over to the serving tables. The food line was beginning to move, and Mary Ann was dishing out the beans. The sun was soft in her light brown hair, so short it barely covered the back of her neck. Her velvet eyes shone bright above flushed cheeks and an innocent smile. With an apron tied around her shapely waist, covering blue denim jeans, the white tanktop blouse revealed a light golden tan on her dainty shoulders and delicate arms.

A shy smile creased Shorty's blocky face. He saw her, all right.

"I'll bet you'd like to get in on a little a' her action, wouldn't ya?" coaxed Morgan.

Shorty was embarrassed, "Aw, Mister Wheeler."

"Don't you think she's lookin' pretty good?" the old man urged.

"Wull...yeah, she's alright."

"She's just your age. Did you know that?"

"Yeah, I know," Shorty mumbled as he scooped prairie dirt back and forth with the toe of his boot.

"By golly, I don't think she had near the build on her last summer as she does this summer, do you?"

Shorty looked at Morgan with an uneasy smirk. He didn't know what to say. His face was red with fluster. It sure was getting hot out.

"How come you ain't rousted that up yet?" teased Morgan.

Shorty searched for an excuse. "I just ain't," was all he could come up with.

"Well, maybe you ought to," the boss advised. "I think she likes ya."

"Yeah, right," replied Shorty.

"Well, I think she does," Morgan repeated. "You didn't see the way she looked at ya when you walked by a minute ago, did ya?"

"No," Shorty answered.

"Well, I did," said Morgan. "Now when you go through the line, there, you talk to her a little bit. I guarantee she'll talk back."

Shorty laughed uneasily under his breath. "I wouldn't know what to say."

"Hell! It don't matter what ya say!" Morgan coached. "Just say somethin'!"

Shorty thought about it for a moment, "I don't know, Mr. Wheeler..."

"Well, I know one thing," said Morgan, "Ya better get over there and get some grub in ya before there ain't none left."

"Yessir," said Shorty as he quickly turned and started to walk away. For the first time, he was glad to get away from Mr. Wheeler. Still, he wondered if the old man might be right about Mary Ann.

"Hold on, kid!" called Morgan.

Shorty turned around.

"I ain't gonna sit in this pickup all damn day! Get my chair outta the back and help me out of here!"

"Yessir, Mr. Wheeler," said Shorty. He drug Morgan's wheelchair from the bed of the pickup and unfolded it. He set it upright by the pickup and opened the door.

Two years ago, Morgan could have walked as fast and far as a man half his age. At eighty-one, he could still rope and ride as good as the very best in the country. After all the years of breaking horses and pushing cows, it wasn't a bad bronc or mad mama cow that put him on wheels. He fell off a windmill. He'd crawled up the very tower by the tank that Shorty just watered his horse from to replace some broken fan blades. The platform gave out beneath him, causing him to fall twenty feet to where his left hip met with the rim of the stock tank. He lay there ten hours before Walt found him and hauled him to the hospital. Morgan came out of it with a shattered hip and his lower back knocked so far out of joint that at his age it was irreparable. He hadn't walked or ridden a horse since. He still got out and drove around his pastures in his pickup, checking on the cattle, pastures, mineral and salt blocks, and the stock tanks, as long as he had Walt or one of the hired hands, or Violet, his wife of fifty-six years, to get out and open the gates.

"Push me up there by the end of the servin' table," said Morgan after Shorty helped him out of the pickup and into the chair. "I'll get one of them ladies to fix me up a plate."

Shorty obeyed.

"Now, get over there and get somethin' to eat."

"O.K.," said Shorty. "See ya later, Mister Wheeler."

"And you be sure and talk to little Mary Ann, now!" Morgan said, loud enough for several people to hear.

Shorty could hear the chuckles and feel the eyes upon him as he took his place in the chow line.

The food looked and smelled good, but Shorty just wasn't all that hungry. He was nervous about Mary Ann. There she was, dishing out the beans, smiling and talking to each cowboy who passed his plate before her. It had never entered his mind until Morgan Wheeler brought it up, but now, as he looked at Mary Ann, she was suddenly the prettiest girl Shorty had ever seen. It was as if she was a completely different person than she'd been at last year's branding. He was dreading having to go by her in line. What could he say to her? He had to say something; Morgan was sitting down at the end watching and listening. He'd give him hell if he didn't say something. But what?

He began to stare at her. Her hair looked so soft. Her eyes so big and blue, her lips so full...

"Would you like two sandwiches or one?"

Shorty looked across the table. "Huh?"

"Two sandwiches or one?" a lady smiled.

"Uh...one," Shorty stammered.

She handed him a plate with a bun piled high with thin slices of barbequed beef. "Help yourself to the ketchup, mustard and pickles," she said cheerily.

He did not answer. Again, he was looking at Mary Ann and wondering what to say. He'd better think fast. He was getting closer.

"Hey, peewee." It was Jake in line behind him.

Shorty hated it when he called him that. He only did it when he was picking on him or showing off. Now he was doing it in front of Mary Ann.

"What'd you do, get lost this mornin'?"

"No, I wasn't lost," said Shorty, not looking up as he put ketchup on his sandwich.

"Then how come my dad had to go back and find ya?" Jake asked with a laugh.

Shorty didn't answer. He had never cared for Jake from day one. He was quickly learning to hate him.

"Huh, peewee? Well, speak up."

Shorty moved down the line. He felt Mary Ann's eyes upon him. He felt his face blush red.

"Or did your horse start trottin' and you fell off?" taunted Jake.

A few of the other cowboys began to chuckle.

"That's alright, Shorty," said one of the older hands, "Jake was green once, too." Although well meant, it only added to Shorty's embarrassment.

"Shoulda' seen the size of the rattlesnake I killed yesterday, Jay," bragged Jake.

Good, at least he'd changed the subject. Shorty felt as if a ton of pressure had been released from his soul as he came to the big pot of beans, and Mary Ann held out her dipper.

"Hi, Shorty," she said in a sweet, soft voice.

The pressure was back on!

His eyes rose until they met hers. Then they quickly dropped back down to his plate. "Hi, uh...," he momentarily forgot her name, "...Mary Ann."

There! He'd talked to her. Just like old Mister Wheeler instructed him to. Now he could move on down the line, which he did.

"Shorty?" he heard her pretty voice again. "Don't you want any beans?"

"Uh..." Shorty searched for the right word. "No."

He passed by the salads and a lady asked him, "What kind of pie would you like?"

He hastily took a piece from the corner of the table, not even realizing that it was rhubarb pie. Shorty hated rhubarb. He cursed himself for being so unfriendly to Mary Ann. She probably thought he was unfriendly or stuck up, or that he didn't like her.

"Better eat more than that, peewee." It was Jake. "You're a growin' boy, remember?" Without waiting for a reply, he turned to Mary Ann. "Hey, cutie. How ya doin'?"

"Just fine," smiled Mary Ann. "And how are you?"

"If I was any better, there'd hafta be two of me," declared Jake.

Shorty watched and listened to the two of them chat. As much as he disliked Jake, he wished he could be like him in some ways. Jake could walk up to any girl like he didn't have a care in the world, and start a conversation. Shorty wondered why he couldn't bring himself to do that. And look at that! Mary Ann was talking back, and smiling. She liked him. He was so undeserving. He didn't care about her. He talked that way to all the girls.

"So what have you been doing now that school is out?"

Why hadn't Shorty thought of saying that?

"Oh, not much," her voice was clear, smooth and pleasant, like a song. "Just riding my horse... and helping my dad put up hay."

"Looks like you been laying out a little, too."

Shorty would never have said that.

"Every time I get a chance."

"Maybe I oughta come over and lay out with you sometime."

A beautiful shade of light pink colored Mary Ann's smiling cheeks. "Oh, I doubt that," she said.

"Yeah, I'll come over and rub some suntan oil on ya."

Now he's being a little too forward, Shorty thought to himself.

"I don't think so, Jake," she answered, showing her annoyance.

"That way I can check out your tan line," he teased as the soft pinkness burned red on her face. "If you got one," he added.

Now he's definitely out of hand, Shorty reasoned. He felt like walking up to Jake and thumping him in the chest and telling him to shut up. That would show Mary Ann where his heart was. But he didn't.

"Jake, you better keep movin'," she scolded. "There are people waiting in line behind you."

"O.K.," said Jake, "but can I call you sometime?"

Call her? Shorty was surprised that Jake would even ask such a question. There's no way she'd want him to call after the rude comments he'd just made.

"Sure!" she said eagerly.

Shorty dropped his pie. It didn't matter. He hated rhubarb.

An hour later, the ladies were already breaking camp. What was left of the beef, beans, and desserts was loaded back into the pickups and trunks along with the card tables and folding chairs.

The propane torch was burning full blast and the branding irons were bright orange hot. The pickups and stock trailers that blocked the entrance to the branding corral were removed and replaced by cowboys, some afoot and some on horseback.

The mounted cowboys were the ropers. They rode their horses into the herd, roped a calf, preferably by the hind legs, and dragged it to the branding area. There were six mounted cowboys. Jake was one of them.

As for the horse-less cowboys, Walt did the branding. If the ropers got too far ahead of him, he'd recruit someone to help him but that didn't happen very often. His wife, Nadine, pulled double duty today. Not only had she done all of the chores that morning, hitched up the trailer, cooked, loaded and hauled the meat, iced tea, lemonade, tables and utensils, she also ran the vaccine gun, giving each calf five cc's of medicine in the shoulder muscle. Nadine and Walt's neighbor and close friend, John Franklin, would castrate the bull calves. He'd carry with him a bucket to keep the testicles in. When the branding was over this evening, the girls would skin, clean, deep-fat fry, and serve them for supper. The flatlanders call them calf fries. In the foothills of Wyoming, they're known as Rocky Mountain Oysters.

The rest of the cowboys, on foot, were the wrestlers. There were six teams of wrestlers, two to a team. As the roper dragged the calf through the branding area by a hind leg, a wrestler put the weight of his knee on the calf's neck, pinning him to the ground, while the other wrestler grabbed one hind leg, and sitting on the ground, braced his foot against the calf's other leg, preventing him from kicking. He then removed the lariat from the leg, and they held the calf down until the brander, vaccinator, and if needed, the castrator, completed their jobs. Then they set the calf free to trot back into the herd and bawl for its mother.

Shorty was partnered up with his buddy, Wade Skinner. Wade and Shorty were good wrestlers, but they'd rather have been roping. Roping was an easier job if you were good, but more than that, there was a certain prestige to being a roper at a branding. The ropers were considered top hands, real cowboys, while any kid with a strong back and weak mind could wrestle. When a roper talked to a wrestler from atop his mount, he looked down on him.

Jake hadn't wrestled calves since he was fourteen, an accomplishment that he was proud of. He wanted everyone to know, especially Mary Ann, that he was, in fact, a top hand. As he waded his horse into the crowded mob of cattle, rope in hand, he watched Mary Ann as she put the last folding chair into the trunk of her mother's car. He didn't want to throw his loop until she was looking. A little white- faced black calf trotted directly through the line of fire. Jake let that one pass. He eased his horse a little further into the milling herd of bellowing mothers and calves. Another one lined out right in front of him. He looked over his shoulder for Mary Ann. She was talking to some lady, still not watching. The other ropers had already dragged at least a couple of calves to the fire. What the heck, she'd be watching later. He cast his lasso over his big bay gelding's ears and snagged a red heifer calf by the neck. He dallied his rope around the saddle horn and pulled the calf to the branding area. Shorty and Wade had just let a calf up and were ready for another one. Jake's calf was on her feet, tugging and bawling, frantically trying to escape. Shorty clenched the taut rope that connected the calf and roper, hung tight and made his way hand over hand to the struggling calf. With his right hand still grasping the rope, he reached over the calf's back to the far-side flank and, forcing his knees under the calf's belly, lifted the two hundred pounder off her feet and flopped her down on her side. At the same instant, Wade clasped onto a hind foot, dropped to the ground, and braced the heel of his boot against the calf's other leg. Shorty now had his knee stuck squarely against the defenseless animal's neck. He took the loop from around her neck and tossed it in Jake's direction. Jake rode back into the herd and, first loop, caught another one by the neck. He towed it into the open and waited patiently as Wade and Shorty's last calf was being processed. As soon as they set her free, he brought the next one by. Again, Shorty flanked the calf and Wade took the hind legs.

Wade looked up at Jake. "Hey, Jake!" he shouted through the noise of the herd, "It'd be a lot easier on us if you'd rope 'em by the hind leg so we don't hafta flank 'em!"

Jake looked down at Wade. "Quit your snivellin," he scowled. "Farmers rope feet, cowboys rope the necks!" and he trotted off.

"What a jerk," said Shorty.

As Jake rode back to the herd, he peered over to where the ladies were gathered. She was looking! Mary Ann had pried herself from the boring talk of the mothers and wives and come over to watch her new hero. Jake seized the opportunity to impress his enthusiastic audience of one. A calf stood alone to Jake's right. He tossed a backward loop that his Grandfather Morgan had taught him, but he missed.

"Damn," he said under his breath as he quickly coiled his rope. He saw another one, an easy target, but by the time he had built his loop the calf had turned and was hidden in the sea of cattle. Jake spurred his steed hard in the belly causing him to spring forward. The cattle parted up the middle as he trotted into the herd. He spotted the small Brahma-looking calf. Too small. He let it go by. There went a good-sized red bull calf. He trotted his horse toward the calf as he threw his loop around its neck. As Jake attempted to jerk the slack out of his rope to tighten the loop around the calf's neck, his horse stumbled. Jake grabbed for the saddle horn as his mount regained its footing. Before Jake could regain control of his rope and jerk it tight, the calf had simply lowered his head and backed out of the loose loop. Jake whacked his horse over the head with the other end of his lasso. "You clumsy son of a bitch!" he muttered.

Mary Ann's enthusiasm waned as she watched the unnecessary scolding.

Shorty and Wade freed their now-processed calf and watched as they waited for another.

"Why's he beatin' on ol' Buck like that?" Wade asked to no one in particular.

Shorty watched and said nothing.

"Now, whoa!" snapped Jake as he jerked back on the reins. Buck stammered and sidestepped. Jake thrashed him between the ears again. Suddenly, he sensed numerous eyes on him. Declining to look up, he tugged gently on the reins and patted his horse on the neck. "Easy,

Buck," he lulled, hoping his father hadn't seen his little blowup.

It was too late to calm his horse. Buck was nervous and jittery, awaiting another rap on the head. "Settle down, buddy," Jake said softly as he stroked his mane and nudged him farther into the herd. Buck pranced sideways, snorting fear with his head held high, eyes and ears scanning all directions. Jake saw a calf in the open. He swung his loop and Buck nearly jumped from beneath him.

"Alright, you dirty bastard!" growled Jake as he whipped his horse across the rear.

Buck bolted forward as Jake yanked back on the reins. Buck backed up and Jake spurred him hard in the guts.

"Alright, that's enough!" Jake heard his grandfather's voice. "You're either gonna learn to ride or you're gonna get another job!" Morgan Wheeler barked from his wheelchair.

Jake stopped instantly and looked at Morgan.

Everyone, including Walt and Nadine, were listening. Although there was a constant roar from the resounding bellows and bawls of the herd, Morgan's crackling tenor voice carried above. "What's the matter with you? You didn't learn that from your Pa! Why, if I could get outta this chair, I'd kick your butt all the way to Colorado!"

"But, Grandpa," pleaded Jake. "He's acting up!"

"He wasn't actin' up! YOU was actin' up!" hollered Morgan. "Now get off him and go tie him up! I'm gonna find you a job you can handle!

"Shorty, tighten up your cinch and build yourself a loop."

Shorty's eyes lit up. "Yessir, Mr. Wheeler!"

Jake bit his lip as he swung his horse around and headed him for the exit.

"Hey!" It was Morgan again. "I said get off the horse and tie him up."

Jake was embarrassed, humiliated and confused. "Huh?"

"I didn't say ride outta here. I said get off. Now get off your horse and lead him outta here!"

Jake did as he was told.

It wasn't a minute and a half later when Shorty returned on Little Red. They wandered easily into the herd and before long, Shorty saw his first catch of the day, a bald-faced red heifer facing away as the cows stepped to either side. Shorty rode up to the calf. As she trotted away from him, he tossed his loop neatly under her belly, setting a trap for the hind feet. As she stepped into the snare, Shorty flipped the rope upward catching both hind feet. He dallied around the saddle horn and pointed Little Red toward the fire. As the slack in the rope became taut, the calf fell to one side and was drug easily to the team of Wade and Jake.

"Get outta the way, Wade," grumbled Jake. "I'm takin' the head."

Wade slipped the rope from the calf's feet, "Here ya go, Shorty." He then looked at Jake. "See how much easier it is this way?" he asked cheerfully. "We don't have to flank 'em."

"Shut up," Jake answered.

An hour passed and Shorty was roping quite consistently. He'd only missed a few and Little Red was working real well. Shorty was so focused on what he was doing he wouldn't have known if Mary Ann was watching or not. In fact, it had never entered his mind.

All of the ropers were doing well. So well that Walt was falling behind on the branding. The wrestlers were waiting on him, and in turn, the ropers were waiting on the wrestlers.

"You need help, Dad?" Jake asked as he held his end of a calf pinned to the ground.

Walt scorched the Wheeler brand, a simple 'W', on the upper right shoulder of the calf. The defenseless hostage bawled loudly and tried uselessly to kick free as the hot iron singed the outer layer of hide, sending white smoke and the rancid smell of burnt hair to linger above and fade into the still Wyoming air. "Starting to look like it," said Walt.

"I'll help ya," Jake eagerly offered.

"You better stay here," Walt replied. "I can't afford to lose a wrestlin' team."

"Tommy Franklin's gettin' old enough to wrestle calves, Dad," implored Jake. "I'll bet John would like for him to learn how. Ain't that right, John?"

John Franklin was castrating a calf right beside Jake and Wade. "What's that?" he asked.

"If Tommy would come and wrestle with Wade, here, I could get Dad caught up brandin'."

John did not look up from the operation he was performing. "Tommy!" he yelled from the side of his mouth.

"Yeah, Dad," a husky twelve-year-old answered from the back of a pickup.

"Wade here's gonna teach you how to wrestle calves."

"You bet!" the boy beamed.

"Alright," Jake said to himself, happy to trade this manual job for an important one. "Here ya go, Tommy. Put your leg here and hold on to his front foot, like this."

Tommy had watched enough to know exactly what to do. He took the foot from Jake and placed one knee on the calf's neck.

Jake went after a hot iron for the next calf as Wade and his new partner held the calf for Nadine to vaccinate. Upon completion, they released the calf just before Shorty rode by, pulling the little gray Brahma by a front leg.

"Hey!" Wade jested. "You're supposed to rope 'em by the hind feet, not the front!"

"Yeah, I know," Shorty apologized. "He about backed out of my rope before I could get to my slack."

Wade picked up the little bull calf and laid him on his side. He couldn't have weighed a hundred pounds. Tommy handled the front end of the calf like an old pro. With the weight of one knee on the calf's neck, he took the rope from its leg, "Here ya go, Shorty!" he said.

"Thanks, Tommy," Shorty yelled over his shoulder as he rode back into the herd, coiling his rope for another catch.

"Something doesn't seem right here," said Wade to Tommy. He thought for a moment, "Oh, we got him upside down," he concluded. "The head has to be on the right...."

He was interrupted by Jake. "You dumb shit, Wade, you got him on the wrong side!"

"I know it!" Wade clarified. "We were just about to roll him over."

"If I brand the wrong shoulder 'cause of you, your ass is grass! You know that, dontcha'?"

Wade and Tommy rolled the little Brahma over.

"Can't you do nothin' without me here to make sure you don't screw it up?" Jake ragged.

"Just shut up and brand the calf!" Wade shouted.

"Hey buddy!" snapped Jake. "You work for me! You don't tell me what to do! It's the other way around! You understand that?" Jake pressed the hot 'W' against the calf's right shoulder. "You can't do nothin' right," he ranted. "I give you a simple job like wrestlin' calves and you can't even get 'em right side up!"

"Oh yeah?" Tommy piped up. "Then if you're so smart, how come ya put the brand on sideways?"

"What are you talkin' about, ya little puke?" Jake challenged.

"Look, Stupid," Tommy said loudly as he pointed at the calf's newly scorched brand. "You put the 'W' on its side, see? The bottoms' where the side should be and the side is where the top should be!"

He was right. Jake had placed a $\geq$ brand on the calf. His face crinkled with antagonism. "Shit," he said quietly as he looked in the direction of his dad.

"Way to go, Ex-Lax," said Wade.

Jake waved the hot iron in front of Wade's face. "Shut up, you asshole," he snarled. "This is your fault. If you'd of had him layin' on the right side in the first place, I wouldn't of got confused!"

"Oh no, Jake," Wade disputed, "you ain't blamin' this on us!"

"Yeah! You moron!" added Tommy.

"Just shut up, Tommy!" ordered Jake. "There's no sense arguin' about it. Hold him still and I'll brand him again."

He hurriedly stuck the iron to the calf's shoulder again. He put it directly to the right of the botched brand, and upside down.

Tommy caught it right away. "Good job, dummy. You messed that one up, too!"

"Huh?" asked Jake as he looked at the brand. "Damn," he whispered. Now, on the calf's shoulder was the brand $\gtrless M$. "Man! I give up!" he whined as he threw his iron into the dirt.

"I'll bet you sure feel stupid!" laughed Tommy.

Jake glared at Tommy. He considered kicking him.

"What's the trouble, boys?" It was Walt.

Jake looked at the ground.

Wade hesitated.

Tommy spoke right up. "Jake messed up the brand twice, Walt, look! He got one upside down and one sideways! He can't do nothin' right!"

Walt let out a long sigh as he studied the brand. "Jake, is this what they taught you in college?"

Jake made no reply.

"Yeah, Jake," Tommy taunted. "Is this what they taught you in college?"

"How in the hell could you foul up a simple job like this?" Walt asked in disbelief.

"Yeah, Jake," Tommy repeated. "How could you foul up a simple job like this?"

"I swear sometimes, Jake," Walt searched for words, "you don't know 'whoa' from 'giddy up'!"

"Yeah, Jake! You don't know 'whoa' from 'giddy up'! Ain't that right, Walt?"

Again Jake glared at Tommy. When he finally spoke, it was through clenched teeth. "You rotten little..."

"Look out!" yelled Shorty from the middle of the herd.

Jake turned around just in time to take a direct hit in the stomach from the hornless head of the little Brahma's protective mother. With a loud grunt, Jake sailed backwards, end over end, over Wade and Tommy, who let go of the calf and were scrambling to get out of the way.

The mama cow stopped and sniffed her baby as he awkwardly got up on all four feet. She looked around and bellowed a warning to anything on two legs. The calf had his head between her front legs.

"Stay back from this ol' cow," cautioned Walt. "She's dangerous! She had Shorty trapped for a half hour this mornin'!"

Jake lay on the ground and struggled to get back some of the air that had been knocked out of him. Tommy was scooting backwards on his butt, and Wade was crawling as fast as he could.

The cow bellowed again and headed out the open east end of the pen toward the hills with her calf hot on her heels.

"Well, hell," said Walt. "We'll need him back. He ain't been vaccinated or castrated, and I don't think there's a damn thing we can do about that brand."

Shorty rode from the herd with another catch on his line. "You want me to go rope him?"

"No, Shorty," said Walt, "we need you here. Jake can get him."

Jake looked up from the ground. He held his stomach as he whimpered, "I think I'm hurt."

Walt took two steps to Jake and kicked him in the rear with his high top cowboy boot. "Get up and mount up!" he ordered. "Hell, I've had worse sores on my lip and kept whistlin'!"

Jake moaned as he slowly got to his feet. He picked up his hat and put it back on his head.

"And hurry up!" Walt added, as he watched the pair cut out across the hills. "It don't look like they'll be slowing down anytime soon."

Jake was still holding his belly with one hand as he walked over to where old Buck was tied.

"No matter which one you rope, the other one's gonna follow you back," his father advised. "I'd rope the calf if I was you. You don't wanna get a loop on that mangy ol' barracuda when you're by yourself." He considered going with him, but he quickly dismissed that thought from his mind. Although Jake messed things up quite often and seldom used good judgment, Walt still wanted to believe that his son could do something on his own.

Jake untied his horse, gathered his reins, and climbed into the saddle. He spurred Buck into a lope, heading south to the hill that the pair had just topped. As he rode along, he cussed the mama cow and her scrawny little ugly baby. Then he cussed his dad and grandfather. And Shorty and Wade and Tommy. He even cussed Mary Ann. He forgot about the pain in his belly as the hate gathered steam between his ears. He thought about how he'd rope the calf and drag him so fast and hard that he'd be halfway dead by the time they got back to camp. He thought about how he wished he was carrying Grandpa's pistol and when the old mama cow charged him, he'd plug her right between the eyes. He would say it was in self-defense, and if anybody questioned him about it, he'd shoot them, too.

He topped the hill just in time to see them duck into a gully heading east. Instead of trailing them, he tapered down the hill to the northeast to head them off. If he could sneak up on them from above and get close enough to rope the calf, he could drag it straight up the wall of the gulch, and the cow wouldn't have a chance of catching him.

He slowed down as he neared the drop-off of the narrow ravine. He silently walked his horse to the edge and peered over. It was about ten feet to the bottom. There was sand, rock and occasional sagebrush, but no cow and calf. He looked up the draw. It sliced from out of the hills and angled across the valley. At the foot of the far wall he could see several entrances to coyote dens. Across from the holes lay a well-worn trail leading out of the small gorge. It was steep, but with care, a man could ride his horse down it. About twenty feet straight out from the crevice stood a sixteen-year-old oak tree. Jake remembered seeing it for the first time as a young boy. He always wondered why it was out here all by its lonesome, and how the seed had made it all the way up here from the river. He quickly turned and looked the other direction down the draw. He could faintly hear the warning of a diamondback rattlesnake. Or was it merely his imagination? His horse nickered.

"Shut up!" Jake whispered. He sat silently in the saddle until he heard something from up the draw and, sure enough, the black mama cow came trotting around the bend with her calf at her heels. Quickly, he prepared his loop. As he waited for the pair to cross below, he decided to tie his rope to his saddle horn rather than to wrap it around the horn after he made his catch. That way, he would be certain not to lose the calf. His Grandpa and Dad had both warned him of the dangers of tying on hard and fast. If one gets ahold of a wild horse or mad cow, there is no quick release should an animal charge or jerk the saddle horse to the ground. Jake had heard stories about animals dying from this method. "But, what the heck," he thought to himself, 'I'm roping a hundred-pound calf, not his mama.

The calf's tongue hung from its mouth as it strived to keep up with its mother. She was on a fast steady trot, never looking up, even when she crossed Jake's shadow on the sandy chasm floor.

Jake let the rope fall directly behind the cow, and the calf trotted into it before he knew it was there. Jake pitched his slack into the air and his loop clenched tightly around the hind legs. He reined Buck around and spurred him away from the gully. The calf let out a short grunt as he was jerked from the ground and dangled upside down on the side of the rock wall. His exhausted mama failed to hear him over the sound of her own heavy panting, and she kept moving onward. Buck continued to move away from the gully, elevating the calf higher and higher. Suddenly, the horse stopped. "Come on, Buck," Jake ordered as he gouged him in the ribs with his spurs. As Buck began to pull again, Jake realized that something was definitely wrong. His horse's head was moving away from him. Instantly, he knew what the trouble was. He'd forgotten to tighten his cinch back at camp in the haste of catching up with the calf. As the saddle slid back on Buck's rear, the back cinch became tight against his flanks. He kicked his back hooves high in the air. "Whoa, Buck," Jake commanded as he fumbled with the rope, uselessly trying to untie it from his saddle horn. Buck turned to the right and sidestepped away from the pull of the rope. The saddle slid down the flustered horse's side and underneath his belly with Jake still partially in the saddle. Jake hit the ground with a thud, as Buck tried to jump away from his still-attached saddle. Jake was drug a few yards before his left foot jerked free of the stirrup. The calf screamed again for his mama as he was drug up the ledge to flat ground. As Buck continued to buck out across the prairie, he drug the calf directly over Jake, rolling him over twice, and kept going. Jake lay on his stomach and did not even bother to holler as he watched his horse top the grassy knoll and disappear into the valley, heading for the barn. Instead he let out a moan of desperation. The saddle would probably be torn to pieces whether it makes it all the way home under the horse or was kicked and scraped off on the trip. If the calf was drug the full six miles to the house, he would surely be crippled or may be even dead.

Jake got to his feet. He was at a complete loss of what to do. How would he explain this one to his dad? Should he even bother walking back to camp? What else could go wrong today?

He heard the thumping of hooves against dry clay and whirled around to see the old cow as she rumbled up the steep trail from the ravine. She frantically bawled for her baby. When she heard no answer, she focused her dark eyes on the enemy. Jake knew what was going to happen next. She charged at him straight ahead from about twenty yards. The oak tree was fifteen yards to the left and was Jake's only chance to escape. The footrace was on. Jake had a head start, but the cow was gaining fast. Clumps of buffalo grass sailed behind her as she bounded after her scrambling target. The tree bounced in Jake's vision with every struggling stride. It was getting closer....and closer.... but the lowest branch was pretty high.

He scampered around the trunk of the tree with the mad cow's head not more than a foot from his rear. Although she wore no horns, Jake knew that she could still thrash and mangle his helpless body with her hooves and stone-blunt head. Two times he rounded the tree before he made one desperate leap. He caught the arm of the bottom branch, but just barely. She swung upward with her head, hitting him in the back of the legs. Hand over hand, he climbed higher out on the branch. Again she swung her head at his legs. He stuck his boots in the middle of her forehead. She snorted and violently shoved up into them. Using this momentum, Jake swung a foot up high enough to get a leg around the branch.

He was safe.

The road leading to the ranch was no more than two wheel ruts worn into the short grass. Buck found and used them at a high lope, dragging the calf behind, occasionally kicking at the saddle hanging loosely beneath his belly and banging him in the back legs. So far, he had ripped off a stirrup leather and most of the padding underneath the seat. The front cinch began to loosen itself, allowing the front of the saddle to flop loose to the ground, but the back cinch remained tight, pressing the back of the saddle hard against his flanks. Finally, the saddle hung low enough that the saddle horn drug into the ground. As it flipped upright beneath Buck's hooves, it shoved deep into his flanks and catapulted him into a somersault. The back cinch snapped in two, freeing the horse and saddle from each other. Buck lay where he landed. He wasn't hurt, just dazed and confused.

The calf lay there for a moment, too. His fetlocks were sore from the tight rope, and the hide of his belly was sore from being dragged a mile and a half, but there were no injuries. He kicked his back legs and the tight rope became loose. He tried to get up and fell on his chin. He shook his head and called for his mama. She did not come. He looked at Buck, still lying there and wondered if that was his mother. He struggled to his feet, this time successfully. His legs were shaky, like the moments after he was born. He wobbled over to the horse and sniffed. Buck grunted as he clambered to his feet. Definitely not mama. Buck headed northwest down the road home. The calf headed southwest at a trot, in search of his mother.

Four strands of barbed wire stretched across the horizon. The calf barely noticed them. He stuck his head between the two bottom wires and kept trotting. His front end stumbled through the fence and the back end clumsily followed. He barely felt where the prickly barbs cut into his hide. He had to find his mama. He kept up the pace until the sun sank behind the Rocky Mountains. Exhausted, he lay down beside a yucca plant and bedded down for the night.

Chapter 7: July 1987

T.J. Jergenson cheered loudly as Bennett McKinney stuck like glue to the famous bucking bull, Rapid Fire. Never had he seen a bull that could leap so high in the air. At the height of his jump his front feet must have been four foot high in the air and the back hooves at least eight. His head was high, his horns were wide and his heart was big. From where the photographer sighted through his lens as he squatted along the far-side arena fence, the huge sign 'Cheyenne Frontier Days – the Daddy of 'Em All' could be partially read underneath the bull's belly.

The camera shutter clicked and this instant of that ride lives forever.

Several eight-by-tens of the eighty-nine point, round-winning ride had been developed and distributed. One of them was in Bennett's own scrapbox in the back of the closet in his parents' guestroom. In the same box were a few other eight-by-tens and some smaller photographs. Some were bullriding pictures, others were just snapshots of Bennett and his friends. One featured Randy, Dave, Shot, T.J., and Bennett all together, standing in front of Shot's old red Ford pickup. There was one of Bennett and his mom and dad at the park at a family reunion, and another one of Bennett as a young boy atop his first horse, Earl. Among these pictures was what had been Bennett's favorite. It was one of himself, along with T.J., standing in front of a Western wear store on a cold snow-covered morning in Roundup, Montana. Also in the scrapbox was an old-time compass his grandpa had given him when T.J. left home to rodeo full-time. "Son," his grandpa had told him, "you go anywhere you want in this world. As long as you've got my compass, you'll always find your way back home." Attached to the circlet of the compass was a safety pin, linking it to the ring given to him by Danielle Dobbins, the girl he left for rodeo. Although he had let a few other women think differently, Danielle was the only woman he had wondered if he was truly in love with. The ring was nothing fancy – a tarnished band with a simple red stone, but it was one that her favorite aunt had given her when she was a little girl. Danielle gave it to him on the same night Bennett gave her a picture of the Cheyenne ride. She wanted his silver belt buckle, but he wouldn't give her that. She had a husband and two kids now and had moved back east. She still had the picture in her photo album. On the opposite page was a picture she snapped when she went on a rodeo run with the boys. It was Bennett and T.J. in front of the Western wear store, that cold snowy morning in Roundup, Montana. Although she looked back on those good old days with fond memories, she didn't wish that the old days were still here.

Bill and Katie McKinney, Bennett's parents, knew nothing of the scrapbox in the back of the closet. They'd find it someday, but downstairs in the living room, sitting on the fireplace mantelpiece, was the Cheyenne photograph, adorned in a gray wooden frame and sitting between two of Bennett's first trophy buckles. Also among these reminiscences was an old photograph of Bennett on Earl, alongside of T.J. on another McKinney horse, Onion. Those two horses had been almost inseparable.

Bill had taken these things down shortly after Bennett died, and put them in a box in the attic. Katie said nothing about it when he did. Two weeks later, he got them all out again and put them back in place. She still said nothing.

The only other Cheyenne photo was on Shot Palmer's bedroom floor among some action shots of Shot fighting bulls, and various pictures of his past wives. Shot had been looking at them last night and thinking, before going to sleep. He'd had a lot of time to think lately. He thought about all of the rodeos he'd missed because of his injuries. He thought about walking again. He couldn't do it yet, but he was determined that it wouldn't be nine months like the doctor said. He thought about sex. He thought he could handle it, but hadn't had the opportunity. He thought about his kids from previous marriages. He wondered what they looked like. Were they tough, or did they turn into sissies without him? He thought about his last ex-wife. He knew why she left and did not hold any grudge against her. Had she left him under normal circumstances, he would most likely have gone looking for her, maybe gotten drunk and beat up her brother. He surely would have done something to get thrown into jail just to prove his love for her. However, with the untimeliness of Bennett's death, he didn't care where she went, or even that she left. It had been three months and he still grieved. It still hurt the way it did two days after it happened. He thought the pain would fade but it hadn't. He tried hard to only think about the good things about Bennett's life, the funny things, the friendship, the wild times, good rides, bad bulls... It always came back around to the one last ride.

It wouldn't have been so bad if his friends were around. Randy and Dave called once in a while. They were traveling pretty hard and doing well.

It was nine o'clock in the morning and Shot lay awake in bed, thinking some more. His thoughts took up where they drifted off into a dream last night. He looked at the picture of his last ex and thought of the advice Bennett offered him years ago. "Shot, ol' buddy," Bennett advised as he threw an arm around his shoulder, "women come and women go. Good friends last a lifetime." Shot's mind could hear Bennett's confident voice. It could see his wide grin, his black cowboy hat cocked to one side and his whiskey glass raised in anticipation of clicking with Shot's whiskey glass. Shot remembered not clicking glasses with Bennett.

Instead he said, "Now, hold on a minute. My folks have been married over thirty years, and so have yers! How can..."

"Well, hell yes, they have," Bennett interrupted. "That's 'cause they're best friends!" Shot's glass met Bennett's in agreement.

His thoughts disappeared when he heard the TV click on in the front room of his trailer house. T.J. had been staying with Shot for a while and sleeping on the couch. Any second he would hear the television go from one channel to the next to the next without slowing down. It hadn't been easy living with T.J. All he wanted to do was sit in front of the TV and flip through the channels. He had yet to offer Shot a dime for all of the food he'd been eating and wouldn't lift a finger to clean any of the messes he made. He said he was going to get a job as soon as he healed enough, but there was no telling how long that'd be. This arrangement was really testing their friendship.

By the time Shot got his special-cut jeans on – the ones with the left pant leg slit up the seam to fit over his cast – and made his way down the hall to the front room, T.J. had been all the way through the channels at least twice.

"Gitcher boots on," said Shot. "We're goin' fishin.'"

T.J. looked up at Shot, cradled between his crutches. The swelling and scabs had long been gone from both of their faces. "I don't fish," he said.

"Well, then it's high time you learned," said Shot.

"I didn't say I don't know how," T.J. argued, "I said I don't fish."

"Gosh-dangit, T.J.," persisted Shot, "it's too nice of a day out there to be sittin' in here. Now get dressed and let's go."

The only movement from T.J. came from his thumb, as he switched channels.

"We'll stop off at the Coffee Cup and get some breakfast."

T.J. looked up at Shot again. "You buyin'?"

Two hours later the boys had Shot's old red Ford pickup unloaded and were sitting on the bank of the creek, fishing poles in hand, and a cooler of beer between them.

"What if I catch a big sucker?" asked T.J. "I don't think my collar bone's healed up enough to reel one in."

"Just give the pole to me," Shot answered nonchalantly. "I'll get him in."

"What if I can't get it to you? I can't reach very far either."

"You ain't gonna catch nothin' that big anyway," said Shot as he looked to the clear blue sky and peeled his shirt off. "The creek's only ten foot wide."

"Well you never know," T.J. assessed. "O.K., I'm gonna cast her deep!"

"T.J., you get that line hung up in the trees, I'm gonna throw yer sorry butt in the water!" warned Shot.

"Bait my hook, will ya, Shot?"

"Bait yer own damn hook."

"I can't. My shoulder hurts."

"Hell with yer shoulder. I'm tired of hearin' about yer shoulder."

"Well, what's the matter with you?" T.J. asked. "You wanted to go fishin'. We're fishin'. Lighten up."

Shot studied T.J. for a moment. He suddenly realized that this was the most he had spoken in over a week. He had to be coming out of his depression. "Alright, give me yer pole, I'll bait it for ya."

T.J. smiled. "Hey, thanks, buddy!"

Shot removed the lid from the beer cooler and pulled out a can of worms. "You want a beer while I'm in here?"

"You bet. Hey, would you help me take off my shirt? I can't get my arm back far enough."

"Who dresses you in the mornin'?" Shot asked.

"I can do it," explained T.J. "It's just hard."

"Well, if you wanna come over here I'll help ya, but I ain't gonna hobble over there."

"Forget it," said T.J. "I can manage." He grunted as he fumbled with the shirt, sliding it from his shoulders and off his arms. He pulled his straw cowboy hat over his eyes and slowly lay back in the tall green grass.

"Here's yer beer," offered Shot.

"Open that for me, will ya pardner?"

Shot disgustedly tossed the can against T.J.'s chest.

"Aww, dammit," T.J. flinched, "them's my broke ribs!"

"Them ribs ain't broke no more! Chrissake, it's been three months!"

"Man, yer cranky today! What the hell's stuck in yer craw?"

"My craw? You don't talk to me for three days," accused Shot, "and now all of a sudden you want me to wait on you hand and foot!"

T.J. tipped his old straw hat back up and looked at Shot. "Well, I'm just tryin' to be sociable. We're here for a good time, ain't we?"

Shot hesitated for a minute. A slight smile shone in his eyes. He shook his head and began to laugh.

"What?" asked T.J.

When Shot's laughter died, he did not answer right away.

"What's so funny?" T.J. demanded.

Shot looked at T.J. Although a grin still lay across his face, there was no laughter left in his eyes. "Oh," he said, "when you said 'we're here for a good time,' it reminded me of what Bennett used to always tell me…"

T.J. knew the saying well, and they said it together: "I'm here for a good time, not a long time."

T.J. opened his beer, took a sip and lay back in the grass again. He watched a single small white cloud slowly float across the treetops. "Do ya ever get to thinkin' that maybe it was your fault, Shot?"

"Huh?" Shot had heard him, but was caught off guard by the question.

"Do ya think it could have been…"

"Hell, no it wasn't my fault," Shot proclaimed. "I did everything I could to save him. Everything I could… It happened so fast, I… Why, do you think it's my fault?"

"No, I don't think it's your fault," said T.J., "but sometimes I wonder if it was my fault."

"Oh." Shot relaxed a little. "Naw, it ain't yer fault, T.J. How could it be yer fault?"

"Well, it was my bull," explained T.J. "The only reason Bennett was there was to help me."

"That ain't no way to talk," Shot dismissed. "It ain't yer fault no more than anybody else's."

"That's what I try to tell myself," said T.J., still eyeing the lone cloud. "Sometimes, though, I just get to blamin' myself… It's bad enough missin' Bennett, and hurtin' for him... and every other thing ya say or think or do reminds ya of him." His lip began to tremble. "But when ya realized that you're responsible..."

"Here!" Shot interrupted. "I told you to quit talkin' like that!" He set his pole aside and focused his attention on T.J. "Now, bullridin' and bullfightin' is a tough business. And me and you and Bennett all knew what we were gittin' into when we started in this game."

"I just..."

"Bennett died doin' what he loved! He lived in the arena and he died in the arena, what's the tragedy of that? That's how I wanna go. There's people who'll live to be ninety and not done the livin' he did... It ain't the length of yer life that's important, it's how much livin' you get crammed into it. We just gotta get on with our lives. We'll never forget him, but we just gotta keep goin'. I'm gonna keep fightin' 'em and yer gonna keep ridin' 'em. Right?"

The cloud in T.J.'s vision was becoming thin and wispy. He watched it slowly disappear. "I don't know, Shot." He squinted at the empty spot in the sky. "I'm thinkin' about quittin'."

"Quittin'? T.J., yer in yer prime. What do you wanna go and quit for?"

"I just don't wanna rodeo without Bennett."

"Oh, man," groaned Shot. "I'd hate to see you lay it down now. Rodeo is what you need right now. Yer too damn good to be quittin'."

T.J. was slow to answer. "My heart just ain't in it anymore."

Shot knew that he could not argue with that. "He was the best, wasn't he, T.J.?"

"He was like the brother I never had."

"What do you mean, the brother you never had? You have a brother. Your brother Ben, right?"

"Nope. Ben's like the brother I never wanted."

"Oh... Well, here, I got your hook baited."

"Then throw it in the water, dummy."

Chapter 8: August 1987

In the northeastern corner of Colorado, all of the roads are straight. No curves. Highways and gravel county roads alike. Not only are they straight, but they run straight north and south, and straight east and west. The surrounding horizon is the same. The blue sky reaches to the ground in an infinite straight line, interrupted only by an occasional farmstead. On a clear day, the grain storage elevators can be seen looming over the small farming towns twenty miles away. The vast landscape was a fading yellow. Harvest crew-cut stubble fields lay idle where a few short weeks ago, an ocean of wheat danced slowly with the warm breeze. Soon, the yellow would be replaced with rich dark gray as the farmers turned the soil over, plowing and discing the land, tilling and cultivating, manicuring and nurturing the earth until it was ready for planting. Each seed of grain would germinate in the fertile dirt under a blanket of white this winter, until the spring sun dissolved the snow and awakened new life from hibernation.

At the corner of one of these fields, where the east-west road met the north-south road, sat the Hotchkin place. Two towering rows of oak trees shaded the gravel driveway from the mailbox to the big green two-story farmhouse, fifty yards away. The house was an old style house, newly painted, with a big front porch and matching double car garage. A newly built patio clung to the back of the house, complete with a picnic table and gas barbeque grill. A lonely tricycle waited patiently at the sliding glass doors for the little girl who lived there with her dad and mom and big sister. The little girl was inside at the kitchen table. She was supposed to be eating her pancakes, but she could see the cartoons on the TV in the front room from where she sat. Her mother was at the sink, funneling powdered milk into a liter bottle.

"Andrea, quit watching TV and eat your breakfast, Honey," Mother said to her daughter.

The four-year-old's eyes never left the television set.

"Andrea!" her mother snapped.

Andrea looked up at her mom.

"Now eat your pancakes, Sweetie, then you can watch the cartoons."

Andrea's big eyes saddened as she slowly spoke. "Mommy?"

"Yes, dear."

"Um, I don't like these pancakes."

"You don't like the pancakes?"

"Uh-uh."

"Well, you've always liked them before," said the mother as she turned on the faucet and ran lukewarm water into the bottle. "What's wrong with them?"

"Um...I...I don't like 'em."

The mother turned off the faucet and with her hand over the opening, shook the bottle vigorously until the powder had dissolved completely into milk. "Well, why don't you like the pancakes, Sugar?"

"Um," the child searched for an answer, "they're rotten."

"Oh, they are not rotten!" she argued as she stretched a rubber nipple onto the mouth of the bottle. "Now, eat your pancakes and you can go help your daddy feed Tuffy."

"Mommy?" Andrea asked again.

"Yes, dear, what is it?" sighed Mama.

"Can I feed Tuffy?"

"If you eat all of your breakfast," she bartered.

Andrea instantly gobbled down the rest of her pancakes. "There!" she said proudly.

"Well, that didn't take long!" exclaimed her mother. "I thought they were supposed to be rotten."

"They are," claimed Andrea, smiling all the while. "I hate 'em!"

"Oh, you..." Her mother took her plate and put it into the dishwasher. "You have to drink all of your milk, too."

"It's rotten."

"Now, there is nothing wrong with that milk," Mother scolded. "You wanted it, you drink it!"

Andrea's eyes dropped to her lap as she began to whimper.

"Tuffy drinks all of his milk," coaxed Mama.

The little girl said nothing.

"Drink your milk, Sweetie, and go tell Kimberly her breakfast is getting cold."

"I'm right here, Mama," said Andrea's sister, older by three years, as she walked in and sat down at the table.

"It's about time," said the mom. "How many pancakes would you like?"

"Forty-two!" Kimberly quipped cheerily. She then covered her mouth with both hands to suppress her laughter.

Andrea looked at Kimberly and said in a somber tone, "That's not funny, Kimmerwee."

Kimberly, always in a good mood in the mornings, found this time of day her favorite time for tormenting her little sister, mainly, because this was the time of day her little sister was in the worst of moods. Kimberly stretched her lips wide with her fingers and crossed her eyes at Andrea.

"Mommy, make Kimmerwee stop it!" ordered Andrea.

Kimberly quickly put her straight face on.

"What are you doing to your sister, Kimberly?"

"Nothing, Mama," she said innocently.

"Yes, she is, Mommy," Andrea argued.

"What was she doing, then, Andrea?" Mama asked as she served Kimberly her breakfast.

"She always..." said Andrea, "...she never...she always, never...she," she searched for the right words, "she...every time she never...always...she..." Andrea forgot what she was talking about. "...she..."

Kimberly began to giggle.

"Shut up, Kimmerwee!!" shrieked Andrea at the top of her lungs.

"My God, what's goin' on out there?" came a masculine voice from the bathroom.

Both girls got quiet.

It was Daddy. At 220 pounds spread across his six-foot, four-inch frame, he was a giant to the girls – all three of them. A gentle giant, and a clean-shaven giant in the mornings. He came out of the bathroom to the kitchen as he did every morning, fetched his seed-corn cap down from the hat rack, and pulled it down on his head. "Andy, what are you screamin' about?"

Andrea, as young as she was, has already begun to master the art of wrapping her daddy's heart around her finger. She gave him her most mournful look. "Kimmerwee's makin' faces at me, Daddy."

He lifted Andrea from her chair and rubbed his huge hand over Kimberly's head, mussing her rust-tinted hair. "Kimber, you pickin' on yer little sister?"

"She's just bein' a baby, Daddy," she answered as she poured maple syrup on her pancakes.

"Not my little Andy," he teased. "Connie, have you got Tuffy's milk ready?"

"Right there on the counter, Paul, dear," said Paul's wife as she began loading the dishwasher.

"Hey, listen," said Paul. "Can you feed Tuffy this morning, honey? I've got to meet with the Land Management people at eight."

"Oh, Paul," Connie sighed, "I've got a million things to do this morning."

"Can I feed him, Mama?" asked Kimber'.

"I don't think so, Honey," said Connie.

"Can I, Daddy?" Kimber' begged. "I'm big enough!"

"Me, too, Daddy," added Andy as her father lowered her to the ground.

"You are not, Andy," argued Kimber', "you're too little!"

"No, sir," Andy retorted, "I'm big enough, ain't I, Mommy?"

"Do you think you can feed him by yourself?" Paul asked Kimber'.

"Yes, I can, Daddy," Kimber' said convincingly. "I can feed real good, huh, Mama."

"Well…" Connie hesitated.

"Be sure and hold the bottle above his head," warned Paul, "otherwise he'll just be suckin' air."

"Then I can?" Kimber' squealed with delight.

"I suppose," her father reluctantly agreed. "As soon as you eat your breakfast."

Kimber' hastily snarfed down her pancakes with a quick milk chaser, and excused herself from the table.

"My goodness," exclaimed Connie. "What'd you do with those pancakes, inhale them?"

Kimber' giggled as Andy squawked, "Mommy, I get to feed Tuffy, too!"

"All right, Andrea," her mother negotiated. "Please, don't scream so loudly!"

Andy screamed with delight, causing her dad to close his eyes and boom, "Little girl, what did your mom just tell you?"

"She said I can feed Tuffy!" she cheered.

Paul lowered himself to one knee and looked Andrea in the eye. "She said don't scream so loud," he said in a calm voice.

Kimberly grabbed the bottle from the counter and ran out the door. "Come on, Andy!"

Andrea squeaked, "Wait for me, Kimmerwee!" at the top of her lungs, and darted out the door behind her sister.

By the time Andrea got to the gate of the white picket fence that surrounded the back yard, her sister had rounded the corners of the big yellow machinery shed. There, in a makeshift twenty- by twenty-foot hogwire pen, a mouse-gray bull calf with the brand ⋛M on his right shoulder anxiously awaited his morning meal. The calf had been here for nearly two months now. Connie found him wandering in the road ditch one morning, too weak to get away. He didn't even struggle when she loaded him into the back of the pickup and rushed him to the house. She tried to feed him milk but he wouldn't swallow. By the time the veterinarian arrived she was afraid that it was too late. The calf lay flat on its side on the basement floor, barely breathing. The vet gave him a shot of penicillin and a couple of vitamin shots. Then he stuck a tube down the calf's throat and force-fed him some milk. When Connie asked the doctor where the calf might have come from, he said that he had never seen that particular brand before. He suggested that she go to the livestock auction barn and look through the brand books, which she did, and found nothing. She figured he'd be dead by the next morning. When she arose the next day and opened the basement door, there he was, standing at the foot of the stairs, waiting for breakfast.

Tuffy had doubled his weight since that day, and little nub horns were beginning to protrude from both sides of his skull. He had long since forgotten about finding his mother, but he did not like it here where he was. He would have liked to be on the other side of the fence. He had tried to move the fence with his head but when it would not budge, he would end up rubbing his ears and shoulders and back against it, partially to scratch himself, but mostly just to while away the long hours of monotony. At first he accepted the woman who found him as his mother but soon she began to seem different and he didn't want to be around her anymore. He would run to her at feeding time, but when the bottle became empty, he would run to the far side of the pen.

His pen was little more than an outdoor jail cell. There was a hydrant and water trough in the corner, which Connie always made sure was full, and a feed bucket with cracked corn in it, which Tuffy would not eat. Paul did not understand this. He didn't know much about cattle, but he thought surely that the calf was old enough to eat by then. What Paul didn't understand was that Tuffy did not know how to eat grain. Eating processed feed is not natural to cattle. Grazing is. Paul had no idea that he needed to sprinkle the corn over hay or grass the first few days until the animal picked up the idea.

"Here you go, Tuffy," Kimberly offered the bottle through the fence as the calf enthusiastically took the nipple in his mouth and began to suck. Once in a while he would shove his nose hard against the bottle, to try to make the milk come faster. Kimberly, having helped her dad plenty of times, knew enough to hold on extra tight to keep from dropping the bottle.

Andrea toddled around the corner crying, "Kimmerwee, I get to feed Tuffy!"

Kimber' did not look away nor loosen her grip. "No, you don't, you're too little!"

Andrea let go a very loud, very mournful howl.

"OK!" said Kimber' as she jerked the bottle from the calf's mouth. "Here, I was only teasin'!"

Andrea's howl dropped to a whimper as her big sister handed her the bottle.

"Now, hold on tight, Andy," warned Kimber'.

Andrea poked the bottle through the fence.

"You've got the bottle too low," Kimber' explained as she tried to grab the bottle.

"No!" Andrea squawked as she pulled the bottle to her chest, guarding it from all intruders.

"Andrea, you hafta hold it up above his head, up here," Kimberly instructed. "If ya don't, Daddy said he'll just be suckin' air!"

"I know!" snapped her little sister. She tried it again, this time sticking the bottle through the highest square in the fence that she could possibly reach. Again, Tuffy took the nipple and began to suck.

"There," said Kimber', "now you're doin' it right."

A smile finally shone across Andy's face.

Preoccupied by the morning's chore, the girls did not hear their daddy as he slammed the door of his pickup, fired up the engine and drove out of the yard.

"You're doin' good!" hailed Kimber'.

"I know!" Andy beamed as she tightly held the bottle above her head.

With the bottle nearly half empty, Kimberly was beginning to want her turn at feeding again. She knew Andy would cry and scream and fuss, and she was doing a good job anyway, so in a rare moment of generosity, she opted to let her little sister feed the whole thing if she wanted to. She watched for a while until boredom got the best of her and she stuck her hand through the fence to pet the calf's head.

Tuffy doesn't like people messing with his head. He let the nipple slip from his mouth as he swung his head from side to side and went back to the bottle.

Kimber' giggled and did it again, causing the same reaction.

"Don't, Kimmerwee," ordered her little sister.

"But it's fun!" said Kimber' as she stuck her hand through the fence and rubbed his head again.

Tuffy, annoyed by the interruptions, swung his head more violently this time and even butted the barbed wire fence before going back to nursing on the bottle.

"Stop it!" Andrea commanded, her smile turned into a frown.

Her sister quit, but Andrea's young mind could sense Tuffy's displeasure, as he was pulling and pushing on the bottle much harder than before.

After thirty seconds or so, Kimber' began to get bored again. "Tag, you're it!" she announced as she poked him on the forehead with her finger.

As Andy began to scold once again, the calf jerked the bottle from her tiny hands and it landed in the dirt at his feet. He backed up a couple of steps and looked at it closely.
"Look what you did!" accused Kimber'.

"It's your fault, Kimmerwee," her little sister said calmly.

Tuffy curiously licked the rubber nipple and then the plastic bottle. He knew there was food in there, if he could just figure how to get it out…he rolled the bottle over with his nose.

Kimber' reached through the fence. Her arm was not long enough so her little sister tried, to no avail.

"I'm tellin' Mommy," she said.

"No!" Kimber' exclaimed. "I can get it!"

"You can't reach it," Andrea pointed out.

"But I can crawl over," she said as she climbed up the hogwire fence.

"I wouldn't do that if I was you," the little girl warned in a very adult-like manner.

The older sister paid no mind, so the younger sister began climbing, too.

"No, you stay there!" Kimber' demanded.

The younger sister paid no mind, either.

As Kimber' lowered herself into the pen, Tuffy backed up a little, confused. No one had ever been in his pen before. Although he yearned to be on the other side of these four walls, this was still his territory and nobody else belonged there.

Although Tuffy was considered a baby still, the bull calf weighed as much as the girls' giant of a father. He backed up two small steps, lowered his head and focused his eyes on the small of the intruder's back.

Kimberly grunted loudly as her frail body was slammed into the fence. She bounced off the hogwire and was hit a second time before falling helplessly into the dirt in the corner of the cage. The animal backed up, snorted, and charged again at his fallen victim. Kimberly tried to scream, but no sound would come out. She tried to grab for the fence as Tuffy swung his head at her, bruising her arm with his inch-long nub horn. He then rooted his head under her body and pressed her face-first against the hard wire panels. She looked up at her sister and mouthed the words, "Help me." In a bloodcurdling, ear-rattling pitch, Andrea screeched, "Mommeeeeeee!!!"

Frightened by the scream, Tuffy bolted to the far side of the pen. Kimberly writhed in the dirt, struggling to catch her breath. Andrea screamed, "Get the bottle, Kimmerwee!" Kimberly's upper lip was swollen from hitting the fence. Blood trickled from her cheek. As she tried to pull herself from the ground she began to sob, and the tears and blood soaked deep into the grimy dirt caked on her face. Her movement drew the little bull back for another charge. Andrea screamed again, stopping him in his tracks. Kimber' was on her knees by now. She clutched the wire and painstakingly pulled herself to her feet. Again Tuffy charged. Again Andrea screamed but this time it did not deter the bull. He rammed Kimberly in the back again. As her body hit, the hogwire panel would give a few inches and spring back. This time she clung to the wire with all her might. Again, Tuffy butted her. And again, as Kimberly unsuccessfully grappled for a foothold on the fence, Andrea screamed at the bull, "Tuffy, stop it! STOP IT!!!" Tuffy brought his head up from the ground, hitting Kimberly in the rear, sending her five feet in the air as she clung tight to the fence. As she came down he met her again with his thick skull.

"You bastard! Get away from my baby, you bastard!"

Tuffy didn't even hear the hysterical voice of the woman who had rescued him from death. He slashed upward from the ground again, this time catching Kimberly on the inside of her left leg, slinging her sideways into the fence. Her tiny fingers were slowly slipping from the wire. Her left hand had let go completely, when her mother latched on to her arm and pulled her up and over the fence to safety.

"It's O.K., Baby," Connie sobbed reassuringly as she cuddled her daughter to her chest. "It's O.K., now, Mommy's got you."

Kimberly wrapped her legs around her mother's waist and clenched her tight around the neck. A moaning cry was interrupted by choking and coughing as she fought to regain her breath.

Andrea squeezed her mama's leg and joined the chorus, out-crying them both.

Tuffy stood facing them, pawing the ground, scooping the east Colorado dirt up on his back, warning all intruders never to come in here again.

"You're alright now, Honey," Connie consoled her daughter as she gently lowered to her knees. "You're O.K., Baby. I'm gonna lay you on the ground now, Honey."

Kimberly's arms and legs locked tighter around the comforting safety of her mother.

"You're O.K.," she reassured. "Mommy'll be right back. Now I'm gonna lay you right here for just a second and I'll be right back, I promise, O.K., Baby?"

Kimberly loosened her grip slightly.

"It'll be O.K.," Connie whispered as she slowly lay Kimber' in the grass. "Andrea will be here."

Andrea's bawling turned to short sobs. She sat beside her sister and then reached down and hugged her. "It O.K., Kimmerwee."

Connie hurriedly walked to the tree grove. She scouted the ground until she found a less-than-perfect club–an old dead branch, three feet long and about three inches in diameter. By the time she got back she was sobbing again. She marched up to the pen where Tuffy still waited, daring her to come in and she reached over the fence and smacked him over the head. The bull snorted, and held its ground. She brought the club way back behind her head this time with both hands and cursed, "Go to hell, you bastard!" as she swung down as hard as she could. When the wood met the hard, bone-armored noggin it made a crashing sound that echoed off of the machinery shed, but the bull never even flinched. This infuriated her even more. It was almost as if he was laughing at her. She whacked him three more times as she roared, "You bastard! You bastard! You bastard!" On the third whack, the club shattered over his head. Tuffy barely felt a thing.

Chapter 9: September 1987

"I Pledge Allegiance to the Flag of the United States of America, and to the Republic, for which it stands; One Nation, under God, indivisible, with liberty and justice for all."

"All right, you guys ready to rodeo?" the announcer prompted over his wireless microphone.

There was little response from the scattered few in the grandstand across the racetrack. Most of the cheers came from behind the bucking chutes, and from the kids who were mounted up, waiting their turn in the barrel racing, pole bending, goat tying and ribbon race.

"Well, it sounds like the contestants are ready," he reported as he stepped down from his makeshift crow's nest – a flatbed trailer – and walked into the arena. "The first event here at the Sixth Annual Labor Day Junior Rodeo is the mutton-bustin'. Who's our first contestant, boys?"

Shot Palmer's old red Ford pickup was backed up to the arena fence just two spots down from the flatbed. He and T.J. Jergenson were kicking back and relaxing in lawn chairs in the back of the truck, beers in hand, a cooler between them. White washboard clouds draped over the northeastern horizon, and the last of the summer sun shone on T.J.'s bare belly. "Wonder what the poor people are doin' today?" mused T.J. as he reared the front legs of his chair off the floor of the pickup bed.

Although it was just a hop, skip and a jump from Shot's trailer house, T.J. almost didn't come to this rodeo today. He wanted to go fishing. In fact, in the last month or so, fishing was all he'd wanted to do. He rarely caught anything, but he still went, day after day. He had big plans to buy a fishing boat. Someday, when he got a job.

Shot, the man who had introduced T.J. to the sport, was sick of fishing. He went along with it, though, and tried not to complain, because, basically, it kept them occupied, and although T.J. still had his down days, he was not near as moody when he had something to do. It kept him from thinking about Bennett. Although Shot was still on crutches, T.J. could probably have been riding bulls by then, if he'd wanted to.

The first sheep rider came out of the chute sitting up on a fast-scattering bundle of wool. After a few yards, the kid let go and fell off the back end, landing face and feet up in the soft arena dirt.

The announcer trotted over to the boy with his microphone and said, "Well, that was a pretty good ride, there, young feller," as he helped him off of the ground, "What's your name?"

The young boy spoke in to the microphone. "Joshua."

"Well, Joshua, was that your first ever sheep ride?" He held the microphone up to the boy's mouth.

The boy nodded his head.

"How old are you now, Joshua?" He held the mike up to the boy's mouth.

The boy held up four fingers.

"Well, here's a dollar for your ride, son. You gonna keep on ridin' sheep?"

Joshua, embarrassed by all of the sudden media attention, snatched the dollar bill from the announcer's hand and quickly walked out of the arena.

"Spoken like a true cowboy," said the announcer, "must be one of those strong, silent types. How 'bout a hand for Joshua? Is our next mutton buster ready to go?"

The next rider was a little blonde girl about Joshua's age. Instead of sitting up like Josh, she lay down over her sheep and had a fist full of wool in each hand. The sheep left the chute at a dead run for the far side of the arena. The little girl clung tight with hands, arms and legs. When they got about halfway down the arena, the six second whistle blew and the sparse crowd cheered.

"OK, get off," the announcer proclaimed. "You rode him!"

She let go of her ride and plowed face first into the arena dirt like a base runner diving for second. She got up smiling and spitting.

"That was a real good ride, darlin', you rode him all the way to the whistle," the announcer congratulated. "Come on over here and tell everybody your name and get your dollar."

The little girl marched right up, took her dollar and spoke into the microphone. "Amanda."

"Amanda, well that's a pretty name for a pretty girl. What's that in your mouth?"

"I don't know," she shrugged.

"Looks like dirt to me. Did you eat a little of that dirt when you got off that sheep?"

"I don't know," she shrugged again.

"You gonna be a bullrider when you get big?"

"I don't know."

The next rider bit the dust and got up bawling, so the announcer didn't even interview him. Just gave him the dollar. The one after that made it all the way to the whistle.

"That was as fine of a ride as I've seen," hailed the announcer. "What's your name, little cowboy?"

"Kenneth," the little cowboy grinned.

T.J. was beginning to get bored already. He held an invisible microphone to Shot's mouth, and in his mock-rodeo announcer voice said, "Well, Kenneth, have you ever seen a grown man naked before?"

Shot laughed.

"Kenneth," T.J. went on, "how come you're such an ugly little shit?"

Shot laughed harder.

"So, Kenneth, are your parents divorced? I bet they don't even love you!"

Shot was cracking up.

"Got a match, Kenneth? I'll teach you how to light your farts."

"S'cuse me..."

T.J. felt a tap on his shoulder. He turned his head to a wide-eyed fidgeting teenage boy with sandy blonde hair poking from beneath a cheap straw cowboy hat. "You're T.J. Jergenson, aren't you?" the boy inquired.

"Yeah, I am," answered T.J. offering a handshake.

The shy young cowboy hesitantly shook T.J.'s hand, "I'm Kid Kaminski. I mean my real name is Kyle, but all my friends call me Kid."

"Pleased to meet you, Kid," greeted T.J. "You in this rodeo?"

"Yeah," the kid said anxiously, "I'm in the bullridin'. I saw you ride one time last year," he went on, "and... well, my dad's not here... and ..."

"And you need some help on your bull?" T.J. concluded.

"Yeah," stammered the Kid, "...If you're not...too..."

"I'd be glad to come and give you a hand, Kid," T.J. volunteered. "Tell you what, I'll be over there when the saddle bronc ridin' starts. They are havin' bronc ridin', ain't they?"

"Yeah," said the Kid, a little more at ease. "But there's only two bronc riders."

"O.K., well, there ain't no use a-gittin' too nervous before then," said T.J., "so I'll see you later."

"Thanks a lot," he said sincerely as he turned around and headed back for the bucking chutes.

"Hey, Kid," T.J. called over his shoulder.

The Kid turned around.

"Relax a little bit," advised T.J. "Yer gonna wear yerself out."

The Kid smiled and nodded.

"Now, where was I?" T.J. asked Shot. "Oh, yeah," he returned to his announcer's voice. "Hey, Kenneth, I hear your mother danced naked with a moose."

Three hours later, after a few more jokes, one more beer and a nap, T.J. put his shirt on and ambled over behind the bucking chutes. Among the young cowboys and future cowboys, he saw Kid Kaminski trying to work some dry rosin into his bullrope, which was hanging from the pipe fence of the back pens. The Kid's eyes lit up when he saw T.J. heading his way.

T.J. asked the Kid, "Didja see your bull yet?"

"Yeah," the Kid answered, a little more relaxed than before. "He's not as big as the other bulls – but he's got horns."

"Don't worry 'bout them horns," T.J. advised. "Do you know anything about him?"

"No," replied the Kid.

"Well, it's just as well," replied T.J. "Probably a young bull with no set pattern, anyway. We'll just take him as he comes." He looked at Kid's old worn-out bullrope hanging on the fence. "Where'd you get this?" he asked.

"An older friend of mine who don't ride no more," Kid answered.

"Hope you didn't pay much for it," said T.J., twisting and shaking the rope. "It's awful raggy. Better buy a new one first chance you get. And when you do, put some tincture of benzoine on the handle. That'll stiffen her up real good. I think it's too late for this rope."

"How many bulls you been on?"

It embarrassed the Kid to admit, "I've never been on a bull…I've been on three steers, though."

"Didja ride 'em?" T.J. asked, encouragingly.

"No," said the Kid as he fumbled with his riding glove, "I almost rode the last one."

T.J. looked down at Kid's glove. "Little loose for ya, ain't it? Why, hell, this ain't nothin' but an old work glove." He did not sense the Kid's embarrassment, as he continued. "Lemme have a look at yer spurs."

With his spurs already hugging the heels of his boots, the Kid turned around and looked over his shoulder.

T.J. dropped to his knees to inspect. "Oh, man, these are bronc ridin' spurs," he denounced. "See this, yer shanks are too short and there ain't enough angle on 'em!" He looked up and saw the worried disappointment in the young greenhorn's eyes. "We'll be alright, though. Ain't no big deal."

It was another hour before the bulls were loaded into the chutes. Kid's bull was a short, dirty colored brown, with no hump and six inch tipped horns that curved forward from the sides of his skull. T.J. climbed down into chute number three and sat on the bull as he showed the Kid, step by step, everything from how to put the rope on to the position a bullrider should be in when he nods for the gate. The young bull wallowed about in the chute as T.J. sat on its back. Not because it was mean, but because this was all brand-new to him. He'd never had a man on his back before, and he didn't like it.

"Now, yer gonna hafta be real quick in here," said T.J. from the back of the still-thrashing bull, "'cause he's gonna fightcha all the way."

The Kid was scared, and T.J. knew it. He climbed out of the chute and put a hand on his shoulder. "Forget about what I said about your equipment," he retracted. "You can ride the baddest bull in the world with a flank rope and a pair of tennis shoes, if you want him bad enough."

The Kid stood motionless.

"Have you stretched out?" asked T.J.

No answer.

"Hey!" he said, nudging the Kid and awakening him from his thoughts – or second thoughts. "I said didja stretch out yet?"

"No," the Kid mumbled.

"You got time. Go stretch out like them other bullriders are doin'. Get good and loose, now."

The Kid did as he was told.

As T.J. looked down at the young bull he suddenly noticed that his own heart was pounding faster and harder. Even though he wasn't getting on, he had the pre-bull jitters. His palms were sweating and his teeth were clenched.

The last barrel racer trotted her Shetland pony out of the arena, and the announcer thanked her. "How about a hand for that little girl, bless her heart…

"Now, let's get set for the bullriding event for the boys aged fourteen through eighteen. We've got five young bullriders here this afternoon and five bucking chutes, so if you'll direct your attention on chute number one, the one that displays the 'Ed's Welding' sign, that's where we're set to go…"

The Kid climbed back up onto the platform behind the chutes beside T.J., saying nothing.

"You pumped up and ready to go?" T.J. asked him.

The Kid nodded weakly.

"You'll be third."

The first young cowboy nodded for the gate. He was on a tall skinny red Brahma bull. The bull bucked in a circle to the left, kicking high and nice.

"See how that boy's got his chin tucked and he stays out over his bull?" T.J. pointed out as the eight-second whistle blew.

The Kid nodded.

"That's how you need to do it."

The bull made his exit and the cowboy tipped his hat to the crowd.

The next bullrider was barely fourteen and could have passed for an eleven-year old. His black hornless bull would be of average size in a regular rodeo string, but it was the biggest one at this junior rodeo.

As the little hopeful straddled his giant opponent and took his wrap, T.J. said to the Kid, "Gitcher glove on, buddy, it's about your time."

The Kid reluctantly did so.

"Remember what I told you about tuckin' yer chin and squeezin' with yer legs." T.J. sensed that the Kid wished he'd never entered. "It's real simple," he calmed. "Just move with him. When he makes his move, just move with him."

The Kid swallowed hard as the chute men swung open gate number two and the big black bull lumbered into the arena, slowly at first, like an out-of-tune truck picking up speed, each backfire a weak attempt to buck. Then, for no apparent reason, the boy slid off the left side of the bull, away from his riding hand. It looked like a pretty tame buck-off. Predictably, the boy should hit the ground, roll, and get up running. To everyone's surprise, though, he was jerked back against the body of the bull, his hand stuck tight in the bullrope. His mother screamed and his father bailed into the arena as the young cowboy dangled helplessly – too short for his feet to reach the ground, too jumbled to find the tail of his rope to yank loose with his free hand. The Kid watched in horror as the bullfighter sprinted toward the action, gaining slowly, as the bull bucked straight down the arena, not wanting to hurt anyone, just trying to shed his clinging intruder. Shot stood up in the back of the pickup on his good leg, instinctively wanting to jump the fence and save the boy, but stopped short, realizing there was nothing he could do. Finally, the bullfighter caught up with the bull. He moved in from the right side, reached up on the bull's back and his hands found the tail of the boy's bullrope. He yanked on the rope with everything he had and the young bullrider's hand slipped free. The boy slid underneath the bull, hitting the dirt on his back, looking up at the big black belly as the bull rumbled over him, unintentionally stepping square in his abdomen. The Kid winced as the cowboy grabbed his guts and folded over in pain, lying on his side.

The bullfighter knelt by his side, "You O.K.?" Of course the boy could not answer.

His father was the next one there. "Lay flat, son, don't try to move," he said as he loosened his son's pants and unbuttoned his shirt. Soon, his mother and a half-dozen other concerned adults gathered around him.

The Kid watched them huddle around the boy as a rancid taste festered in the back of his mouth. He shivered as a raw chill spread from his spine throughout his body, leaving goose bumps beneath cold sweat. He looked down at his bull, rocking back and forth in its enclosure. He wished that he was anywhere but here.

"Relax," T.J. advised in a quiet tone. "Looks like this may take a while." He paused and then said, "Think about what yer gonna do, now, run it through yer mind."

The only thing running through the Kid's mind was the boy hanging up and getting stomped. He thought about telling T.J. that he had changed his mind, that he didn't want to ride after all, but doing that would mean admitting that he was afraid.

The big black bull found the catch pen gate and exited quietly as the announcer filled dead space with his voice. "We all hate to see something like this happen. As we know, rodeo can be a dangerous sport. Hopefully, this fine young cowboy isn't injured too bad. Probably just has the wind knocked out of him... Still, every precaution must be taken... While I've got a minute, I'd like to thank the Clear Creek Tree Farm for supporting this rodeo and for donating the beautiful belt buckle that some lucky cowboy is going to win in the bullriding today... And folks it looks like good news. He's up and on his feet! How about a hand for this young man, as that's all he's going to be taking home with him today."

Contestants and parents alike cheered and applauded as the boy slowly made his way to the arena gate, flanked by his mother and father.

"And our next bullrider – Kyle Kaminski in chute number three…"

The Kid shuddered at the announcement of his name.

"OK, Kid," T.J. encouraged, "let's get after it!"

The Kid didn't move.

"C'mon Kid," urged T.J., slapping him on the back, "let's go!"

The Kid slowly and reluctantly climbed into the chute, over the back of the bull.

The flankman stood beside T.J. "Better stay away from him," he told the bullfighter as he hung the flank rope loosely on the bull. "He's never been bucked before."

The Kid lowered himself down until his butt touched the bull's back. The bull jumped, sending the Kid scrambling out of the chute. He was stopped by T.J.

"No, stay down on him," said T.J. "Yer alright."

The Kid looked at T.J. apprehensively. His legs and hands shook.

"Don't let him scare ya." T.J. said quietly in the Kid's ear. "This bull ain't nothin'."

He lowered himself down again. When the bull felt contact he bounded forward again. The Kid started up the chute again and felt T.J.'s hand on his shoulder.

"Stay there!" snapped T.J. "Now sit on him. Put yer legs clear down on his sides. This son of a bitch ain't gonna hurt you!"

The Kid did as he was told as the bull rocked back and forth.

"See, that ain't so bad," T.J. coached. "Now hand me the tail of yer rope."

Trembling, the Kid did and then stuck his gloved hand into the worn, frayed handhold.

T.J. pulled on the rope, tightening it around the bull's belly. "Tell me when that's enough," he said.

"That's enough!" was the immediate answer.

"Ya sure?" doubted T.J. "That ain't very…"

Suddenly the bull ducked his head out and leaned hard on the side of the chute. The Kid wailed in pain as his leg was pinned between the bull's rib cage and the wooden slat. "My leg!"

T.J. pulled his hat from his head and swatted the bull between the eyes with it. The bull bellowed and snorted and then stood straight.

The Kid was up and out of the chute before T.J. could stop him.

"Kid, you gotta stay down on him!" said T.J. impatiently. "The longer you mess around in the box, the worse he's gonna get!"

The Kid clutched his calf muscle with both hands and moaned, "Ooooh, my leg…"

"Well, cowboy up and put it outta yer mind," urged T.J. "It's get even time!"

The Kid sat on the top rail of the chute.

"Come on, buddy," said T.J. "Now's the time. Look at that! He's standin' good now."

The Kid stared at the back of the bull to avoid looking T.J. in the eye. "My leg," he sobbed again, "it hurts!"

"It's a rough sport," argued T.J. "Sometimes yer legs are gonna get hurt. Now, are you gonna get on?"

The Kid fumbled for an excuse. "I can't feel my toes."

"You don't *need* toes to ride bulls, that's why spurs was invented!" grumbled T.J. "Do ya want him or not?"

The Kid hung his head in shame.

The flankman piped in, "Come on, boy, yer holdin' up the rodeo."

No answer.

"Hell," said T.J. to the gateman as he undid the rope and stripped it from the bull, "turn him out."

The gateman looked to the flankman for final orders.

"You heard him," he said as he walked past the Kid to the next chute.

The Kid glared through tears as the bull walked nonchalantly into the arena and was trailed through the catch pen gate.

T.J. walked back to the pickup, leaving the Kid moaning in self-pity. He crawled into the pickup bed and plopped down in his lawn chair. He was disgusted and trying not to show it. "Everybody's got to believe something, Shot," he stated wisely as he opened up the cooler. "I believe I'll have another beer."

"So what happened to yer little pardner?" asked Shot. "He get hurt?"

"Nope," said T.J. popping a top. "Just lost his heart."

The announcer introduced the next young bullrider and a small white bull with black spots spilled from the chute, straddled by a skinny, long-legged cowboy. The bull bucked straight down the arena, double-jumping and kicking under his belly. The youngster squeezed hard with his knees and legs, as his legs were too long to get a good hold with his spurs. His chest stuck out and his free arm pumped wildly over his head. His cowboy hat was pulled so low that his eyes could barely be seen, but he bared his teeth in determination. The whistle sounded and he threw a long leg over the bull's head as his fist turned loose of the rope. He spun around in mid-air and landed on his feet. Then onto his butt, his back, his head, and he was on his feet again. He glanced over his shoulder to make sure the bull wasn't after him, before taking off his hat, looking to the heavens and giving thanks.

"That guy rides a lot like you," observed Shot.

T.J. looked over at him. "What kind of a crack is that?"

"Wasn't a crack," said Shot. "I just said he rides like you."

"Oh," said T.J. after thinking about it, "I just got out over my bulls more."

"You do the first couple jumps," noted Shot, "But t'ords the last of yer rides yer almost sittin' on yer pockets, just like he was."

"No, I don't," argued T.J.

"Sure ya do."

"Do not!"

Shot chuckled lightly to himself and contended, "The heck you don't, T.J."

"I got films of me ridin'," T.J. defended, "and on every one of 'em, I'm way out over my bulls!"

"No, yer not."

"Yes, I am!"

"Are not."

"Up yers!"

"Where are them tapes of you ridin'?" Shot inquired.

"I think they're at yer place."

"How old are they?"

"Five or six years," T.J. answered.

"Who was doin' all the filmin'?"

"'Member that girl Bennett was haulin' around for awhile? Danielle Dobbins. 'Member her?"

"Oh yeah, I remember Danny," Shot smiled. "She was a sweetheart."

"She went on a winter run with us one time. Filmed every single bullride."

The announcer introduced the last bullrider and they watched as a young cowboy got dumped on his head off of a spinning bull and sprinted back to the chutes. Shot and T.J. paid no attention to the announcer as he congratulated the winner and bid everyone a thank you and a safe trip home.

"Where is she, now?" asked Shot. "I always thought Bennett just might hook up with her for good."

"I think she thought so, too, for awhile," said T.J. "She couldn't handle Bennett's cowboy ways. She wanted a farm. Wanted him to stay home and run it. I don't know where she is now. I wonder if she knows about Bennett."

"He should have married her," said Shot.

"Married her?" T.J. repeated. "What for?"

"Well, 'cause she's a good ol' girl," Shot answered.

T.J. looked at Shot like he was crazy. "That ain't no reason to marry a girl. Didn't I just tell you she wanted him to stay home and run the farm?"

"Yeah," explained Shot, "but what he shoulda done was just marry her and then never stay home. That's how I always done it."

T.J. scoffed, "Well, that's how come you been divorced three times, ya big dummy!"

"Aw, that ain't got a thing to do with it."

"It ain't?"

"No, it ain't. The reason I been divorced three times is 'cause I kept gettin' into bad marriages. I kept marryin' bitches. They kept tellin' me what to do."

"Kept tellin' ya to stay home."

"That's right...no, that ain't right...well, yeah that is right, kinda, I guess."

"So if ya blowed it so many times," reasoned T.J., "how come ya figure Bennett shoulda' got married?"

"I just think she's a good ol' girl. Hell, I'da' married her," said Shot. "We oughta get out them tapes tonight and watch yer rides."

T.J. stared out into the empty arena. "Naw, we don't need to do that."

"You don't want to?"

"Not really."

"Why not?"

"Just rather not."

Shot studied the look on T.J.'s face. "I'd kinda like to take a look at 'em. See who's right about the way you ride. I still say you didn't get out over yer bulls that much, 'specially t'ords the end of yer rides."

T.J. said nothing, so Shot asked, "What rodeos did she tape?"

T.J. listed the towns: "Spokane, Tacoma, Portland, Great Falls, and then we hit Denver on the way back."

"That's right," recounted Shot, "I was clownin' Denver. You guys bunked with me that night." His skinny lips twisted into a grin. "I was tryin' to get Bennett drunk enough to pass out so's I could slip off down the hall alone with Danielle."

T.J. looked at Shot in disappointed amazement, "You dog!"

"Aw, hell," Shot searched for an excuse, wishing he'd never brought up the subject. "It ain't like he'd never had none 'a my wives."

"Bullshit!" T.J. contended. "He wasn't never with yer wives while you was married to 'em."

"No, but before and after."

"At least he had enough sense not to marry 'em," said T.J. "I can't believe you'd low-crawl him like that!"

"Oh, settle down!" growled Shot. "Nothin' come of it. I ended up passin' out before he did." He quickly changed the subject. "So, let's git them tapes out tonight."

"I already told you," said T.J. "I don't want to watch no rodeo films."

"Well, why not?" Shot inquired.

"I don't feel like it."

Shot could see irritation cover T.J.'s face. "Well, what's wrong with ya?" he asked, unsympathetically.

"There ain't nothin' wrong with me, I just don't wanna watch no bullrides...let's go fishin' instead."

Shot stared at T.J., trying to figure him out.

"And quit starin' at me," said T.J.

Shot lifted the cooler lid and pulled out another beer. "I know what yer problem is," he theorized. "Yer afraid yer gonna git to...want a beer?"

"Got one," T.J. declined.

"Yer afraid," continued Shot, "that yer gonna git to cravin' bulls again, aintcha?"

T.J. gazed at the empty grandstand across the arena. His mind filled them up with people – fans and families, best friends and girlfriends, churchgoers and hellraisers – all cheering and applauding simultaneously at the good rides, all "oohing" and "aahing" in chorus at the bad wrecks. His mind envisioned the lanky young cowboy who had ridden the little spotted bull as himself, and the jump-kicking bull as a twisting, spinning ball of fire! To the left, hard and high, right out of the latch! The crowd was on its feet, the bull switched directions, the rider never loosened! The buzzer sounded, the rider bailed, landed on his feet, threw his hat...the crowd disappeared and T.J. gazed at the empty grandstands.

He took a swig of beer and said, "Hell, no, I ain't cravin' no bulls."

"But yer afraid that cravin' might come back if ya watch them tapes, aincha?" Shot insisted.

"The only reason I don't wanna watch them tapes is 'cause I seen 'em before," claimed T.J. "Let's git outta here."

"Might as well," said Shot, as he rose from his lawn chair and hopped to the open tailgate of the pickup, and with beer in hand, cautiously jumped to the ground using only his healthy leg. Unbeknownst to his doctor, Shot had attempted on more than a few occasions to walk without the use of his crutches, but not for very long. The weight of his body had ignited an unbearably sharp pain in his left kneecap, a warning that it just wasn't ready yet. According to the doctor, it would be at least four more months before Shot could start walking with a cane. According to Shot, any day now. Only the kneecap knew for sure. Shot hopped along the box of his old red Ford and opened the passenger side door. "If ya wanna stop at the bar, I'll beat yer ass in a game of pool," he challenged.

"Yer on," said T.J., already behind the wheel. He fired up the pickup and pulled onto the dusty exit trail behind a fancy blue pickup pulling a matching, gooseneck stock trailer.

As the traffic slowly made its way to the outlet gate, Shot spied young Kid Kaminski walking towards the pickup. "There's yer little buddy now," he pointed.

"That ain't my little buddy," said T.J. "Look at him. Said he hurt his leg. Hell, he ain't even limpin'."

The Kid had his gear bag hefted up on a shoulder. He was relaxed now, grinning, as he walked up to the driver's side door and said, "Thanks for the help, T.J."

T.J. stopped the pickup. "I didn't end up doin' much," he said. "How's yer foot?"

"It's my leg that's hurt," said Kid. "I think it'll be O.K."

"So, you don't think they'll hafta amputate?"

The Kid forced a small chuckle. "Boy, that was weird when I couldn't feel my toes."

Shot piped up, "Maybe ya oughta' check your boots. They coulda' fell off!"

His grin tapered. "Lucky thing for that bull that he hurt me in the chute. I'da' spurred the hair off 'im!"

Shot laughed and rolled his eyes, and T.J. looked in the rear-view mirror. Although no one was behind him, he said, "Well, I better get outta here. Hate to hold up traffic."

"Before you go, I was wantin' to ask ya," the Kid sought. "Earlier you said somethin' about my rope and glove and spurs not bein' very good...I was wondering where can I buy that kinda stuff."

"You mean yer gonna keep ridin'?" T.J. asked.

"Heck, yes," replied the Kid. "It's in my blood."

"Y'know, Kid," T.J. searched for diplomatic words, "maybe you should try tennis or bowlin'. Rodeo's a rough sport."

Kid swung his gear bag from his shoulder and set it on the ground. "I just wanna ride bulls," he said. "I have ever since I was a little kid."

"Well, you sure didn't show it today," said T.J., not as diplomatically.

The grin completely disappeared. "Huh?"

"You pussed out," T.J. accused the Kid. "You didn't even want that bull."

"He hurt my leg," reasoned Kid.

"He didn't hurt yer leg," T.J. argued.

"Yes he did, he mashed it against the chute."

"You ain't even limpin', Kid."

"Well, it still hurt," the Kid defended.

T.J. was getting irritated. "Kid, you don't know what pain is. I've rode with busted ribs, pulled muscles, torn ligaments, broken toes...man...you were bucked off a' him before you ever got on. Before he ever mashed yer leg, you were jumpin' out every time he twitched a muscle. When you get on a bull, you gotta do it with determination, you gotta be aggressive. You gotta not let *nothin'* get in yer way. Ya just gotta bear down and cowboy up. Ya gotta want it so bad you can taste it..."

The Kid looked T.J. in the eyes and said nothing as the words of confidence soaked into his brain.

"...Kid, I hate to be preachin' atcha this way. It's just that...I lost the best friend I ever had to this sport and I miss him and it hurts. It hurts *bad*. And I been injured all summer, but now the injuries are gone and there ain't nothin' left but the pain...but I can ride with pain. And when I come back I'm gonna come back strong and hard. I'm gonna ride tougher than I ever have. My hammer's gonna be *cocked*, boy, I'm gonna tuck my chin and lift on that rope and if he gives me any shit in the chute I'm gonna get that much madder and ride that much tougher!"

T.J. took a breath and summed up his feelings. "*That's* how ya go about it...If not, then ya might as well be bowlin', or playin' tennis, or fishin'."

The Kid stood expressionless before T.J.

For the moment, T.J. could detect a whole new attitude about the kid. Once a wide-eyed scared 'wannabe', now just maybe, he was a confident, young 'will-be'.

The Kid stuck his hand out. "Thank you, T.J."

T.J. reached out the window and shook his new friend's hand hard. "Thank *you*, Kid." He put the truck in gear and began to roll away.

"I'll be seein' you around!" the Kid called out.

T.J. hollered back out the window, "I hope so!"

Shot sat silent, awaiting a comment as they pulled out of the rodeo grounds onto the highway that headed for home.

When T.J. said, "Shot, I think I'll pass on that pool game," Shot smiled, knowing what T.J. would say next. "I got some rodeos to enter."

Chapter 10: October 1987

The noon sun swung a fraction lower in the wide Nebraska sky than it did a week before. The days were shorter and cooler. The flatland corn south of the Platte River had transformed from verdant green to golden blonde. Wheat germinated below rich brown soil. Alfalfa hay had had its last cutting of the season. North of the Platte, the cattle and horses alike were beginning to gain weight, and their coats were becoming thick on their hides in preparation for another harsh Sandhills winter. The line separating the two regions is a half mile wide in some places and a foot deep in others. Sometimes the river bed breaks into separate streams, parting three, four, five or more times, like a frayed rope, only to intertwine with itself miles downriver. Other times, the Rocky Mountain melt water will rise above its banks, flooding fields, roads and houses.

Mike Fanner's place got flooded this past summer. Heavy snows in the mountains last winter followed by an extremely hot summer took the blame for his alfalfa field being under water, as well as the basement of his house, floor of his barn, his driveway, and his roping arena. But that had been months ago. The flood waters had subsided, the basement had been pumped out, the driveway was clear, the arena was dry, and the dirt was disked and raked to a soft even texture, providing solid footing for Mike's good roping horses, allowing them to be at a full run in less than ten yards and slide to a quick stop with ease.

His roping chute sat at the west side of the arena, and his calves were in the alley, ready to be run through for Mike and his brother Brad to practice their roping and tying skills on, as they did every weekday afternoon in the fall.

The Fanner brothers were rodeo cowboys. In the arena they did two things–rope and tie calves, and they were fast. Because they had to haul their horses everywhere they went, plus Mike's wife, Janine, and her barrel horse, they were not able to attend as many rodeos in a year as their roughstock riding counterparts. They also had to spend a lot more money throughout the year, what with pulling a loaded gooseneck trailer down the road behind their dually club-cab pickup, plus the veterinary bills, feed, and the price of their practice stock. The positive side of the coin was that calf ropers are a lot less prone to injury.

The young men were practicing alone. Mike's wife helped push calves when she could, but three days a week Janine waited tables at the cafe in town.

Mike warmed up his horse by loping him in a slow circle in front of the chute. In his early thirties, Mike was of medium build, straight brownish-blonde hair, and a wide toothy smile under a worn-out straw cowboy hat. The horse he was riding was a four-year-old black gelding that he'd bought from a neighbor to the north. A little skittish, but a fast horse that really paid attention to cattle. Mike called him Shazaam and saw a lot of potential in him.

Brad was the older brother by two years. He was the same height as Mike, but much heavier, and most of the excess weight was around his belly. He wore wire-rimmed glasses and his medium-length black hair poked out from beneath a white ballcap. He lived by himself a few miles down the road, but spent the majority of his time here, roping with his little brother as he had done since the age of ten. His two horses were saddled and tethered to his horse trailer. They waited patiently, anticipating their almost daily ritual of loping in endless circles while the rider would swing his loop around and around, for no apparent reason at all – until the rider would back into the roping box, bolt after an escaped calf, skid to a halt while the second the rider tossed his swinging loop around the calf's neck, and held the rope taut; then their master would leap off his mount, throw the calf to the ground, and tie its legs together – only to let the calf loose again, so they could do the same thing to another calf. This rite had become second nature to the older horses. Their simplistic brains did not have the ability to wonder why they did this again and again. They just did it.

Brad emerged from the barn carrying a propane bottle and a hot-iron tray. He took them to the edge of the arena and set them down. "Where's that brandin' iron?" he asked his brother.

"It should be hangin' in the tack room, right next to the stairs," Mike answered.

The boys had a calf to brand today. Twelve of the thirteen calves here had been branded with a bar X, a registered mark of the previous owner. The thirteenth calf was a little gray Brahma, just brought in the night before by a friend from Colorado, Paul Hotchkins. Paul wouldn't take any money for the calf, just wanted to get rid of it. He said he didn't pay anything for it anyway, said the calf had pinned his daughter up against a fence a month or so ago, and had roughed her up a bit. Ever since he'd been worried that it would happen again. He had no explanation for the strange ⋝M brand on the bull calf's right shoulder and the brothers could not find it in the brand book, so they decided to burn a line down the side of the sideways 'W' and make a 'B'. That way the BM could stand for Brad and Mike.

Brad brought the branding iron from the barn and laid it in the iron tray. The swift October breeze blew out three matches before he could get the propane torch lit. He set the flame to the desired temperature, all the way up, and placed it in the hole at the end of the tray, pointing the blaze at the branding iron. In a matter of minutes, the simple 'I' brand would be sizzling enough to add to the 'W'.

"Is your horse warmed up?" Brad asked his brother.

"We're ready to rope," said Mike before he put the piggin' string – the small rope he needs to tie his calf with – to his mouth and clenched it with his teeth.

Brad walked over to the roping chute where the first calf was already waiting. "This is that fast little bugger," he warned as he climbed over the alley fence and lowered himself down behind the calf. He crowded the calf up toward the front of the chute. His job was to open the spring-loaded front gates and to shove the calf out should he balk.

Mike backed Shazaam into the box beside the chute. The jet-black horse was prancing with nervous excitement, as he did every time he anticipated chasing down a calf. His ears fluttered every which way until his rump came in contact with the back of the roping box. Then he suddenly became very relaxed and calm. He focused on just two things – the calf and his master's commands. His neck was curved in such a way that his head was high, yet his nose was low, tucked under, just inches from his chest. Mike held tight on the reins. He sat poised, forward in the saddle. Along with his horse, he focused on the calf. When the calf was standing the way Mike wanted and looking forward, he nodded his head slightly and Brad tripped the latch by pulling on a rope that hung directly in front of his face, automatically springing the gate open and sending the calf fleeing into the arena. As if they were one, horse and rider bounded from the box in hot pursuit of their helpless prey. As Brad had said, the calf was a fast little bugger. Had Shazaam not been a fast horse they might not have caught the calf before he'd made it to the far end of the sixty-yard long pen. But he was, and midway down the arena he had Mike within five yards of the calf. Mike reached over his horse's head and threw his swinging loop around the calf's neck. With his lasso tied to the horn of his saddle, he pitched its slack into the air, tightening the snare around the calf's neck, ensuring that the little bugger could not run through the loop. A millisecond later Shazaam dug his heels under his belly and slid to a stop as Mike sprang from the saddle, connecting with the ground at a full run, like a jet plane coming in for a landing. Four steps later he'd reached the struggling calf. With his left hand on the rope and his right hand on the calf's far-side flank, he lifted him from his feet and slammed him down on his side. He then quickly gathered the legs – two hind and one front – and, jerking the piggin' string from his mouth, slipped the small loop tight around the ankles, made two fast wraps and tucked the third wrap under the second one and thrust his hands to the sky. His job was done. He casually walked back to his horse, who still had a tight line on the calf, mounted, nudged the horse forward and waited six seconds – the legal time allowed for the calf to kick free.

"Good run!" hollered Brad from the chute.

Mike looked over his shoulder, "I run him a little farther than I wanted to."

"I told you he was a fast little bugger."

"I think he's gittin' faster," Mike commented as he dismounted, took the loop from the calf's neck and freed him of the piggin' string.

The calf jumped to his feet and trotted to the east end of the arena.

"How's Shazaam lookin'?" asked Mike as he climbed back aboard.

"Boy, he's lookin' real good, Mike. Smooth."

"Last week he was hittin' the brakes a little soon," said Mike. He rode back to the roping box while coiling his rope. "I think I got him over that."

Brad closed the spring-loaded chute gates, went back and climbed into the alley again, behind another calf. "Hey, this is that calf Paul brought in. When you rope him, leave him tied and I'll get the iron."

The gray bull calf was five months old now, and weighed nearly three hundred pounds. He had grown miserable in the last few months. So miserable, in fact, that he would charge the fence of his twenty- by twenty-foot hogwire pen when anyone came near. Then they quit bottle-feeding him and he began to hate the people who held him prisoner there, especially the little girl who had invaded his territory that morning. Before long, the only one who would come around with feed and water was the man. So he spent his days – every day – staring through the squares in the fence. Like the horses, he had no ability to wonder why things were the way they were, but he knew that he longed to be free from the solitude of his enclosure. Sometimes he got so restless in there that he would scamper about in his pen, jumping high in the air, kicking behind him and snorting at intruders who weren't there. The rest of the day he would rub his sides against the fence, sleep, get up, have a drink of water. The first four days that he was off the bottle, he just sniffed the cracked corn in his feed trough. Then he got hungry enough to lick it, and slowly taught himself to eat from a trough. Every evening, when the sun had settled below the pink horizon, he paced back and forth along the fence until the sky was pitch black.

Then, the day before, a horse trailer had backed up to the pen and the man took away part of the fence. The man tried to chase him out of the pen, but instead he chased the man out of the pen – right into the trailer. He followed him in but the man got away and slammed the door behind him. When he realized he wasn't in his pen anymore, he wanted to go back. This pen was smaller and darker – and moving. He was afraid. He bawled the way he did when he was a baby calf, looking for his mama. He bawled that way all the way here. When the trailer doors were opened, he saw calves. He wasn't sure what they were, but they looked like him, sounded like him, and smelled like him, and he was glad to see them. He ran to the herd and nudged his way to the middle.

"Get up there, little gray," commanded Brad from behind.

The little gray didn't want to go up there and leave the other calves. He held his ground. Brad whooped and smacked him on the rump with an opened hand. Instantly, he kicked behind with a well-placed blow to the groin that sent a jolt of throbbing pain swirling through both of Brad's life-givers.

"Ahhhhhh!" Brad exhaled as he held what hurt and bowed over frontwards. "Ahhhhhh!!" he repeated, backing out of kick range.

Mike spurred Shazaam to a trot to the roping box. "You O.K., Brad?"

"Ahhhhhh!"

Mike knew what had happened, but he didn't know what to do, so he just looked solemnly down on his brother.

After a moment of quiet, Brad let go of himself with one hand and gripped the fence rail. He slowly tried to straighten his back, stopping midway. Momentarily he lifted his head. His face was beet red, his eyes were crossed and his lips were puckered. In a tortured, spasmodic shrill voice he stammered, "I'm...gonna cut...his nuts...............out."

As Mike looked down on his brother, his face slowly evolved from solemnity to guilt-ridden amusement. He bit his lip and fought the uncontrollable urge to laugh. He whirled Shazaam around and loped to the middle of the arena, twirling his rope and trying to hide the fact that it struck him as hilarious – not that his brother got kicked, but the distorted look on his face and the high pitch of his threat.

Brad stood up straight now, and let go with his other hand. He steadied himself against the wooden rails on either side of him, tilted his head back and peered through the redness of his eyelids, closed against the burnished sun. He leaned to one side, opened his eyes and stared at the ground for awhile, wondering if he was going to be sick. He took a deep breath and let it out sharply. Then he looked at the calf and whispered, "You son of a bitch."

Although still dizzy and still throbbing, he had regained most of his composure. He stood sideways in the alleyway, reached out with his right foot and rammed the heel of his cowboy boot against the base of the bull calf's tail. The calf kicked back, this time missing. Brad's jaw stuck out in anger. He muttered some profanities as he lifted both feet from the ground with the support of the sides of the calf alley, and stomped hard on the rear end of the calf. The calf returned with a two-footed kick beneath Brad's feet and then darted into the chute. Brad quickly dropped his feet to the ground and slammed the gate behind the little gray. "There!" he exclaimed victoriously. "Gotcha now, runt!"

Although the extreme throbbing in his crotch told Brad that everything was still there, he reached down and felt, just to make sure. With a shaky sigh of relief he looked up to see if Mike was watching. Good, he wasn't. Just loping Shazaam in a tight circle and nonchalantly twirling his lariat. Brad cleared his throat and tried to hide the lingering pain in his voice, "You 'bout ready?"

Mike held his head low, hiding his grin under his old straw hat. "Yeah," he answered, "I'll be right there." As he walked his horse to the box he could not persuade his mind to erase the cartoon-like image of his brother's pain-twisted face.

Brad looked at the calf through the bars of the gate he had just slammed. He knew he had to get in there with him. Might as well get it over with. He slowly opened the back gate and slipped behind him.

The little gray had his nose through the front chute gate. He wanted out of there badly. He felt a hand on his rump and kicked behind him with one foot. He felt a 'thunk' and heard the man yelp in pain. Then he felt the man's body up against his. He kicked several times and connected on most of them, but the man was too close for his kicks to connect at full impact. He persisted in trying, though. Soon he felt his tail being twisted and tightly curled up over his back. The paralyzing pain caused him to cease fighting and stand still.

Mike and Shazaam backed into the roper's box. Again the horse was completely focused. The amusement of Brad's agony-stricken face was gone from Mike's mind. He licked his lips, pulled the reins tightly, leaned over the saddle horn, looked over at his brother and burst into uncontrollable laughter.

"Oh, for God's sake, Mike!" Brad blasted. "Let's go! The little prick is kickin' the shit outta me!"

The more Mike tried to stop laughing, the worse it got. He finally rode out of the box.

"Shit Mike! What's with you?"

Mike couldn't answer. He loped Shazaam to the far end of the arena and back. The delirious giggling had ceased, but he could not hide the grin across his face.

"Are you ready, now?" asked Brad impatiently. "I ain't gonna stay in here all day!"

Again, Mike backed his horse into the box. This time he was careful not to look at his brother. When the horse and calf were standing right, he nodded his head and the gate sprang open.

The calf shot from the chute like a bullet from a forty-five. He could see another calf at the far end of the arena and he could hear horse hooves pounding close behind him. He caught a glimpse of a rope as it dropped in front of his eyes and tightened around his neck. He kept racing until he hit the end of the rope. He saw nothing but sky as he was jerked over backwards and before he knew it he was lying on the ground. He could see Mike, already off his horse and charging down the tight line, directly in front of him. So he scrambled to his feet and charged back. The top of his head collided with one of Mike's legs just above the kneecap, sending him somersaulting over his back. Instincts would have allowed most calves to run away at this point, but they kept this one here to finish the fight. He spun around bellowing and rammed heads with Mike. Stars fluttered before Mike's eyes as he grabbed for the rope connecting his horse and the calf and called out to Shazaam,

"Back! Back!" Shazaam did as he was told and soon he had pulled the hostile attacker off of his downed partner.

This time it was Brad who was laughing as he hurried into the arena to see if his brother was all right. The last thing he expected when he trotted by Shazaam was for the gray calf to attack him, too, which was the first thing that happened. He spun on his heels and hot-footed it for the fence, arms pumping wildly, whooping and yelping and keeping an eye on the calf from over his shoulder. The calf's three-inch upturned horns were inches from Brad's oversized, jostling butt when he hit the end of the rope and was jerked to his back again. By the time he had recovered his feet, Brad was clambering up the fence. He snorted at Brad and pawed the ground beneath him. Before, he was charging out of self-defense. Now, he was mad and wanted to hurt someone.

He turned and saw Mike slowly prying himself off of the ground, his straw hat in one hand, rubbing his head with the other. He took a run at him, but, tethered to Shazaam's saddle horn, he could not escape the circumference of the circle in which Shazaam was the pivot point. He turned and faced the only living creature he could get to. Shazaam stood silent, facing the calf, keeping pressure on the rope, just like he was supposed to do. The calf lowered his head and headed for the horse's knees. Shazaam's eyes widened. He back-stepped as fast as he could, but not nearly fast enough. An instant before the calf butted him, Shazaam jumped sideways in the air and hit the ground in a dead run. The calf chased after him until, again, the rope tightened around his neck and he fell, dragging across the arena dirt, no longer able to keep his feet under him.

Brad bailed from the top of the fence, back into the arena, hollering, "Catch that horse or he'll drag him to death!"

Mike was to his feet, racing at the horse at an angle, trying to cut him off against the fence. "Whoa!"

Shazaam slowed when he heard his master's call, "Whoa, now, buddy, easy, there."

When the horse slowed down to a trot, the calf made it to his feet and charged him again, sending him sprinting down the arena again.

"Whoa, Shazaam," Mike called as the calf nosed into the dirt and slid on his side behind the confused and panic-stricken horse. "Whoa, pardner, easy."

Shazaam, wary from the last time, did not ease up this time.

Brad lumbered behind them, yelling to his brother, "Try and corner him!"

Shazaam rounded the far end of the arena and headed back down the fence line, dragging the calf like a sled. He saw Mike, directly ahead, his arms flailing, his anxious voice at the top of his lungs, "Whoa, Shazaam! Whoa!"

He slowed up, apprehensively, and Mike relaxed and dropped his arms with anticipation of calmly walking up and seizing the reins. Undecided on whether to 'whoa' or 'giddup,' the horse stayed in a slow lope until he was just a few feet from Mike, when he decided to pick up speed again. Mike reached for the saddle horn, grasped it securely and swung himself to the saddle – almost. When he landed on the confused horse's rump, it propelled Shazaam back into a dead run. Mike's legs, once straddling the animal's backside, slid behind. He stretched out over the back of the horse, clinging to the horn, his chin bouncing off the back of the saddle with every stride. He hopelessly tried to pull himself up and into the saddle, but the jostling speed made it impossible. He knew that if he let go now, the calf would be dragged over him, possibly causing bodily harm to both of them. His bouncing eyes could see the end of the arena nearing in a blur. He knew that Shazaam had a choice; he could crash into the fence or curve sharply to the right. Mike turned his head to the side and closed his eyes. At the last possible instant, the horse swept right, the rider swung off the left, his overpowered fingers parting from the horn. He let out a groan before he even hit the ground, ricocheting off it, his body whirling upside down into the fence in a heap. He opened one eye, just in time to catch a glimpse of the calf plowing past, missing him by less than two feet.

Brad stopped running long enough to dig his pocketknife out of his jeans pocket and open up the blade. He hoped to cut the nylon rope as Shazaam dragged the calf by. Puffing and wheezing, Brad was just too slow and out of shape to head the horse off as he rounded the curves and headed back into the straightaway.

Mike slowly rolled over to his knees and, with the help of the fence, pulled himself to his feet. He felt useless for the calf. They'd never catch that horse until he was played out, and by then it would surely be too late. He felt sickened that a calf was dying at his hands – the calf that Brad felt like killing just moments before. He looked at his horses tied to the trailer. Would he have time to sprint over there, cinch up, bridle, and get back before the calf was strangled to death? Very doubtful. He was going to try anyway, when he saw Brad's other catch rope hanging on the post, right in front of his face. He snatched it away and built a loop as he rushed toward Shazaam again. He knew, as the horse rounded the far end of the arena, that he would be back this way again. He swung the lasso over his head and waited. As Shazaam passed between him and the fence, Mike tossed the loop over the horse's ears. The back of the loop settled over his neck but the front of it was still lying across the fleeing horse's nose. Mike ran at him and fed all twenty-five feet of the rope out until he just had ahold of the knot at the end. Mike watched the loose loop slide down the horse's nose until it dropped over the end just before the rope ran out of slack. He clung to the rope's knot with all of his might and was jerked face first into the dirt, dragging beside the calf.

"Hang on, Mike," Brad wheezed encouragingly as he pushed his exhausted body onward. "I'm coming!"

Hanging on madly to the end of the rope, Mike could not hear the words of his brother. The only sounds he was conscious of were the continuous 'thumps' of the dirt clods, kicked up by Shazaam and exploding against the brim of his cowboy hat. With the hat being his only protection right then, he knew better than to lift his head or open his eyes. He felt the earth shift as Shazaam rounded the curve again. His legs kicked uncontrollably as his body rolled over to his back. He could feel the back of his shirt and jeans filling up with dirt. He kept his fingers, eyes, and mouth clenched. He could hear something ripping. It was the brim of his straw hat, tearing away from the crown. And finally, he could sense the horse was slowing down.

Brad had slowed to a half-walk. Between his heavy gasps, he tried to 'whoa' the horse, but the only sound Shazaam heard was his gasping for air. He held his hands high as he approached the slowing horse, his pocketknife still in his right hand, ready to cut the rope, in case Shazaam tried to bolt again.

The calf's legs were limp. His tongue hung out of the side of his mouth, caked with dirt.

Shazaam slowed to a trot, and Mike opened his eyes. He could see the strangling calf dragging beside him, but he dare not let go of his own rope. A layer of dirt camouflaged his face to the arena floor. His entire body was concealed in dirt, inside his clothes and out. The brim of his hat was around his neck. Only the crown was upon his head, like a high-topped Stetson monk hat.

Brad coaxed the horse to a stop, gently walked up to him and retrieved the reins. With a half-sigh, half-panting wheeze, he backed Shazaam up two steps, untied the calf's rope from the saddle horn, and his own rope from the horse's neck. Both Mike and the calf lay still as

Brad let the exhausted horse loose, and walked to them. "You O.K., Mike?" he puffed, folding his knife and slipping it into his jeans pocket.

Mike rose to his hands and knees, hacking up dirt and spitting mud. He dizzily looked up at his brother. "Yeah," he slurred, "yeah, I'm alright. We better see if we can save this calf."

Brad dropped to his knees in front of the calf, and still fighting for his own air, removed the rope from its neck. "He's...he's breathing," he said as the calf sucked as much air as he could muster. He cleaned the calf's tongue with his forefinger, then opened its mouth wide and reached far inside to make sure its throat passage was not blocked off with mud. "Mike," he said, "Get me a twig or a piece of straw or somethin'. His nostrils are packed tight."

Bruised and beat up as he was, Mike wasted no time finding something to dig out the compressed dirt from the calf's nose. "This oughta do it," he said of the rusty bailing wire he untied from the arena fence.

Brad gently held the calf's head up as Mike ran the wire up a nasal passage until one side was clear. "There," Mike said quietly, "Now, the other side..."

Brad was beginning to breathe easier. He sat on the side of one foot, tucked under. "You'll be alright, little guy," he reassured.

The little guy let out a short sneeze and his head shuddered. Life began to shine in his eyes.

"Pump on his chest a little, Mike, that might help."

"Can't hurt," agreed Mike as he laid his palms against the rib cage and pressed sharply.

"There ya go," said Brad, "Keep that up for awhile."

A few pumps later the calf bawled and swung a hind foot.

"Grab him!" Brad barked as he pressed a knee down hard on the animal's neck and hung on to a front leg, "He's gonna try to whip us again!"

Mike seized the struggling hind foot with both hands, "I don't think he's gonna put up much of a fight this time."

'Thock!' The calf's other hind foot nailed him squarely in the kneecap. He grimaced in pain. "You...sonuva..." He quickly sat his butt on the ground and pressed the front of the heel of his boot against the back of the calf's leg, holding him steady, "...bitch! Gitcher knife out, Brad!"

Brad sat atop the calf, motionless.

"I was thinkin' 'bout lettin' you go, you sorry little bastard," Mike roared wildly, "but now, them nuts are comin' out! Gitcher knife out, Brad!"

Brad studied his brother. He could nearly feel the heat generating from Mike's boiling blood. He knew that underneath the thick layer of dark gray-brown terrain, Mike's face had to be beet red. The way his own face was a few minutes ago when he was bent over hanging on to his crotch. After all that they had just been through, Brad was deathly afraid of what was undoubtedly going to take place next. He felt an uncontrollable laughter building up somewhere in his chest. The same feeling Mike had hidden from him moments before. He tried not to look his brother in the eyes, because they were crossed. Like his own were a few minutes ago in the chute. Brad swallowed hard and the edge of his lip began to quiver. He tried not to notice the straw hat brim Mike wore like a giant clown collar or the brimless crown scrunched down on his head, nearly covering his crossed eyes. He clamped his lips tight and made short snorting sounds as the laughter escaped from his nose.

Mike looked at Brad in amazement covered by rage. "What's the matter with you, Brad? Gitcher knife out!"

One more long snort and Brad completely and helplessly surrendered to the urge that possessed his body and mind. Every horse's ears stood up and flicked his way as Brad's howling cackle burst across the arena, bounced off the barn and sailed into the trees across the river.

Mike's jaw dropped open. He thought his brother had lost his mind. He wanted to say something, but could not find the words.

Brad's shoulders shook. Then his belly. Soon his entire body was jiggling like jelly atop the little gray calf. The jiggling continued even when the sound faded into the wind as he fought to stop and catch his breath again. He glanced at Mike and exploded into roaring, merciless merriment.

Mike simply could not believe it. What was Brad laughing about? Did he enjoy seeing his brother in pain? He looked down at his dirt-strewn hands and clothes. They were all the same shade of gray. He felt the dirt clods in his jeans. He realized he had so much dirt in his boots that he could just barely move his toes. He looked at his brother who was hopelessly trying to hide his side splitting laughter and his anger dropped to an aggravated bewilderment. He felt something foreign around his neck, and realized for the first time that the brim of his hat was not protecting his eyes from the sun. Still clinging tightly to the calf, he reached up with his other hand and pulled the top of his hat from his head and stared in disbelief. He tucked his chin to his neck and dropped his eyes to the straw hat brim enshrouding his shoulders.

Suddenly he felt like the court jester, complete with the face-paint and silly costume. He looked back up at his brother, a breathless, red-faced, teary-eyed, jiggling mound of mirth, and his guts began to tremble. He shook his head. This couldn't be happening. It came on fast and furious and he knew he could not fight it. A giant guffaw ripped through Mike's lips like air out of a whoopee cushion as he gave in to the common undeniable force with Brad, and together, in the middle of the arena, sitting on a calf, they laughed loud and long.

A flock of Sandhill cranes made its way south across the blue Nebraska sky. It took over two minutes from horizon to horizon. And the boys were still laughing.

A small group of Canadian geese were slow-circling specks above the Platte River as they shopped for a place to land. They finally settled in a corn stubble field and picked at the loose grains of corn left over from last week's harvest. The laughter began to subside.

"Oh, God!" Mike howled as he held his aching ribs with one hand. "Oh, God!" he repeated just before his guffaw was replaced with a hacking cough. His cheeks hurt more from the laughing than his kneecap did from the kicking. "I can't believe this," he said between coughs, nearly choking on his own words. "Gitcher knife out, Brad," he grinned.

Brad still could not answer. He shook his head from side to side and let out a loud high-pitched half-wail, half-sigh.

Mike sat giggling, waiting for his brother to regain his composure. When the howling faded, he said again, "Gitcher knife out, Brad."

Again, Brad shook his head. He found his breath and said, "We can't cut him, Mike."

"The hell we can't," argued Mike, still smiling, "Gitcher knife out."

"We can't, Mike," Brad stressed, trying to get serious. "He's been through too much today. We damn-near drug him to death. If we cut him now, the stress could kill him."

Mike started to argue, but stopped short. He knew his brother was right. The grin on his lips slumped to bitter disappointment. There would be no revenge today.

"Besides," added Brad, "this calf's meaner'n hell and he don't give up. We leave his nuts in and he might make a rodeo bull someday."

"We ain't in the buckin' bull business," Mike retorted.

"I know we ain't, but this'n has a lotta potential. You know ol' Roy Tisdale's kid is always gettin' on practice calves. Let's see what this one'll do with him."

Mike thought for a moment. Reluctantly he said, "Alright...but I'm gonna tell you somethin' right now; this little son of a bitch ever kicks me again, I swear, I'm gonna cut his head off!"

"I don't blame ya," agreed Brad. "I feel the same way about him. But right now we've got a bigger problem."

"What's that?"

"We still need to brand him."

"Good!" Mike beamed vengefully. "I'm gonna enjoy this!"

"You wanna get the iron, or sit here with the calf?"

"If you think you can hold him alone," Mike volunteered, "I'll get the iron. Can ya?"

Brad no sooner answered "Yeah," than Mike was to his feet and heading for the hot branding iron. "Be quick, though, Mike, he's starting to fight!"

Mike stepped outside the gate, turned off the valve to the propane torch and removed the scalding iron by its long handle from the tray it cooked in. By the time he got back, the calf was putting up quite a struggle.

"Hurry every chance ya get!" Brad coaxed, impatiently.

Mike trotted up to the calf and lined up the points where the 'I' would look best on the 'W' and was inches from pressing the blistering hot iron against the calf's hide when Brad yelled, "Hold it!"

Mike stopped instantly. "What's the matter?"

"I'll never hold him by myself while you're brandin' him. Tie him up with yer piggin' string."

"I got a brandin' iron in my hands," argued Mike. "What am I s'posed to do with this?"

"Give it here," said Brad, "I can hold it with one hand and hang on to a foot with the other."

"You sure?" Mike questioned apprehensively, as he handed his brother the iron.

With the weight of his entire body perched on the calf's neck, Brad relieved Mike of the iron. "Now, slip yer loop over his front foot and gather his hind legs."

"Easy for you to say," Mike commented as he pulled the small rope from under his belt. He stepped up to the calf's back and fastened the loop snugly around the front foot. After three tries and one kick to the hand, he managed to push and pull the two back legs far enough forward to tie them securely to the front foot. "There!" he said as he stood up over the calf and wiped his hands in victory.

Brad relieved the calf of the weight of his body as he lifted his frame from its neck. "Alright," he said, "I'll slap this line on him and we'll be through..."

"Hold on now!" interrupted his brother. "*I'm* brandin' him! You won't let me castrate him, at least give me the pleasure of burnin' him!"

Brad shrugged his shoulders. "Makes no difference to me," he said as he handed Mike the iron.

Mike's grin was evil as he slowly and carefully lined up the iron with the existing brand and pressed it to the hide. The calf bellowed in pain for a split second and ceased immediately – although the iron still sizzled against his skin, it also burned his sensory nerves, leaving him oblivious to the crackling flesh and smoldering hair.

It was an empty victory for Mike as he tossed the iron to the side, for he knew that the calf did not experience near the pain he had wanted to inflict.

"Looks good," said Brad as he inspected the perfect ℬM on the bull calf's shoulder. "Brad and Mike." He turned and walked toward the fence. "I s'pose you might as well untie him now."

"Wait a minute, wait a minute," his brother responded immediately. "Get back here!"

"It don't take two of us to untie him," said Brad.

"Then *you* untie him!" argued Mike.

"I didn't tie him up, buddy. *You* did."

"You shit-head," Mike cursed as he watched his brother climb up on the fence. He looked down at the calf, then back at Brad. "I can't believe you ain't gonna stay and help me with him."

"No use both of us gittin' run over," replied Brad, as he took a seat on the top rail of the fence. Then he offered some advice. "You might be able to jerk that loop through and haul ass back to the fence before he gits up."

The worry lines in Mike's forehead showed heavily through the dirt. "I doubt it," he murmured. "I tied him awful damn tight. Haven't I gone through enough today?"

"Just untie him and get it over with," his big brother ordered.

Mike took an uneasy breath as he reached down for the thick nylon string that held three of the calf's legs together.

The calf lifted his head and his dark eyes met with Mike's. Mike hesitated as he felt the calf daring him to pull the string. He yanked on the string and began to bolt for the fence, stopping short, realizing the string had not come untied.

Brad said nothing as he watched from the fence. Shazaam

peered silently from the far corner of the arena. The only sound to be heard was the soft autumn breeze shaking the dry toasted leaves from the giant river oaks.

Mike approached the calf again. This time he latched onto the rope with both hands and yanked with all of his might. The rope came loose and the calf's feet sprang free. Mike bolted for the fence where his brother sat watching. Immediately the calf was on his feet. He spun around, lowered his head and bore down on the only moving target. Mike was halfway to the fence.

"Come on, Mike! You can make it!" cheered Brad from the sideline.

The calf was going fast and furious.

"Yer almost here, buddy! Pull it out!"

The arena fence bounced in Mike's vision with every stride he took.

Ten yards...

Five yards...

He felt a sudden pressure against his butt, sending him off-balance. He went to his knees, then slid face-first into the dirt, inches away from the fence. He heard the calf bawl and he grunted as the calf jabbed his small horns into his back.

"Grab the fence!" yelled Brad from above. "Grab the fence and pull yourself up!"

Mike fumbled for the fence until his hands found it. One hand over the other, he began to heft himself up along the fence, the calf still pounding on his ribs and back.

"Keep climbin', buddy!" Brad encouraged, "You're almost here!" He lowered himself partway down the fence and kicked the calf in the head, diverting his attention. As the calf swung his head at Brad's foot, Mike crawled to the top of the fence.

"Git outta here, ya sonuvabitch!" Brad hollered at the calf as he brought his foot back over the fence.

Mike slowly climbed down the other side of the fence and sat down in the weeds.

The calf snorted a couple of times and trotted off down the fence line.

Brad grinned at Mike from atop the fence. "Little brother," he said, "I just saved yer life."

Mike shaded his eyes from the sun as he looked back up at Brad. "Shuddup."

Chapter 11: November 1987

"Get up, Bennett!" screamed Shot Palmer.

The chute gate swung wide. The bull's front feet were in the air. T.J. Jergenson was planted firmly in the middle of the bull's back. Bennett McKinney rolled to his stomach. Shot was running toward Bennett. Before Genghis Khan's front end came to the ground, he saw Bennett scrambling on the ground. Bennett moved in slow motion. Hours passed as he kicked dirt behind him, struggling to get to his feet. His mouth was open but no sound came out. His eyes were wide. Genghis bore down like a locomotive. Nose to the ground, the bull was less than two feet from his helpless prey when Shot bolted upright in his bed, sweating and trembling in fear.

It was over.

Thank God. Usually it lasted longer. Sometimes it just wouldn't go away. There were nights when he heard "Get up, Bennett!" over and over and over...

"What's the matter, Honey?" a woman's voice asked in the darkness.

For a moment, the room was as silent as it was dark.

"Were you having that dream again?"

He'd dreamt it so many times, now, that he'd named it "Yeah," he sighed shakily, "it was *that dream* again."

She reached behind him and fumbled for the light on the night stand. Her brown eyes squinted as her bedroom was filled with light.

Shot let his head drop forward and he rested his teary eyes in the palms of his hands.

She ran her long fingers over his upright back. "My God, you're soaking wet!" she exclaimed. "Is it that hot in here?" Almost immediately she felt his body begin to shiver. "Honey, lay down," she said in a calm, soothing voice. She reached up and took hold of Shot's wrist, pulling it to her body. "It's O.K., baby," she half-whispered. "It's O.K." She ran her hand up his bare back to his shoulder and tried to pull him to her. He resisted and she pulled harder until he gave in to her.

He snuggled like a child to her long, thin body and looked at her through sobbing eyes. "Oh, Rachel," he whispered in a broken voice.

For a long time, nothing was said as Rachel protected Shot from his fears.

Rachel understood what Shot was going through. Not really, but that is what she had been telling him for nearly a month and a half. The fact that she didn't understand was not for lack of trying. The more she tried to understand Shot, the more of a mystery he was. The bigger the mystery, the more the intrigue. Although she hadn't said so, Rachel wanted her last name to be Palmer instead of Hewitt. She didn't know that Shot had already harbored thoughts of making her wife number four. Her long black hair covered the pillow where she lay her head, encircling her tiny face, long thin nose, and the square jaw that affirmed her Sioux ancestry.

"Are you O.K?" she finally asked.

Shot sniffed and nodded his head.

"Can I get you anything?"

He slowly moved his head from side to side. "Just lay here with me," he said in an easier voice.

Rachel slid deeper into the bed, until her forehead rested against Shot's. "Do you want to tell me about it?"

"You've heard it all before," he said.

She pulled the blankets up over the top half of his still-shaking body. "Tell me about this Bennett."

He did not answer.

"You've told me about how he died, and you've told me about the dream you keep having, but you've never told me about Bennett."

Shot thought for a moment. "He was just a real good friend of mine," he said. "Not much to tell...We raised a lotta hell together."

Rachel searched his face for a story. "How did you meet him?" She saw a faint glimmer in his eye, like kindling in a campfire that may either glow with warmth, or smolder and die out. She fanned the spark. "Did you grow up with him?"

"No," he finally answered. "Met him at a rodeo I was clownin'."

"Where at?" she coaxed.

"Was down in Clinton, Louisiana," he said quietly. "I'd seen him before, knew who he was. This was about five years ago, I guess. I shoulda' kicked his butt that day but I didn't."

Rachel looked surprised. "Kicked his butt? Why?"

A slight smile found its way to one corner of Shot's crooked lips. "Well," he said, "I knew who Bennett was. I'd seen him around. Even said howdy to him a time or two. Anyhow, Bennett and T.J., and a couple of bronc riders, Dave Whitney and Randy Corey, were up in the slack that mornin'..."

"Up in the slack?" Rachel interrupted.

Shot had forgotten that Rachel had only been to a few rodeos in her lifetime, never been behind the bucking chutes, and had never dated a cowboy before. "Slack," he explained, "is when they got too many contestants to put 'em all in the performance. Understand?"

Rachel shrugged a shoulder. "No."

The trembling had left Shot's body and voice. "Well...O.K., let's say it's a two-performance rodeo – Saturday night and Sunday afternoon – and they're only lettin' twenty bullriders in each performance..."

"Why would they do that?"

"Either because the stock contractor ain't got enough bulls to go around," said Shot, "or there just ain't enough time. If they let everybody in the perf, the rodeo could take all day long. Anyway, say you got twenty riders each perf but sixty riders entered up. Can't run 'em all in the perf, so they have what they call the slack performance. It's usually before or right after the regular performance. The public ain't invited, no clown acts. See what I mean?"

"Mm-hm," Rachel nodded.

"Anyway, they were up in the mornin' slack – what Bennett used to call 'bulls for breakfast' – in fact, Bennett won that rodeo..." Shot's voice trailed off.

"Is that all?"

"Oh, no, that ain't all," Shot said, completely calm and relaxed. "I had divorced my second wife and I had this little gal with me that I was fixin' to marry. Well, after the slack was over, them boys went down to the bar and proceeded to get drunk – 'cept for Randy, he don't drink. They got back about the time the rodeo was fixin' to start. I was headin' into the arena for the introductions and I seen Bennett leanin' on Joni's pickup door – Joni's the gal I was gonna marry – and he was a-sweet-talkin' her, I could tell. But what could I do? I couldn't leave the arena. Little later I had my umbrella open and I was tight-rope-walkin' the arena fence, and I looked past the race track and, by God, there goes Joni's pickup, out the gate and Bennett's drivin' it and she's scootched clear up against him. But what could I do? I couldn't leave the arena...He got her back in time to watch the bullridin'."

"Did they..." Rachel hesitated, "do anything?"

"Hell, yes, he took her down to the swamp and bred her!"

"And you became friends with that guy?"

"Yeah," said Shot, "We got to be good friends shortly after that."

"I can't believe you didn't beat him up!" said Rachel.

"I didn't have time after the rodeo." Shot rolled to his back and put a hand under his head. "By the time I got all my stuff put away and got paid, them boys was long gone. 'Sides, at the time I didn't know for sure if they'd done anything. Joni was pretty quiet on the way home, that's for dang sure...And, it's like Bennett told me a few months later; if it wasn't him, it woulda' been somebody else. She was pretty much bringin' it on. She didn't think I paid enough attention to her when I got around my rodeo buddies."

"Was she right?" inquired Rachel.

Shot pondered the question for a moment. "Yeah, I'd say so."

"Are you going to be that way with me?"

"Are you kiddin'?" Shot cradled her head under his arm. "I could never ignore you, darlin'."

Rachel looked at his profile – the crooked nose, broken many times; the thin, twisted lips; the lobe-less ear, the one he says his brother cut off and fed to the cat. Such a rough facade surrounding such innocent eyes. "I'll bet you say that to all the girls," she said.

"Yeah, I do," said Shot, his eyes searching the ceiling for cracks. "But it's different, now...I mean it, this time."

She watched his eyes wander from one corner of the room to the next. Sure, he means it now, but will he still mean it at the rodeo? "So whatever happened to Joni?"

"We stayed together another week or two," Shot replied, "But we both knew it was pretty much over. I'da' got rid of her sooner but I needed a place to stay. I finally told her 'Adios' and she tried to hook up with Bennett, but he never did haul women down the road."

"Why not?"

"He says it's like takin' a sandwich to a barbeque."

"Sounds like a great guy," Rachel said sarcastically.

"Oh, he was," Shot agreed, not catching Rachel's meaning. "In fact, he said he left with her that day with me in mind. Said he wanted me to know what kind of girl she was before I married her..." His eyes looked off into nowhere. "Friends like that don't just come around every day."

Rachel rolled her eyes. "With friends like that, who needs enemies?"

Again, Shot missed the point. "Not me," he said thoughtfully. "I got plenty of 'em already."

She shook her head. "Want me to shut off the light?"

"I'll get it," he said, as he reached over and flicked the switch of the table lamp.

"Good night, honey," she said.

He kissed her on the forehead. "'Night, darlin'," and rolled over. His wide eyes stared at the blackness of the room. After awhile he rolled over again and stared some more. Soon he rolled to his stomach. Then to his back. He picked up his pillow and fluffed it with his fist. He put it under his head. Then he took it out and...

"Shot, will you lay still?"

...fluffed it again...

"I can't sleep."

"Neither can I, with you bouncing around like this."

He ran his fingers along her silky smooth face. "Wanna make love?" he asked.

"Again?...Honey, I've got to go to work in less than two hours."

"Good way to start the day," he suggested.

"Shot," she whispered, "I just want to go to sleep. Good night."

Shot lay silent for a while, then interrupted the quiet. "Wanna play cards?"

With an impatient sigh, Rachel begged, "Why don't you just go to sleep?"

Like a young boy searching for an explanation, he somberly admitted, "I'm afraid I'll have *that dream* again."

"Shot, honey," she lectured, "you can't go on like this! It used to be a few times a month, this is the third time this week!"

"Well, I wish I knew what to do about it," said Shot, "other than stay awake."

"Turn on the light," she told him.

When the room became bright, he said, "You know, what gets me is I never dream about that bull gettin' *me*. Son of a bitch shattered my knee, broke my collarbone, tore off half my face and all I ever dream about is him bearin' down on Bennett and me not bein' able to get there. I just get T.J. straightened out and now *I'm* all screwed up.

"Did I tell you T.J. won Phoenix? He's in Waco, Texas today and then headin' up to Butte, Montana.

"I always figured I was a better man than that."

"Better man than what?" asked Rachel.

"I always figured," said Shot, "that I had the mental toughness not to let that kind of thing screw with my head."

"Shot," Rachel contended, "You watched one of your best friends get killed while you were responsible for his safety. Who *wouldn't* that mess with?" She thought about what she'd just said, and wished she would have left out the part about 'responsible' and 'safety.' She tried to cover it up. "You wouldn't be near the man you are if that didn't mess with your head a little."

"I guess so," Shot conceded. "It's still two months before my first rodeo. I just hope I can do O.K. there at Rapid City," and his weary frown flexed and stretched into a smile.

Rachel's eyes were so close to his face that she saw two blurred smiles. "What?" she asked.

"Hmm?"

"What are you smiling about?" she demanded.

"Oh, I was just thinkin' 'bout the last time we were in Rapid."

"What happened?"

"Bennett claimed," he told her, "that when he dies, he's gonna come back as a bull...a rodeo bull."

Rachel giggled. "Was he serious?"

"You bet he was," Shot went on. "Even said he had proof."

"What kind of proof?" she inquired.

"He had a tattoo on his right arm. His initials – just a plain ol' BM. He said someday we're gonna see a bull with a BM brand on its right shoulder. Says that'll be him."

"Do you believe him?"

"No," Shot chuckled. "But then again, I wouldn't put anything past Bennett. Wanna play cards?"

"I told you I don't want to play cards."

Chapter 12: December 1988

SCOTTY REDWOOD'S
WORLD CHAMPION
BULL RIDING
SCHOOL

It appeared in Western and rodeo magazines all over the country;

Special Holiday Edition
December 27-29
✓Unlimited livestock to meet your individual needs
✓Instant video replay
✓Heated indoor arena
✓Classroom and hands-on instruction by Scotty Redwood,
Two-Time World Champion Bullrider

Below the telephone number, tuition fees and location of the school was a black-and-white photograph of the great Scotty Redwood riding a bull at the National Finals Rodeo from eleven years before.

Over thirty bullriding hopefuls called and tried to enroll. Only the first dozen were accepted.

At ten a.m. on Tuesday, the twenty-seventh, all twelve young men, ranging from fourteen to twenty-one, gathered behind the bucking chutes in the big yellow indoor arena, and clung to every word of the legend, Scotty Redwood. "For those of y'all who've been livin' in a cave for the last dozen years or so, my name is Scotty Redwood, two-time World Champeen Bullrider and three-time runner-up, and I'll be yer bullridin' instructor for the next three days." When he spoke, his voice was low, and, even indoors, his breath danced with the cold December air. "Now, if you boys listen to me and do as I tell ya and take my advice and criticism with an open mind and watch the films of yerselves ridin' and of me and the other greats ridin', then you'll get the most out of the school. If you don't want to listen and pay attention, suit yerselves, it's yer tuition money."

The thing that stood out the most about the legend was the glittering gold belt buckle, edged in silver, a diamond guarding each of the four corners. Golden dust storms swirled around the silver inlaid ribbons that seemed to flow from the framework, inscribing, 'World Champion Bullrider' veiled across the top, and 'Scotty Redwood' gleaming along the bottom, all in burnished turquoise overlay. Although the date, dancing on the left side, said that it was eleven years old, the gleaming trophy buckle shone like it did the night he first cinched a belt to it.

Below this centerpiece, Scotty's tight blue jeans were tucked inside his high heeled, high topped black cowboy boots. Above it, he wore a light tan, leather jacket, open in front, proudly exposing the belt buckle. Dark brown fringe hung a good six inches across the back and all the way down the sleeves of the jacket. Red and white Indian beadwork flooded his shoulders and chest. His hands were covered with matching tan gloves, complete with heavy gauntlets that were adorned with matching brown fringe and matching Indian beadwork. A bald eagle feather stuck out from the red and yellow beaded hat band on the gray Stetson that concealed the tiny balding spot on the north by northeast section of his head.

"The first thing I want to do is take a look at all of your equipment. I'll have you hang your ropes up on that fence there by the buckin' chutes." The only wrinkles on Scotty's face were hidden behind rose-colored sunglasses. A deep heavy line cradled each eye. The rest of his face was as smooth as a still spring pond. His nose was narrow and long, the bridge as straight as a ruler. Beneath it, a drooping brown mustache covered his top lip, and his bottom lip could be seen only when he spoke. "Get your gloves and spurs out, too. I'll give 'em an inspection and talk to each one of y'all individually. After that we'll go into the meeting room and see some bullridin' films. By that time this building ought to be warmed up enough for y'all to get on some bulls."

As the young cowboys fumbled through their gear bags and dragged out their bullropes, one of Scotty's assistants called to him, "Hey, them fellers with that try-out bull is here."

"Have 'em back up to the alley out there," Scotty instructed. "Put him in that far corner pen with the other young bulls."

The assistant's face was red from the subfreezing winter winds outside. He wore a thick orange hunting cap with the earflaps down. He pulled his blue bandanna up over his nose and turned the collar up on his heavy sheepskin coat before stepping outside. He trotted to the alley gate and motioned for the driver to back the stock trailer to it.

The packed snow squeaked and crunched beneath Mike Fanner's pickup tires as he lined up the trailer and backed it up to the gate. He rolled down his window as the red-faced man approached the pickup. "How are you, Sam?" he greeted.

"Cold," the man answered from beneath his bandanna. "How you doin', Mike?"

"Pretty good," Mike said through a toothy smile as he shook Sam's hand. Nothing had changed in the last year and two months about Mike, except the hat. He threw away his brimless straw the day the little gray Brahma calf had worked him over, and bought a thirty-X black felt. "Is yer cousin around?"

"Yeah, Scotty's inside," said Sam, "but he's talkin' to a bunch of students right now."

"Well, just tell him I brought that bull he said he'd try. If he bucks, tell him I'll deal on him. If he don't, send him back."

"I'll tell him," said Sam. "Hey, where's Brad?"

"He's home doin' chores and lookin' after the livestock," Mike answered.

Sam's eyes smiled. "He has to stay home and work while you get to do the runnin' around, huh?"

"Slick as them roads was just this side of the state line," Mike contended, "I was startin' to wish I'd stayed home and let *him* bring that bull."

"That bad?" Sam answered.

"Wasn't a lotta fun," said Mike. "Listen, this bull's horns ain't been tipped yet and he's pretty hookie. I'd put him in a pen by hisself if I was you."

"Sounds good," agreed Sam. He started hopping from toe to toe, trying to keep warm. "Hey, what's his story, anyway?"

"Me and Brad had him as a ropin' calf, but he was just too damn mean. Tried to kill my brother," Mike fibbed his way out of his own embarrassment. "Yeah, he was just a little bit too much calf for ol' Brad to handle. We took him to a neighbor's for his boy to practice on but his mom would never let him git on. We figured he'd be..."

"Mike, I hate to interrupt ya," Sam interrupted, still hopping on his toes, "but I'm gonna git him unloaded and git inside before I freeze my feet off."

"O.K., Sam." Mike smiled and began to roll up the windows. Before the glass reached the top of the door, he concluded, "Good to see ya again."

Sam waved and scurried to the back of the trailer. He swung the alley gate open, and then the trailer gate. "Come on, bull," he commanded as he peeked through the slats of the trailer.

The first thing he saw was a pair of perfectly shaped horns protruding in opposite directions and curving straight upwards to the trailer top, above large gray flopping Brahma ears. Black-tipped horns, pencil-sharp. The next thing he noted was a gray mound of Brahma hump, piled six inches above the rest of the bull's back.

"Git outta there!" Sam ordered again as he beat on the side of the trailer.

The bull stuck his head out and looked around. He casually stepped from the trailer to the frozen muck and walked down the alley toward the bull pens.

When he had arrived at Mike and Brad Fanner's roping arena, he was five months old and weighed three hundred pounds. He had since more than tripled in age and weight. He had a slow and easy demeanor now. Tall and lanky, he had not filled out into a full grown mature bull yet, but it would not be long. Day by day, his neck had gotten thicker, his feet bigger and his back wider. Curtains of loose hide hung like the front of a king's robe from his neck all the way down his chest and belly.

Sam latched the alley gate behind him, shut the trailer door and waved Mike farewell, as he considered his words of caution: "This bull's horns ain't been tipped yet and he's pretty hookie. I'd put him in a pen by hisself if I was you." Sam looked around. No empty pens. He remembered his cousin's orders: "Put him in the far corner pen with the other young bulls." He stepped up on the gate to get a better view of the far corner pen. Pretty spacious, and only three bulls in there now.

His mind heard Mike's voice, "...pretty hookie..." He looked at the gray Brahma at the far end of the alley. "...ain't been tipped..." He doesn't look so mean. "I'd put him in a pen by hisself if I was you." A deep chill was frosting through Sam's fingers and toes. "Well, you ain't me," he thought back. "He's goin' in the far corner pen and I'm gittin' inside where it's warm!"

He hopped off the gate and walked around the corrals to the far pen. Three three-year-old bulls huddled in the corner with their tails to the stinging northeaster. One was a small red Hereford with no horns. The other two were taller black bulls, one with a white face and down-turned banana-shaped horns; the other, all black with wide horns, curving forward slightly and tipped at the ends. Sam clambered over the fence at another corner, making sure not to disturb the beasts. They saw him, and paid no mind. They didn't want to mess with him any more than he wanted to mess with them.

The new arrival eyed Sam as he opened the alley gate to the pen and stepped behind it.

"Come on, bull, git in there," Sam commanded.

The bull stood there.

"Hey, bull, git in the pen."

The bull wiggled his floppy ears and then swung his head up and down.

"Don't make me come and git you!" Sam threatened. He stepped out from behind the gate and cautiously walked toward the new bull. If he could get by him, he wouldn't have to crawl over the fence and walk all the way around the corrals to run him in. Most bulls – even bulls that have a reputation of being dangerous in the rodeo arena – show a non-aggressive respect for cowboys in the small back pens. Sam took another couple of steps.

The bull lunged at Sam, slipped on the hard frozen dirt and fell awkwardly to his belly. In the same instant, Sam backpedaled furiously until he too lost his footing, landing on his rear, flipped over every bit as gracefully as a snapping turtle and belly-crawled under the fence.

He suddenly felt rather stupid. The bull hadn't charged him at all. He was bluffing. There he was, still standing in the middle of the alleyway, waving his horns in Sam's direction. Sam got to his feet and looked around. At least no had been watching. He eyed the bull. For the first time, now, he noticed a BM brand on its right shoulder. He didn't know what it was about the bull – maybe it was the untipped horns, maybe the way he stood his ground, or the look in his eye when he lunged at him – but he didn't trust him. His heart thumped fast and he had to pull his bandanna from his face to let the bitter wind cool his flushed face. He realized he had just been afraid for the first time in many, many years. He decided it might be better to go the long way around. He clumsily stood up, walked back across the pen and climbed over the fence.

As soon as Sam had left, the bull ambled down the alley, beheld the open gate, and invited himself in. The small red bull never looked up. The black bulls looked him over and the white-faced one mooed him a greeting. The BM bull never heard the gate latching behind him as he walked over to the three in the corner. The red bull, half-snoozing, sensed BM's presence and glanced at him from the corner of his eye, and ignored him.

Sam watched from the gate as BM took his place next to the white-face with the down-turned horns. "Hell, they'll be alright," he said to himself as he turned and headed for the door.

The all-black bull wanted a closer look at BM. Suddenly uncomfortable among the two bigger bulls, BM turned around and headed for the gate. The all-black bull followed. Realizing there was no longer an opening where there had been before, BM began to circle in the pen, searching for a way out, with the black bull directly behind. BM stopped at a corner and peered through the rails of the steel fence corrals. The big black rammed him in the hip with a blow from a blunt horn. BM grunted and wheeled around, swinging his horns in warning, and trotted down the fence-line.

Sam heard the commotion and stopped short of the door to see what was going on. "Hey, knock it off!" he hollered as he trotted back to the pen.

As BM rounded the pen in the opposite direction, the big black again followed, not from directly behind, but to the inside of the circle, the way a boxer will keep a weaker opponent against the ropes.

The white-faced bull stood in the middle of the pen, rotating around, watching the action, while the red bull stood, uninterested, in the corner.

BM shifted into a lope as he approached the corner where the red Hereford stood. The big black was hazing him tighter to the fence. Unable to get around the Hereford, he broadsided him, gouging one horn into his flank and sinking the other deep between his ribs. The Hereford bellowed in pain as he was momentarily lifted from his feet and slammed into the corral fence.

"Hey! You son of a bitch!" roared Sam as he jumped up on the fence, flailing his arms like a madman.

Blood ran bright red from both holes in the squirming Hereford's side as BM himself was knocked into the fence by the black bull's dull horns. He seized this opportunity to scramble out of the corner.

As Sam ran to open the gate, cursing loudly, the big black had BM pinned against the steel fence, exerting eighteen hundred pounds of his own weight through two quarter-sized blunt horn tips against BM's shoulder and ribs, jabbing again and again. BM wailed as he swung his head back and caught the black bull with a horn, just deep enough to penetrate the hide and send the bull running. Suddenly, BM felt in control, and if the enemy was going to run, then he was going to chase him.

Sam had opened the gate. The black white-faced bull still just stood in the center of the pen. The little red was glad to get out, followed by the big black, with BM hot on his tail.

Sam tried to shove the gate closed before BM made it through, but it was too late. The gate bounced off the bull's shoulder and swung back on its hinges, nearly knocking Sam off his feet.

A jagged crimson trail followed the Hereford bull up the alleyway, and formed two steaming puddles below him where he stopped, trapped at the dead end. The big black right behind spun around to face off with his opponent, but was not given enough time. BM charged broadside and stabbed him in the lower belly, shoving him into the Hereford and pinning them back against the locked gate. He stepped back and charged again, opening another bloody hole in the black bull's belly. As he gouged and ripped at the black's guts, the Hereford squirmed from the corner and slipped unnoticed past the attacking bull, fleeing back down the alley to his pen, not even slowing down as he sped by Sam, who was swearing at the top of his lungs.

BM continued to maim the near-helpless bull, ripping at his intestines and lifting his hind end off the ground. The bull's cries for help were as useless as Sam's mindless profanities – both could be heard by no one except the onlooking bulls in neighboring pens.

Sam finally decided that the big black was not going to escape and he had better go for help, when, somehow, the black bull broke free and got away. As he bounded down the alley, he carried his head low. His tongue hung from his mouth and the snot flowed from his nostrils almost as fast as the warm blood from the numerous gaping wounds. A long, sorrowful bellow gurgled in his throat.

Of course, BM was not through yet.

Sam stood behind the open gate and watched the broken, scared bull race down the alley with his assailant in hot pursuit. He knew that his only chance of separating BM from the other bulls was to slam the gate shut just as soon as the black bull's rear crossed into the pen. A split second too late or too early and the gate will bounce back to him and the fight will still be on. The black bull loped by. Sam shoved the gate hard and scrambled up the fence behind him. The steel gate met the latch an instant before BM crashed into it, hitting it with enough force to bend the rails. He ricocheted off the gate before regaining his balance, where he faced his victim through the bowed rails and waved his blood-soaked horns in defiance.

"There, ya no-good piece a' shit!" Sam scowled from atop the fence. He looked at the three bulls in the pen. The little Hereford's bleeding had already slowed considerably, but the big black bull's underbelly was smeared with red as each grisly gash oozed forth and trickled to the ground, mixing with manure and snow. "Damn," he said out loud to himself, "I better get Scott." He swung over the fence and headed for the door, all the while wondering how would be the best way to break the news to his cousin. He knew he would be mad. Real mad. As a part of his mind searched for the right words, another part of his mind would interrupt with the voice of Mike Fanner: "I'd put him in a pen by hisself if I was you."

He opened the door and peered inside. Scott was behind the chutes with his students lecturing on the importance of proper equipment. Sam hesitated before taking a deep breath and entering the building. He walked up to where the group of boys were gathered around his cousin and stood behind them, saying, "Scott?"

Scott had one of the boys' bullropes in his hand. "Not now, Sam," he said. "Now, what this here rope needs is some tincture of benzoine poured on the handle and let it soak in the sun for a couple days. That'll stiffen 'er up real..."

"It's important, Scott," Sam interrupted again. "We got problems."

"Sammy, I'm giving a lecture to the boys. Can't it wait?"

"We got a bull down and hurt. It ain't lookin' good."

Scott dropped the bullrope to the ground. "Which one?"

Sam's voice cracked with nervous guilt. "The big black bull," he said. "He's losin' a lotta blood."

"Well, shit," Scott growled, as he headed for the door. "What the hell happened?"

"He got to fightin' with that new bull that Mike Fanner brought in," Sam explained as he followed Scotty outside.

"God...damn, Sam!" whined Scotty as he looked at the bull ahead, lying on its side in a soupy pool of its own blood, yellow and orange intestines overflowing from gaping wounds and streaming to the dark red puddle. "How could you let somethin' like this happen?"

The bull shuddered and his body stiffened. One last long puff of steam surged from his open mouth, and in a slow, sorrowful moan disappeared with the wind.

Sam fumbled for an honest excuse, but had none. "Mike Fanner said they'd be alright together," he lied, "so, hell, I didn't think nothin' about it. I did all I could to get 'em apart, Scott. Really, I did."

Scotty took the gray Stetson from his head and drew back as if he was going to slam it on the ground, but didn't. As he slapped it back on his head, he saw the little Hereford standing in the corner, dried blood a dark, dirty brown matted into his hair, below a small puncture wound in the rib cage. "What about this'n?" he demanded.

"He just got in the way of 'em," Sam explained. "He was just in the wrong place at the wrong time. It was the black bull that started it anyway, Scott, that Braymer didn't want no part of none of 'em...I don't think this red bull looks hurt too bad, do you?...I don't think them wounds are very deep...Do you?...Scotty?"

Scotty glanced around for something to throw but there was nothing handy. "Where's the son of a bitch that did it?" he hollered.

Sam swallowed hard. "It's that gray Braymer in the alley."

"Hell, his horns ain't even tipped!" roared Scotty. "God-damned guys bring me a bull and his horns ain't even tipped! No wonder he tore him up so bad! Son of a bitches just cost me a bull! I can't believe they'd bring me a bull without tippin' his horns! I'll tell you one thing – Mike Fanner can just pay for the son of a bitch! Sam, you git that Braymer inside, in a chute, and whack them horns off!"

"Yessir," Sam complied.

"And if that Braymer son of a bitch don't buck," Scotty vowed as he tramped to the door, "he's hamburger!"

Sam stood motionless until he heard the door slam. As he glanced down at the dead bull, inanimate on the frozen ground, he tried to tell himself that it didn't matter. Lazy ol' bull never bucked worth a damn anyway. That's why he's at a school for kids right now, instead of at a real rodeo with the toughs. Good riddance. One less hay-burner to feed.

Sam pulled his bandanna back up over his face. He knew he'd need help driving the Brahma into the chute – the bull had no respect for humans – but he didn't dare ask Scotty for help. He trudged over to his pickup and opened the driver's side door. From behind the seat he pulled an electric cattle prod. Yellow in color, a three-foot-long, plastic wand with the batteries encased in the handle end and two prongs of bare steel on the business end, the 'hot-shot', as the cattlemen called it, was capable of convincing even the most stubborn animal to move. He returned to the building and lifted the overhead door, then hurried around to an alleyway gate, where the bull faced him from the other side. "Buddy, ya got one chance to git in there on yer own," warned Sam. "Ssssst! Hyah!" He threw his arms in the air.

BM didn't move, didn't flinch or even blink.

Sam pushed the button with his thumb and tested the hot-shot against the steel gate. A sharp, snapping buzz and a purple spark popped from each prong. "You asked for it," he said as he poked it through the gate and touched it to the bull's bare nose. A quick five volts of electricity slapped his nose like the crack of a whip. He jumped backwards instantly before spinning around and bounding inside the building. Sam was quick to get through the gate, get down the alley behind the bull, and slam the overhead door from the outside, before BM had a chance to turn around and bolt back out. "There!" Sam gloated through the door, "I'll teach *you* the meaning of respect!" He hurried over and entered the building through the walk-in door, and pulled his bandanna from his face, glad to get in out of the cold.

"Sammy," Scott ordered from where he was back talking to his students, "after you git them horns tipped, you better call the renderin' plant and tell 'em to come and git that dead one."

"O.K., Scotty," said Sam, extra obligingly.

"Then git that Hereford bull in and put some iodine on them wounds," he went on. "We better not buck him for a day or so."

BM stood in the holding pen snorting at Sam as he walked up and, from the outside of the pen, pulled open the slide gate to the narrow alley leading to the bucking chutes. The bull walked over and inspected the opening, but did not enter. Sam moved over along the fence to where he could reach the bull's hind-end with the hot-shot. He stepped up on the fence a couple of rungs and commanded, "Git in there!" as he zapped him on the rump. Automatically, BM kicked behind himself, knocking the hot-shot from Sam's hand and sending it sailing through the air. Sam quickly stepped down from the fence and stuck his little finger in his mouth, kissing the tip of it. "Dang, that hurt," he whispered.

Before the hot-shot had ever hit the ground, BM was trotting up the narrow alley to the bucking chutes. He didn't stop until he came to the dead end at the last one. He heard something behind him as the slide gate was slid shut, trapping him in his standing-room-only cage. He put his nose to the ground and blew dirt around as he searched for a way out. But there was no way out, so there he stood. Every so often he'd wallow back and forth and side to side in the chute, ramming the front of the chute and rattling the side rails with his horns, but the steel bars would not move. He attempted to turn around once, getting only his head cocked backwards and his horns stuck in the rail. It took awhile for him to get loose and when he did, he just stood and waited and watched and listened.

At first he heard just one human voice, as Scotty lectured the boys about the finer points of bullriding. Then the group broke up and there was a lot of movement behind the chutes. Some of the boys would walk up and look at him and he would glare right back into their eyes. He was a little afraid, and he could tell that they were, too.

Without warning, one soft cotton rope was looped around both of his horns and jerked tight at the base. He threw his head left and right, his horns clanging against the steel barrier. Soon, he could not throw his head to the left any more, as three young men had the rope snubbed around a rail and pulled up tight. Every time he would throw his head to the right, they would pull the rope tighter until he had no head movement at all. With the side of his face pinned against the side of the chute, he could hear the sound of the crosscut saw as its teeth hacked through the outer layer of his spike, and he felt the painless rumble in his skull. Only once did he try to shake loose. Overpowered, he knew he had no choice.

As Sam shoved and pulled the saw back and forth across BM's left horn, he warned the students watching from the inside of the arena, "Better stand back, blood's gonna be a-flyin'!"

About that time, his sawteeth found their way to the other side of the horn and the black-tipped, pencil-sharp end of BM's horn and four inches that spread from it, fell to the ground. The flat-tipped end of his left horn was now a little larger in diameter than a quarter, and from three tiny pinholes, streams of blood squirted five feet above the bull's head and eight feet into the arena.

Sam went to work on the other horn.

"Are you going to do anything about the bleedin'?" one boy asked.

"Them holes'll dry up and quit bleedin' pretty quick," assured Sam. "He ain't gonna bleed to death."

Again, BM felt the dull vibration in his skull as Sam sawed four inches off of his other horn. Young cowboys scrambled to get out of the way as blood gushed overhead.

Sam backed away with his saw. "Let him loose!" he told the three boys who had BM's head snubbed tight to the side of the chute. The boys let loose of the rope and scattered as the bull shook his head from side to side, spraying blood in every direction, drying immediately on the hats, clothing and faces of the three scattering cowboys, turning their good shirts into work shirts. The boys who had escaped the red dots laughed and pointed at the boys who didn't. The boys who didn't laughed also.

The carrying-on was interrupted by Scotty Redwood's low, authoritative voice. "Sammy."

"Sir?" answered his cousin.

"I'm gonna take these boys into the meeting room. We're gonna watch some bullridin' films and have a little talk while yer doctorin' that hurt bull, and gittin' the dead one hauled out."

"Yessir," Sam obliged.

"If you boys want to follow me," Scotty said as he walked toward the door beneath the grandstands, "I got the video tape set up and ready to go. I want everybody to sit up front where you can see and hear real good."

The boys filed into the meeting room and found their seats.

"Before I start the tape, do any of y'all have any questions for me?"

A young man of seventeen raised his hand. "Mister Redwood?"

"Mister Redwood?" Scotty repeated in mild surprise. "Son, the only Mister Redwood I know is my daddy and he ain't here. Y'all can call me Scotty, boys. Try to forget that I'm a two-time World Champ, if ya can. Hell, I put my boots on one at a time just like y'all – only difference is I got six pair an' they're all custom-made. I put these jeans on one leg at a time, too – only difference there is, I cinch mine up with one a' my World Championship buckles. ...You had a question, son?"

"Yessir," the young cowboy asked. "How soon are we gonna get to get on some bulls?"

"In due time, boy, in due time." Scotty started to reach for the 'on' button of the VCR but stopped short and looked at the boy. "What's yer name, cowboy?"

The young man answered, "Kid Kaminski. My real name's Kyle, but all my friends call me Kid." A few inches taller, his hair a few shades darker, and his voice a few octaves lower, Kid had developed a whole new confidence since meeting up with T.J. Jergenson last year.

"Well, Kid," asked Scotty, "How many bulls you been on?"

"Twenty or twenty-five this past summer," he answered. "But I ain't been on nothin' for the last couple of months, now. I'm kinda cravin' 'em."

Scotty's eyebrows raised. "Twenty or twenty-five, huh? How many do you think I been on in my life?"

Kid shrugged, "I'd hate to guess."

"Well, go on, guess anyway," Scotty coaxed.

Kid squinted a thoughtful eye. "Couple thousand, I 'magine."

"Couple thousand?" Scotty chuckled, "Try about three times that."

Kid tried to appear impressed as he searched for the point that Scotty was making.

"Six thousand bulls," Scotty estimated. "Twenty-two years of rodeo, million or so miles, two World Championships, three-time runner-up, and more belt buckles than I can count..."

Kid decided there was no point to this story – the Champ just liked bragging on himself.

"...Son, in the next three days I'll have you on so many head you may never want to see another bull for as long as you live."

The Kid grinned.

Scotty pushed the 'on' button. A country-rock guitar blared above a heavy beat as a bull and rider exploded onto the screen. The rider's brown, drooping trademark mustache and long, narrow nose made him easily recognizable as he conquered bull after bull in this opening sequence. It was two-time World Champion Scotty Redwood. A voice overlaid the whine of the electric guitar. A low voice with a slight southern drawl. The voice of two-time World Champion, Scotty Redwood.

"Buckle up, chap up, cowboy up...ride up! Hello, future bullriders, this is Scotty Redwood, two-time World Champeen, three-time runner-up, and in the next thirty minutes I'm going to show you some of the best bullrides in the world and tell you how I did it, and I'm going to show you some of the most common mistakes other bullriders make and how to avoid 'em." The music slowed and the screen changed from a great Redwood ride at the National Finals to a quiet scene of Scotty walking in front of empty bucking chutes, saying, "Every bullrider alive dreams about makin' it to the National Finals and winnin' the World Bullridin' title, but only a few ever make it, some of us twice..."

The live Scotty in the classroom watched the Scotty on the screen with fascination. "It takes more than a strong arm and quick reactions to become a World Champion. It takes guts and determination and want-to and try. It takes drivin' all night and ridin' with pain and injury. Sometimes it takes writin' hot checks to pay yer fees, livin' on rodeo dogs and Coke, not bein' home or seein' yer family or gittin' yer mail fer months at a time. Somtimes I wonder why the hell I did it." The on-screen Scotty had a somber look on his face. "But I'm reminded," the live Scotty's mustache spread wide over his grin, "ever' mornin' when I strap on one a' these Gold Buckles. You wanna be a Champ? I can tell you ever' thing I know – the rest is up to you."

A chute gate from somewhere in the U.S. appeared. It swung wide and a big cream-colored Charolais bull exploded into the arena beneath a determined nameless cowboy. Five jumps into the ride, the cowboy was slung face-first into the dirt.

Same bull, same rider in slow motion, Scotty's voice: "One of the most common mistakes bullriders make is sittin' on their pockets. When you're on a big lungin' bull like this, you need to be up over his front end, reachin' forward. When the bull blows into the air, you want to be leanin' forward, just like those English-style horse riders that jump over bushes and fences and such. When the horse goes into his jump, they're leanin' up over his neck, and there's even a little daylight between the rider's butt and the horse's back. It's the same way with ridin' bulls. See how this rider's leanin' back and he's a foot-and-a-half off his bullrope? Ya can't cheat them big bulls outta no power that way. The bull gets him to the end of his arm and slings him over his head."

At a different rodeo, another chute gate flew open. A small, wide-horned Corriente-cross bull barely left the chute and was spinning like a top. The rider stayed on for half of the allotted time, and was slammed back into the chute he came from.

Again, the action is replayed in slow motion. "Most every bull is built different and bucks different," came Scotty's commentary. "When you get on a bull this little that spins this fast and this flat, and by flat I mean there's very little kick at his rear end, you need to be sittin' straight up and down on him. Otherwise, centrifugal force is gonna slow you down and cause you to get outta time with your bull, just like it did to this cowboy. He was too far out over this bull. He shoulda' realized it and corrected."

Out of another chute at another rodeo came a high-kicking hard-bucking Brahma-Longhorn cross bull spinning to the right, with a long, lanky cowboy on his back and riding in good form. Suddenly, the bull switched directions, bucking the cowboy into the eye of the spin, knocking him to the ground with a horn and stepping on his leg.

Kid Kaminski watched intently at the wreck. His eyebrows raised at the familiarity of the tall awkward form of the fallen rider. As the slowed-down version of the same ride began, he pondered who the long-legged bullrider could be. Three jumps into the ride, the cowboy's gray felt hat sailed from his head, revealing the dark complexion, crooked nose, and big lower lip of none other than T.J. Jergenson. Even though the Kid had chickened out of the bullriding that Labor Day before last, the lecture T.J. gave him afterward had been with him ever since... "When you get on a bull, you gotta do it with determination, you gotta be aggressive! You gotta not let *nothin* get in yer way! Ya just gotta bear down and cowboy up! Ya gotta want it so bad, ya can taste it..."

But right now, Kid was hearing Scotty's voice. "This cowboy starts a real nice ride. Mighta took him all the way to the pay window – if the bull hadn'ta fooled him. When the bull switched directions, the cowboy never got ahold with his inside spur. That's what got him thrown down in the well. The moral is: always feel yer feet. Keep 'em movin', keep 'em workin', and keep gittin' ahold."

The live Scotty pressed the 'pause' button. "I wanna add a little somethin' here, before we go on. See how tall that last man was? He's too damn tall to be gittin' on bulls. Why, I'm five-eight and he's damn-near a head taller'n me. It works against ya. Puts yer center a' gravity too high and yer legs are too long to get ahold of anything. That's why he bucked off that bull. He oughta be playin' basketball. Bein' a tall bullrider is worse than bein' a fat bullrider. At least if yer a fat bullrider you can lose the weight."

The Kid raised his hand. "Mister Redw....er, Scotty?"

Scotty directed his attention to Kid. "Yeah, son, what's on yer mind?"

"Well...can't, uh...ain't it possible..."

"If ya got a question, boy, you best ask it," Scotty said impatiently.

"I don't quite know how to put it," Kid stammered as he searched for the words. "Can't you make up for your...if things ain't real good in one part, can ya...well... never mind."

"Has it got somethin' to do with this last bullrider?" Scotty asked.

"With him bein' too tall, it's gonna hurt his bullriding," the Kid reasoned, "but can't he compensate for that?"

"Well, son, you ain't but about five-and-a-half foot. Why are you worried about it?" Scotty inquired and without giving Kid a chance to reply, asked, "You plan on growin' a bunch in the next couple years?"

"My mom's pretty tall." This provoked a chuckle from Scotty and the rest of the class. Suddenly Kid felt a little embarrassed.

"Yer mom's pretty tall, is she?" Scotty grinned from beneath his mustache. "Yer mom a bullrider?" That comment encouraged more laughter from the boys.

Kid looked around the room. "Hell, no," he said, as a hint of a smile lifted one corner of his lips. "She's too damn tall!"

Everyone in the room laughed except Scotty. "So what're you tryin' to say, boy?"

"That just 'cause you're too tall doesn't mean you can't be a bullrider. If you want it bad enough, you can overcome your obstacles."

Scotty's eyebrows raised. "I like yer attitude, son. And he's right," he said to the rest of the class. "I rode my last three bulls at the National

Finals with a busted ankle. Rode 'em all, came away with my second world title. I did just what this young man said; I overcame my obstacles. 'Cause I wanted it just that bad.

"But," he added, "as far as that lanky cowboy in the last clip goes, he'll never be a Champ."

This surprised the Kid. "Why not?" he asked.

"Because I know this bullrider," he replied, "and he ain't got the attitude of a Champion. He's in it for the party. He ain't got the grit and determination of a World Champion," he stated as he reached for the button to turn on the tape.

"How do you know that?" Kid challenged.

Scotty's hand stopped short. Although he didn't bother to remember Kid's name, he said, "Kid, is this guy a friend of yers or somethin'?"

"I know him," answered Kid. "He's T.J. Jergenson."

"Well, you got that right," Scotty said. "You take some advice from me: you wanna be a champ, you don't follow in the footsteps of T.J. Jergenson."

"Maybe you're wrong," Kid replied.

The room got eerily quiet. The kid sitting next to Kid slumped in his chair, embarrassed to be next to him. Around the room, students' eyes widened and jaws fell open. They couldn't believe that this teenage boy would argue with two-time World Champion, Scotty Redwood.

Scotty forced a laugh and said, "Well, boy, maybe I am wrong. But I'll bet two Gold Buckles against anything you got that I ain't." His face began to redden. "T.J. Jergenson ain't never even been close to makin' the National Finals. Yeah, he's hit all the big rodeos, but when the pressure's on, he pressures up and peters out." He stopped talking for a moment, as if the lecture was over. Then he continued, "The first thing he needs to do is git off the booze. He prob'ly don't know what it's like gittin' on a bull sober." To most of the students, Scotty's word was gospel, but Kid wasn't buying any of it about T.J.

Scotty continued, "You know his old runnin' buddy, too?" he asked the Kid. "Bennett McKinney? He was just as bad as T.J. Died on the arena floor at the Houston Stock Show three years ago. Drunk on his ass. Wasn't even ridin'. He thought he was out there fightin' bulls for T.J. or somethin'. Too drunk to be in the arena and too damn drunk to know it."

Surely he's lying. "Were you there?" Kid asked.

Scotty pointed a finger at Kid "I don't have to be there, boy,

I know what goes on at rodeos." The same finger pressed the 'on' button, and the tape continued.

Throughout the rest of the film, Kid had a hard time paying attention to the details and the finer points of riding that Scotty was pointing out. Scotty's voice kept resounding in his mind about how T.J. was only in it for the party. That doesn't sound like the T.J. that lectured him about 'try' and 'want-to' at that Labor Day rodeo. And that part about Bennett McKinney being drunk in the arena. Although Kid had never met Bennett, he had heard of him, and had heard no stories that coincided with Scotty's.

When the film was over, Scotty had some closing words. "What it all boils down to, boys, is this: you can be a mediocre bullrider or you can be a Champion bullrider. Now, I realize that most y'all ain't gonna be a World Champ. Hell, probably *none* of ya. But ya still gotta set goals for yerselves, and ya might as well set 'em high. If ya don't set goals, ya ain't gonna ride to yer potential and if ya ain't gonna ride to yer potential, then ya might as well be sittin' at home.

"We're gonna take an hour break, now. There's a cafe just down the road from here called Jim Bob's. Eat light 'cause we'll be gittin' on bulls right after dinner."

Throughout most of lunch, Kid didn't have much to say. He sat with two new friends he'd met that morning. Tyler, a short, heavyset young man of sixteen, sat beside him in the booth, while Chase, a taller cowboy who had been riding bulls for six years, sat across the table. The boys all ate light, just as Scotty had instructed. Kid and Tyler split a hamburger, and Kid didn't even eat all of his half. As they lingered and slurped the last of their Cokes, Tyler and Chase started talking about bulls, and the school so far, and finally about Kid talking back to the Champ.

"What the hell were you thinkin'?" Chase asked him.

"What?" Kid asked back.

"Talkin' back to Scotty like you were."

"Yeah," Tyler added.

"I think he's full a' crap," said Kid.

Chase rolled his eyes and said sarcastically, "Oh, yeah, he's full a' crap all right. That's how he won two world championships!"

"Yeah!" Tyler added.

"Two world championships," the Kid repeated and took a drink of Coke, "two world championships. I bet he's told us that twenty times already. How come he's gotta keep rubbin' our noses in it?"

"To show us what we can get done if we really set our minds to it," Chase replied.

"Yeah," Tyler added.

"Well," Kid said thoughtfully, "that might be part of it, but I think he just likes to brag."

"If you rode as good as Scotty," claimed Chase, "you'd brag, too."

"I bet I wouldn't," the Kid argued. "Just because he rides bulls so good, doesn't make him a better person than us. He just seems so conceited. He acts like he's so much better than us."

"Kid," Chase reminded, "it's like he told us this mornin'; you can take it in and learn, or you can...not take it in and don't learn...somethin' like that. It's yer money."

"Yeah," Tyler added.

"Shut up, Tyler," Chase snapped.

Kid tipped his glass up to his mouth and let the remains of the faded Coke-flavored ice slide to his teeth. He set the empty glass down and munched and deliberated. "I don't like the way he talked about T.J. Jergenson. I bet he don't even know him."

"Do you really know him?" asked Chase.

Kid looked at his empty glass as he told a half-truth. "He helped me down on my very first bull."

"Didja ride him?" Chase inquired.

The next lie showed all over the Kid's face. "Al...almost."

"All he said was he's too tall to be ridin' bulls," said Chase.

Tyler listened quietly. He had nothing to add.

Kid's eyes met Chase's. "That ain't all he said. He said T.J. ain't got the attitude of a champion. That he ain't got grit and determination. He makes him sound like he's just an old drunk, and it ain't true! He said practically the same thing about Bennett McKinney!"

The boys in the next booth over and at the table across the way stopped their idle conversations to hear what the Kid had to say. "It takes alotta guts to cut down a dead man, don't it? Remember when he got killed? I heard all about it and read all about it, both, and there wasn't nothin' about him bein' drunk."

Chase spoke quietly. "There's probably a lotta things them papers don't print..."

"He was pullin' T.J.'s rope and got knocked off the chute, is what happened," Kid went on. "He'd just got off his own bull! He wasn't drunk! Died from massive head injuries. The bull was Genghis Khan and he almost killed T.J. and a bullfighter! I seen the video replay!"

"O.K., O.K., easy, Kid," said Chase. "You didn't even know Bennett. Why're ya gettin' so worked up?"

The entire cafe had turned its attention to their booth. Tyler broke the silence, adding, "Yeah."

Chase slid out of the booth. "Lunch is over, guys," he said as he lifted his heavy winter coat from the rack. "We better git to school."

Back at the arena, BM stood quietly waiting in his chute. The pinholes in his now blunt-tipped horns had long since dried and clotted shut. For nearly forty-five minutes, the place was quiet, except for the wind whistling through a gap above the overhead door. The monotony was broken as a door opened and slammed and Sammy Redwood walked up to the bull's small confine. "How ya doin', buddy?" he asked in an extra friendly voice, the one he used to talk to dogs and horses when no one else was around. He poked his finger through the steel rails, up by BM's face. The bull snorted and tried to whack it with a horn as Sammy instantly jerked it back. "Easy there, fella," Sammy smiled. "Thought you mighta' had time to simmer down by now." He climbed up the chute gate, reached over and patted BM on the hump. The bull tossed his head back, trying to hook Sammy's hand with his horns. Again Sammy pulled his hand back. "Might as well get used to it, partner," he said quietly. "As much trouble as you caused this mornin', yer lucky Scotty didn't have me haul you to the killers." He rubbed the bull's back, out of range of his horns, and held his ground when BM slung his head and lunged and snorted. After a few minutes of fussing, the bull came to realize it was doing him no good and began to settle down.

"There ya go, bud," Sammy said softly. "Now, yer learnin'." He took his hand from the bull's back and straddled the rails above him. "Relax now, ol' buddy," Sammy soothed. "I'm just gonna sit down on yer back, real nice and easy." He talked to BM as he slowly slid his legs down each side of his rib cage. The bull began to wallow back and forth again. "Settle down, now, buddy, make it easy on both of us." Still hanging on to the top rails, he continued to lower his body until his butt came into contact with the bull's back. As BM lunged and bucked in the chute, Sammy moved with him, steadying himself on the side rails. "You ain't gonna throw me off in here."

A pair of students came through the door and quietly walked behind the chutes and watched Sammy work with the young bull. With BM still squirming below him, Sammy peered between the slats. "Which one a' y'all's gettin' on this'n?" he asked. Neither one spoke up. They continued to watch as more young cowboys came in from the cold. By the time all twelve had gathered, the bull's jumping and bucking had dulled to minor fidgeting. "Well," said Sammy, as he raised himself from the bull's gray hide, "I think I got him tamed down enough for one a' you boys to git on." The bull snorted a warning and tossed his head as Sammy crawled over the backside of the chute. "Scotty oughta be here any minute, now," Sammy announced. "I'm gonna need a couple of you guys to help me load chutes. I got chute help comin', but they ain't showed up yet. The rest of y'all might as well gitcher gear on and git good and loose and git ready to ride."

Kid Kaminsky hunched down on his heels and unzipped his gear bag. On one side of him, Chase, nearly the oldest of all the students, appeared calm and relaxed as he pulled his flashy blue and silver chaps from his own gear bag. On the other side of him, young Tyler sat on the ground, mouth open, tongue curled down and cocked to the left over his bottom lip, as he awkwardly tried to strap a spur to his boot.

"Y'know, Tyler," Chase demonstrated, "if you'd stand up and just put yer foot on the rail of this fence, like this, ya might have a lot better luck."

Tyler watched the older cowboy, and did the same.

"Put 'em on snug, but not too tight," Chase warned. "Ya need a little give, otherwise yer liable to pull a groin."

Tyler looked at the high-horned BM bull in the first chute. "I hope I don't hafta git on him," he said.

"I ain't gittin' on him," Chase stated. "I didn't come here to git on no try-out bulls."

Kid faced the bull as he buckled his chaps around his waist. "I'll git on him," he said in relaxed determination.

From the meeting room door below the grandstands strolled Scotty Redwood, followed by an entourage of chute help and a bull-fighter. "Gitcher bullropes rosined, boys," he announced. "We'll be ridin' real shortly. Somebody might as well be puttin' a rope on this bull-killer, here," he said, waving a finger at BM. "Who wants him?"

Scotty grinned at the stale silence of the young wannabes. Then, his eyebrows were raised in mild surprise as Kid Kaminski stepped forward. "I'll take him," he volunteered.

"You got him, son." Then he turned to the men standing be-hind him. "Charlie, put a flank rope on that bull. And you guys go help Sammy load bulls."

BM watched with one eye at the activity to his right. He saw the group split up and a man walk toward him. He stood restlessly as he felt a soft rope draped over his left hip. Tired of fighting his steel cage, he did not put up a fuss or even look back to see what was going on. The man fed the hook through the bottom rail and caught the bottom end of the cotton rope with his long wire hook and pulled it to himself underneath the bull's belly. He then unhooked the rope and, leaving it hanging across the bottom slat of the chute, he climbed up the chute and, using the same hook, reached down beside the bull and pulled the rope up and tied it snugly around BM's hips.

By this time Kid was chapped up and almost ready to ride. His plaited bullrope hung from the top rail of the back pen fence, his bull-bells strapped securely to the loop. He pulled his steerhide riding glove onto his left hand and bound it in place with a thin rawhide strap around the wrist. From his gear bag he drew out a black sock. With the open end tied shut in a knot, it contained powdered and chunk rosin. As he patted the leather handhold of his bullrope with the sock, the powder sifted through the material and formed a microthin layer on the handhold. He then powdered his own gloved hand before grabbing the handhold and yanking on it repeatedly, the friction causing the rosin to heat up and become mildly adherent, enough to help him maintain a better grip on his bullrope, but not enough to 'hang him up' when the ride was over. As he went through this process, he thought of the lanky gray bull. He had no idea of what the bull would do, having never been bucked before. He'd have to be ready for anything and everything. His heart began to thump in his chest. He shed his jacket as the cool air inside the building suddenly seemed hot. He replayed the basics of bullriding in his mind. Lift. Squeeze. Reach. Charge...

"You about ready, Kid?" asked Scotty.

"About," the Kid answered. "I just need to stretch out a little."

Scotty pulled a round container of tobacco from his hip pocket, pulled the lid off and took a pinch. "I ain't gonna hurry ya none," he said as he tucked the tobacco behind his lip. "I would like to git it done today, though."

Sammy and his chute help had the other five chutes loaded and had three more bulls waiting in the alley. "Let's git it on, bullriders!" he roused.

"Sammy, I'll have you flankin' these bulls," Scotty said to his cousin. "Charlie and Larry can swing chute gates and Rod can run the catch pen."

"Alright," Sammy agreed. "Hey, what are ya gonna call that gray Braymer?"

"After the shit he's caused us this mornin'," said Scotty, "he's gonna be hamburger if he don't buck good."

"I got a feelin' he's goin' to," Sammy replied.

"We'll see."

"So, whatcha gonna name him?" Sammy asked again.

Scotty shook his head. "I ain't gonna worry 'bout a name. First he's gotta save himself from the meat processin' plant."

"Hamburger, huh?" Sammy thought out loud. "Well, he's got that BM brand already on him. How 'bout Big Mac?"

Scotty refused to answer. "You ready, son?" he asked Kid.

"Yep," Kid answered as he untied his bullrope from where it hung on the fence. "You wanna pull my rope, Chase?"

Chase nodded as Scotty announced, "I want all you bullriders to gather 'round where ya can see from behind the chutes. I'm gonna go in the arena and give directions. Go easy with this bull, Kid, it's his first time. Make sure he's lookin' when you nod yer face. And you gatemen, give him a slow gate. Make sure he sees some daylight before ya throw it wide."

BM clambered in his cell as he felt Kid's jingling bull bells slide down his rib cage and the bullrope dangling against his thick hide. He bellowed to no one in particular as the rope was pulled beneath his belly and snugged around his chest. When he felt Kid's legs slowly moving down his sides, he settled down a little. He'd been through this before. Soon, the bull was supporting all one hundred and thirty pounds of Kid's weight on his back. He stood calmly until he felt the bullrope tighten around his chest. He lunged forward and kicked the wall behind him as he tried to no avail to shed his tormentor. The rope came tighter and he came up on his haunches and tried to bail out over the sides of the fence. He was slapped on the nose by a felt hat and returned to all four feet. All the while Kid never moved from his back. He felt Kid move forward, closer to his shoulders. He felt the legs tighten against his body. He heard people yelling all around him. He looked to the left and realized he was not trapped in a cage any more. At first he hesitated as the gate was only opened about four feet, but there was a man standing in that gap, near enough to catch. He hit the gate with his left horn, jerking it out of the gateman's hand and swinging it wide open. He spun around and charged as the gateman leapt up on the next chute gate to safety. As BM blew by him, he realized that he still had an unwanted rider clinging to his back. Instincts told him to bolt into the air. As he did, he felt the rope around his hips squeeze and put pressure on his flanks. He kicked high above his head to shed himself of this annoying parasite. As his front hooves met the arena dirt, he thrust himself into the air again, this time even higher, his tail and back hooves snapping like a whip in a streak of gray. He hit the earth again with the weight of the rider still upon his back, spurs still scratching his ribs. When he blew into the air again, he cocked his head to the right and turned in that direction, putting every muscle he had into it, from his nose to his toes. From the corner of his eye he could see the blur of Kid's chaps and free hand, and his own feet behind him. For two powerful high leaps, he chased his tail in one spot. His antagonist was still scratching and clawing to stay aboard. So he switched directions. As he launched himself to the left, he felt one spur-hold give way and another one slide clear back to his hip, and suddenly the rope around his belly loosened. As he kicked over his body, he felt a hoof connect with a 'thud' as his opponent sailed through the air behind him. He spun around in time to see the Kid plummet to the ground, flat on his back. The bullfighter scampered between him and the downed cowboy. He charged at the bullfighter, his head low, a foot behind and gaining. His prey cut left. BM sliced his horn upwards, to the seat of his pants – and missed. He stopped in his tracks and looked around. Kid rose to his feet and headed to the fence, so he chased him. He darted after him at an angle to the fence, and was quickly overtaking him. At the instant his target was about to jump to safety, BM's horn slashed through the air – and missed again. He wheeled around, but it was too late. Kid was over the fence. He held his head high as he trotted around the arena, looking for another victim, or a way out.

Kid watched the victor scouting the arena. Although he had lost this battle, his entire being was filled with the adrenaline rush that begins before getting on and lasts long after a ride is over. He knew he'd made a few mistakes during the ride, and paid for them by getting thrown, but he was not discouraged. After all, he told himself, you learn by making mistakes, and he was at this school to learn. As he became aware of the rest of the world, he could hear the rest of the cowboys cheering their approval for both him and the bull. It was then that he began to realize that it had been quite a ride, almost.

As BM found the catch pen and cautiously exited the arena, a grin spread across Kid's face. He crawled back over the fence and sensed a stinging pain below his left rib cage. He didn't even care. All Kid wanted was another bull. He walked to the middle of the arena to pick up his bullrope and headed for the chutes.

"You made a helluva try," congratulated Scotty as he hopped down from his perch on the fence.

"Thanks," Kid modestly accepted.

"Did everybody see what he did wrong?" the instructor asked the rest of the crowd.

A few of the students shrugged their shoulders. Finally one said, "No."

"How 'bout you, son," Scotty picked a cowboy from the middle of the bunch. "Wha'd he do wrong on that bull? What got him throwed off?"

Like a kid in a classroom having no idea the answer to a math problem, he considered a wild guess, and then admitted, "I dunno."

Scotty folded his arms and cocked his head, "Anybody else?"

Each student considered the situation thoughtfully. Finally an older cowboy spoke up, "The bull just beat him."

"No bull 'just beats' a cowboy," Scotty lectured. "Everything happens for a reason. For every move the bull makes, you've got a countermovement. How 'bout you, Kid? Do you know why that bull throwed you off?"

The Kid took a chance on a wild guess, "Did I blow my feet?"

"I dunno, did ya?"

He thought back over his ride. "I don't think so."

Scotty put his hand on the young man's shoulder. "No, you didn't blow yer feet. What he did," he said to the rest of the class, "was he just didn't react when the bull switched the direction of his spin. You were makin' a real nice ride goin' to the left, when he switched direction on ya. You weren't *even* ready. And ya gotta be ready for *anything*."

The bullfighter walked up and patted Kid's back. "You damn near took a hookin'," he said.

Sammy spoke up from atop of the empty bucking chute. "You damn-near took a hookin' yerself!" he said to the bullfighter. "You boys wanna know *how* close you were to gettin' hooked?"

"Pretty close," agreed the Kid.

Sammy jumped down inside the chute. Down in the dirt lay the four-inch-long pointed tip of one of BM's sawed-off horns. He picked it up and through the slats of the chute he showed the bullrider and fighter alike. Holding the base of the horn in one hand, he touched the spiked end with his fingertip. "He missed you by *that* much," he emphasized. "That bull just didn't know how to gauge the new length of his stabbers yet – otherwise, he'd a' tore you up!"

Kid examined the weapon. "Shit!" he exclaimed with an uneasy laugh.

"Alright," intervened Scotty. "Who's next?"

One boy volunteered, "I'm ready!"

"Let's go, then," he commanded.

"Hey, Scotty," Sammy called as he climbed out of the chute, "You gonna name that gray bull?"

Scotty scratched his jaw. "Well, he bucks too good to make him into hamburger, that's fer damn sure. What was it you suggested?"

"I figure Big Mac," proposed Sammy, "bein's he's already got a BM brand on him."

"Big Mac...that name oughta' suit him fine," Scotty returned his attention to the bucking chutes. "Anytime yer ready, son."

Chapter 13: January 1989

"Eight ball – corner pocket," announced Randy Corey as he chalked up his cue stick.

"You'll never make it, Corey! You'll never make it!" Shot Palmer screeched from across the pool table, loud enough to be heard on the street outside the bar.

Randy's pool partner, Dave Whitney, stood on top of his chair, a glass of Old Crow and water in one hand and a cue stick in the other. "Bullshit!" he yelled just as loud as Shot. "Corey ain't never missed a shot like this in his life! Gitcher money out, boys!"

T.J. Jergenson made not a sound as he crept up behind Whitney and, grinning ear to ear, jerked the chair out from beneath him.

Dave's feet sailed behind him with the chair as his body toppled face-first to the hardwood floor, shattering his drink, leaving a wasted whiskey and slivers of glass in a puddle beside his head. He did not even look up to see who the culprit was as he spoke, "Goddamn you, Jergenson, you sorry sonuvabitch!"

"Yeeee-ha!" whooped Shot as Randy shook his head in mild disgust.

T.J. was in a giggling fit as he hunched down to help his little buddy from the floor. "Gosh," he hefted Whitney to his feet and turned him about-face, and with his best 'it was an accident' look, offered, "I sure am sorry 'bout that."

Dave looked T.J. in the chest and in a drunken slur said, "Screw you, buddy. You owe me another drink!"

"I'll gitcha another drink!" agreed T.J. as he picked Dave's pool stick from the floor and slapped it into his hand, "But you oughta' be kickin' all that broken glass underneath the pool table before one a' them bouncers comes by and sees what you did!"

"What I did?! Whaddaya mean..."

But it was too late to argue. T.J. was already walking away. A man on a mission, T.J. Jergenson had thirsty friends to buy drinks for, and pockets full of money to spend on them, having won the second go-round at the Denver Coliseum less than two hours before. Earlier in the week, he had tied for second and third with another bullrider and was going into the final round in the bid for the average. His next and final bull at the National Western Stock Show and Rodeo would be the following night. T.J. could have waited around after the rodeo to find out which bull he would be getting on, but he didn't.

"Can't do nothin' about the draw anyway," he had told his friends as they piled into his new blue Ford custom van in front of the Coliseum. He had confidence that no matter which bull he drew, he was going to ride. There was only one bull in the entire circuit that actually scared him enough that he would pay the turn-out fine and decline to get on. That bull was Genghis Khan of Sonny Joe Barker's Stingin' B Rodeo Company, and he wasn't there. T.J. had started out the new year real strong. He'd already placed in the money at Bullhead City, Arizona; Dayton, Ohio; and Spokane, Washington; and won a first at Lafayette, Louisiana.

Dave Whitney cussed his lanky buddy through the twang of the country band's lead guitar. "Ya know what pisses me off?" he complained to both Randy and Shot. "That's the third time he's pulled that chair out from under me since we got here!" Unlike T.J.'s bullriding, Whitney's saddle bronc riding had not won a dime yet all year. He placed just out of the money here at Denver earlier in the week and was thrown off this afternoon. The previous year had been only mediocre for Dave. He won enough to get by, but not much more than that.

His best buddy and pool partner, Randy Corey, had had a good last year, while he was riding, but had wrecked a knee in the early summer while wrestling steers and was out of competition for nearly three months. The Denver Stock Show was treating Randy pretty fair, with a first place in the steer wrestling and a fourth in the saddle bronc riding. He arched over the pool table and, closing one eye, focused his shooting stick on the cue ball. "Well, Dave, if you'd quit standin' on chairs, he wouldn't be able to jerk 'em out from under ya," he said as he sent the eight ball into the corner pocket.

"Nice shot, podna!" Whitney whooped as he hopped up onto another chair. "Hey, bullfighter!" he gloated to Shot Palmer. "You guys know any *hard* games?"

Shot grumbled as he dug into the pockets of his blue jeans for quarters. "You damn bronc riders just got lucky. I'd be kickin' some butt if my partner could shoot worth a damn," he said, motioning to T.J. at the bar. "It's a good thing he's buyin' the drinks or I'd tell him to hit the road!" He put two quarters in the slot and released the pool balls. Other than his pool game, things were going well for Shot. He was fighting bulls real regular, and had been since summer. Although he had gotten his share of aches and pains, he kept them to himself, and while he was not quite as quick on his toes as he once had been, he was much more instinctive and reactive than ever before. He had married Rachel Hewitt last fall after the Kansas City Rodeo, making her his fourth and, he swore, his final, wife. T.J. stood up for him at the ceremony, after spending most of the night before trying to talk him out of the marriage. Shot took her with him to all of the rodeos at first, but she quickly became tired of the road. He called her every night, when he got a chance. This night he didn't get a chance. "O.K., we're goin' five bucks a stick!" he announced as he placed the balls in the rack, "and I'm through messin' around!"

"Shot!" hollered T.J. from across the room, "You ready for another beer?"

"Hell, yes, I'm ready!" Shot yelled back. "And I'm tired of carryin' you in these pool games! We're playin' for money, now!"

"How 'bout you, Randy?" asked T.J. "You want a Coke or somethin'?"

Randy waved him on, "No, I'm alright."

"One good thing about Corey," T.J. said to the barmaid across from him, "he's a cheap date."

The barmaid chuckled as she served up the drinks. She wore a very low-cut flowered blouse, which she filled out nicely, above tight red denim jeans tucked into sapphire colored high heeled cowboy boots. She was very short, very cute, and in her mid-twenties. Her bleached blond hair was blown into place over hazel eyes. A sly smile tugged at one corner of her lips as she studied the action over at the pool table. "Who's that cowboy?" she boldly asked T.J.

"Which one?"

"The one racking the balls," she said, eyeing Shot Palmer, "with the hat tipped to one side and the funny ear."

"What the hell do women see in him, anyhow?" T.J. scowled as he shook his head from side to side. "Hell, *I'm* better-lookin' than he is!"

He lay a ten-dollar bill on the bar and she slid it back to him, waiting for an answer.

"He's married," said T.J.

"Where's his wife?" she questioned with piercing eyes.

T.J. hesitated, and looked toward the front door. "She'll be here any minute."

The barmaid read through his lie. "She's not even in town," she said.

T.J. pushed the ten spot back to her side of the bar. "Here, you better take this."

Again, she slid it back to him. "I don't want the money," she said. "I wanna know who he is."

"Listen," implored T.J. "He's in his fourth marriage and this'un's goin' good. Let's not screw things up for him."

The woman's eyes drifted back over to the cowboy with the funny ear. "He sure looks like he'd be a lotta fun," she murmured.

"*I'm* a lotta fun," T.J. urged, "and I'm single...My name is T.J." She wasn't listening. "I'm winnin' the bullridin' here...leadin' the world standings, too."

Her eyes never left her intended victim as she said to T.J., "Tell me his name and set me up with him, you cowboys can drink free here all night."

"Shot Palmer," T.J. acknowledged without hesitation.

"Shot Palmer," she repeated, approvingly. "I could use a shot a' that. What's he do?"

T.J. put the ten-dollar bill back in his pocket. "He's a rodeo clown."

"Well, well," she said smoothly, "A cowboy with a job. I like that. You tell him that Christy's buyin' tonight, and tell him I *will* be free for a dance or two."

T.J. tried one last time. "Ya sure ya don't wanna trade him in for me? It might work out best all the way around."

Christy winked and walked away.

With two beer bottles in one hand, and Dave Whitney's drink in the other, T.J. made his way back to the pool table. "Drink up, boys," he generously invited, "There's plenty more where this came from!"

"It's about time!" scolded Dave. "A man could die of thirst waitin' on you!"

Randy Corey drew his stick back and hit the cue ball has hard as he could into the racked pool balls. A resounding 'CRACK' sent the balls scattering about the table, rebounding off the banks and sinking three colored balls.

"Thanks for the beer, T.J.," said Shot, having just finished his last one and reaching for the new. "So, who was that ol' girl behind the bar you was talkin' to?"

"Just an ol' bar rag," said T.J. "I talked to a couple fellers about her," he went on. "They said she's trouble. Said she's had every disease on the books – syphilis, herpes, V.D., you name it. Definitely one you wanna stay away from."

"Thanks for that information, pard. I think I'll wander over there and say 'howdy' to her."

As Shot walked away, T.J. said to Randy and Dave, "That's the last we'll be seein' of him tonight."

"Well, shit," said Dave. "What're you gonna do? Shot was your pool partner."

"You guys just play each other," T.J. suggested. "I'll sit out this'n and play the winner."

"O.K., Corey," Dave challenged. "Git ready to git yer butt kicked!"

Randy said nothing as he nonchalantly downed two more balls in the same shot.

"Better get 'em while you can, Goliath, 'cause when little Dave takes over, yer gonna be on the ground!" Dave warned. Randy walked around to the table, studied the outlay of the balls, slowly leaned over the table as he lined up a shot, and casually slammed down another ball.

"Don't count yer chickens before they're hatched, big guy!" said Dave in desperate confidence. "The pressure's on!"

Randy had only one more ball to make before the eight ball. He made it easily.

"Here's where he chokes!" Dave told T.J. "He can't run the table on me! Betcha a buck ya miss, Corey!"

Randy Corey surveyed the table.

Dave followed Randy around the table. "Betcha a buck ya miss!"

"Eight ball," he deliberated as he slowly chalked his stick, "off the bank – side pocket."

Dave closed his eyes and crossed his fingers. "Miss, miss, miss, miss, miss, miss, miss, miss, miss, miss..."

Randy studied the angle of the trajectory from the ball to the table's cushion back to the intended pocket, as Dave continued his chant. He extended his upper body over the table and lined up the cue ball to the precise point needed to connect with the eight ball. He slowly drew the pool stick back, letting it slide smoothly between his thumb and forefinger, and shot.

Dave opened his eyes just in time to watch the eight ball fall into the intended hole. "This is a stupid game," he said in disgust.

"Nice shootin', Corey!" T.J. congratulated as he dug into the pocket of his blue jeans for quarters. "I guess I'm up next."

"You go ahead and play Dave," Randy smiled. "I'm gonna head on back to the motel room."

"You sure?" asked T.J.

"Yeah, I got a steer to wrestle tomorrow," said Randy as he put his stick back in the wall rack, "and I'm gonna get up early and go joggin'."

"You chicken-shit," Dave accused. "You just don't wanna play me, 'cause ya know you'll gitcher ass kicked!"

Randy laughed as he walked to the door.

"Ya need a ride to the motel?" offered T.J.

The handsome cowboy turned around and faced his buddies. "The motel's only a block away," he said obligingly, and left.

"Well, Dave," T.J. said to the little drunken bronc rider, "looks like it's just me and you."

"I'm tired of this game," Whitney protested, "It cuts in on my drinkin'. Let's just sit down and have a drink."

T.J. followed him to a small table midway between the pool tables and the dance floor.

"Want a shot a' tequila?" Dave proposed.

"No, thanks!" T.J. replied without hesitation.

"Well, I'll have one. Ma'am?" He hailed a passing waitress. "A shot of José and an Old Crow and water for me. He's buyin'," he pointed at T.J.

"I'll be right back with that," she said without slowing down.

Dave took a swig of his Old Crow and water, and sat back in his chair to watch the women going to and from the ladies' restroom. T.J.'s eyes scanned the crowded dance floor. Already, he had spotted Shot Palmer two-stepping with the cute little barmaid, Christy.

"T.J.," Dave said as he held out his glass for a toast, "you made a great ride, today."

"Thank you, Dave," T.J. returned. "He was a good bull to get on. A lotta fun."

"You rode him just right," slurred Dave. "Yer gonna win the world this year."

"I'm sure gonna try. If I can stay healthy and keep my head screwed on straight, I think I got as good a chance as anybody."

"Yer *gonna* do it, buddy. It's in the bag."

"It's a long time 'til December," T.J. reminded him. "A lot can happen in a year."

Dave sucked down the second half of his drink. He smiled, but it was a sad, troubled smile. He looked away when he saw T.J. looking back at him.

T.J. studied the unsettled demeanor of his comrade's face. He hoped that Dave would bring up the problem so he wouldn't have to ask, but he knew Dave better than that. "You O.K.?" he finally asked.

Dave slowly looked up from the ice in the bottom of his glass. "What the hell's wrong with me?" he asked in a sorry tone.

T.J. thought before he spoke. "Is there somethin' wrong with you?"

"I'm ridin' like an old lady," said Dave as he leaned forward and rested his elbows on the table. "What's happenin' to me?"

"Aw, hell," T.J. reassured, "Everybody goes through a slump now and then. You rode into it, you just gotta keep gettin' on and ride out of it."

"I ain't picked up a check in three months, T.J. And all last year I was barely breakin' even."

"You need a loan?" T.J. volunteered.

"No, I don't need a goddamn loan," Dave answered.

" 'Cause if ya do, I can sure give ya one."

"Well, in that case, maybe I do," conceded Dave. "But that ain't what this is about. I use'ta be able to ride better'n any a' them guys today. What am I doin' wrong?"

"Well, Dave," T.J. searched his mind for the right words, "it don't seem like yer chargin' at them broncs like ya use'ta do. Yer not spurrin' 'em as hard and yer not keepin' up with 'em. It's like you've lost yer timin'."

"I know I'm gettin' behind," said Dave. "I just can't figure out why."

The waitress showed up with Dave's mixed drink and his shot of Cuervo. She sat the drink on the table and handed him the full shot glass, which he immediately downed. "That'll be five-fifty," she told T.J.

"That barmaid, Christy, is buyin' the drinks tonight," T.J. told her. "She owes me a favor."

"Lord, I don't know how that girl makes any money," the waitress said. "She's always buyin' cowboys drinks. And then she's always on the dance floor dancin' instead a' servin' drinks..." She was still grumbling as she made her way back to the bar.

T.J. turned his attention back to Dave. "Well, I don't know for sure, Dave," he said, "but I think I might know one thing that's hinderin' yer bronc ridin'."

"Yeah?" said Dave as he tipped his glass to his lips.

"Maybe it's this stuff."

Dave gulped down a third of the drink and set it on the table. "What stuff?"

"All this whiskey you been drinkin'," said T.J.

"Nah, that ain't it."

"You sure?"

"Hell, yes, I'm sure," Dave maintained. "I been drinkin' since I was a kid. I rode tough 'til just the last couple a' years. We all drink, 'cept for Randy."

"I know we do, Dave, and you've always been known as a partier and a hell-raiser..."

"...and a bronc-ridin' sonuvabitch!"

"...and a bronc-ridin' sonuvabitch, but you use'ta not drink like ya do now.. I mean, you really been hittin' it hard lately. Yer drunk more often than ya are sober. And ya been gittin' on broncs with a pretty good buzz lately and it's showin'. Hell, at Sioux Falls you were damn near too drunk to crawl over the chute gate."

Dave waved a finger in T.J.'s face, stating, "I know when to quit, bud."

"Ya didn't at Sioux Falls."

"O.K., *one* time..."

"That ain't the only time," said T.J., "You been doin' it more and more. You got too much talent to be throwin' it away like that. I been wantin' to talk to ya 'bout it for a long time, now, but I was afraid I'd make ya mad."

"You *are* makin' me mad," declared Dave. "I got it under control! You don't need to be tellin' me how much I need to be drinkin'. There you are, sittin' there with a beer in yer hand, tellin' *me* I need to quit drinkin'!"

"I never said you need to quit, Dave, I just think you oughta slow down."

Dave swallowed the remaining two-thirds of his drink and slammed his whiskeyless glass on the table. "More whiskey!" he bellowed at the bar. He then grinned defiantly at T.J. and said, "I do what the hell I want."

T.J. took a pull from his beer bottle and directed his attention to the dance floor. He could see Shot Palmer dancing close and holding tight to his new girlfriend. He could hear the mumblings of his intoxicated friend – "Ain't nobody tells Dave Whitney what t'do..." He looked back across the table at him. "I didn't mean to upset ya, Dave," he said apologetically. "But, *yer* the one that asked me what's wrong with ya."

"Don't worry 'bout it, pardner," Dave forgave. "Let's have another drink."

"What the hell," T.J. relented, "yer drunk anyway...Ma'am?" He motioned for another round.

"Y'know, Dave," he said thoughtfully, "I think I know when it happened to you."

"When what happened?" Dave inquired.

"When ya went from bein' a good-timin', after-the-rodeo drinker to what you are now."

"And just what am I now?"

"A drunk."

"What makes..." Dave started to argue the point, but stopped short. He didn't have a case. "Alright, smart-ass, when did it happen?"

"Right after Bennett died."

Dave's lips stiffened and his eyebrows drew together. A hint of a quiver touched his voice as he said, "Don't talk about Bennett...We're here to have fun. I don't wanna hear nothin' about Bennett."

"That's my point," said T.J. "You been tryin' to have fun ever since Bennett died. If you'd quit tryin' so hard to have fun and concentrate more on yer bronc ridin'..."

"I said, don't *talk* about Bennett!" boomed Dave as he slammed his fist on the table, hard enough that T.J. had to catch his beer before it bounced to the floor.

"Talkin' about him might help," T.J. suggested. He waited for a reply, but got none. "Me and Shot talk about him all the time... I *like* talkin' about him. Sometimes when we talk about him it's almost like he's there with us...laughin' and carryin' on. I remember his favorite sayin' – 'I'm here for a good time, not a long time.' They should a' put that on Bennett's headstone."

"Shut up!" Dave brought both fists down hard on the table, this time bucking his glass, the ashtray and T.J.'s beer off the table. "SHUT the FUCK UP!" he cried as he beat on the table again. Tears flowed freely down his face as he raised his fists above his head and brought them crashing down once more onto the teetering table.

T.J. reached across and grabbed Dave's wrists. Dave jerked back, cursing and squirming in a fit of rage. With a tight hold on Dave, T.J. rose to his feet, sending the table toppling to the ground. "Easy, Dave," T.J. tried to calm, "yer gonna get us kicked outta here!" One of Dave's wrists slipped free of T.J.'s grip. He spun around, kicking at anything within reach. Bar patrons scrambled to get out of his way. T.J. locked his arms around Dave from behind and clamped down tightly as he struggled to restrain him. Blinded by tears and deafened by roaring fury, Dave couldn't hear T.J.'s "Cool it, the bouncers are comin'!" nor could he see the bouncers or would have even cared as they overpowered and separated the two of them. As Dave continued to wail and wallow, T.J. tried to explain, "It's all right, boys, we was just leavin'. Dave gits a little worked up now and then. I got him under control..." all the way out the door.

The long-haired lead singer of the country band never missed a poignant word of 'Silver Wings' as he witnessed the scuffle between the bouncers and the two drunken cowboys. Now that that scene was over, he returned his attention to the friends and lovers swaying slowly in each other's arms on the crowded dance floor. From the three-foot-high bandstand, he and the other three members of the group nightly witnessed broken hearts rebounding, relationships beginning, adultery proceeding, fights ensuing, and drunks being escorted to the door. He watched as two young sweethearts closed their eyes and wrapped their souls around each other and moved as one, oblivious to all but the love in their hearts, the bass and steel guitars, and the smooth voice of the man who was observing them. He watched an old cattleman dressed in a four-hundred-dollar suit, a thirty-X gray felt Stetson, and wearing a diamond-encrusted ring shaped like Texas, dancing with a young brunette who could pass for a Dallas Cowboys cheerleader. He saw the barmaid he had spent the early morning hours with in his motel bed. She winked at him as she danced by the stage, her head resting against the chest of a cowboy with thin crooked lips, a funny ear and his hat cocked to one side.

As the song came to a close, she squeezed Shot Palmer's butt and said, "I'd better go to work before I get fired."

The band drifted into an old Hank Williams tune.

"Maybe I have time for one more," she reconsidered.

As they glided around the edge of the dance floor, Shot looked over to the pool tables. "Hey, my friends are gone," he whispered in Christy's ear.

That sly smirk tugged at the corner of her lips again as she queried, "I wonder where they went."

"I dunno," said Shot with a crooked grin. "But I bet they don't come back."

"Where are they stayin'?"

"I have no idea," he said innocently.

She knew he was lying, and happy to play along. "Have you got a place to spend the night?"

Shot tilted his head down and lightly rubbed his jaw against her head. "No, I sure don't."

"You buy me breakfast," she bartered, "you can come to my house."

He tried to act surprised and grateful, "You'd do that fer me?"

Christy looked up and smiled. "Only if you promise to be good."

Shot said as he kissed her on the forehead, "I'll be the best you ever had."

Chapter 14: February 1989

The creaking and squeaking of the old wood-framed windmill could be heard for nearly a mile above the soft north Texas breeze. Tin fan blades powered by cool mellow winds revolved sluggishly around the gears singing out for lubrication as, little by little, they pumped pure translucent water from the underground rivers, up through the long iron rod deep in the earth, into the wide aluminum-sided stock tank.

Nearby, prairie dogs popped from their burrows like jack-in-the-boxes, enthusiastically greeting the morning sunshine before scampering to neighboring mounds for a day of social chatter.

Off to the west, midway to the valley, a small herd of pronghorn antelope whiled away the morning, a few of them up and grazing in bunch grass, most resting motionless on their bellies, enjoying the comfort of the rays upon their backs.

They were so relaxed and content that they completely disregarded the dozen lumbering creatures not seventy-five yards to the south of them. Nor did the great bovines acknowledge them. Bulls of different colors, shapes and sizes, they all had one thing in mind as they followed each other up the trail, as they did every morning at that time – water. Every day started with the trek to the water tank, where they lounged around for an hour or so, ignoring the prairie dogs and replenishing their bodies. Then, they'd all wander off together, in any given direction, to spend the rest of the day wherever the grazing was the choicest.

Once a week, their routine was interrupted when horses carrying cowboys with bullwhips and lariats came out to gather and trail them east to the practice arena, where they were loaded into bucking chutes for jackpot bullridings. Lazy by nature, the bulls would just as soon stay out on the prairie, but when they saw mounted horses coming their way they knew the routine, and headed for the home pens out of habit, with little resistance.

So far, there had been no sign of any humans as they leisurely made their way up the gradual incline from the valley. Leading the herd was the bull the cowboys called T Bar, the largest and oldest, a short-horned cream-colored Charolais with a "T–" brand on his hip. Following the leader was a black Angus-cross bull with a white face and downturned banana-shaped horns. Wipe Out was his handle to the young cowboys who showed up weekly to practice and try out new stock, although his action fell exceedingly short of his name. In back of Wipe Out strolled a little red Hereford bull with no horns that they called Red River. Although he was as old or older than half of the animals in the herd, he was by far the smallest. Healed-over bumps of sewn-up puncture wounds on his left flank and lower rib cage were reminders of a cold day not long before when he happened to be in the way of two battling beasts in the back pens of a December rodeo school. And behind him sauntered the lanky young Brahma who was responsible for Red River's wounds. The mouse gray, high horned bull, though not yet two years old, was as tall as most full-grown Brahma bulls and was filling out profusely. His ears hung below his ivory like palm leaves, and the ridges of thick skin above his eyelids sloped inward, bestowing him with a sinister demeanor. Having only been bucked out of the chute a few times, Big Mac was quickly attaining a big reputation among the local cowboys. Having a longer gait than the smaller red bull, he would occasionally lower his head and prod Red River on as they neared the watering tank. Tagging along behind Big Mac ambled eight more of Scotty Redwood's uncaring hopefuls.

The windmill made one last dying squeal as the breeze dissipated and the pump slowed to a stop. T Bar approached the tank and casually dipped his thick lips into the water, followed by the next three bulls in succession. Big Mac lowered his nose to the dark green tinted tank water and decided he didn't want the water where he was standing – he wanted the water next to him, where Red River stood, so he clubbed him in the shoulder with a blunt horn. The little red quickly backed away from the tank and went around to the other side. Big Mac moved over, next to the big black bull. He lowered his mouth to the water and decided that this, too, was not the water he wanted. He jabbed Wipe Out in the neck, moving him over until he bumped into the leader, T Bar. T Bar swung his head around and clipped Wipe Out in the nose, sending him also to the other side of the tank. Big Mac looked at T Bar, the boss of the mob since long before Big Mac was part of this group. No bull had dared to challenge the big Charolais since he battled the last leader for the position nearly a lifetime ago. But Big Mac wanted what T Bar had – his water, his position, and although he did not know it yet, his cows. He lowered his head and rammed T Bar in the ribs. The older bull whirled around and faced off with the younger bull. For nearly a minute the two stared each other down as the rest of the bulls sipped their water and the windmill made a weak attempt to lift a few more drops from the ground. The nearby prairie dogs halted their chatter as they stood up on their haunches and watched the stand-off. Both bulls lowered their heads. Their breaths whispered puffs from their nostrils as each sized up his opponent. Big Mac scooped dry Texas dirt up on his back with a big front hoof. T Bar backed up a couple of steps as if to get a run at the challenger, and then sidestepped a ways before turning away and trotting around to the far side of the tank. Big Mac bellowed a warning and waggled his head so vigorously that his ears flapped against his face. He had this entire side of the tank to himself, as he would every morning from then on. With the other side already occupied with sipping bulls, the ex-leader stood back and waited his turn.

A half mile to the east, over the rise, Scotty Redwood and his cousin Sammy trotted their mounts toward the windmill. The trophy saddle that Scotty sat in straddled the back of a big Palomino mare called Laramie. Braided horsehair reins draped from Scotty's leather-gloved hands to the horse's silver-inlaid curbshank bit below a concho-studded headstall. Fringe hung as thick from his heavily beaded buffalo hide coat as it did from the shotgun chaps that covered his legs. The design of the silver Mexican-style spurs at the heels of his high-topped ostrich skin cowboy boots matched that of the bit in Laramie's mouth.

Sammy rode a good old, solid, rough-out saddle on a good old, solid, white-faced sorrel gelding named Baldy. Baldy was as tall as Laramie, certainly as quick, and with more 'cow sense.' He just wasn't as good to look at. Sammy's blue bandanna lay draped around his neck and the earflaps were folded up on his orange hunting cap. A month's worth of reddish-gray beard covered his face. Motor oil and blood stains permanently graced his winter work coat, unzipped down the front to reveal a checkered flannel shirt. From his chaps hung no fringe, no beads, no conchos. The only visible stitching was from a repair job from a horse wreck that would have required as many stitches in his leg had he not been wearing those chaps. Unadorned metal spurs with dull rowels clung to his leather workboots.

They said nothing as they rode over the top of the rise together and spotted the bulls at the windmill. They had done this many times over; nothing needed to be said. As they neared the herd, they veered off from each other, Sammy to the north and Scotty to the south. They partially circled the bulls, and closed in. Right away Big Mac and a few of the others began to move down the trail. The rest of them waited until the cowboys got closer to crowd them along.

"Hey bulls, git to movin'!" Sammy whooped as he waved his lasso in the air.

The bulls lazily turned and followed Big Mac.

Sammy noticed that the big Charolais was slow to get started this morning. Usually, he was the first one to head home. "I think somethin's wrong with T Bar," he told Scotty. "Look how he's movin'."

"Hmmm." Scotty observed the bull trudging along, his head held low. "He sure ain't lost no weight this winter...He's just gittin' old. Let him drop back if he wants to. We won't even buck him today."

Slowly heading down the trail, they passed T Bar up, allowing him to go back to the tank, stop and graze whenever he wanted. He followed the herd.

Half an hour later, the bulls filed into the corral behind the bucking chutes. From atop his horse, Sammy swung the wooden gate shut, leaving the old Charolais in the pasture.

Already, local bullriders were rosining their bullropes, gathering directly behind the chutes.

"Howdy, boys," greeted Scotty as he rode by. "Glad you could make it." He spurred Laramie over to the hitching post at the edge of the yard in front of his trailer house and dismounted. Newcomers to the Scotty Redwood Ranch were often surprised at how a world champion who dressed so lavishly, rode fancy horses and drove fancy pickups, in contrast, lived in an outdated, single-wide trailer house with a wife and two kids, and had a pole-shed for a barn. He tied the reins to the post and went in the house. When he returned moments later, he had a clipboard with waiver forms for the contestants to sign, clearing him of responsibility if anyone should get injured, and a coffee can with markers inside, each one with the brand of a different bull, to be used for the random draw of the bucking stock.

By then, Sammy had the three wooden bucking chutes loaded and Big Mac was the first one in. He'd only been bucked three times before, but he knew the system well – when the chute gate opens, do everything you can to shed your rider, then chase him down, run him over, maul him around, then find the catch pen gate, and go back to your pen and relax.

"How many riders we got today?" asked Scotty as he approached the small group of cowboys.

"There's just seven of us," one of them spoke up.

"That's enough for a bull ridin', I reckon," he said as he set the clipboard and coffee can on the makeshift table – a giant cable spool lying on its side. "Forty dollar fees. Thirty of that goes in the pot, ten goes for stock charge. Pay two places. Sixty-forty."

"Take checks?" asked one cowboy.

"Cash only," Scotty stated. "You know that, Jesse."

Jesse nudged his buddy. "Lend me forty bucks, Dan."

The first cowboy stepped up and handed Scotty two twenty-dollar bills.

"Sign that paper," said Scotty as he stuffed the money in his shirt pocket. The cowboy did so without reading what it said. Scotty held the coffee can in the air and the cowboy reached in and pulled out a poker chip with a piece of masking tape clinging to it. Written on the tape in felt-tipped marker was a 22. "That'd be Devil's Disciple," Scotty told the cowboy. "Know him?"

"No, sir," he said.

"He's that tiger-striped brindle. He's usually to the left."

The next cowboy gave him the money, signed the waiver, and drew from the can. "Red River," said Scotty. "You been on him before."

The next entry was Jesse. He'd scraped up enough money from his friends to get on. The tape on his chip had a BM written on it.

Scotty smiled slightly at Jesse. "Big Mac. He's the bull to win it on." He motioned with his head to the chute the bull was standing in. "He's waitin' for ya."

Jesse looked at the high-horned Brahma. "Is he a new one?" he inquired.

"I've bucked him three times," said Scotty. "Twice at the last school I put on and once out here. Ain't nobody made it to the whistle on him yet."

Jesse's buddy Dan stood behind him in line. "That's alright, Jesse," he said. "Ain't nobody that can ride worth a damn got on him."

Jesse gathered his rope from the fence and walked over to where Big Mac patiently waited in the chute.

The young man acting as the bullfighter that day approached him and advised, "You'll wanna be movin' when you get off a' this bull, Jesse, he's pretty hookie."

"O.K.," agreed Jesse as he crawled up on the chute and lowered his rope down beside the bull.

Being a quick learner, Big Mac gave Jesse very little trouble in the chute as he snugged the bullrope up around his chest.

Having done that, Jesse climbed from aboard the bull and out of the chute to stretch out his muscles and psych up his mind.

With the entry fees all paid, waivers signed and bulls drawn for, Scotty announced, "Let's ride!"

They started the action two chutes behind Jesse and Big Mac. A young man bucked off a small white bull dotted in black. Next was the big black banana-horned bull, Wipe Out. He had a soft trip and his rider handled him with no trouble at all, for the low score of sixty-seven points.

Then it was Big Mac's turn. He stood motionless in the box as Jesse slid his feet down both sides of his back and had Dan pull the tail of his rope up snug.

"Bear down, Jesse," encouraged Dan. "Charge him, now. Be aggressive."

"Better cock yer hammer for this bull," warned Scotty from the flank. "He's a buckin' sonuvagun."

The gate was barely open when Big Mac exploded from the chute like a keg of dynamite. All eyes were wide, especially Scotty's, as he watched his bull leap high into the air and spin around like never before. Jesse pumped fiercely over his head to keep up with his loose-hided, twisting, jumping, kicking, head-slinging package from hell, when his handhold was jerked from his hand and he found himself sailing through the air toward the middle of the arena. Like an airplane coming in for a landing, he hit the ground on his feet and never slowed down as he high-tailed it for the nearest fence. Big Mac spun around on his front feet and stopped on all fours for a split second, long enough to scope out the situation. He saw the bullfighter facing him from ten yards away and the bullrider running past him, not looking back. He charged at the bullfighter, who, at the last instant stepped to one side, leaving nothing in his sights but the fleeing bullrider. He bore down on his victim, rapidly gaining ground. Jesse could hear the bull's pounding footsteps above the yells from competitors and spectators alike, to "Run!" and "Look out!" as he sprinted for safety. He was not five yards from the fence when he felt himself being scooped up by the seat of his jeans and flying through the air. His arms flailing wildly, he soared over the arena fence and crash-landed on the hood of a Dodge pickup. The cries of warning from the crowd and cowboys turned into cheers of amazement and laughter, from everyone except the young lady in the cab holding her infant son, as she rolled down her window and warned, "You better not scuff my husband's pickup with your spurs!"

Big Mac snorted through the fence at his humbled opponent, and trotted off to the out-gate.

Scotty watched the bull in awe as he left the arena. "That son of a bitch is buckin' better every trip!" he stated dumbfoundedly to no one in particular. He heard someone say back, "If he keeps improvin' at this rate, nobody ever *will* ride him!"

Jesse's friend Dan was the first to arrive at his side, followed by Sammy Redwood.

"You O.K.?" asked Dan as he helped him down from the hood of the pickup.

"Yeah, I guess so," replied Jesse, somewhat shaken. "What happened?"

Sammy declared, "Big Mac just threw a double-tough trip at ya, partner. You didn't really make no mistakes, he just threw yer ass off, that's all there is to it!"

An hour later, the rest of the bulls had been bucked, the winners paid off, and young cowboys sat around on the tailgates of their pickups enjoying a beer, conversation and the unseasonably warm weather.

Scotty and Sammy tightened their cinches and climbed aboard their horses to trail the bulls back out to the pasture.

"Whaddya think?" Sammy asked his cousin as they rode to the bull pen.

"I think I'm gonna give ol' Sonny Joe Barker a call tonight," Scotty mused. "I'll bet he's got a spot on his team for a bull like Big Mac."

Sammy reached down from atop his horse, unhooked the latch to the big white gate to the pasture and swung it wide. "How much money do ya reckon he'll bring?"

"Top dollar," said Scotty. "Nothin' less than top dollar."

Big Mac was the first to meander out of the pen and up the hill to the west pasture, followed by the rest of the herd, single file. T Bar waited quietly along side of the trail as each bull strolled by him, and took his place at the end of the line.

Chapter 15: March 1989

The blackness of the night faded with time into the dreariness of a windy gray morning as Dave Whitney headed his old black Ford pickup north along the two-lane blacktop. Dave was traveling alone this morning, going to visit with a friend. His trusty bottle of Old Crow lay on the seat beside him, although he hadn't had a pull from it in over twenty miles. Stopping only for fuel, he had been on the road for nearly four hours, leaving directly from the house party, the one that started after the bar closed for the night. He'd had a fairly good time at the bar, with his co-workers from the livestock auction barn and their friends, but it was nothing like being with his rodeo buddies. It had been two months since he had been with his own kind, and he missed them as much as he missed the lifestyle. Sure, he liked the guys he worked with, but they liked to 'wind down' after a hard week's work. They would rather sit in a booth to drink their beer, smoke cigarettes, talk about their jobs, and cuss their boss. Dave longed for the days when every time he and the boys stepped into a bar it was a celebration! And even on the rare occasions when none of them won any money, they could still find something to celebrate about. Their special kind of freedom and their special kind of friendships – they celebrated these two blessings constantly, even when something seemingly more important came along, like the first place check, or the latest trophy belt buckle. Dave told himself that he still had plenty to celebrate about – he was alive and healthy and had a steady job, but when he tried to celebrate, he just couldn't get into it like he used to. He didn't have a lot of fun at the party that commenced after the bar closed. There were no cowboys, although a lot of them wore the hats. There were only a few decent-looking women there, and they each were surrounded by three or four young horny hopefuls. No one cared that he was a bronc rider and a damned good one and no one cared when he told them that he was only going to work until June, when he would have enough money saved up to rodeo hard, just in time for the big summer run. All that they wanted to talk about was race cars, football and Dave's least favorite sport – if it could be called a sport – in the entire world, fake wrestling. Not everything about the party had turned out bad. He did win some money playing poker – enough for a tank of gas and a couple of pieces of beef jerky. When he left the party unnoticed at three in the morning, he fully intended on going home to his apartment in town, but when he got to the stop sign just up the street from his house, he had turned left instead of right, and he'd been heading that way since.

Dry faded corn stubble protruded through a thin snow cover along both sides of the highway. Dave yawned and rubbed his bloodshot eyes. The broken white line and the hum of his engine were so constant that they became an abstract presence in his conscious mind, blocked out by memory after memory of days gone by.

He remembered the very first bucking horse he ever got on – just a little hop-skipper named Yellow Rose – and how he knew right then that a bronc rider was what he wanted to be. He remembered his uncle Jake coaching him on the finer parts of saddle bronc riding, like setting the stirrups and lifting on the hack rein. He remembered winning the state high school rodeo bronc riding title as a freshman and going to Helena, Montana, for the National High School Rodeo Finals. That was where he first met Bennett McKinney and T.J. Jergenson. Although Bennett was a senior and T.J. a junior, they took Dave under their wings, showed him the ropes and got him drunk for the first time.

He remembered the first time he talked to rodeo clown Shot Palmer. Shot cornered him at a rodeo dance and asked him where Bennett McKinney was. Dave knew that Shot was mad and planning on beating Bennett to a pulp because Bennett had had a sexual interlude with Shot's fiancée down in Clinton, Louisiana, so he told him that Bennett was at the only motel in town, and then he just made up the number of the motel room. Shot went to the motel, broke down the door, and broke the nose of the rodeo announcer he'd worked with that very evening, before he realized he had the wrong man.

Dave tried to remember the first time he'd met his bronc riding partner, Randy Corey, but he couldn't. He'd just started seeing Randy at rodeos now and then. Randy, being very quiet and unassuming yet congenial and always smiling, was just a little harder to get to know than the rest of the bunch. Dave had known who Randy was for six months before he ever actually even talked to him. Not long after that, Randy was throwing his gear in the van and going down the road with the boys.

Dave's thoughts of Randy drifted to a time at a big dance hall down in New Mexico when he told Randy, "You pick her out, big buddy. You go up to any woman in this entire place and tell her I wanna kiss her titties, and we'll just let the guts fly with the feathers!" Being quiet, reserved and sober, like Randy always was, Dave didn't think he'd do it, but Randy scouted around and found the biggest, stoutest, meanest-looking woman in the whole place, pointed Dave out to her, and told her what Dave had instructed. She liked the idea. She grabbed Dave, danced one dance with him and took him straight home. Although he would never admit it, he had fun that night, but what really stuck out in his mind was the embarrassment and humiliation he suffered the next day when she brought him back to the rodeo grounds, and even walked with him to the chutes. She was wearing a big yellow dress. Bennett said later that if she had been wearing one big red earring, she would have looked like a school bus. A week later, Dave thought he'd get even by smearing Vaseline all over Bennett's clutch and brake pedals in his van and T.J. ran it through a motel room wall.

He reminisced about the women – the really nice women – that he was certain he would have had a chance with, had he not driven them off with his fast-living, hard-drinking ways. Oh, well. If they didn't want him as he was, it never would have worked out anyway. Still, he considered, as he looked at the whiskey bottle on the seat beside him, if he didn't drink so much, he could surely have had a steady girl to be with in the evenings when he was feeling so alone. And, with that speculation, he unscrewed the top of the one-third full bottle and helped himself to a generous swig of harsh, amber liquid. He screwed the lid back on, set the bottle down and made a left turn onto a gravel road.

He drove slowly over a small knoll. Over the hill, in front of the rows of pine trees, above the entrance, was the sign, *Prairieview Cemetery*. It had been nearly two years since Dave had been to this place – on the day they lowered Bennett's body into the ground. He crept his pickup up to the gateway and shut off the engine. He sat for a minute and watched the trees swaying against the cold winter wind. He buttoned his coat, turned its collar up, and pulled his seed corn cap down low. He took another pull from his whiskey bottle and laid it back on the seat. Then he picked it up again, slid it into his coat pocket and stepped out of the pickup. As he made his way through the big open gateway, the wind and whiskey made him stumble sideways into the flagpole. He hung onto it with one arm, took a deep breath and regained his composure before trudging on, past the grave of the Unknown Soldier. He made his way up the narrow pathway toward Bennett's headstone, leaving his bootprints behind him in the thin skiff of snow. The only other signs of life became still as two cottontail bunnies nestled behind grave markers and nervously watched Dave go by.

He tried to remember just where it was that they'd buried Bennett. He envisioned the open tent above the casket, the congregation of friends and family, the preacher, and Bennett's parents sitting up front in their folding chairs, their hearts in such pain that it hurt Dave to think about them. It seemed like Bennett's spot was just north of one of the tallest pines in the place. He looked to the waving treetops. Three exceptionally high trees reached up to the bitter gray skies. He approached the closest one and scouted to the north, but none of the stones were chiseled with Bennett's name. As he walked toward the second tree, he saw a gravestone at the end of a row. It was about three-and-a-half feet tall, the color of a light blue roan horse. In the right-hand upper corner a heart was etched in the stone. Inside the heart was a silhouette of a bucking bull and rider. Dave stepped around to the front of the stone.

Bennett William McKinney
Born – October 7th, 1960
Died – April 8th, 1987

For the longest time, he just stood and stared at the words engraved in the headstone. He searched his mind for words of his own. His nose wrinkled and his lips disfigured. His tears left a sideways trail as the flurries swept them across his face. He tried to speak but cut the first word short. He swallowed hard, sniffed and looked to the gray sky above. As if his legs suddenly had given out from beneath him, he dropped to his knees and wept out loud. He wept until his voice was hoarse and his tears were dry. He felt weak from sorrow and suddenly very dizzy and unstable. He felt as if the breeze had become a whirl-wind and was trying to knock him down from all directions. Bennett's headstone began to spin around him. He teetered to one side and put his hands on solid ground. He slowly lowered his butt to the grass and rested on an elbow. With his back against the wind, he lay with his head on the base of the stone. As the spinning world slowed down around him, he shivered and looked up again at the blurry outline of pine trees swaying back and forth as they, too, moaned in sorrow.

He began to wonder why. Why did it have to happen? Why Bennett? Why couldn't it have been me? Why couldn't I have gotten to him in time? He pictured the scene: Bennett lying helplessly face-down on the arena floor, Genghis Khan bearing down on him. He pictured it again, and again. The third time around Dave saw himself sprinting into the arena – the whole scene in slow motion – and taking the full force of Genghis' charge just below the hips. With a mighty heave, the bull slung his head upward, tossing Dave, spinning head over heels, high into the air.

It was at that split second – or eternity – when thoughts fade into dreams, that Dave found himself being thrown over the fence, over the grandstand, through the rafters and ceiling of the Coliseum, high over the city, over mountains, spinning vertically through the clouds, losing track of up or down, seeing water, the sky, land, sky, fields, sky, clover, and more clover. He found himself lying in a field of green clover with little white and yellow flowers blooming all about. He felt a smile on his face as the warm sun caressed and relaxed his weary body and mind. In the distance, snow-capped mountains filled the space between the clover and the blue, cloudless sky. Clover, mountains and sky. And quiet, except for the occasional whippoorwill song from out of nowhere. At the edge of the clover, much too far away to see, he noticed a figure – a man – walking in this direction. Immediately, the man was close enough to recognize – it was Bennett – and suddenly he stopped just a few yards away. He was youthful looking, like when Dave met him years ago, and he wore no hat. He smiled. Not the wide ornery grin that was imprinted in Dave's memory, but a thoughtful, knowing smile.

Dave made no attempt to get up from the cushiony comfort he lay on. "I thought you was dead," he said.

"Well," Bennett replied, "there you go thinkin' again," and his smile widened to the ornery grin that Dave was accustomed to. "How're the boys?" he asked.

"They're all doin' good, 'cept me," Dave answered.

"What's wrong with ya?" Bennett inquired.

Dave ignored the question. "How you doin'?"

"How do you think I'm doin'?" replied Bennett. "I'm dead."

"You always gotta be a smart-ass, dontcha, Bennett...Some a' the guys miss ya..."

For a while they just looked at each other, as if the other was a photograph to reminisce upon. Finally Dave broke the silence. "Say it one last time for me."

"Say what?" asked Bennett.

"You know," Dave requested.

Bennett knew. With a ceremonious 'click' of invisible shot glasses, he winked at his buddy and announced, "I'm here for a good good time, not a long time." He turned to walk away, and was gone in an instant.

Dave felt a chill go through his body. He looked up and gray clouds began to block out the blueness of the sky. The sun disappeared and the clover lay over flat beneath the strong gale. Soon, the clover was no longer clover, but grass, and the mountains were the gravestone where he laid his head. He slowly sat up and looked around the graveyard. He rubbed his eyes and wondered how long he'd been asleep. He scooted his body up closer to the headstone and leaned against it as he pulled his whiskey bottle from his coat pocket. He unscrewed the lid and downed half of what was left. He sat the bottle on the base of the stone where his head had been, and sluggishly got to his feet. He patted the top of the stone, said good-bye in his mind, and stumbled away. When he made it to his pickup, he crawled inside, but did not fire up the engine right away. Instead he sat and watched the familiar pines swaying in the wind. The two cottontails waited, patient and motionless, until he started the pickup and slowly headed south.

Chapter 16: April 1989

When Scotty Redwood backed his covered stock trailer up to the back pens of Sonny Joe Barker's private rodeo arena, Big Mac – the only passenger on the trailer – peered through the slats at the other bucking bulls lazing about and waiting for the action to start.

"Whoa!" Sonny Joe stopped the driver at the open gate to the wood corral hallway, "That ought to do it, Scotty."

Scotty killed the engine of his new Dodge diesel and opened the door. The familiar custom-made high top, high heeled cowboy boots stepped to the ground, below blue jeans so tight that they looked painted on to Scotty's butt instead of slid into. His World Champion Belt Buckle sparkled in the bright spring sunshine as did the mirrored sunglasses beneath his familiar gray Stetson.

He ambled to the rear of the trailer and greeted Sonny Joe with an open hand. "Been a long time, Sonny. How'd ya winter?"

Sonny Joe grabbed Scotty's hand and shook it firmly. "Good, Scotty, real good. How 'bout you?"

"I must be gittin' old," Scotty grinned beneath his thick drooping mustache. "Seems like these winters are gittin' longer and harder every year."

"Well, then you know what you got to look forward to when you git to be my age," returned Sonny Joe, who was in his mid-fifties and fifteen years Scotty's senior. "How's yer cousin, Sammy, doin'?"

"Gittin' lazier every day," Scotty replied. "If ya can't do it from the back of a cowhorse, he don't wanna do it."

"Well, let's take a look at this bad Braymer bull you been tellin' me about," Sonny Joe suggested.

Scotty motioned with his head toward the inside of the trailer. "He's right here."

Sonny Joe looked between the strips of iron at the tall gray bull. "He ain't very fleshy."

"He's only a two-year-old," said Scotty, "but he'll fit right in with yer A-team."

"Naw!" Sonny Joe refuted.

"Hell, yes," proclaimed Scotty. "You can take this bull to the finals!"

"Not this year..."

"Don't bet on it," said Scotty as he unlatched the trailer gate and swung it open.

Big Mac stepped to the edge of the trailer and surveyed the grounds.

"Big Mac!" Scotty coaxed, "Git outta the trailer!"

Big Mac casually stepped to the ground and moseyed down the hall.

Sonny Joe was quiet as he studied the bull. After a moment he said, "He's dang-sure a rodeo-lookin' sonuvagun." He looked at his own reflection in Scotty's sunglasses. "Wha'd you give for him?"

Scotty hesitated. Three months ago he had lied to Brad Fanner on the telephone, saying the bull didn't buck very hard, but would work as a practice bull for young students. He had bought the bull for beef slaughter price. "I gave five thousand for him." His lying eyes twitched behind his shades. "But he's worth twice that much."

"Ten thousand?" Sonny Joe exclaimed. "I ain't *never* paid that much for a bull!"

"If you don't," reasoned Scotty, "somebody else will."

Sonny Joe looked the bull over again. He considered telling Scotty just to load him up and take him back home. Instead he said, "Well, we might as well watch him in action." He squeezed through the opening between the stock trailer and the fence, and shut the alley gate behind him. Big Mac turned around and faced him as he called out to his chute help. "Open up them slide gates, men, we're gonna buck this gray bull."

"Watch him, Sonny," Scotty warned from the outside of the gate, "he's plenty..."

Just then the bull charged down the hall at Sonny Joe. He stopped short when his intended victim scrambled to the top rail of the gate.

Scotty finished his warning... "hookie."

Sonny Joe crawled down the safe side of the fence. "Why the heck didn't you tell me that, before I got in there?"

"Hell, I didn't know you was goin' in, Sonny," said Scotty. "I was just headin' to the pickup to get my bullwhip." With that, he went to his rig and retrieved a twelve-foot braided leather whip that hung from the gun rack. "This here's about all he understands," he asserted as he returned to the fence. "Big Mac!" he ordered, as he climbed to the top of the fence. "Move outta here!"

The bull faced him, challenging him to come down from the safety of his perch. Scotty swung the whip around his head and snapped a warning into the air.

Big Mac backed up a few steps before whirling around and loping to the far end. Immediately Scotty bailed off the fence and ran after the bull, still cracking his whip as he chased him up the narrow alley way to the bucking chutes. When Big Mac had made it to the last chute, the slide gate was slammed shut behind him.

"There!" said Scotty as he climbed out of the chute behind Big Mac.

"Who wants to get on this bull?" he asked the group of cowboys who had gathered at Sonny Joe's for the weekly practice session.

"What's he do?" inquired a young bullrider.

"Oh,..." Scotty hesitated again as he downplayed the bull's ability, "...he might turn back, might kick a little."

The young man stood quiet, undecided.

"Hell, he ain't nothin' but an old mama cow's calf," Scotty coaxed. "Git on the sumbitch."

"O.K., I'll take him," he answered. He started to gather his bullrope from where it hung on the fence, when Sonny Joe walked up and put his hand on his shoulder.

"Hang on, partner," Sonny Joe interrupted, "I got another bull for you. I'm gonna let Wiley get on this'n."

"Who's Wiley?" Scotty asked.

"Wiley Paz," said Sonny Joe. "A little Mexican kid. He's only nineteen and ain't even been ridin' for a full year yet, but this kid is *sticky*, now."

"Nineteen years old?" Scotty repeated with a sarcastic smile. "Good Lord, I hope he don't hurt my bull!"

Sonny Joe chuckled, "Come on, I'll introduce ya to him."

Toward the other end of the chutes, the young Mexican cowboy was working dry rosin into the hand-hold of his bullrope.

"Wiley," Sonny Joe called to him, "I want to introduce you to somebody."

Wiley let go of his rope and met the two of them halfway. He was about five foot three and could not have weighed over a hundred and twenty pounds.

"Wiley, this here's Scotty Redwood. Scotty, this is Wiley Paz. He's one of the best new bullriders to come down the pike in a long, long time."

Unimpressed this far, Scotty extended his hand.

Wiley smiled up at Scotty and shook his hand. "Pleased to meet you, sir," he greeted.

"So you think yer gonna ride Big Mac, huh?" Scotty questioned.

Wiley looked confused. "Big Mac?"

"He's a bull Scotty's tryin' to sell me," explained Sonny Joe. "He's the gray Braymer in the first chute. Ol' Scotty claims he's pretty wolfie."

Wiley peered around Scotty's shoulder to see the bull. He looked back at Sonny Joe with a confident smile, claiming, "I can ride him."

"If you do," said Scotty, "it'll be the first time anybody has."

Sonny Joe patted the young cowboy on the back. "Just give it yer best shot, pard."

"Always," he returned. Then he said to Scotty, "You seem familiar. Have we met before?"

Scotty's eyebrows raised. A bullrider who didn't know who the legendary Scotty Redwood was? "No, boy," he said, "we ain't met, and I doubt if I'd remember if we did."

"Seems like I've heard your name before. Are you from around here?"

Scotty rolled his eyes to the sky, and back to the little cowboy. "No, I ain't from around here," he grumbled.

"Did you used to ride bulls?"

"Did you just arrive from Mexico?" Scotty snapped back. "I'm a two-time World Champion bullrider and three-time runner-up!"

Wiley's eyes widened in surprise and his lips turned to the frown of a scolded schoolboy. He quietly uttered, "I'm sorry. I didn't mean..."

"And I'll bet the price of that bull that he'll toss yer sorry beaner ass back across the border where you belong!"

Wiley slowly raised his head. His guilt-ridden frown transformed into tight-lipped anger and his wide eyes narrowed to slits as he pointed his finger at Scotty and announced, "I will ride your bull and spur holes in his lungs!"

Scotty chuckled without smiling. "We'll see, boy. We'll see."

The two of them turned around and walked away from each other, leaving Sonny Joe standing alone with his thumbs in his pockets, shaking his head.

Wiley gathered his bullrope from the fence and headed toward the bull. Sonny Joe stopped him halfway. "I apologize for the way ol' Scotty's actin'," he said. "I've know him fifteen years, but I never had any idea he was such a prejudiced sonuvabuck."

"That's O.K.," Wiley assured, "we'll show him," and started to walk off.

"Well, it makes me mad," complained Sonny Joe. "He had no call to talk to you that way."

Wiley turned and faced Sonny Joe. "It's not your problem, Sonny. He's a jerk. This kind of thing happens more often than you'd think."

"Well," Sonny Joe mumbled...

Wiley smiled reassuringly and left Sonny Joe standing alone again.

Sonny Joe pondered the situation. "Doggone it, it's just not right." He grinned slightly at Scotty's shock when the young bullrider did not know who he was. Still, that did not make it right. Sonny Joe walked over to the pickup where Scotty was retrieving a flankrope to hang on Big Mac. Scotty glanced at Sonny Joe, then looked back down into the pickup bed.

"Kind of a cocky little shit, ain't he?" commented Scotty.

Sonny Joe leaned against the pickup. "Oh, I don't know," he said. "Maybe yer just mad because he don't know who you are."

"Maybe I am," said Scotty. "I win the world two times and that ignorant little shit who calls himself a bullrider don't even have the common courtesy to know who the hell I am!"

"Scotty, that was might-near a dozen years ago," Sonny Joe pointed out. "To a nineteen-year-old, a dozen years ago is a *long* time."

"I don't give a shit," growled Scotty. "Damn foreigner learned to read and write American, you'd think he'd catch up on the news!"

"That kid was born in Texas!" Sonny Joe snapped. "He's as American as me and you!"

Scotty looked Sonny Joe in the eye. "He may be American to you, but he just looks like another beaner to me."

Sonny Joe squared up to Scotty and poked him in the chest, hard enough to make him back up a step. "That's twice," he said. "You ever call him that again, I'll whip ya, and if I can't do it alone, I'll get help!"

Scotty quickly forced a smile. "Settle down, now, Sonny. I didn't mean to piss you off. Now, you can call that boy American, Mexican-American, Texan, any nationality you want, but if he's gonna call hisself a bullrider, then he's gonna hafta prove hisself."

"He has," said Sonny Joe. "Many times over."

"Yer awful damn sure of him, aintcha?"

"Yes, I am."

"Well, I'll say it again," said Scotty. "If that...boy can ride Big Mac, I'll *give* him to ya!"

Sonny Joe paused, and asked, "Are you serious?"

"As a heart attack," Scotty answered.

"Yer awful sure of that bull, aintcha?"

"Yes, I am."

"And if he bucks off?"

"Twenty thousand," Scotty bartered without hesitation.

"If that bull can throw off Wiley Paz," said Sonny Joe, as he closed the deal with a handshake, "he's worth twenty thousand."

Scotty let go of Sonny Joe's hand and took his flankrope to where Wiley was securing his bullrope to Big Mac's back. He climbed up on the platform on the back side of the chute, and as he hung the flankrope loosely around the bull's hips, he said to the young bullrider, "Ol' Mister Barker's gonna be countin' on you."

Wiley said nothing as he sat on the bull's back and adjusted his loop.

"You hear me, boy?" insisted Scotty. "I said Sonny's really gonna be countin' on you."

"This has nothing to do with Sonny," said Wiley as he went about his business. "This is between me and the bull."

"The hell it don't have nothin' to do with Sonny," Scotty contended. "All *four* of us are in on this deal."

Wiley slid the loop of his bullrope to Big Mac's belly and climbed out of the chute. "What do you mean?" he asked Scotty.

"I mean this is gonna be a twenty thousand-dollar bullride," said Scotty. "If you can ride him, I give the bull to Sonny, free of charge. On the other hand, if you ain't cowboy enough to stay on for eight, this bull is sold to Sonny Joe Barker for a whoppin' twenty thousand dollars!"

Wiley just looked at Scotty, dumbfounded.

"You ever ride for twenty thousand dollars before, boy?" Scotty taunted. "Pressure's on now, boy. Yer gonna make or break Sonny Joe Barker."

Wiley jumped from the perch to the ground and strode over to don his chaps and riding glove.

By then a group of cowboys, aware of what was at stake, had gathered at the chutes to encourage the talented young bullrider. Two appointed rodeo officials took their places in the arena, on each side of the chute. The informal bullfighter, clad in blue jeans and football cleats, jumped from toe to toe in the middle of the arena. The official timekeeper, up in the crow's nest, set her eight second timer to zero-point-zero. Sonny Joe entered the arena, saying nothing to Scotty as he walked by chute number one.

Wiley Paz hopped back upon his platform, tied his deer hide riding glove snugly around his wrist, and eased down onto Big Mac's gray, loose-hided back.

Sonny Joe stepped up to the chute and said quietly as he reached through the rails and patted Wiley on the knee. "Just relax and ride like you always do, partner. Just have fun on him."

"Yessir," Wiley half-whispered as he handed the tail of his rope to his helper.

Sonny Joe watched the young man through hopeful eyes. He had no more advice, so he backed away from the chute.

Scotty Redwood snugged the flank rope around Big Mac's haunches and tied it off. He leaned over and whispered in Wiley's ear, "How're you at ridin' under pressure, boy? Bullridin's easy when yer ridin' for a brass buckle in a forty dollar rodeo. Twenty thousand dollars worth a' pressure kinda takes the fun out of it, don't it, boy?"

Wiley worked the rosin into his glove and rope as Scotty continued to harass him.

"I'll tell you what's the shits of it; you ain't gonna git a damn thing out of it! You want in on some of the action? I'll betcha a hunnerd bucks you fall off. Hell, I'll bet two hunnerd! Wanna go five?"

Wiley tried to block Scotty's remarks out of his head. "O.K., pull," he said to his assistant.

"You were pretty cocky a while ago," said Scotty. "Struttin' around like a big ol' rooster. You wanna bet five hunnerd...? Or didja turn into a little brown chicken?"

"Alright!" Sonny Joe fired. "Quit messin' with my bullrider!"

Scotty grinned at Sonny Joe as if he didn't care about the outcome of the ride.

Wiley laid the bullrope across the palm of his hand, around his fist and through his hand again. He clenched the rope and cocked his thumb securely against the knuckle of his forefinger.

"Good luck, boy," Scotty said loud enough for everyone to hear. "Yer gonna need it."

Wiley slid his crotch against the back of his hand, took a deep breath, tucked his chin and nodded for the gate.

Both rider and beast drank in the exuberant rush of violent freedom as the gate swung open, and, together, they exploded from their cage in a frenzied mayhem. As the bull's front hooves pounded the ground and he twisted around to the left, Sonny Joe yelled from ten yards away, "Be there, Wiley! Ride! Ride!" Wiley flung his right spur to the bull's shoulder and pumped his free arm furiously over his head. Scotty stood on his perch behind the chute, biting his lip with anticipation. Big Mac bailed into the air again and swung his rear end around, behind and over his head. Every time his big front hooves connected with the earth, he slung his nose to the sky, his antlers dancing inches from Wiley's nose, as he continued to dive over his own shoulder. With each descent, Wiley's riding arm was yanked straight by the pressure of the whipping force of Big Mac's reeling backbone, only to re-cock as Wiley flung himself with every effort in his being back to his bullrope every time the bull would gather his back hooves underneath him for the next launch. Five seconds clicked by.

"Buck him off!" Scotty hollered, as he began to panic. Sonny Joe's eyes widened as he realized the young cowboy was doing it – he was riding Big Mac! As Wiley pumped over his head and thrust his hips toward his rope, he felt confident and in control. For every move the bull made, Wiley had a countermove. Suddenly and instinctively, simply riding this bull was not enough. He let go with his right leg, on the outside of the spin, let his foot sail dangerously away from the bull and then jammed his spur back into Big Mac's rib cage. Again, he pulled his boot away from the bull's hide. With no warning, the bull slung his head around and switched directions. With Wiley's right leg gripping nothing, and the full force of the momentum going left, Wiley saw nothing but the arena floor when it smacked him in the face. Dazed and confused, he instinctively scrambled to his hands and knees when he was stomped back into the ground by Big Mac's descending back hooves. Again, he struggled to get out from underneath the raging trampling beast when a horn thumped him in the rib cage and catapulted him through the air, sending him rolling fifteen feet away. As Wiley lay on his back with his feet toward the bull, he felt helpless and paralyzed by fear as he watched Big Mac lower his horns and rush him. Suddenly, from out of nowhere, the bullfighter darted across both the downed cowboy's and the bull's vision. Big Mac took the bait, and chased it all the way to the fence, while Sonny Joe and another cowboy dragged Wiley to the safety of the open bucking chute where this contest had begun.

"Better close the gate on us. He might come back huntin'," said Sonny Joe to the gateman as he lay Wiley down on his back. "Lay still and breathe deep, Wiley. Just relax."

As Wiley struggled to get his breath back, he uttered, "Did...did I ride him?"

Sonny Joe looked up at Scotty. "Did he?"

Scotty looked up at the time-keeper. She looked at her stopwatch and announced, "Seven-point-eight-eight."

The other young cowboys moaned in disappointed disbelief.

Scotty just smiled

"I'm...sorry, Sonny," Wiley stammered.

With a hand on Wiley's shoulder Sonny Joe returned, "You did your best, Wiley."

"I shouldn't have spurred him..."

"Spurrin's just aggressive bull ridin'. That's the way yer s'posed to ride 'em. Ain't a man here that coulda' rode that bull as far as you did," declared Sonny Joe. "Includin' Scotty Redwood."

Scotty's smile disappeared.

Big Mac trotted arrogantly around the arena, looking for the out-gate or another victim, either one. He found one, and exited the arena.

Wiley's air found its way back into his lungs and he tried to sit up.

"Just lay here, Wiley," said Sonny Joe. "Where do ya hurt?"

"I'm O.K.," Wiley told him. "My back's just gonna be a little sore for awhile." He winced with pain as he sat up on his own. "My ribs, too."

"They broke?" asked Sonny.

"I don't think so," Wiley answered.

"Can ya walk outta here?"

Wiley clasped Sonny Joe's hand and let him help him to his feet. "Yeah."

Before helping Wiley from the arena, Sonny Joe looked him in the eye and said, "You were ridin' him like a champ. I'm proud of ya." He took his young friend behind the chutes where someone had laid a trash barrel on its side for Wiley to sit on. He then walked over to where Scotty was waiting at his pickup.

For an uneasy moment, neither one said anything.

Then Sonny Joe spoke, "You didn't lie. He's one helluva bull."

"Well," Scotty returned, "yer cowboy ain't no slouch, either."

After another awkward pause, Sonny Joe said, "My banker likes me. I'm gonna go see him in the mornin'. You'll have yer twenty thousand by Tuesday at the latest. You wanna hang on to Big Mac 'til then?"

"Hell, Sonny," said Scotty, "I trust ya. Might as well leave him here now, as haulin' him home and then back again."

The two shook hands, and Scotty got in his pickup and drove out of the yard.

For nearly a week, Sonny Joe kept his new bull penned up and on a strict diet of a high protein food ration consisting of silage, dry corn, and molasses. He thought about hauling him down to the

Beaumont Rodeo, with the rest of his 'A' team', but decided against it. Big Mac was only a two-year-old, and although big for his age, he was not a mature bull. Let him wait a year, Sonny decided, before taking him into the big leagues. At his tender age, he might not handle the road-miles well. If the traveling affected his bucking performance, he could start getting ridden often, and spurred, which, at this stage of his life, could possibly drive the desire to buck away from him and ruin him for life.

So for the first days, Big Mac stood alone in his pen, sleeping, eating his high-ration feed, peering over the fence at the grazing meadow where he would rather be, and staring back at Sonny Joe when he would come visiting in the evenings to just size up the bull, study and admire him.

Then, one morning Sonny Joe showed up, like he did every morning, only this time without the usual bucket of feed that he poured into the trough from over the fence. Instead of feeding the bull, he opened the gate to the pen, and stood behind it. Big Mac looked at his trough. No feed. He looked through the open gateway to the meadow. Sonny Joe waited patiently while the bull thought over the situation. When he finally ambled from his pen out into the pasture, Sonny Joe quietly shut the gate behind him and went on about his business.

Big Mac did not walk far from the corrals. He did not need to – there was plenty of grazing right there. He grazed on the lush prairie hay until the sun was high above. Then he stopped and looked around. It was time for water. He strolled across the pasture, directly away from Sonny Joe's arena and corrals, until a worn cow trail intercepted his course and he followed it for nearly a mile to a winding creek shaded by huge budding oak trees. He ignored the water snake slithering through the mud to get out of his way, and the song of the whippoorwill accompanying the bull as he lumbered to the middle of the shallow flowing stream. He drank slow and leisurely, and when he was done drinking, he just stood there in the cool water, batting at the flies with his long, drooping ears, and swatting them off his rump with his tail. Finally, he slowly trudged out of the water, through the mud, to the knee-deep grass that encompassed the winding trail of water. A huge gray oak tree reached skyward and spread its leaves wide. Big Mac grunted a sigh as he lay down beside it and, with a cool spring breeze on his face, went to sleep.

When he awoke, the shade of the giant oak had moved behind him. The whippoorwill still sang to him from above and magpies called to each other in the distance. He paid them no mind. Through the softly rustling leaves he heard some sloshing about in the creek upstream. He raised his head and looked around. From his vantage point he could see little more than grass and trees. He slowly rose to his feet. A hundred yards upstream, around the bend of the creek, Big Mac saw another of his own kind. He bellowed at the bull. The bull bellowed back and so did another bull, one that was hidden in the trees. And then another one. Big Mac started walking toward the bulls. Before he got there he spotted another bull standing on the creek bank. Then a couple of them lounging in the water, and another one scratching his rear against the rough bark of an old oak tree. He stopped and looked across the creek. A whole herd of bulls, of different colors, shapes and sizes, dotted the meadowed hillside. One of them from the creek came up to look him over. Big Mac lowered his head and dug up a clump of grass from below his nose. He was glad to be with more like him, but they had better keep their distance. The bull heeded his warning and stopped. The other bull–the first one Big Mac had seen – tried to sneak up on him from the flank. Big Mac whirled around and gave him the same warning. Then, with his back turned away from the bull from the creek, that one moved toward Big Mac again. Big Mac waited until the bull was close enough and spun around and clubbed him in the neck with a horn. The bull let out a short cry and galloped back down to the creek, so Big Mac did what came natural – he chased him. The bull stopped in the middle of the creek and looked over his back. When he saw Big Mac loping down the creek bank at him, he darted up the other side and hightailed it into the thick of the herd. Big Mac splashed through the water and stayed after the bull until he was about halfway through the herd. There he saw something that made him stop in his tracks.

It was a dark-red, wide horned Watusi-Brahma cross bull, standing directly in his path, staring him down. To the rest of the herd, this bull was known as the leader. He decided where they grazed, where and when they drank, and he was always the first to drink. The leader didn't go around anyone. The biggest, baddest bulls stepped aside when the leader came through. To the rodeo world he was known as Triple Zeros – the infamous Genghis Khan, the most treacherous, dangerous bucking bull going down the road. A bad chute fighter, quick as a cat, meaner than hell, who liked to hook riders from his back with his extra long horns. Bullriders hated to draw up on him, and most turned him out, ever since he'd killed a cowboy named Bennett McKinney over two years before in Houston, Texas.

Although Big Mac had no recollection of ever seeing the bull before, he stood motionless in panic-stricken fear. Genghis bellowed to him. He did not answer. The older Watusi-cross bull outweighed the young Brahma by four hundred pounds. He ripped at the grass with his front hooves and tossed it behind him while Big Mac remained still. He lowered his head and charged. Big Mac's eyes widened as he attempted to spin around and run. Genghis rammed him broadside with enough force to knock him to the ground and roll him completely over. Big Mac struggled to get to his feet, and was almost there when one of Genghis' big club horns bashed him in the hip, sending him to the grass again. The impact had spun him around so that he lay on his belly, directly facing his attacker. He looked up and saw Genghis not ten feet in front of him. He closed his eyes, lowered his head and braced himself for the impact...but it never came. He peeked up at Genghis. The big bull held his fighting stance, his head low, and snorted as he dared Big Mac to get up. Big Mac bellowed a helpless call for help. The other bulls never looked up from their grazing. The two stared each other down. Big Mac had fear in his eyes. Genghis Khan had no fear. Sheer exuberance shone from his eyes. Violent, aggressive exhilaration. Like a high noon showdown, the underdog knew he had to make his move. He bolted to his feet. Genghis charged. The thud of their heads crashing could be heard a mile away. For the first time ever, Big Mac saw stars and felt like his neck had been jammed all the way back to his hips. His legs wobbled as he backed up. Again, Genghis stood his ground, this time his legs in a wider stance and they, too, seemed to be a little shaky, and his head was bobbing, like he was waving it at little fluttering stars that did not exist.

Big Mac whirled around and ran toward the creek, never looking back to see if he was being followed. When he got to the creek, he sloshed across it, climbed up the other side and kept going. He found the trail leading back to Sonny Joe's corrals. He never stopped running until he had made it to the closed gate of his pen. By that time, his tongue hung limp from his mouth, his entire body was wet with sweat, and snot and saliva ran freely. It was over an hour until his breathing slowed to normal. He stood in that one spot, his head hanging low, the rest of the afternoon, and all through the night.

Chapter 17: May 1990

"Hey, Terry! I don't think the people here in Bakersfield, California, are too smart!" Rodeo clown Shot Palmer's voice reverberated through the speakers and across the arena and grandstands, thanks to his brand new wireless microphone headset. It had cost him over six hundred dollars and was well worth it. Now he didn't have to yell his jokes up for the announcer to repeat.

"You don't think these people here are smart?" the announcer replied, between calf-roping runs. "Now, Shot, that's no way to talk about the good people of Bakersfield."

"Well, it's just that when I was drivin' down the road yesterday, I seen a cowboy ridin' his horse across the pasture, and he was holdin' his hand over his eye, like this."

"Holding his hand over his eye?" the announcer followed along. "Was he injured?"

"Well, that's what I wondered," continued Shot. "I pulled over and hollered to him, 'Hey? You hurt?' He says 'No.' I says, 'Then how come you got yer hand coverin' yer eye?' He says, 'Cause, the boss sent me out here to look for an old black cow with one eye!' "

The joke drew a little laughter from the packed stands of southern California, but not the loud enthusiastic belly laughs he expected, so he tried again. "I drove a little farther and seen two guys workin' along side the road. One guy was diggin' holes with a post-hole digger and the other'n was behind him fillin' the holes back up!"

The announcer, of course, played the straight man. "That doesn't make a lot of sense, Shot. Why were they doing that?"

"Well, that's what I wondered," Shot went on, "I pulled over and hollered, 'Hey! How come yer diggin' them holes and this other feller's fillin' 'em in?' He says, 'Well, we're part of a three-man fence buildin' crew, and the man who puts the posts in the holes is out sick today!' "

That one got less response than the first one. Shot began to think the wireless microphones aren't so great after all. At least before, when his jokes wouldn't go over good, he could blame the announcer for not relaying them right.

One man who was laughing was T.J. Jergenson, as he watched from behind the bucking chutes. He slapped his buddy, Randy Corey, on the back and exclaimed, "I never heard that last one before! Where does he come up with that stuff?"

Randy was not listening to the jokes nor watching the calf roping. He was watching the blue sky fade to orange as the sun slowly set over the Sierra Madre Mountains. A cool breeze sifted in from the San Joaquin Valley and carried the stirred-up dust slowly to the south end of the arena. Randy was competing that night in both the saddle bronc riding and the steer wrestling, and was finding it difficult to meditate with T.J. constantly nudging him in the ribs and saying things like, "Did you hear that last joke? That sonuvagun gets funnier every time I hear it!"

"Hey, Terry!" Shot Palmer's voice amplified from the loudspeaker. "Whattaya call a good-lookin' woman in Bakersfield?"

"Oh, listen to this," T.J. told Randy. "It's a good'un!"

"...a tourist!"

T.J. doubled over with laughter.

Randy smiled – more at T.J. than at the joke.

"Man!" T.J. simmered to a chuckle. "Ol' Shot's on a roll tonight!"

"On a roll?" Randy was quick to disagree. "Yer the only one laughin'!"

T.J. looked around. "By God, yer right...That's because I'm among a bunch of fun-haters! Where's Whitney? He'd enjoy this!"

Dave Whitney was sitting above a back-pen fence, studying the bucking horse he would be getting on later that evening. He had seen the horse buck a few weeks before at Oakdale, and was confident he could win the rodeo on him.

Dave also had looked over the bulls. Although he had lost his desire to ride bulls after he got on his first one years ago, he was always around to pull T.J.'s rope, and he knew the names and characteristics of all of Sonny Joe Barker's older bulls. He had found the bull that T.J. was to get on that night – number forty-four, a small, high-kicking spinner called Magnum. He saw a few bulls that he did not recognize. One of them that really stood out was a large gray Brahma bull. A majestic-looking beast with wide shoulders, a big hump, perfectly shaped upturned horns and piercing eyes that followed Dave everywhere he went. That bull, Dave noticed, was not branded in the same manner that the other ones were. While the rest of the herd had numbered brands on their rumps, this one had a BM imprinted on his right shoulder.

Then Dave saw the bull that he hated the most. More than anything alive – Triple Zeros, Genghis Khan.

The color of dried blood, he stood alone at one end of the pen as the rest of the bulls crowded the other. Dave's mouth became dry and his eyes hardened with contempt as he watched the despicable monster rubbing a deadly horn back and forth against a steel pipe fence-post as if he were sharpening it in anticipation of another kill. As Dave glared at the bull, his mind's eye brought the vision of Bennett lying limp and lifeless on the arena floor. He saw T.J. slumping over Bennett's dead body, fighting for his breath as his tears dripped onto Bennett's face, mixing with his blood. Most of all, he saw the stagnant look in Bennett's eyes, a look that he wished he could at least put in the back of his mind. After three years, that same, non-existing stare was so real, so repulsively fresh, so vivid and close, that he felt like he was back in Houston, in that coliseum, at that time. Cold chills hit his entire body at once, and sweat beads clung to his pale, white face. He saw this sickening vision over and over and...

"Hey!"

...He snapped back to here and now.

"You O.K., man?"

Dave turned partway around. It was a black-hatted cowboy that he didn't know. "Y...yeah, I'm O.K."

"You look like you seen a ghost!" the cowboy observed.

Dave blinked and looked away.

"You know these bulls?" the stranger asked.

"Most of 'em," Dave answered.

"Which one is Big Foot?"

Dave peered over the herd. "See that big black Braymer? That's him. He's a good'un. Goes both ways." Then he announced proudly, "I seen Bennett McKinney win Houston on him."

"Alright. Thanks, bud."

Dave looked solemnly at the ground. "About ten minutes before he got killed," he murmured.

He got down from the fence and walked over behind the chutes. There his saddle sat, upright, beside Randy's, rosined and ready to go. The broncs would be loaded soon, and the two of them could saddle up. He strolled down the fence line, past countless cowboys just sitting around, telling stories, relaxing or psyching up for their coming event.

"Got a good'un, Dave?" one of them looked up and asked.

"I think so," said Dave, as he walked by. "Crazy Snake."

"Stick it on her," encouraged the cowboy.

He stepped up on the platform, where Randy Corey was watching the calf roping and T.J. was laughing and carrying on as if he didn't have a care in the world, let alone a bull to twist later tonight.

T.J. laid a long arm across Dave's shoulder and quizzed, "Hey, whattaya call a good-lookin' woman in Bakersfield?"

"Heard it," was Dave's reply

"O.K.," said T.J., "This one ol' boy is ridin' out across a pasture with one hand over his eye..."

"Heard it," interrupted Dave.

T.J. didn't even slow down. "One guy's diggin' a hole along the highway and another guy's..."

"Heard it! Jesus Christ, T.J., I been watchin' Shot for eight years now. I know every joke he's ever told!"

"That one about the guy with his hand over his eye," T.J. protested, "is a new one."

Dave rolled his eyes. "I told it to him!"

"Oh," T.J. conceded. "Well...it ain't very funny, anyhow," and turned his attention to the arena.

"Sheesh!" Dave said to Randy, "Where'd we get him?"

"I don't know," laughed Randy. "But I wish you'd take him back. Didja find yer horse?"

"Yeah, I sized her up. Looked at the bulls, too. Found yours, T.J. Forty-four, Magnum. Have you see him?"

"Ain't been back to look at him," T.J. answered. "But I know him."

"Ol' Sonny's got some new stuff back there," Dave commented. "There's one big gray Braymer that looks like he'd be pretty waspy. He's a rank-lookin' sonuvagun."

"What do they call him?" T.J. asked, without turning his attention from the arena.

"I don't know," returned Dave. "He didn't even have a number on his butt – just a BM on his shoulder."

Both T.J. and Randy's faces went blank.

"Wha'd you say?" Randy asked, certain that he must have heard wrong the first time.

"I said he didn't..."

Suddenly, Dave was grabbed by the collar and slammed up against the slide gate. T.J., still clutching his collar, had his fist pressed tight against Dave's throat. "Don't you *ever, ever* mess with me like that again!" was T.J.'s warning.

Dave looked up into T.J.'s eyes and could see he meant business. With a fist against his throat, he could barely breathe and did not attempt to speak. T.J. slowly let go and eased the pressure off of Dave's throat, but held his stare in Dave's face.

Dave's voice was slightly hoarse when he began to speak. "What the hell was that all about?"

When T.J. refused to speak, Randy admonished, "That wasn't funny, Dave."

"What wasn't funny?" Dave demanded, "Wha'd I say?"

Jergenson's chest heaved slightly now as he breathed. Dave had never seen a more deadly serious look in his eyes – not even when he was about to nod his head on a bull. "Just don't do it again!" he cautioned for the second time.

"You better tell me what the hell is goin' on here!" asserted Dave.

"I'll take yer head off!" T.J. threatened.

Randy squeezed between the two. "Hey, guys," he said as he pushed them apart, "just leave it alone."

Dave sidestepped around the slide gate and backed up. "What's the matter with you, Jergenson?"

"Easy, T.J.," Randy calmed as he kept his body between them. "He didn't mean nothin' by it."

T.J. just stared for a while. Then, slowly, he detached his eyes from Dave and looked around. A few cowboys had gathered. Some prepared to break up the fight between the best of friends, if need be, and others just watching the potential excitement. As his heart and breathing rate slowly dropped, T.J. backed up a step, raised his palms in a surrender fashion, said "O.K.," and turned and walked away.

Randy turned and faced Dave, who was staring back, speechless and dumbfounded. Randy gave him a disgusted glance, stepped around him and began walking in the other direction.

Dave followed. "Come here!" he ordered as he grabbed Randy by the arm.

Randy spun around, "I don't think we should talk right now!" he snapped.

"Corey," Dave implored in desperate confusion, "somebody has got to tell me what is goin' on!"

A look of bewilderment slowly transformed Randy's face. He suddenly realized that Dave was not playing a sick joke on them after all, but honestly did not know what was going on. "Dave," he said, trying to figure things out as he spoke, "you really don't know about the BM?"

Dave let go of Randy's arm. "I know there's a bull back there with a BM brand on his shoulder," he replied.

"Dave, if you're screwin' with my head, *please* don't do that," Randy implored.

"Corey, I ain't screwin' with nobody's head. What's got into you guys?"

"Show him to me," Randy demanded.

"Huh?" Dave grunted, still as confused as ever.

"Where's that bull with the BM brand?"

"He's back there in the bullpen," Dave answered.

"Let's go," ordered Randy as he headed that way.

They walked past the line of lounging cowboys, around the corner, and climbed to the top of the bullpen fence.

"O.K.," asked Randy, "Where is he?"

"See that tall gray Braymer over there?" Dave pointed out, "That's him."

"I don't see no brand on him," Randy scoffed.

"It's on the other shoulder," said Dave. "Go around, if ya don't believe me."

Corey crawled off the fence and walked around to the far side of the pen. He peered between the planks of the wooden fence at the bull's right shoulder. His mouth dropped open and his whole body felt numb as he saw Bennett McKinney's initials imprinted into the bull's thick gray hide. He stood up straight, and as his eyes stared past the sky and horizon, his mind traveled back in time to that night at the Rapid City Holiday Inn, when Bennett had peeled his shirt off, revealing a simple BM tattoo on his right bicep. "If you ever see a bull with a BM brand on the right shoulder," Bennett declared, "you'll know it's me."

"There," said Dave as he hopped down from the fence. "Now, are you satisfied?"

Randy didn't know what to say. He looked at Dave. Then at the brand and then back at Dave again.

Dave walked around the pen, over to Randy. "What's wrong?" he asked with a concerned demeanor.

"Dave," Randy spoke slowly as he backtracked through his mind, "do you remember that night in Rapid City..." He stopped to gather his thoughts.

"Which night in Rapid City?" asked Dave. "The night I whupped that smart-ass race car driver in the hot tub?"

"No, not that night..."

"He had it comin,'" Dave continued. "He kept tryin' to mother up to the girl I was with."

"I'm not talkin' about that night..."

"B'sides, I had to whup him. He said race car drivers are tougher than cowboys and there was a bunch of people around and I was afraid they'd believe it."

"I'm talkin' about a different night..."

"It ain't my fault he got all that blood in the hot..."

"Whitney, will you shut up for a second?" Randy impatiently cut in. "I ain't talkin' about when you whupped the guy in the hot tub! Do you remember the time...?"

"The time that ol' drunk fell down the stairs three times and me and T.J. kept helpin' him back up?" Dave laughed as he slapped Randy on the back.

"No, not that time either!" scolded Randy. "Whitney, does everything you ever remember happen after the rodeo? Don't you ever remember what happened during the rodeo?"

"Oh," Whitney conceded. "Did this happen during the rodeo?"

"Well, no," admitted Randy. "This happened after the rodeo."

"Was it the time you and Shot picked up them chicks and yers was married to a city cop?" Dave quizzed.

"No!" hollered Randy. "Damnit, just listen!...Remember when T.J. got busted for indecent exposure and drivin' without a license by that black lady cop?"

"Yeah, I remember that."

"O.K., then," said Randy, "Remember the night before?"

Dave thought for a moment, "No."

"Come on," coaxed Randy, "you remember the night before."

"No, I don't, Randy," declared Dave.

"Yes, you do," Randy implored. "It was about three years ago."

Dave thought hard and said, "Sorry, man, I don't remember the night before."

"You gotta remember, Dave. Bennett was showin' us his tattoo and..." Suddenly, it came back to him. "...Of *course* you don't remember! You were passed out!"

"I was?"

Corey looked back at the brand on the bull's shoulder. "Dave," he said, "I got a story to tell you. It was a couple of months before Bennett got killed. I remember now, you were passed out on the bed right beside him when he showed us his tattoo."

"Tattoo?"

"Uh-huh," Randy turned his attention back to Dave. "A BM on his right arm. He said that when he dies, he's gonna come back as a Braymer bull. Well, we all said he was fulla shit, and he showed us his BM tattoo and said if he dies first and if we ever seen a bull with a BM brand on the right shoulder, it'd be him."

After a pause, Dave said disbelievingly, "Reincarnation?"

They looked at the brand together.

"That's why T.J. went off on ya," explained Randy. "I guess we all figured you knew about it, too." He looked at Dave. "Whattaya think?"

Whitney's eyes wandered from the brand to the rest of the bull. He looked up at the massive hump and majestic horns. He saw the proud stance, piercing eyes and the loose-skin dewlap flowing from his neck and chest. In quiet amazement he said, "He doesn't even look like Bennett."

"Of course he doesn't look like Bennett," said Randy. "Whadja expect – glasses and a big nose?"

Dave didn't answer the question. Instead he said, "This is too weird for me. I'm gittin' outta here," and headed back for the bucking chutes.

"Wait for me!" Randy ordered his little buddy as he hurried behind him. "We gotta tell T.J., ya know."

"No, *you* gotta tell T.J.," corrected Dave, not even looking back. "He 'bout beat the hell outta me last time I mentioned them letters."

By then, Sonny Joe and his chute help were loading bucking horses and Randy's bronc was in her chute.

"Let's saddle up," said Randy as he lifted his saddle from the ground and laid it on the platform. As he grabbed his headstall and hopped up on the platform, he asked Dave, "You think T.J.'ll be back to help us on our broncs?"

"I dunno. He was pretty fired up when he left," replied Dave, as he crawled over the fence into the arena. "My horse is still in the backpens. I'll be able to help ya."

As Randy slipped his headstall over his bronc's nose and buckled it securely over her head, he asked, "Do you think it could really be Bennett?"

Whitney hesitated to answer the question. Finally, in a philosophical tone, he said, "Yeah...yeah, I think it could be...Do you?"

Corey picked up his saddle. He, too, thought about it for a few seconds before answering, "Naw," and lowered his saddle down on his horse's back.

Dave snugged up the saddle's front cinch and buckled its back cinch around the mare's belly. "Me neither," he offered.

Just then Shot Palmer snuck up and poked Whitney in the ribs. With his microphone turned off, he encouraged, "Ride up, you guys."

"You know it," agreed Randy, before asking, "Hey, do you know any of Sonny Joe's new bulls?"

"I ain't seen nothin' of Sonny's since last November," said Shot.

"Didja notice anything strange about one of 'em?"

"How strange?" asked Shot.

"*Real* strange," answered Dave.

"Not that I can think of. Why?"

"We got a *big* surprise for you," Dave predicted.

"Well, I'll be ready for him," declared Shot as he walked away.

"Maybe," Randy said to himself, "and maybe not." He turned around to see Sonny Joe Barker dropping a wool-covered leather flankstrap over his bucking horse's haunches.

"You got a good little bronc here," Sonny commented to Randy. "Ride her right and she'll take you to the pay window."

Ignoring Sonny's words of encouragement, Randy inquired, "Sonny, where'd ya get the gray Braymer with the BM brand?"

"Ol' Big Mac? Bought him from Scotty Redwood, a little over a year ago. Paid twenty thousand for him."

"Twenty thousand?" Whitney exclaimed as he crawled back over the chute. "For Bennett?"

Sonny Joe gave him a strange eye.

"Where'd Scotty get him?" Randy interrogated. "Do ya know?"

"He bought him from Mike and Brad Fanner, up in Nebraska," revealed Sonny Joe. "I don't know where they got him. How come you bronc busters suddenly took an interest in my bull?"

"Oh, no reason," Corey lied, not wanting Sonny to suspect that he was crazy, stupid or both. "He just kinda caught my eye."

"That bull catches alotta eyes," Sonny said proudly. "Just wait 'til you see him buck!"

"I can hardly wait!" Randy assured him.

Moments later Randy and Dave rode their broncs, and successfully, without the help of T.J. Jergenson. Shortly after the bronc riding, T.J. showed up behind the chutes and began working rosin into his bull rope and glove.

As Randy exited to the timed-event side of the arena to compete in the steer wrestling, Dave leaned against the fence and pondered on whether or not he should try again to tell T.J. about the BM brand on the side of the mysterious new bull. Hell no, he decided. He'd almost gotten his butt kicked the first time he tried. Let T.J. find out for himself.

He tried to watch the rodeo for awhile, but just couldn't get the brand, and the story that Randy had told him, out of his mind. No wonder T.J. was so shook up.

"Hey, T.J.," he offered. "You gonna need a hand gettin' down on yer bull?"

T.J. looked over at his comrade. "Yeah, I will." Like Dave, he felt the tension in the air. He felt bad about losing his temper earlier, but he meant every word he said and was not about to apologize. "Will you pull my rope?"

"You bet," said Dave as he nervously shoved his hands into his pockets.

"By the way," added T.J., "you made a damn nice ride tonight. I was watchin' over by the concession stand."

Dave's wide eyes smiled. "Thanks, buddy."

The announcer's voice rambled obliviously above their heads until a familiar name caught their attention. "Randy Corey backs his horse into the box..."

The two walked over to the fence to watch.

"Randy hails from Monticello, Idaho," the announcer went on. "He needs to be faster than five-point-four to take the lead in the round..."

Randy nodded his head. The front chute gate sprang open and the eight-hundred-pound steer bolted into the arena on a dead run. The borrowed horse that Corey rode quickly caught up and ran beside the steer as his rider slid from the saddle and grabbed the fleeing steer by the horns. Randy let his feet drop to the ground and his heels slid though the dirt in front of him as he brought the steer to a halt. Then he arched in his back, twisted the steer's nose to the sky, and pried until the steer was lying in the dirt with all four feet in the air.

"Yeah!" T.J. yelled out enthusiastically.

"That was a fast time!" exclaimed Whitney. "Way to go, Corey!"

Randy let his steer up and then picked himself up from the ground and walked back to the doggin' box as he dusted the front of his shirt off with his hands.

"Listen to this, folks, we have a new leader!" reported the announcer. "Randy Corey bailed off his horse and threw that steer to the ground in a time of four and one-tenth seconds, ladies and gentlemen!"

Corey tipped his dusty brown felt hat to the cheering crowd.

"Alright!" approved T.J. as he walked back to his gear bag and bullrope.

Dave leaned against the fence and grinned over Randy's winning steer wrestling run. Hopefully, they'd all three pick up a pretty good check that night. He peered over his shoulder and could see that T.J. was still smiling and joking with the other bullriders as he knelt to strap on his spurs. Now might be a good time, Dave considered, to show Jergenson the gray Braymer, and let him see for himself. He's got to find out sooner or later...Naw, let it be later. Why mess with his head before he crawls on Magnum? Show him afterwards. Sonny Joe should be loading bulls any time...

His thoughts were interrupted by the sound of bull bells clanging as bullriders anxiously carried their bullropes to the just-filled bucking chutes.

He hurried to T.J.'s side. "Yer bull in yet?"

"He ain't in the chute," answered T.J. as he strapped on his flashy red chaps. "But he's in the back alley, three or four bulls back. A little black muley. He's standin' behind a big gray Braymer."

"Gray Braymer?" Dave said aloud. He looked to the back alley past the hustling cowboys. Sure enough, Forty-four Magnum was standing right behind the BM bull.

T.J. gathered up his bullrope and headed for his bull. "Got a hook?" he asked his assistant.

"No, but I'll get one," Whitney replied. He grabbed a long rebar hook hanging on the fence and crawled over the alley as T.J. straddled the bull with the support of the rails on either side and lowered the bell and loop of his bullrope down the right side of Magnum.

Dave snatched the loop with his hook and pulled it to him underneath the bull's belly and, hand over hand through the rails, climbed it up Magnum's left side until T.J. could reach it and string the tail of his bullrope through. T.J. then slid the bell and loop so that they were directly under the bull's belly.

"Look alright?" Jergenson asked from above.

Dave inspected the placement of the loop. "Looks alright."

T.J. pulled the rope up snug and tucked the tail securely under the hand-hold, climbed down from the alley and walked over to his gear bag, where he began stretching exercises and pre-playing his ride through his mind.

Left standing alone, Dave tried not to think about or look at the big gray Brahma standing in front of Magnum. Surely it was just a coincidence. Or maybe somebody was playing a sick joke on all of them. Sonny Joe would never do a thing like that. Shot Palmer? No way. Those guys loved Bennett too much to pull such a stunt. Maybe the brand wasn't even there. Maybe Dave was just seeing things. Maybe it was temporary insanity for all the whiskey he'd been drinking all those years. But if that was the case, how could Randy Corey have seen the brand? He didn't even drink.

Dave walked up beside the bull and stared at the brand. He rubbed his eyes and looked again. His hand trembled slightly as he reached through the rail and touched the initials.

"Bennett?" he whispered.

The bull snorted, wallowed from side to side and then butted the bull in front of him.

Just then, a young cowboy crawled over the bull, rope in hand. "You know this bull?" he asked.

Whitney's first instinct was to say yes, he knew him well. He looked up at the cowboy. "Nope," he answered, "never seen him before," and walked away.

By the time Dave made his way over to where Jergenson was, Randy was already there.

"There he is!" Dave grinned as he walked toward his friend. "You doggin' sonuvagun!"

"I drew a pretty nice steer," Corey said modestly as he reached out to accept the congratulatory handshake from Dave. Although he tried not to show it, Randy was slightly embarrassed when Dave passed up the handshake and embraced him. "Easy there, cowboy," he blushed, "I don't want nobody to get the wrong idea!"

"I'm proud a' ya, buddy," said Dave when he let go, "and I need to talk to ya," his eyes motioned, "over here."

The two of them stepped away from T.J.

"Didja see where Jergenson's bull is?" Dave quietly asked Randy.

"Yeah," he answered, "right in front of...you know."

"Man, this is just too weird for me, Randy," confessed Dave. "What are we gonna do?"

"Well, for now," advised Randy, "I don't think we should say anything to T.J. about it. I'm afraid it'll screw with his mind, and he don't need that before he gets on his bull."

"That's what I was thinkin'," Whitney agreed. "I just hope he doesn't see the brand before his ride. I gotta admit, Randy, this thing is screwin' with my mind."

"Me too, a little," said Corey. "But me and you didn't let it mess with us 'til we was done competin'. Hell, maybe T.J.'d be alright with it."

"Maybe," said Dave dubiously. "But I doubt it."

"I guess there ain't nothin' we can do about it if he does,' Randy commented. "To tell you the truth, I'd rather he seen it for hisself than for me to hafta tell him."

"We ain't gonna tell him," Dave corrected as he crossed his arms. "We're gonna show him. Shot's gonna shit his pants, too, when he sees it. He don't know nothin' about it yet, either."

"That's right," Randy realized, "and as goofy as he is anyway, he's *really* liable to go off!"

"Man, this ain't gonna be good," Dave feared. He glanced over his shoulder and did not see T.J. "Hey, where's Jergenson?"

Randy looked both ways. "I didn't even see him leave."

Saying nothing, they hurried over to where Magnum and BM were waiting patiently. Seeing no sign of T.J., they both hopped up on the rail and peered over the other side of the alley.

T.J. lay semiconscious on the ground while the cowboy who had asked Dave about the big gray bull fanned him with his hat.

Dave and Randy bailed over the alley.

"You O.K.?" asked Dave as he knelt beside T.J. and lifted his head from the ground.

T.J.'s eyes rolled and he muttered incomprehensibly.

"Relax, T.J., breathe deep." Randy put his hand on T.J.'s chest and asked the cowboy, "What happened?"

"He was helpin' me put my bullrope on," the stranger said. "All of a sudden he stood up straight, said he bent somethin', and fell over backwards!"

"Bent somethin'?" asked Corey. "Bent what?"

"I dunno. He just said he bent it and passed out!"

"Bennett?" asked Dave.

"Yeah, bent it!"

Dave and Randy looked at each other and said, "He's seen the brand!"

T.J.'s mumblings slowly became understandable. "Bennett..."

"You're alright, T.J.," Randy assured. "Now, tell me what happened."

"I saw Bennett," slurred T.J.

"Where?" asked Randy.

"There!" T.J. answered as he pointed to the BM brand. "Help me up, guys."

Dave and Randy stood him upright and steadied him as he made his way to a fence to lean on.

As the color began to fade back into Jergenson's complexion, he said to Dave, "Man, I'm sorry I got so mad at ya earlier, buddy."

"I understand," Whitney accepted. "I s'pose I woulda done the same thing. The important thing for you right now is to forget about them initials and just ride this little black bull."

"Right," agreed T.J., his mind still a little cloudy. "I won't even think about them initials."

"Attaboy!" said Dave. "You better relax for awhile. The bullridin' is comin' up purty quick."

"I'm just gonna relax, then," T.J. confirmed, almost as if he were intoxicated, as his buddies helped him over the alley. "And I ain't even gonna think about them initials."

"You sure yer O.K.?" asked Corey.

"Yeah, I'm O.K.," T.J. answered. "I just need to rest a minute, get my blood pumpin'."

His legs grew steadier as he walked to the end of the chutes. He suddenly felt a burst of energy within. "Hey, I'm feelin' good now, boys," he announced. "I think I just need to walk around for awhile."

He looked like he was doing alright, so the boys let him be. He paced alone behind the chutes. He sized up his bull, Forty-four Magnum, in his mind. He imagined himself on the bull, spinning hard to the left, his right arm pumping vigorously over his head. His train of thought was interrupted as the BM brand flashed through his memory. He thought hard about Magnum, switching directions and spinning the other way, kicking high above his head. Again, the BM imprinted itself foremost in Jergenson's mind. He stopped.

He restarted his ride on Magnum from the beginning, complete from the head nod and the swinging gate to the explosive first jump from the chute, when his mind switched channels to Bennett McKinney taking off his shirt in the motel room, revealing his simple BM tattoo.

"Damn," T.J. said aloud. He concentrated on Magnum. He pictured the bull in his mind. He felt the bull bucking and twisting beneath him. He heard Bennett's voice: "If you ever see a bull with a BM brand on the right shoulder, you'll know it's me." T.J.'s face contorted as he stopped in his tracks, clenched his fists and closed his eyes. It was no use. The harder he tried not to think about the brand or the tattoo, the more vivid they became in his head.

He looked around. There was Sonny Joe Barker at the flank of his first bull to buck tonight. Maybe a little conversation would keep T.J.'s mind off of...you know.

He stepped up on the platform and sidled up next to Sonny Joe. "Howdy, Sonny," he greeted. "How ya doin'?

"Good, T.J.," returned Sonny as he watched the last barrel racer enter the arena and charge her horse for the first barrel. "How you been? Ya been beatin' 'em?"

"Best year ever, so far."

"I'm glad to hear it. Wha'd ya draw up on tonight?"

"Magnum."

"You'll like him," assured Sonny Joe. "They win alotta rodeos on him. He's quick and real flashy, 'cause he kicks so high and spins so tight, but he ain't got the power to throw off the tough riders." He leaned in close to T.J. and vouched quietly with a wink, "You'll win this rodeo on him."

"Alright," Jergenson grinned. "That's what I like to hear."

As the barrel racer exited the arena and the rodeo committee men came to haul the barrels out, Sonny Joe mentioned, "Hey, I got a new bull that's fixin' to be the star of the string before long."

"Ya do?"

"Yeah, I call him Big Mac," Sonny Joe went on. "The buckin'est critter I've ever owned." He pointed over his shoulder with his thumb. "Big gray Braymer in the alley, there. He's got a BM brand on his right shoulder. Wait 'til you see him buck!"

"I gotta go," said T.J., without hesitation, as he walked away.

"Are you folks ready for some bullriding?" urged the announcer to the cheering crowd. "Well, that's good, because we've got some of the toughest bulls and bullriders in the country here tonight. First I want to introduce to you folks the man without who this rodeo would not be possible. He owns not only the bulls and bucking horses you've seen perform tonight, but also the roping calves and the steer wrestling steers. Please, give a nice, big, southern California welcome to the founder, owner and president of the Stingin' B Rodeo Company, Mister Sonny Joe Barker!"

Sonny Joe tipped his gray Stetson to the appreciative crowd and then snugged up the soft cotton flankrope around the first bull's haunches.

"And the next man I'd like to introduce, well, you've already met," the announcer went on. "You know him as the funny man of the rodeo arena, but this part of his job is as serious as a heart attack. Here he is: the cowboy protector, Shot Palmer!"

Shot trotted into the arena, this time without his wireless headphone, and thanked the enthusiastic crowd with a tip of his little black derby.

The first bull set to go, Shot knew well – a small one-horned Hereford cross. "Let me open the gate on this one," Shot said to the gateman at the latch, "'cause I gotta grab him right here, as he comes outta the box."

The gateman gave Shot his position and took a seat on top of the fence.

Shot watched intently through the rails as the rider wrapped the tail of his rope around his hand and slid to his bullrope. As soon as the rider nodded his head, Shot threw the gate open, stepped toward the bull, grabbed his horn and yelled his name. "Stubby!" The bull lunged into the air and slung his head in Shot's direction. Shot let go, stepped back and yelled again, "Stubby!" Automatically, the little bull stayed hooked in that direction, and went into a spin.

For the first few seconds, the bullrider stayed in the middle of Stubby's back, eventually slipping ever so slightly to the outside of the spin. Suddenly centrifugal force began to tug on his upper body. He scratched and clawed with his inside spur and pumped urgently over his head. It was too late, for he had neither the strength or agility to fight his way back to the middle of Stubby's back. With his left hand clinging to the bullrope, the rider was flying off of the right side of the spinning bull. As the rider parted company, realizing he had just lost, he was jerked back to the bull, and swung around the outside of the spin.

He was hung up. His bullrope had rolled forward over his fingers, twisting the wrap tight around his hand, making it impossible to let go. As the bull spun tight and the rider was slung around him at the end of his arm, it was next to impossible for Shot to get to the tail of the bullrope. He hollered at the bull and grabbed his one horn again, hoping to bring Stubby out of the spin, so that he could have a chance to get in and grab the rope. The bull yanked his horn from his hand and kept right on spinning.

Shot stepped back, but not enough to miss the cowboy's knees as they swung around and knocked him to the ground. Bouncing to his feet, he knew that he must make a bold move and that he must do it now. As the bull continued to spin, Shot waited until his back hooves slashed through the air inches from his face, and then he dove for the middle of his back. Just as he clenched the loose tail of the bullrope with both hands, Stubby's head shot around and caught him just below the knees, catapulting him feet first through the air. With a death grip on the rope, Shot sailed upside down over the bull. When he came to the end of the rope, he felt the tension give for a split second and he knew that he had freed the rider's hand from the bullrope.

He landed facedown in the dirt beside the scrambling cowboy. He lifted his head in time to see one of Stubby's back hooves stomp down in the middle of the cowboy's back. Shot leapt to his feet, hopped over the helpless cowboy and slapped the bull across the nose. "Come on, Stubby!" he yelled and this time the bull followed him all the way to the catch pen.

As the medics carried the injured cowboy from the arena, the announcer praised Shot for his heroism and the crowd cheered. Shot barely acknowledged their applause. He was mad at himself. Although he knew he had done all that he possibly could to save the rider from injury, he was still upset. He just hated to see one of his cowboys get hurt.

He wiped the last ride from his mind and looked ahead to the next one, a new bull that he was not familiar with. Shot looked up at Sonny Joe.

"If he don't turn back in three or four jumps," said Sonny, "Go to him and see if ya can't bring him around."

Shot backed up and waited.

The rider called for his bull and as the gate opened, the bull blasted from the chute. He bailed high in the air, one, two, three jumps, four, and kept going. Shot sprinted toward the bull's head. When he was within three feet, the bull turned his head toward Shot, so Shot slowed down just a fraction, ready to lead him in a circle, but then the bull kept going straight. Again, Shot caught up with the bull, and again the bull threw a fake at him and kept going. He ran to the bull yet again, this time grabbing a horn, hollering and smacking him in the forehead, to no avail. The buzzer sounded, the rider bailed off, and the bull headed for the far end of the arena.

Shot cussed the bull, and apologized to the rider. So far, he was not having a good evening.

Meanwhile, T.J. Jergenson stood behind the chutes, planning the perfect ride on Magnum.

Dave Whitney stood at his side, offering these words of encouragement; "Ride tough, now. Move with him. Just let it all hang out and have fun...Don't even think about that BM brand."

"Shit, Whitney, don't even bring up that brand!" snapped T.J. "How are I supposed to not think about it if you keep talkin' about it?"

"Never mind buddy, just ride up."

T.J. wagged his head and cursed again, "Shit."

The next rider nodded his head. The bull made two straight, high-kicking jumps, spun to the right for a couple of rounds, and came out of the spin for the last few seconds, unable to shake his rider loose.

"One more before ya," Sonny Joe warned T.J.

T.J. pulled out his leather riding glove and slid it over his hand. He took a couple of deep breaths and punched himself in the chest. He stared at his bull. That was the one to have, the one to win the rodeo on. He momentarily glanced at the bull in front of Magnum – the big gray with the brand. He shook his head until all thoughts of the brand and the bull rattled from his mind.

Randy Corey lay a supporting hand upon T.J.'s shoulders and encouraged, "Stick it on 'em, cowboy!"

Another man and beast tangled, and it was T.J.'s turn.

As he crawled over the chute and eased down on the back of Magnum, his lip curled, revealing clenched teeth and his breath became a low growl. He handed the tail of his bullrope to Dave and ordered, "Pull!" He slid his gloved hand fervidly up and down the heavily rosined rope, kindling valuable heat in both leather and nylon. "Slack!" he said and as Dave loosened the rope around the bull's belly, T.J. worked the warmth into the leather handle of his bullrope in the same fashion. With his little finger lined up directly with Magnum's backbone, he slid his hand under the handhold and said to Dave, "O.K., pull." Again Dave tugged on the tail of the rope until T.J. said, "That's good." He took the tail from Dave and laid it along the top of his handhold. He then wrapped it around his hand and across his palm, squeezing tight and cocking his thumb over his forefinger. He slid to his rope and as he sucked in one last lung-full, he glanced over Magnum's head and through the upright bars of the slide gate in from of him to...

The mouse gray back of the BM bull.

He looked back down at Magnum and took another breath. And another.

Anticipating eyes engulfed T.J. as, for a few seconds, the world stood still.

"He's standin' good for ya," yelled Shot, from the arena. "Nod yer face!"

T.J. nodded for a split second and the BM brand flashed across his mind.

Magnum sprung from the chute, took two high leaps, and went into a tight left spin, right into T.J.'s riding hand. T.J. watched the bull's head as he threw his free hand over his own. With his hand securely in his bullrope, his body snug against his hand and arm, his legs and spurs gripping and squeezing the bull's hide and rib cage, T.J. felt comfortable and in perfect control. He loosened up with his outside foot and began to spur the bull in the shoulder. He could not hear the roar of the crowd as he concentrated on nothing but riding his bull and riding him well.

Then the brand fluttered into his consciousness. His free arm stopped moving for a jump. His inside spur slipped and slid back a foot from his rope, and his hips slid to the outside of the spin. He jammed his foot back into place and pumped wildly over his head, but he was out of sync with the bull. He stopped spurring and started scratching for anything he could get a solid hold of, but there was nothing. His butt slid back to the flank rope and his hand was jerked from the handhold. He landed on his hands and knees and immediately scrambled to his feet and ran to the fence, cussing himself all the way.

"Folks, that is something you just don't see very often," spoke the announcer. "All this cowboy is going to be taking home with him tonight is what you give him. Let's pay him off, shall we?"

As the Bakersfield spectators offered T.J. a consolation round of applause, Shot fetched his bullrope for him.

"What the hell happened, T.J.?" he asked as he handed him the rope, "You were in there, solid."

"I dunno," said T.J. "Just havin' a bad night, I guess."

"You ride better'n that on yer worst night," Shot responded.

T.J. said nothing as he coiled his rope and walked out of the arena.

By now, Sonny Joe was pulling up the flank rope on the pride of his string, the big gray Braymer – Big Mac.

Shot strolled up to the chute to have a look at the new bull and to gain some guidance from Sonny Joe.

"Just stand back and watch the fun," advised Sonny, "but get in there as soon as this kid gets throwed off. He's pretty hookie."

Shot nodded and backed up.

"Hey, Shot," yelled Dave Whitney from behind the next chute, "see if ya notice anything strange about this bull."

A young bullrider slid to his rope and called for Big Mac. The chute gate had barely opened when the bull shoved it wide with his mighty head. He bailed from the chute with such intense energy, swapping ends in mid-air, kicking so high, snapping back to the ground so fast, that Shot whispered, "Wow!" under his breath just before the defeated cowboy went sailing through the air.

Shot sprinted to the bull's head and sidestepped around his right horn. Big Mac took the bait and chased him along the row of chutes, sending judges and gatemen scrambling up the fence for safety. Shot cut to the left and Big Mac stayed with him, head low and horns inches from the seat of Shot's baggy britches, fervent with anticipation of running him down and mauling him into the ground – doing what comes naturally. Just as the bull believed that he had caught his prey, Shot switched directions. Again, Big Mac struggled to catch and harm his nimble opponent. At that instant, Shot was in his glory. Saving cowboys and stepping around charging bulls was what he lived for and when he was not doing it, he was dreaming about it. As he stayed barely one step ahead, he could feel the bull's hot breath at his heels, and he could feel his horn brushing against the seat of his pants. He was in the pocket – the fine line between a ballet and a wreck. So close to danger and yet safe where he was. He reached behind him and grabbed Big Mac's right horn and led him around in a circle, as the bull began to tire and slow down a little. As Shot flitted around the bull, he could see a brand on his right shoulder. It said BM.

"Bennett?"

Shot hesitated, as for a microsecond his mind flashed back to the Rapid City Hotel and Bennett revealing his tattoo, saying, "If you see..." Suddenly, he was clipped below the knee and found himself on his head in the arena dirt. As he looked up between his own legs, he barely had time to see the gray underbelly of the bull when both back hooves collided with his back in forward momentum and rolled him over onto his face. Before he had a chance to move, he heard himself let out a heavy grunt as the same two hooves came crashing down in the middle of his back. Shot's pain was muffled by his impassioned desire to breathe. He lifted his face from the dirt. He could see the bull, still bucking, eight feet away and returning for another trampling. He clawed and scratched at the ground in front of him, kicked and wallowed in the dirt behind, but his spine would not lift Shot's hips from the ground. The bull lowered his head as he charged. Shot buried his face back in the dirt, covered his head with his arm, and awaited the impact...

The impact never came.

Slowly, Shot opened his eyes, lifted his head and peered over his shoulder. Not two feet away, the big gray bull stood, guarding his helpless victim. As Shot began to gasp again for breath, the bull snorted a slimy warning at his face and trotted off to the catch pen. Shot could see the BM brand, bouncing back and forth on his right shoulder.

Dave Palmer was the first to reach Shot, followed by Randy Corey, T.J., and the paramedics.

"You O.K.?" Dave asked as he knelt beside, not knowing what to do.

Shot struggled to answer, but his voice was lost, as well as his ability to breathe.

Dave held on to his buddy's arm and began to roll him off of his stomach.

"No!" screamed a lady medic. "Don't move him! He could be paralyzed."

"Stand back," said her male partner. "Give me some room."

"Yer gonna be O.K.," assured Dave as he backed up, still on his knees.

The medics lay a stretcher beside Shot on the ground. On "One...two...three," they simultaneously rolled his body onto the stretcher and promptly strapped an oxygen mask to his face. "O.K, we'll need some help carrying him out of here," she commanded. T.J. and Randy joined Dave and the medics. "On three," she said. "One...two..." On "three" they lifted Shot from the ground and carried him toward the ambulance just outside of the gate.

"Still with us, Shot?" asked Randy. "You still with us?"

Shot looked up at the friends and medics between the glare of arena lights. Unable to speak, his eyes said, "I don't know..."

Chapter 18: June 1990

"...You with us, Shot...Hey, you awake?" A familiar voice drifted across Shot Palmer's semiconscious thoughts. "Hey...Shot...you awake?" He slowly lifted his eyelids. A fuzzy form appeared beneath a brown felt cowboy hat. It took Shot a few seconds to realize that it was his buddy, Randy Corey, speaking to him. "Hey guys," he heard him say, "I think he's comin' to!" Two more faces appeared before him – T.J. Jergenson and Dave Whitney.

"It's about time," said Dave as he put his hand on Shot's shoulder. "You gonna sleep all week?"

Shot's voice was weak and cracked, "Where...where am I?"

"Yer in the hospital," T.J. told him. "Do ya remember what happened?"

As Shot's eyes began to focus, he looked around the room. Undecorated white walls supported a textured white ceiling. In one corner of the room was an open doorway to the hall, another to the toilet. The curtains on the window to his right were pulled back, revealing a half-dozen palm trees stretching their necks toward the blazing California sun. "Huh?" he asked, to no one in particular.

T.J. repeated, "Do ya remember what happened to ya?"

"Yeah," Shot hoarsely half-whispered. "What happened to me?"

"Ya took a pretty good stompin'," said Randy.

"I know that," maintained Shot. "I meant what's wrong with me?"

Randy and T.J. looked at Dave, and for an uneasy moment, no one spoke.

Finally, Dave said, "Well, Shot...You tell him, T.J."

T.J. looked at Randy. "Go ahead," he insisted.

Shot groaned a mournful sigh. He felt a cold pain throughout his neck, shoulders and upper back. He knew it was bad news.

"Shot," Randy cleared his throat. "You broke yer back in two places."

After a painful pause, Shot optimistically rationalized, "So, I'll be out of the game for awhile."

"The doc says you gotta find a new game," Whitney piped up. "He says yer outta this'n fer good."

Disappointment covered Shot's entire face. Then he stubbornly said, "What the hell does he know about bullfightin'? It ain't like I'm gittin' on 'em and gittin' bounced around every time."

"He's a specialist," said T.J. "He seems like he knows what he's talkin' about."

"I don't care if he is a specialist," Shot protested. "If he had any brains at all he'd a' been a cowboy instead of a doctor!"

Randy Corey and the others suspected that Shot might be wrong, but none of the men could really argue with his point.

The pain in Shot's upper body expanded and intensified. "So what are they gonna do?" asked Shot. "Operate?"

"They already did," answered Corey.

"Already did?" repeated Shot. "When?"

"Saturday night."

"What day is this?"

Randy thought for a second and said, "Thursday."

"Thursday?" Shot echoed. "Jeeze, it seems like it was just last night!"

"You been in a coma for five days," Dave informed him. "Somethin' 'bout not gittin' enough oxygen to yer brain."

"In a way yer pretty lucky," added T.J. "That bull coulda' done a lot more damage to you if he'd a' wanted to."

"I know," agreed Palmer. "I remember him stoppin' right before he got to me the second time."

"To tell you the truth," said Randy, "I don't think he stomped on you on purpose. But you were right underneath him, and he couldn't help it."

"Yeah," concurred Dave. "He wouldn't have done..." He stopped in mid-sentence, wondering if everybody else was thinking what he was thinking.

T.J. sat down in the chair next to the bed and said, "Shot, me and the boys noticed somethin' real strange about this bull. Did you?"

Immediately Shot thought of the BM brand on the bull's right shoulder. "Like what?" he inquired.

"Well," Jergenson said as he leaned back and laid his foot across his knee, "Whitney seen it first. He ain't branded like the rest of the bulls are. His brand ain't on his butt, it's up there on his right shoulder. And instead of numbers, he's got letters."

"BM," Shot stated.

Randy walked to the neighboring bed and sat down.

"So, you seen it too," pressured Dave.

"Right before he caught me," Shot confessed.

"So," Corey asked. "Whattaya think?"

"You mean do I think it was Bennett?" asked Shot.

"Sonny said he was real surprised that the bull didn't just keep on maulin' ya," stated T.J. "He says that was the first time he's ever passed up a chance."

Dave looked at T.J., then at Shot and asked, "Think it's 'cause he knew ya?"

Instead of answering, Shot asked, "Where'd he get that bull, anyhow?"

"He said he got him from Mike and Brad Fanner, up in Nebraska," Randy answered. "But he don't know where they got him from. So...whattaya think?"

Shot didn't answer.

"How you feelin'? Jergenson inquired.

"I'm feelin' fine," lied Shot, "and I'll be fightin' bulls again. I don't care what that doctor says. Did you guys go to Clovis, New Mexico?"

"We're leavin' tonight," said Dave. "We been here all week."

"All week? Where ya been stayin'?"

"A motel down the street," T.J. answered. "We been takin' turns stayin' here with you."

"Hell, you guys didn't need to do that," Shot protested.

"Wasn't no problem," allowed Whitney. "We drew outta Mesquite. Nobody drew up worth a damn and it's too far to go out there anyway. Plus, they got a lotta good bars in this town."

"So, whattaya think, Shot?" Randy asked anxiously.

"I think I'm pissed off, Corey," Shot returned. "I'm sick and tired of hospital beds."

"I know what you mean," agreed T.J. "Last time you were in one a' these places, I was in a bed next to ya."

"Yeah, and you were a pain in the ass, too," said Palmer. "By the way, did anybody call my ol' lady?"

"Which one?" asked Dave.

"Whattaya mean which one?" Shot grumbled. "Rachel, ya bonehead."

"Nope," Dave answered.

"Good," said Shot, "I don't wanna worry her."

"That's what we figured," Randy concurred. "But dontcha think she'll worry that ya never call?"

"Hell," Shot declared, "I never call her anyway."

Randy got up from the bed and began to pace the floor. "Dammit, Shot, I gotta know what you think about this bull!" he ranted.

"Well, I don't know what I think for sure, Randy. I been in a coma. I ain't had as much time to think about it as you. What do you think?"

That one stumped Corey.

"I'll tell you what I think," T.J. offered. "A month before Bennett got killed, me and him was headin' up to South Dakota so I could go to court on that indecent exposure deal. Well, on that trip – I'll never forget it – we made a vow to each other that we were goin' to the National Finals together. And then he died. Well, boys, I believe that me and Bennett are still goin' to the Finals together. Not only that, but we're gonna win the world."

Whether they believed it or not, the boys gave T.J.'s story serious consideration.

"You remember the night Bennett told me he was gonna come back as a bull?" Randy reminisced. "You said he was fulla shit, T.J. You wouldn't have any part of it."

"I know it," Jergenson admitted. "And when he showed us that tattoo, and said he'd prove it to us, I still thought he was fulla shit. But when I seen that brand – hell, that's proof enough for me."

Randy sat back down on the bed and slowly shook his head back and forth.

"Don't you believe me?" asked T.J.

"It ain't that I don't believe ya," granted Corey, "I'm just tryin' to figure out how it coulda' happened."

"Some things ain't meant to be figured out," T.J. said somberly.

"But there's got to be some kind of an explanation," insisted Randy. "Sonny Joe didn't brand him?"

Dave spoke up. "I talked to Sonny right after they hauled Shot off. When he bought him, he was already branded that way. You guys ever hear of Mike and Brad Fanner?"

"Never heard of 'em," grunted Shot.

"It's prob'ly just a coincidence," Randy tried to convince himself.

"I don't care how he got that brand," declared T.J. "It's a sign. Y'all seen the tattoo and heard Bennett's story..."

"'Cept me," Whitney interrupted.

"...and if that ain't proof enough for you, then I don't know what is!"

"It's just that I believe in the Bible," said Randy. "I was brought up where ya don't question the Bible. It's s'poseta be the only real proof, and the Bible don't say anything about reincarnation."

"How do you know?" quizzed Shot. "Have ya read it?"

"Well...no," Corey admitted. "Not clear through. Have you?"

"Nope."

"I started to, once," announced Dave.

"Which one?" asked Randy.

"Whattaya mean 'which one'?"

"The Old Testament or the New Testament?"

"I dunno," shrugged Dave. "It was kind of a new-lookin' book."

"How'd it start out?" Randy asked.

"With God creatin' the universe and the world."

"That's the Old Testament," stated Randy. "Why'd ya quit?"

"Well, the more I read," explained Dave, "the more skeptical I got. And then, ya know the part about Noah and the flood? Well, that was pretty farfetched. And then a little later, there was this part about Noah gittin' drunk and passin' out in his tent naked and one of his boys walks in and sees him, and just 'cause of that, his boy's s'poseta be burnin' in hell through eternity, and I said, 'bullshit', and shut the book and never opened it back up."

Shot's and T.J.'s eyes moved from Dave to Randy.

"A lotta things in the Bible have been proven," Randy insisted.

"I'm sure they have," Dave responded, "but a lotta things I just ain't gonna buy. I'll tell ya; I don't know how or why we were put here, other than to rodeo, but I do know that life's a big ol' mystery and the only ones who are truly full a' shit are the ones who think they got it all figured out."

"Jeez!" exclaimed T.J. "I ain't never heard you talk this much, sober!"

Dave was suddenly embarrassed. He walked over to the window and peered out at the palm trees.

"What do you think, Shot?" asked Randy. "Not about the bull, just about life and death in general."

"I dunno," Shot pondered. "I just don't know. Some people believe we come back and live again in this world. Others think we go on to another world. I s'pose the reason folks believe these things is 'cause it's comforting. I mean, if you love somebody who dies, it's a lot easier on you if ya believe that they went on to a better place. Even for your own death – I 'magine we'd all like to think we're goin' on with it...another chance to enter up, or whatever."

"Is that how you feel?" Randy inquired.

"I'd like to...but in truth, I don't," Shot sighed as he looked toward the ceiling. "I reckon we only go around once so, we better do it up right while we can. It's like Bennett always useta say..."

The others joined in, "'I'm here for a good time, not a long time.'"

Shot's thin lips curled to a smile and it soothed the aching pain in his back. "Y' know," he related with a faraway look, "I think more about how I'm gonna die than what's gonna happen afterwards."

Dave's eyes came back from the palm trees and settled on Shot. "How are you gonna die?"

"I wanna die in the arena."

"Really?" Dave asked, only mildly surprised.

"Yep. Goin' down in a blaze a' glory, doin' what I love..." His eyes saddened. "It shoulda' been me."

"What shoulda' been you?" asked T.J.

"Insteada Bennett," Shot moaned. "It shoulda' been me."

"Aw, Shot, don't talk that way," Randy pleaded. "Bennett prob'ly wanted to go out in a blaze a' glory just as bad as you did. Most all bullriders do."

"Not me!" argued T.J. "I wanna live to be an old man!"

"Well, I know one thing. I will fight bulls again," Shot stated. "Even if it kills me."

Considering that, Randy added, "I don't know how or when I'll die, but I know that when I do, I'll see Bennett again in heaven. I hope to see you boys up there, too."

"Yeah, whatever," Dave dismissed. "We better git goin'. It's gonna take us all night to get to Clovis."

"I s'pose yer right," said T.J. as he lifted his lanky body from his chair. "Besides, it's just about time fer Andy and Barney to come on T.V."

Randy hopped up from his seat on the bed, and extended his hand to Shot. "Hate to leave ya here, buddy. Just glad you come outta yer coma before we left. Give Rachel a call."

"I will." Shot's smile was as weak as his handshake.

Dave came over and lay his hand upon Shot's shoulder. "Take care, pardner. Let us know when they release ya. We'll come out and haul ya home."

"I 'preciate it, but I know yer schedules are too busy fer that," said Shot. "Rachel can come and git me."

"See ya."

"Take care."

"So long."

And they left.

The pain in his back, ribs, and shoulders intensified. He stared at his surroundings and mumbled in disgust. He saw the blank T.V.

screen staring back at him, waiting for permission to speak. Shot found the remote control and clicked the television to life. The news and weather was on. He flipped channels. A cooking show. He flipped again, just in time to see Barney accidentally lock himself in jail. Experience advised Shot not to laugh with his ribs and back in such a condition. It didn't matter. He didn't feel like laughing anyway.

Chapter 19: July 1990

"Hello everybody, this is Jeff Stevens for WYO news, and I am at one of America's biggest rodeos, the Daddy of 'Em All, here in Cheyenne, Wyoming." The newscaster looked out of place in his red checkered shirt and his brown high-crowned felt cowboy hat perched atop a head full of gray-black streaked, permanent-wave curls. "And with me is the young man not only leading in the bullriding here in Cheyenne, after his first two bulls, but unofficially he has moved into first place in the world standings for nineteen-ninety, Wiley Paz."

The young Mexican-American cowboy, a full head shorter than the newscaster, appeared nervous as he tried to smile at his first-ever camera interview.

"Wiley," the newscaster went on, "tell us about your first two rides."

Wiley cleared his throat. "Well, I rode my first bull...and won the round on him. And then I rode my second bull, and won a third in the second round."

Jeff Stevens paused. He was expecting a little more discourse from his interviewee, who had seemed so cool and relaxed before the cameras were rolling. "That's great, Wiley. Tell me; were they hard to ride?"

"Uh..." Wiley looked into the camera lens which stared back at him like a big round eyeball, "yeah...I mean, yessir...one of 'em."

"Which one was harder?" smiled the newsman as he shoved the microphone back in front of the bullrider's face.

"Uh...the second one."

Already, the interviewer realized that he was not going to get much of a conversation from this tense bundle of embarrassment. He changed the subject. "How old are you, Wiley?"

"Uh, twenty. I'll be twenty-one, uh, next year."

"Yes. Very good...and how long have you been riding bulls?"

"Three years."

Jeff Stevens looked cynically at his producer, who was beside the cameraman, motioning with his hands, "Stretch it out. Stretch it out..."

"That's quite a feat," Jeff hailed. "A young rookie such as yourself leading the world standings, midway through the summer. How does that make you feel?"

Wiley pondered the question and replied, "Uh...good."

Still smiling and trying to look as interested as can be, Jeff said, "Wiley, as of your last ride, you have surpassed the money earnings of veteran bullrider T.J. Jergenson, who is less than two hundred dollars behind you. Will you be able to hold on to your lead?"

"I dunno," Wiley responded. "I hope so...I'm sure gonna try."

"You've got two more bulls to ride here at Cheyenne to win the average and the buckle. Have you got a game plan?"

"I've got a real good bull today," said Wiley. "I'm just gonna do my best to ride him."

"Spoken like a true cowboy," Mr. Stevens concluded, ignoring the producer's "Stretch it out" signals. "And here you have it, folks; the leading bullrider here in Cheyenne, as well as in the world standings, a man of few words, Wiley Paz. Back to you, Ted."

"O.K....we're clear," announced the producer. "You cut the interview a little short, Jeff. We really need to try to get at least three minutes per interview."

"Do you think you could get me somebody who might at least talk to me?" Jeff requested with bitter sarcasm. "I might as well have been talking to myself. Thanks, Wiley, you were great. Who's next?"

Wiley walked away, relieved to be out of the limelight. He took a deep breath and let it puff from his cheeks as he joined his fellow bullriders who had been watching the interview.

"Good job, Paz," one of his friends razzed him. "You sure do seem at ease in front of the camera."

"Yer a natural star," another commented.

Wiley's lips spread to an embarrassed grin. "Aw, hush."

"Were ya scared?"

"Heck, no," Wiley denied. "I just ain't got much to say, that's all." He happened to look toward the boardwalk that bridges over the catch pen alley way. He saw a man he recognized. Coming down the steps in black high-topped boots rising nearly to his knees with his tight blue jeans tucked into them, World Champion belt-buckle, pin-striped shirt beneath a fringed leather vest, an oversized red, white and blue bandanna draped around his neck, drooping brown mustache, mirrored sunglasses, and a long bald eagle feather sticking out past the brim of his gray felt cowboy hat, was a man almost every bullrider recognized. It was two-time World Champion Bullrider

Scotty Redwood. On Scotty's arm was the prettiest bleached-blond buckle-bunny Wiley had even seen, dressed up even fancier than the legend himself. Behind him was an entourage of Scotty's acquaintances and fans who preferred to call themselves his friends. Wiley recalled his first impression of the Champ – the cocky, bigoted smart-ass who made him feel like a second-class bullrider, or worse. Still, Wiley was not a man to hold a grudge, so, just to be friendly, he said, "Hi, Scotty." Scotty nodded in Wiley's direction as he strolled by.

"Mister Redwood," he heard the producer greet, "we've been expecting you."

"Let's get this over with," said Scotty as he sauntered to the front of the camera.

The producer shook Scotty's hand. "Mister Redwood, I'd like you to meet our anchorman, Jeff Stevens," he introduced. "He'll be conducting our interview today."

"It's a pleasure to make your acquaintance," welcomed the newsman. "I'll start off by introducing you, two-time World Champ, three-time runner-up, then I'll ask you how you would compare rodeos today as opposed to the rodeos of yesterday."

"Whatever," said Scotty nonchalantly, "I got an opinion on just about everything."

"Could we lose the shades?" suggested the producer. "And tip your hat back? Let the home viewers see what you look like."

Scotty thrust a forefinger to the brim of his Stetson, raising it a couple of inches and removed his glasses, revealing bag cradled, bloodshot eyes.

"O.K., let's go ahead and keep the shades on," the producer contradicted himself. "They're an extension of your being. People are used to seeing you in that way."

The newscaster sidled up next to the Champ and they both posed for the camera.

"Ready?" signaled the producer. "O.K....you're on!"

"Jeff Stevens, once again, here at the Cheyenne Frontier Days Rodeo, and I am talking with one of the greatest bullriders of all time, two-time World Champion Bullrider, three-time runner-up, Scotty Redwood. Mister Redwood, do you..."

"Son, the only Mister Redwood I know is my daddy and he ain't here," Scotty recited. "Y'all can call me Scotty."

"Fair enough. Scotty, it's been a dozen years since you've won a World Championship Gold Buckle. Tell me, has rodeo changed much since those days, and in what way?"

"Rodeo has definitely changed since I was ridin' the circuit," stated Scotty as he pulled the microphone from the newsman's hand. "In some ways, for the better – more money, mostly. When I was goin' down the road, a lotta these rodeos paid a little more than half of what they do now, and I predict it's gonna get better as time goes by. In some ways, rodeo has gotten worse. The cowboys are softer than they used to be. They ain't as tough. A hard travelin' bullrider today might hit a hunnert and twenty-five rodeos a year, max. I use'ta hit twice that many. There wasn't no limit on how many you could go to, to make the finals, plus, they didn't pay as much, so you had to hit twice as many rodeos to win the same amount of money. Yep, we were tougher back then. You been talkin' about little Wiley Paz and T.J. Jergenson bein' one an' two in the standin's. Now, they're pretty fair bullriders, alright, but the reason they're one an' two in the standin's is 'cause I ain't competin' against 'em."

"You're saying that if you were still competing that they would be two and three in the world standings?"

"Figure it out."

"With all due respect, Scotty," Jeff Stevens pressed, "don't you think you're being a bit boastful?"

"It might sound that way," Scotty answered, "but I'm just speakin' the truth. Yeah, Jergenson and the little Mexican kid are good bullriders, I'll give ya that, but the bullriders today just ain't the quality bullriders that we had a dozen years ago. They ain't outta the same mold. They ain't got the same grit."

"You announced your retirement a month after you won your last World Championship. People say you were in your prime, and could have easily won two or three more. Why'd you quit?"

"I had a lotta reasons for steppin' down. One, what else did I have to prove? I proved I was the best in the world, and I proved it wasn't no fluke when I won it the second time. Two, I had too many irons in the fire. Between my product endorsements and my rodeo schools and my own roughstock string, I just didn't have enough time. When I'm travelin' hard and ridin' bulls, I do nothin' but travel hard and ride bulls."

"Any advice for the young, up-and-coming bullriders?"

"If yer gonna ride like a Champ, you gotta learn from a Champ. I put on six bullridin' schools a year, complete with video playback so ya can watch yer rides, positive attitude lectures, and bulls to fit every size, age and ability. I can be reached at..."

"And unfortunately that's all the time we have. I have been visiting with two-time World Bullriding Champion, three-time runner-up, the legendary Scotty Redwood. Back to you, Ted."

"We're clear," the producer said. "Great interview, Mister Redwood, very informational."

"Yer boy cut me off," growled Scotty.

Jeff Stevens hung his head and quietly skulked away.

"Yes, and we're very sorry about that," the producer apologized. "We've only got an allotted amount of time for each interview, and we've got to make time for the T.J. Jergenson interview."

"You cut me off for T.J. Jergenson?" blustered Scotty. "Has he ever won the world? Has he ever been runner-up? If you think the American public would rather listen to a wannabe bullrider than a World Champ, then I guess that's yer dumb ignorance. What's he gonna talk about, what it feels like to be a loser? He can't tell ya 'bout bein' a winner. He don't know!"

Everyone was quiet but the still-apologizing producer as Scotty turned to leave. Just to the side of the crowd, leaning on the white panel fence, he saw T.J. Jergenson quietly waiting his turn in front of the camera. T.J. raised his eyebrows and grinned, "Howdy, Scotty."

Scotty grumbled, "That's *Mister* Redwood, to you," and he walked away.

"O.K., which one is Mister Jergenson?" the producer asked the group of cowboys.

"That'd be me," T.J. volunteered.

"Mister Jergenson, such a pleasure to meet you," greeted the producer as he shook T.J.'s hand and led him to his spot. "I'd like you to meet our newsman for WYO TV. This is Jeff Stevens."

"Good to meetcha," hailed T.J.

"Likewise," said the newscaster. "Is there anything in particular that you would like to talk about?"

T.J. thought for a moment. "I guess not," he said. "Whatever you wanna ask me."

The producer was already next to the camera. "Ready?...You are on the air...now!"

"And once again this is Jeff Stevens for WYO News here at the Daddy of 'Em All – Cheyenne Frontier Days, held the last full week of July, and I am standing here with bullrider T.J. Jergenson. T.J., it looks like a tight race between you and rookie bullrider, Wiley Paz."

"Yessir, it is a tight race," agreed T.J., "but not just with me and Wiley. There's a handful of guys that are knockin' on the door and they ain't too far behind, and it's a long ways to December, so anything could happen."

"How long have you been riding bulls, now?"

"Oh, seventeen or eighteen years. It sure don't seem like that long."

"And yet you are virtually an unknown coming into the race. Your biggest threat, Wiley Paz, has been riding bulls for a mere three years. What took you so long?"

"Y'know, sometimes I ask myself that question. I wish I had the fire in me when I was twenty that ol' Wiley has in him. I guess I always wanted to win, but I didn't have that deep-down cravin' to win like I do now. I was just ridin' 'cause I loved ridin'. And if I could pick up a check here and there, pay my way down the road, I was more than happy. Me and my buddies – we were just havin' fun and livin' free."

"Obviously, something has changed, T.J. What brought about that change?"

"Things ain't really changed that much. I'm still havin' a lotta fun, love it as much as I ever did. I finally just set myself some goals, and I'm goin' after 'em. See...I went through a rough time a couple years ago...I even quit for awhile."

"Injury?"

"Well, that was part of it. I lost my best friend in a bullridin' accident...and about a month before that happened, me and him made each other a vow that we was gonna quit screwin' around and we was gonna make it to the National Finals together...and then he got killed...so it's up to me."

The interviewer could see the emotion welling up in T.J.'s eyes, so he changed the subject. "Can you explain, in words, what it is like to strap yourself to the back of a two thousand-pound bull?"

"I doubt it," said T.J., glad to be talking about something else. "It's one a' them things ya gotta do to really know what it's like."

"What goes through your mind? Are you nervous? Are you afraid?"

"It's a helluva rush, I'll tell ya that much. I guess I'm a little bit afraid, only I don't like to call it afraid. I like to call it 'pumped up.' See, I take the fear and I turn it into a positive thing. It's a whole lot of adrenaline. Ya don't hafta gitcherself pumped up to ride bulls because you already are. I'll tell you what, when you sit down on a bull in the chute...and ya can just feel the muscle and power in him. Even though he's just standin' there. And they got this smell, they smell...mean and rank. And then ya work that rosin into yer bullrope and feel it heat up in yer hand and ya know yer ready, and that the moment of truth is comin' right up." T.J.'s fists and face clenched as he spoke, "And then ya nod yer head and ya both blow outta there like..." He caught himself, and settled down. "...There's not a better feeling...It's what I live for."

After a short pause, the newsman concluded, "Wow. While I'll never know exactly how it feels to ride a bull, at least now I think I have some idea why you guys do it....This is Jeff Stevens for WYO News. Back to you, Ted."

Chapter 20: August 1990

Mary Jo Jergenson lay her newspaper over the arm of the couch. "Who could that be this time of night?" she asked herself as she got up and headed for the door. She wrapped her housecoat around her and peered out the window. Outside, T.J. awaited with his friends Randy Corey, Dave Whitney and their newest traveling partner, Wiley Paz. She opened the door and with outstretched arms greeted, "Well, Tommy! For goodness sakes!"

"Howdy, Maw," said T.J. as he hugged his mother's head against his chest. "Surprised to see me?"

"I certainly am!" She backed away and looked up at her son. "I wasn't expecting you until next month for our rodeo here in Enid! Why didn't you call? Your father's already in bed."

"We didn't know if we'd make it this far," explained T.J. "We didn't wanna..."

"Who are your friends? Come on in, boys, don't be shy! I've got a pan full of fudge brownies I just made tonight. You are staying the night, aren't you?"

T.J. followed his mother into the kitchen, and the boys followed him. "Yeah," T.J. said, "We were plannin' on it, if it's O.K."

"Don't be silly," she giggled. "Of course it's O.K."

"Maw, you remember Dave and Randy, dontcha?"

"The bronc riders? You boys are lookin' good. Everybody stayin' healthy?"

"Yes ma'am," smiled Randy.

"All of us 'cept for Shot," Dave added.

"I heard about that," lamented Mary Jo. "Pity. Seems like he'd just healed up from his last accident."

"And this here," T.J. introduced, "is Wiley Paz."

"It's a pleasure to meet you," Wiley nodded with a smile and a handshake.

"Well, it's nice to meet you," she returned. "You're quite a bit younger than the rest of the boys, aren't you?"

"Yes, ma'am," said Wiley. "I'm only twenty. These guys are kinda showin' me the ropes."

"You're with good company," she said as she opened the refrigerator door. "Now, you boys set yourselves down at the table." She pulled out a jug of milk and, as the cowboys found a place at the table, went to the cupboard and got four large glasses. On the countertop, between the toaster and the breadbox, sat a rectangular pan covered with tin foil. She peeled the foil back, revealing still-warm fudge brownies. "I must have known you were coming. I don't bake very often anymore." A thought suddenly crossed her mind. "Have you boys had supper? We've got some leftover ham and I've got plenty of eggs and bacon."

"That's O.K., Maw," said T.J. "We ate right after the rodeo, just a few hours ago."

"Where were you boys rodeoing tonight?" Mary Jo inquired as she cut the brownies into equal-sized pieces.

"Coffeyville, Kansas," T.J. reported. "Tomorrow night we're in Lawton, Oklahoma."

"Lawton," she repeated as she stopped cutting for the moment. "Your great-uncle Hylo lives in Lawton. You better give him a call tomorrow. Maybe you could stay at his house tomorrow night."

"Yeah, I might do that," said T.J. unenthusiastically. T.J. hadn't seen Uncle Hylo since high school graduation. Hylo was the big fat guy who advised T.J. that rodeo "ain't no way to make a livin'. If ya want a job with a real future I might be able to git ya on at the power plant."

T.J. changed the subject. "How's Paw doin'?"

"He's just doin' fine," she said as she finished slicing up the brownies and put them on individual plates. "Keepin' real busy. He'll be glad you're here. He's got some square hay bales to load and stack in the mornin'." She grabbed four forks from the kitchen drawer and served each of the boys their dessert, along with a glass of milk. "Eat up, there's plenty."

The boys politely thanked her and dug in.

"Sure is good," said Dave after devouring his in no time, without the use of his fork. "I ain't had homemade brownies since I don't know when."

Before Dave had finished speaking, Mary Jo slid another piece from her spatula to his plate.

"Maw?" T.J. asked about Bennett's parents. "Have you talked to Bill and Katey McKinney lately?"

"I see them every now and then," she said in a somber tone. "They seem to be doing alright. Bill has his moods when he's really down. I guess he's never been quite the same since it happened. You really ought to stop in and see them tomorrow, if you get a chance."

"Yeah, I s'pose I should," agreed T.J. "Maybe we'll do that."

"How are you ranked in the world standings, Tommy?" she asked her son.

"I'm leadin' the world, right now," T.J. reported, "but not by far."

"Well, you just don't get hurt," she coached, "and there's not another bullrider in the world that can catch you."

"I dunno, Maw, I got some tough competition. There's one guy in particular who ain't gonna make it easy for me."

Mary Jo sat the pan on the counter and sat down at the head of the table. "Oh, he hasn't got a chance," she encouraged. "Who is he, anyway?"

T.J. pointed past his shoulder with his thumb, "It's ol' Wiley, here," he grinned.

Mary Jo's eyebrows raised. "It is? Well, good for you, Wiley!"

"Thank you, ma'am," he said shyly and washed down his brownie with a swig of milk.

"And only twenty years old..." suddenly she became a bit embarrassed about saying 'he hasn't got a chance.' She covered for it, adding, "Well, you both just do your best. You know what your father says, Tommy; you can't control what the other bullriders do, anyway. Just ride everything you get on."

"That's what we try to do, Maw," agreed T.J.

She looked at Dave and Randy. "How are you boys doing?"

Dave spoke up, "We're scrapin' out a livin', but that's about it."

"As long as you're havin' fun and can make a livin'," she stated, "that's what's important. More brownies, anyone?"

"No, thank you," Randy declined.

"None for me," said T.J.

"They sure were good, though," commended Wiley.

"Hell, I'll eat another'n," Dave requested.

Mary Jo chuckled as she got up and went to the counter. "Are you boys tryin' to starve little Dave out?" she asked as she sat the whole pan in front of him.

"He's just a bottomless pit," said Randy, elbowing Dave in the ribs.

"Well, in the morning," she announced, "you're going to have some real food. A good ol' homecooked meal. You boys are all too skinny. Every one of you."

"I never did know a fat bullrider, Maw," T.J. responded.

"I'll bet you boys are on a regular diet of hot dogs."

"Aw, that's only partly true," said T.J.

"I drink a beer now and then, too, Mrs. Jergenson," teased Dave.

"My goodness, I hope it's not a light beer!" she replied. "Well, I'm going to turn in. Tommy, we've got the couch, the spare room and the bunkhouse. You know where the extra blankets are. Goodnight, boys."

"O.K., Maw, g'night."

"'Night, Mrs. Jergenson."

"Thanks for the brownies."

Mary Jo exited the kitchen and retreated down the hallway. When Dave Palmer heard the bedroom door close behind her, he said, "Paz, run out to the van and get the beer!"

"Gitcher own damn beer!" Wiley replied. "I ain't old enough to drink anyway."

"I been tellin' ya ever since ya jumped in with us," Palmer contended, "if ya wanna git drunk, it's O.K. with me. Hell, I'll even buy!"

"I don't wanna git drunk," Wiley stated. "This big ol' glass a' milk's good 'nuff for me."

"Shit, you ain't even been weaned yet," Dave grumbled. "T.J., I can't believe we're runnin' with *two* non-drinkers, now. It was bad enough when there was only Corey...What's this world comin' to?"

"I don't know," said T.J. "But I don't think I want another beer tonight, either."

Dave wagged his head in disgust. "Are you turnin' lightweight on me, too? You only drank two of 'em on the way down here!"

"Well, I'm in my parents' house, Dave," T.J. explained, "and they're *here*. I don't wanna git loud and keep 'em awake."

"Well, does anybody object if I have a beer?" Dave challenged.

"You drink all the beer you want," T.J. consented.

"Paz!" Dave snapped. "Run out to the van and get the beer!"

Wiley Paz raised his middle finger in front of Whitney's face.

With a disgusted sigh, Dave slowly rose from the table. As he headed out to the van, he complained to no one in particular, "These young kids just don't show no respect anymore."

Randy Corey laughed, "Don't take any shit off him."

"I don't," Wiley stated proudly. "That's just what he's wantin'."

"I think Paw's got some cards around here someplace," T.J. offered. "Anybody wanna play some poker?"

"I dunno how to play poker," confessed Wiley.

T.J.'s and Randy's eyes lit up. "That's O.K., Wiley," T.J. generously replied. "We'll teach ya." He got up and went into the next room where he fumbled through some desk drawers until he came up with a deck of cards. When he returned to the kitchen, Dave was on his way in with the beer.

"Sure nobody wants one?" Whitney offered one last time. With no takers, he said, "Good. Makes that much more for me. Looks like we're gonna play a little poker, huh?"

"Five card draw alright with you guys?" asked T.J.

"Dealer's choice," stated Dave as he plopped down in his chair and sat his partial twelve-pack on the floor beside him.

"No dealer's choice," Randy corrected.

"Dealer's choice!" Dave demanded.

"No dealer's choice!"

"Dealer's choice!"

"Shoot, Whitney," complained Corey. "Every time it's your deal, we gotta play that damn Indian poker!"

"What's Indian poker?" inquired Wiley.

"You'll find out," said Dave. "Dealer's choice!"

"O.K., dealer's choice," conceded T.J., as he shuffled the cards. "But it's my deal, now, and it's five card draw. Cut?" he offered Dave.

Dave cut the cards and pulled his wallet from his back pocket. "Gitcher money out, boys, and kiss it goodbye. I'm feelin' lucky tonight!"

"Ante up, guys," reminded T.J. "You wanna just start with quarters?"

Randy felt around his pockets. "I don't have any quarters."

"Yer gonna need a bunch of 'em if yer gonna play with me!" boasted Dave as he popped open a can of Coors.

"Maw's got a quarter jar on the 'fridgerator," said T.J. as he got up from the table. "Just gimme five bucks apiece."

"Five bucks?" repeated Wiley, looking somewhat reluctant.

"Five bucks is just a start, sonny boy," declared Dave. "We'll be throwin' twenty dollar bills in there in no time!"

"Not me," denied Wiley. "I don't even know how to play the game!"

"You just do what I tell ya," advised Whitney. "Ol' Uncle Dave'll teach ya the game."

"Yeah, right," added Randy as T.J. sat the jar in the middle of the table and the boys divvied up their change.

"O.K., Wiley, pairs are good, straights are good, flushes are good," explained T.J. "The higher the cards, the better."

"Huh?"

"We'll help ya out as we go," assured Randy.

T.J. set the money jar on the floor and quickly dealt out five cards apiece.

Randy looked at his cards and pondered, "Oh, man..." He discarded three. "I'll take three cards."

"You watchin' this, Wiley?" asked T.J. as he dealt Corey three more cards. "It's yer turn."

Wiley looked confused, "What do I do?"

Dave leaned over next to Wiley. "Lemme see yer cards." He pondered the situation and pulled two cards from the young man's hand. "Git rid a' these two."

Paz discarded the two the way he had just seen Randy do, and answered, "I need two."

Before T.J. could deal Wiley the new cards, Randy reached for the old ones, saying, "Let's see whatcha had."

Dave slammed his open hand down on the back of Randy's, contending, "You don't need to see that!"

Randy jerked his hand from under Dave's and slid the cards to his chest. "A five and a seven," he observed, "why wouldn't ya want me to see that? Let's see yer hand, Wiley."

"Bullshit!" argued Dave as Wiley showed Randy his cards.

"Five, six, seven!" Corey exclaimed. "He had two pair, and ya threw 'em away!"

"Ya cheatin' little shithead!" added T.J.

"I'm just helpin' him learn the hard way!" Dave defended. "How's he gonna learn anything if we keep tellin' him what to do?"

"Re-deal!" called Randy. "Wiley, this time, you listen to me."

"Go ahead and deal 'em, Randy," said T.J. "This time, everybody put in a quarter. You get the idea, Wiley? Pairs are good. Four of a kind is better. And a straight, like ten, jack, queen, king, in the same suit, is real good."

"I think I'm catchin' on," maintained Wiley, as he threw his quarter in the pot.

"Same game," announced Randy as he dealt out five cards apiece.

Wiley picked up his cards and looked them over. He had a king, five, nine, five, and an ace. He thought about it for awhile and tossed in the nine. "One card," he requested. Randy slid him another card. Wiley was surprised to see another five.

Dave discarded two and Randy replaced them.

"Three," said T.J., as he threw out his bad ones.

"Hell, I don't know what to do," said Randy. He finally threw away two of them and replaced them. "O.K., Wiley. What're ya gonna do?"

"What am I supposed to do?" asked Paz.

"You wanna raise the bet?" asked Whitney.

Wiley looked at his cards again. Ace, king and three fives. "Uh...I guess not."

"Well, I'll raise a quarter," Dave answered proudly, as he tossed one into the pot.

"I'm out," said T.J.

"Me, too," Randy followed. "How 'bout you, Wiley?"

"I think I got a pretty good hand," he speculated. "Naw, I'm out, too."

"If ya got a good hand," Whitney advised, "throw in yer quarter. Ya might beat me."

Paz studied his hand some more. "Naw, I'm out."

"You sure?" asked Dave.

"Yeah," Wiley assured, "I'm sure."

"Whattaya got?" Dave inquired.

"Ace, king," Wiley answered, "and three fives."

"Oh, Paz," bemoaned Corey, "You should a' bet on that. That's a good hand!"

"But I didn't know if it was the best hand," Wiley reasoned.

"You should a' took a chance," advised T.J. "A hand like that's worth a raise or two."

"I thought you was s'posed to be helpin' him!" Dave jumped in. "Corey, yer s'pose'ta be tellin' him to raise and call!"

"I would of, if he'd of asked," Randy came back. "Why, what do you have?"

Dave slapped his cards on the table. Ace, king, queen, jack, ten. "Right off the bat!" he exclaimed.

"Would I'd a' beat that?" asked Wiley.

"Hell, no, ya wouldn't a' beat that!" Dave growled, "but with a hand like yers, ya should a' at least upped the bet a few times!"

T.J. and Randy began to laugh as Wiley said, "But then you'd have won more money from me."

"Well, that's the idea, dummy!"

"To lose money?"

"No! It's..." Dave shook his head in disgust, "It's yer deal."

"Well, look at it this way, Whitney," chuckled Corey as he passed Wiley the cards, "ya won three whole quarters!"

Two hours and eight beers later, Whitney folded, flat broke. "This is the dumbest game I ever played in my life," he complained. "Where do I sleep, T.J.?"

"You know where the bunkhouse is," presumed T.J., "dontcha?"

"Yeah, I r'member," slurred Dave as he took his last beer and stumbled toward the door.

"You might want to open up some windows," T.J. reminded. "It's prob'ly a little stuffy in there."

"I think I'll hit the sack, too," said Randy, as he pocketed his money and got up from the table.

"Hell, Corey, you still got plenty a' money," T.J. pointed out. "It's only one-thirty. The bars ain't even closed yet."

"They are in Nebraska," he replied, and headed for the door.

"Well, Wiley," said T.J., "It's me and you. Wanna keep playin'?"

"Oh, I don't care," Paz granted, "whatever you wanna do."

"Let's not, then," T.J. opted. "It ain't the same with just two players." He cocked his thumb over his shoulder toward the door that Randy Corey had just exited the house from. "Does he know that we're in Oklahoma?"

"I don't think so," Wiley joked back, "The dummy thinks we're in a bar in Nebraska!"

"Hey," T.J. reminded with a childlike grin, "we got more brownies!"

"Well, git 'em over here!" Paz smiled eagerly.

T.J. put the pan in the middle of the table and said, "I'll get the milk out, too."

As Wiley dug into the brownies, he asserted, "You sure know how to make a feller feel at home, T.J. I'd like you to meet my folks sometime soon."

"Lookin' forward to it," replied T.J., as he sat and poured two glasses of milk.

"I 'magine they'll come to the finals to watch me ride. Papa never liked the idea of me ridin' bulls 'til just lately, when he seen how much money I'm makin'. He come up from Mexico, and busted his butt every day of his life. He didn't think it was right for me to be runnin' around and havin' so much fun. He couldn't imagine that it could ever pay off."

"He's come around though, huh?"

"Yeah, pretty much. He smiles and shakes my hand, now, when he sees me. He used to just think I was a bum. Mama, she still don't like it. Thinks I'm gonna get hurt. After the finals, I'm gonna buy 'em a lotta nice things."

"Like what?" T.J. inquired.

"Whatever I can afford," mused Wiley. "New cars and pickups. Maybe a house."

"You better hold quite a bit a' that money back," warned T.J. "I don't mean to bust yer bubble, but some years just ain't gonna be as easy as this'un. I know yer a helluva rider, and yer ridin' tough, drawin' good, stayin' healthy, and everything's goin' yer way, but it ain't always gonna be that way. You'll go months where you can't draw a money bull to save your life, and when ya do, you'll buck yerself off. And yer mama's right, Wiley; you stay in rodeo long enough, yer *gonna* git hurt."

With a glass of milk in one hand, brownie in the other, Wiley Paz froze in time as hurtful confusion flowed through his face.

"Don't get me wrong, Wiley," T.J. tried to explain himself, "I'm just sayin' that some people pay their dues before, and some pay their dues after, but, no matter what, the dues are *gonna get paid.*" He searched Wiley's face for that easygoing smile. "Look, I'm just sayin' hang on to some a' that money. I ain't preachin' at ya, I'm just givin' ya some financial advice."

Wiley slowly took a drink of milk and then smiled thoughtfully. "I never looked at it that way before," he expressed. "Thanks, man!"

T.J. laughed a friendly laugh of relief and patted Wiley on the back. "Any time, ol' buddy."

"T.J.?" Paz looked up to T.J. He wanted in on some of his knowledge, his experience.

"Yeah, pard."

"I been hearin' you guys talk about this Bennett every now and then. Who was he?"

T.J.'s eyes smiled mellow. "Bennett was the bullridin'est, whiskey-drinkin'est...He was the best man I ever knew. And the best friend I ever had."

"Tell me about him."

"Well, he was just...he was just always good to be around. Always willin' to help ya. He was just one a' them guys that...that was here for a good time, not a long time. In fact, he use'ta say that all the time. It was always a good time with Bennett. Always."

"What happened to him?"

T.J. looked down into his milk glass. "A bull killed him in Houston."

Wiley became silent. He suddenly felt sorry for T.J., and everyone else who had to lose this man. And then he felt regret that he had never been able to meet Bennett himself.

"I'm responsible for his death," added T.J. "It eats at me every day. For awhile I told myself it wasn't my fault, but I know it was. I know it. Randy and Dave don't say so, but they know it. Shot Palmer damn sure knows it...I feel so bad for his parents. But I can't face 'em. I ain't goin' over there tomorrow."

Wiley studied T.J.'s face. Suddenly he looked to Wiley like an old guy. The worry lines below his beat-up straw cowboy hat bunched up in the center of his forehead. The unshaven frown drooped below weary eyes – one less open than the other – both cradled by dark lines reaching for the edges of his face.

Wiley did not know if he should ask or not. Finally, he did. "What do you mean, you're responsible?"

T.J. let out a long sigh. "I was ridin' the bull at the time. You know the bull, Genghis Khan?"

"I've seen him," Wiley said.

"Sonny Joe shoulda' put a bullet in his head. I can't believe he's still buckin' him." He went on to explain, "I'd just took my wrap when that bull lunged up in the air and knocked Bennett off the chute gate into the arena. Well, I didn't know Bennett was layin' in the arena, and I nodded my head, and when they opened the gate, he went straight for Bennett and killed him."

Wiley searched for the right words. "Wow," was all he could come up with.

"That ain't the whole story, though," T.J. continued as he set his glass on the table. "You know the bull, Big Mac?"

"Yeah," said Paz. "I been on him.

T.J. looked at Wiley, dumbfounded. "You have not!"

"The hell I haven't," Wiley defended his word.

"When?"

"'Bout a year-and-a-half ago."

"Sonny Joe wasn't even buckin' him a year-and-a-half ago!"

"No, but Scotty Redwood was." Wiley argued. "Matter of fact, I'm the reason Sonny had to pay so much for Big Mac. If I'd a' rode him in Sonny's practice pen, Sonny'd a' got him for free. He slammed me down and Sonny bought him for twice what Scotty was askin'. That bull *bucks*, now."

"Damn right he does," agreed T.J. "So, you got on him when he was just a two-year-old, huh?"

"Yeah," Wiley answered. "He wasn't near as big as he is now."

"Anyway, lemme tell ya the rest of this deal about Bennett," T.J. backtracked. "One night when we was gittin' drunk, Bennett told me that when he died that he was gonna come back as a buckin' bull. Everybody thought he was full a' shit, 'cept for me. Well, I thought he was full a' shit, too. Anyway, he showed me his BM tattoo on his shoulder, for Bennett McKinney. He said if we ever see a bull with a BM brand on his right shoulder..."

"And Big Mac has one!" Wiley interrupted.

T.J. flicked both wrists in the air as if to rid himself of the conclusion, leaving it suspended in the air for Wiley draw on.

Wiley grasped at the concept, "Can they do that?"

T.J. shot a disgusted sideways glance at Paz, "Can *who* do that?"

"Well, I mean...how's that work?"

Closing his eyes in mild frustration, T.J. said, "Hell, I don't know how it works! All I know is, three months ago this bull shows up with a BM brand and he's the buckin'est sumbitch I ever seen!"

"No..." Wiley said in awe, "shit..."

"But, there's a part I forgot to tell ya," T.J. went on. "Before Bennett got killed, me and him made a solemn pact that we was goin' to the National Finals together." He raised his eyebrows to Wiley in 'get the picture?' fashion.

Wiley searched for the meaning. "So...didja go to the finals together?"

"Hell, no, we didn't! He got killed!"

Wiley was lost.

"Look, Wiley," T.J. impatiently explained, "we made a pact to go to the Finals together. He died. He came back as Big Mac. Understand? We're still goin' to the Finals together!"

"Ohhhhhh," Wiley said slowly as it sank into his brain. "Now I see. Man, this is wild! You ain't makin' this up, are you?"

T.J. leaned over to Wiley and looked him in the eye. "You think I'd lie about something like this?"

Wiley didn't know, but the look in T.J.'s eyes said that he wasn't. "No," Wiley answered. "No, I don't think yer lyin'."

T.J. sat back and drank the last of his milk. "Well, pardner," he said in a relaxed tone, "you didn't get to meet him as a man, but you got to meet him as a bull."

"He must a' been a good man," Wiley reflected, "'cause he sure is a good bull."

As T.J. gazed off into the nowhereness of the middle of the kitchen, and things to come, Wiley looked again at his new amigo. It's strange, he thought, how T.J. no longer looks like the old man who moments earlier was still in mourning over the loss of his dear friend. The worry lines were gone with the frown. The dark lines beneath his eyes were suddenly lighter. A squint still remained in one eye, but it was a youthful, 'smacked-by-a-bull' squint.

"Wiley," T.J. asked, "do you believe in fate?"

"I dunno," said Wiley. "Never really thought about it. I ain't even real sure what it means."

"It means that some things are just gonna happen," explained T.J., "and no matter what you do to try and stop it, it's just gonna happen anyway. And there ain't nothin' you can do about it."

"Oh. No, I don't think I believe in that."

"I use'ta not believe it either," said T.J. "But since this BM thing, I been believin' a lotta things that I didn't use to."

"So, you believe in fate now?" Wiley asked.

"Uh huh."

"Do you know your fate?"

"Yeah, I do," claimed T.J., as his gaze returned to Wiley. "I sure do. I finally got all this figured out. There's a reason Bennett died that night, and there's a reason I started ridin' so good and winnin' all this money, and there's a reason he came back as a bull, just like he said he would. Wiley, I'm gonna win the world this year. I'm gonna be the World Champion Bullrider. There ain't no way around it.."

"But what about me?" appealed Wiley. "I wanna be World Champion!"

"You can be runner-up," shrugged T.J. "or you can be World Champ some other year. Yer young, you got a lotta chances to win the world." He jabbed his thumb against his own chest. "Nineteen-Ninety is *mine!*"

Chapter 21: September 1990

"T.J. Jergenson – Bullridin.'"

"T.J. Jergenson," repeated the Enid, Oklahoma rodeo secretary, as she scanned the sheet of rodeo contestants. "Here you are, T.J. That'll be sixty dollars."

T.J. already had three twenties out, and laid them on the table.

"Thank you very much," she responded, "and you've drawn bull thirty-four, Widow-Maker."

T.J. stepped aside and Wiley Paz moved forward to the table and handed her a fifty and a twenty. "Wiley Paz in the bullriding."

Again she checked the contestant sheet. "O.K., Wiley Paz. Here's your change and your bull is BM – Big Mac."

Wiley looked up at T.J. in time to see his face go blank. "Alright!" he said confidently as he made room for the other contestants behind him. "It's payback time!"

As they walked together back to the van to get their gear, T.J. didn't know what to say. He wanted his partner to do well, but deep down, he didn't think his little buddy could ride Big Mac, and Wiley could sense this feeling, so nothing was said.

Although it was nearing seven-thirty in the evening, the temperature still sizzled around the one hundred degree mark, as the die-hard fans began to fill up the shaded grandstand across the arena. A little breeze would be welcomed there – would have been all day. As the rodeo announcer made his final mike-check – "Testing. Testing. One-two-three. Can you folks at the end of the arena hear me O.K.? Up a little? How's that?" – the water tank truck made laps in the arena spraying the ground with a last coat of moisture in an attempt to keep the dust down.

As Jergenson and Paz approached the van, they both recognized the man who was sitting in the entrance of the van's side door.

"Paw!" T.J. hailed as Jim Jergenson stood up to shake his son's hand.

Just as tall as T.J., but with a much straighter posture, broader shoulders and meatier frame, Jim seemed to be twice the size of T.J., and three times the size of little Wiley Paz. He sported a thick red mustache, chubby red cheeks, and reddish-gray hair poked from beneath the back of his new straw cowboy hat. "How ya been, Tom?" he greeted as they clasped hands.

"Just great," grinned T.J. "How 'bout yerself?"

"I been hot, boy, hotter'n hell, but there ain't nothin' I can do about that. Wiley Paz! You little dickens! Is my boy takin' good care of ya?"

"Well, he's doin' his best," Wiley returned as he, too, shook Jim's giant paw. "It's good to see ya again!"

"You too," said Jim. "You two gonna be around awhile? I got more hay to put up."

"I 'magine we can stay around tomorrow and part a' the next day before we gotta leave," said T.J., "as long as ya don't work us *too* hard."

"Where's yer bronc-ridin' buddies?" he asked.

"They drew outta this'un to go to Mesquite," T.J. answered.

"Oh, well," Jim confirmed, "they didn't work as hard as you guys anyway. 'Specially that shorter one of the two, Dave Whitney."

"Where's Maw?" T.J. asked.

"She's up in the stands, where *I* oughta be," responded Jim.

"You're swingin' chute gates again this year, aintcha?" assumed T.J.

"Hell, yeah," returned Jim, "and you boys better ride up. If ya don't I'll be right there to kick yer asses!"

"Right there's reason enough for me to ride tough!" chuckled Wiley.

"Well, I better git goin'," said Jim. "It's dang near show time. I just wanted to come over and tell you boys good luck."

"Thanks, Paw. See ya later."

Two hours later, Oklahoma dust rose behind sweaty barrel horses, despite the efforts of the water trucks prior to the rodeo.

T.J. Jergenson's bull, Widow-Maker, waited quietly in chute number one. T.J. had seen the bull go several times before. A big red and white bull with no horns, he generally spun real hard to the left and threw a lot of power.

Normally, at this time T.J. would be doing a few exercises and stretching out, but as hot and muggy as it was, he decided to save every bit of his energy for the big ride. As he sat against the wooden fence, his straw hat draped over a knee, the dust clung to the large sweat stains beneath his armpits.

Even as hot as it was, Wiley Paz paced back and forth in front of T.J.

"Wiley, why dontcha relax a little bit?" recommended T.J. "You'll be the last bullrider. They always close the show with Big Mac."

"I can't relax," claimed Wiley. "I got the best bull in the herd."

T.J., already clad in chaps and spurs, slowly stood up and slid his riding glove onto his hand as the last barrel racer darted out of the arena. "Pull my rope, Wiley?"

Wiley nodded his head in agreement as he hopped over the chute to the left side of the bull.

Sonny Joe Barker was already at the bull's flank. "Win y'self a pile a' money, now, T.J.," he encouraged.

"Ladies and gentlemen, are you ready for some bullriding?" boomed the announcer from above the chutes.

Mild applause and some wild cheering resounded from the grandstands.

"Folks, I know you can do better than that," coaxed the announcer. "This is the event we've been waiting for all night! Now, I'm going to ask one more time – are you folks ready for some bullriding?!"

This time the crowd responded much more enthusiastically, whistling and whooping and cheering and clapping.

"That's what I wanted to hear," the man behind the mike responded. "Folks, you know the rules – eight seconds, one hand – other than that, anything goes. It's bullriding time in Enid, Oklahoma, and the first player tonight happens to be the number two bullrider in the world, born and raised right here in Enid, T.J. Jergenson!"

Again, a surge of spirited excitement reverberated from the bleachers.

As T.J. crawled over the top rail of the chute, he saw his father looking up at him from the gate latch.

"Didja go over and talk to Maw?" big Jim asked.

"Yeah," T.J. answered as he sat down on the bull's back. Widow-Maker's back was so wide that T.J. barely had enough room to drop his legs down beside the bull. Luckily, the seasoned bull stood extremely well in the chute and T.J. was able to push him back and forth with his knees in order to get his legs down where he wanted. "I talked to Grandma Flourke and Aunt Tessa, too," he added as he warmed up the handhold of his rope.

"Well, cowboy up and win yer hometown rodeo, son," coached Jim. "There's still a lotta single local girls who want ya to spend all that money on 'em at the dance tonight."

"Pull," T.J. said to Wiley without looking up.

Wiley lifted on the end of T.J.'s bullrope and T.J. slid his gloved hand up and down along it until he felt the glove and rope begin to bind together. "Slack." He slid his hand into the handhold again, and ordered, "O.K., pull." Wiley steadily tightened T.J.'s bullrope, until T.J. halted him. "That's good." Wiley still held the rope securely while T.J. jerked the leather-entwined handhold back and grabbed handfuls of the bull's loose hide and pushed it forward, away from the rope. "Pull a little more," he commanded. Wiley did so, and T.J. took the rope from his hand, and wrapped it around his riding hand.

As Wiley hopped down from the chute and stepped past Jim, he prompted, "Now, *ride*, T.J.!"

Again, T.J. had trouble sliding to his rope as Widow-Maker's back was so wide. Little by little, he inched his way to the handhold of his rope, leaned forward, took a deep breath and nodded his head.

"Go git 'em, boy!" hollered Jim as he threw the gate open.

Widow-Maker rocked back onto his hind legs and bailed high from the chute. As he did, T.J. hunched up over his shoulders and prepared for the jolt of the bull's front feet when they hit the ground. Suddenly, a 'thunk!' and a rush of pain flooded T.J.'s right kneecap as it crashed into the steel gate post as Widow-Maker tried to rub him off on the chute gate. This intentional cheap shot forced T.J.'s body back two feet from the bullrope before his knee slid past the post.

At that point a cowboy could grab down, bail off and declare a foul, for which he would be awarded a re-ride, if he chose to take it.

It never entered T.J.'s mind.

As Widow-Maker's front hooves collided with the ground, T.J. thrust his hips as hard and as far as he could forward to the rope. He gained nearly a foot. When the bull leapt into the air again and made a left turn, T.J. lost all that he had gained. Again, when the bull hit the ground, T.J. used the momentum to fight his way back closer to the bullrope, and this time he refused to give back the inches that he conquered. But the bull took them anyway. Fueled by the fire in his soul, T.J.'s eyes reddened as his thick bottom lip tightened and rolled inside out, revealing jagged snarling teeth. He grunted in desperate determination as he charged forward with every ounce of 'try' in his being, scratching and clawing the bull's thick hide with the blunt lock-rowels of his spurs, gaining inches, losing a few of them with each jump and gaining a few more back, reaching forward, pulling back, digging and thrusting until he was inches from being in control. As Widow-Maker continued to lunge forward and to the left, T.J.'s right foot lost everything it had a hold of, slid up the bull's side until it spurred T.J. in the rear. As he instantaneously jammed his foot back down to the bull's side, he had already been slid a foot and a half back from his rope again. As he courageously struggled to get to the rope again, he felt the bull's momentum increase. Trying with all of his might, T.J. did not have the strength to pull his body forward. He found himself fighting just to hold his position where he was. As his body strove fervently to stay aboard this massive twisting chunk of muscle and bone, T.J.'s conscious mind possessed one thought – "buzzer…" From the day he began riding bulls he was told never to anticipate the eight-second buzzer. Although his grip on the bullrope never weakened, his arm was straight and stretched to its limit. His butt was all the way back to the flankrope and his legs awkwardly clung to the bull's hips. At a fraction of an instant before his feet slid completely up behind him and his free arm slammed down upon the bull's shoulders, T.J. heard the sound he had been waiting for – the buzzer.

While Widow-Maker stayed circling to the left, T.J.'s body was thrown off of the right side of the bull – away from his riding hand, and T.J. knew immediately that he was hung up. About the time his feet and knees hit the ground, he was jerked back up into the air, his fist bound tight to the back of a raging hurricane. As the buzzer continued to tell him to get off, T.J. had one other thought on his mind – "bullfighter…" When the bull made his descent to the ground, T.J. grasped for the flopping tail of his bullrope, catching nothing but air. Again, he was jerked back to the bull – so hard that his head flopped back like that of a rag doll – and his feet sailed over his head. For an instant, he felt a hand on his wrist. Then he felt a tugging on his bullrope. Suddenly, he was free, and somehow on his feet and running toward the fence.

As he realized he was safe from the bull, T.J. found that the pain in his right kneecap – the one that crashed into the gate – had agonizingly returned to his consciousness. He almost dropped to the dirt, but held himself up by bracing the fence.

As soon as the bullfighter led Widow-Maker from the arena, two paramedics, armed with a white bag of tools and a gurney, trotted to T.J.'s aid.

"I won't need that carryin' board," T.J. grunted as cordially as he was able, "but you can help me out of the arena."

With a human crutch under each arm, T.J. hobbled from the arena amidst a standing ovation from his hometown crowd.

"Ladies and gentlemen, he is up, he is O.K., as we look to our judges for the score...a respectable eighty-two points! What do you say we pay off T.J. Jergenson one more time!"

Wiley Paz met T.J. at the gate. "You O.K.?" he asked.

"Hurts like hell," T.J. grimaced. "I'll be alright."

The medics insisted on taking a look at the knee, but T.J. refused them. He just wanted to sit down for a while, which he did.

Nearly fifteen minutes later, by the time Sonny Joe's chute help had run Big Mac into the narrow alley way to the chutes, T.J.'s knee had swollen and stiffened considerably.

"You gonna be able to pull my rope?" Wiley asked him as he gathered his bullrope from where it hung on the fence.

T.J. had just finished packing away his gear into his own rodeo bag. "Yeah," he answered hoarsely, trying to conceal the strain of his swollen joint, "Is he in, yet?"

"Yep," Wiley confidently announced. "The last chute."

One by one, four more riders left the chutes with glorious dreams of victory on their minds. Two stayed on for eight seconds, two bit the dust, but no one in the night's performance had surpassed T.J.'s eighty-two point marking.

"Friends, we've saved the best for last," the announcer divulged in a low and quiet manner, coaxing anticipation from the audience as his voice and rhythm became faster and louder. "Big Mac, of the Stingin' B Rodeo Company, one of the top-ranked bucking bulls in the country has drawn up to a young bullrider by the name of Wiley Paz, who just happens to be *the* number one ranked bullrider in the world!" He continued as the crowd cheered encouragement for both rider and bull. "Wiley Paz, weighing in at one hundred and twenty-five pounds and all of twenty years old, has won more money than any other bullrider, *including* T.J. Jergenson who is in a close second in the race for the world title and is winning this very rodeo. Big Mac is a three year old Brahma and *he is mean!* This will be the bull's seventy-third trip in professional competition. Of the seventy-two previous trips he has been ridden – never! Yes folks, seventy-two professional rodeo cowboys have nodded their heads on this bull, not one of them was there for the eight-second whistle. Will Wiley Paz be the first to conquer this unconquerable beast? If he does, he will increase his lead over second-place T.J. Jergenson. If he cannot, however, ride this bull, T.J. again will be in the lead for the world standing. Which way will it be, folks? Bull – or rider?"

Wiley heard none of this as he slid his legs down alongside of the bull and worked his rosined glove and rope together. He noted right away that he had a wider spot to sit on this time, and Big Mac definitely took up more room in the chute than he did a year and a half before, back in Sonny Joe's practice pen. The hump on the bull's shoulders was higher, his horns wider. Even as Big Mac stood still, Wiley could feel muscle and raw power that was not there before. "Slack," he commanded T.J., at the tail of his rope.

T.J. let the rope go limp. He searched for words of encouragement. Although he didn't think his partner could ride the bull, he did know the power of positive thinking, and if Wiley truly believed that he could do it, then just maybe he could.

"O.K., pull," Wiley told him.

"Be there, Wiley," Sonny Joe encouraged from the flank. "If anybody can cover this bull, yer the man."

Wiley took the tail of the rope from T.J. and wrapped it around his hand.

"Now, *ride*, Wiley," T.J. whispered loudly in Wiley's ear before he climbed from the chute and limped back down the fence line.

"It's in yer hands now, son," Jim Jergenson half-yelled from his place at the gate. "Make it happen!"

Without hesitation, Wiley slid and nodded.

As big Jim threw the gate open, Big Mac hesitated in the chute. Wiley tightened up and watched the bull's head as if it were a short fuse burning toward a keg of dynamite. The explosion would be any second...When the bull leapt from the chute, the soles of his massive hooves were four feet from the arena floor. As his dirty gray hump reached its highest peak and he began to descend, Big Mac slung his head skyward, sprung his backbone earthward, and kicked high behind himself, snapping all of his eighteen hundred pounds to the ground with such intense force that Wiley's neck muscles failed to keep his chin tucked against his chest. His teeth clicked together and his head and body felt rattled from the jolt as the bull beneath him pounded the ground and instantaneously bailed high and into a left spin. Wiley felt his feet bouncing uselessly along Big Mac's rib cage and gripping nothing when the bull snapped back to earth again. He felt completely out of control as he vigorously pumped his free arm over his head. Half a jump behind, Wiley struggled chaotically to get back into the bull's rhythm. As Big Mac plunged to the ground for the third time, Wiley felt the handhold of his bullrope slip from the palm of his hand, halfway to the ends of his fingers. Again, he threw his arm wildly, scratched and clawed with his spurs, strove to keep his head down, his arm cocked, his grip...Together, man and beast blew into the air. When the bull hit the dirt, the cowboy was sailing backwards, head first and upside down, through the air.

Big Mac was not through yet. Immediately, he spun around on his front hooves in time to see his newest prey land in front of him like a sack of potatoes. The bullfighter darted in front of his face but he paid no attention. Experience had taught him not to chase an upright victim when a downed one was available. He lowered his head and charged. As his target rose to his hands and knees and looked over his shoulder, Big Mac saw and recognized the open-mouthed, wide-eyed look of fear. He heard a grunt upon impact and slung his horns to the sky, sending his helpless victim sailing again. As Wiley landed clumsily on one foot and dropped to his knees, Big Mac never lost sight of him. He charged again. Lowering his head and slinging his horns, he heard the familiar grunt, and was surprised at the absence of pressure against his head, as he followed through with his swing. At the last instant, Wiley had dove to one side of the bull's deadly horns, and was now hightailing it to the nearest fence. As Big Mac spun around and rushed the boy, the bullfighter once again came into his view. As he was closer, and running slower, the bull let Wiley go for the seemingly easier prey.

Wiley scampered up the fence where he paused to catch his breath and to cuss himself for failing to ride Big Mac.

"You O.K., cowboy?" someone asked from the safe side of the fence.

Wiley didn't even look up. "Yeah," he muttered.

"There is nothing to be ashamed of," consoled the announcer, "to get thrown from a bull of that caliber. All Wiley Paz is taking home with him tonight is what you give him." The crowd was already cheering and clapping as the announcer urged, "So how about a big round of applause for this young cowboy! And after seventy-three trips, the winner and still champion, what do you folks think about Big Mac of the Stingin' B Rodeo Company?"

Wiley's youthful pride felt crushed as the crowd's polite and respectful applause erupted into a wave of ovation that danced throughout the arena and lingered with the dust clouds long after the handsome gray bull had exited the arena.

Chapter 22: October 1990

"Shot sure is gonna be glad to see us," T.J. smiled as he pulled into the trailer park. "I ain't even talked to him since he broke his back at Bakersfield. Wish Randy and Dave was with us, he'd be glad to see them too. Yer gonna like Shot, Wiley, he's a good sonuvagun."

Wiley Paz had been hearing this, and words like it, for the last ninety miles, when T.J. decided that they had time to take a little detour on their way to the next rodeo and stop off to visit with his old running buddy, Shot Palmer.

"He was a bullfightin' sumbitch," T.J. carried on. "Always in the right place at the right time."

In the last hour and a half, T.J. had built Shot Palmer's name into legendary proportions in the ways of bullfighting, fist fighting, womanizing, drinking, and hellraising. So much so, that Paz was pretty nervous about even meeting the man.

"This woman he's got with him now is better lookin' than any of 'em that he married," Jergenson rambled. "Kinda Indian lookin'. I think her name's Rachel." He pulled into the empty driveway of an old yellow trailer house and shut off the van. "His pickup ain't here...Dang it, I hope he's home," he said as he opened the door and got out.

Wiley crawled out, too, and stretched his legs beside the van as T.J. walked up the plank steps and beat on the door.

"Shit," T.J. cursed as he peeked through the small door window. "There ain't even no lights on. Sure is a mess in there." He twisted the doorknob. "It's locked."

A slight breeze rustled the orange and yellow leaves of the young sapling in the yard beside the house. Wiley buttoned his jacket and looked westward at the fading pink remainder of the day. Some of the neighboring houses had little pictures of witches and skeletons and ghosts in their windows. The trailer across the street even had a scarecrow in the yard. Shot's house had no Halloween decorations at all.

"I think I still got a key to the house in the glovebox," said T.J. as he returned to the van. He opened the glovebox and dug around a little. "Here it is."

Wiley followed T.J. back to the house. T.J. stuck the key in the hole, lifted, jiggled and twisted. "Honey, I'm home," he announced as he opened the door and entered. "Shot never was much of a house-cleaner," he told Paz as he surveyed the crumbs on the ugly green carpet, empty beer cans on the coffee table, and the used silverware and paper plates on the kitchen counter.

Wiley finally spoke up. "No, I guess he ain't." His eyes scanned the living room, stopping at a black-and-white, eight-by-ten photograph on the wall. "Hey, is this him?"

T.J. came and looked at the picture. It was Shot, in full clown regalia, running toward the camera, looking over his shoulder at a little black fighting bull that was hot on his heels. "That's him," he said. "I think that's at North Platte, the first year they had a bullfightin' competition there."

Wiley scanned the wall for more pictures. "Here's one of you, T.J., and Dave and Randy, and a couple of other guys."

"That's Shot," T.J. pointed out, "and this other'n is Bennett McKinney, the guy I told you so much about."

"You all look like a bunch of wild-asses," noted Wiley.

"That's about all we amounted to, back then," attested T.J.

Wiley's eyes followed the wall around the corner and stopped. "Looks like somebody still is." He pointed out a fist-sized hole in the white plaster wall.

"God-dang." T.J. shook his head. "I wonder where he is."

Wiley snooped into the kitchen and opened the refrigerator. "Jesus!" he exclaimed as he slammed the door shut. "He ain't been here for awhile! The bread's green and there's somethin' in there that's growin' fur!"

T.J. looked around. "But the heater's still on. He must a' left in a helluva hurry."

"You s'pose he's in jail?" mused Wiley.

"That's just what I was thinkin'."

"Where's the bathroom?"

"Down the hall and to the right."

Wiley excused himself, leaving T.J. alone, wondering what could have happened to Shot. Let's see; the heater was on, the furniture was all still here...It wasn't like Shot to leave like this. Well, actually it was. He used to pull this kind of stuff all the time. But, you would think that living with Rachel might have settled him down a little. Not really, none of his other three wives did. T.J. decided to call the jailhouse. He picked up the phone receiver and held it to his ear. No dial tone. So much for that idea. He put the receiver down and walked into the living room. Another hole in the wall. Also, a lamp propped upside-down above a crumpled lampshade and shattered bulb. T.J. shook his head. He pictured Shot and Rachel in a messy fight. He did not know Rachel very well, but he did know Shot's temper. He heard the toilet flush as Wiley finished up. At least the water bill is paid. Maybe Shot was just on a weeklong drunk and was at the bar. Maybe he was just road-tripping. Maybe he'd found a job and would be home from work any minute now.

"T.J.!" he heard Wiley yell, "Who's this?"

T.J.'s heart clenched like a fist. He pictured Rachel or Shot, lying unconscious, or worse, as he hurried down the hall and peeked around the corner into Shot's bedroom.

There stood Wiley, laughing at another photograph he had found. "Here's a picture of you when you were a young punk! Lookit that Beatles haircut!"

T.J. let out a thankful sigh and leaned weakly against the door. "Wiley..."

"How old are you in this?" asked Paz in semi-amazement.

T.J. surveyed the picture. "Thirteen or fourteen."

"Man!" Wiley exclaimed and tossed the photograph onto the bed where he had picked it up. "There's pictures all over the floor," he noticed.

"Shot use'ta get 'em out and stare at 'em for hours when I was livin' with him," T.J. remembered aloud. "He's got to miss fightin' bulls somethin' terrible."

"Here's another one of you," announced Wiley as he picked it up from the floor.

"Yep," said T.J. "Me and Bennett. In Roundup, Montana. Bennett's only serious girlfriend took that of us."

"Did he marry her?"

"Nope."

Wiley dropped to a knee, pulled another picture in close, and slid it right-side up. "This is a heckuva bullridin' picture," he claimed. "It ain't you, his legs ain't long enough. Is this Bennett, too?"

"Sure is," T.J. said proudly. "At Cheyenne Frontier Days. He won the round on that bull."

"That bull is *bailin'*, now," Wiley said in awe. "Bennett must a' been a damn good rider."

"He rode just like you do," claimed T.J. as he squatted down beside Wiley. "Exact same style. You look so much alike when you're ridin', that sometimes I think I'm watchin' Bennett. It's unreal."

Wiley took T.J.'s words as a great compliment. Not knowing how to express his gratitude, he said nothing.

"Wanna watch Bennett ride?" T.J. asked.

Wiley looked at T.J.

"Shot's got a lotta rodeo footage of me and Bennett," T.J. explained. "They were really Bennett's tapes but Bennett didn't have no VCR."

"Heck, yeah," agreed Wiley. "Let's have a look. Maybe I'll learn somethin'."

"Alright!" said T.J. as he rose and left the room. "Follow me!"

"Hey, do you think we should call the copshop and see if they got Shot in there?" Paz asked as he walked behind T.J.

"Already tried," T.J. answered without looking back, "but Shot's phone's been disconnected."

"S'pose we oughta go down there?"

"Not really. I got a few unpaid traffic tickets here. Besides, if we get him out now, he's just gonna wanna get drunk." Beside the television set was a cardboard box full of video tapes. T.J. stooped over, picked out a tape, and read the label. "Pocatello, Idaho; Calgary and Medicine Hat, A.B., C.N. That must be Alberta, Canada. Wanna watch 'em?"

"Sure," answered Wiley, as he dusted off a spot on the couch.

T.J. turned on the TV and the VCR and stuck the tape in. A bronc rider was getting set in the chute. "You wanna watch Dave and Randy ride broncs?" he asked.

"Not if you don't," Wiley declined. "I've see them guys ride plenty of times."

"Me neither," said T.J., as he found the remote control, fast-forwarded the tape and settled back in Shot's recliner. "She only taped Randy and Dave's bronc rides, but Bennett had her get all of the bullridin'." He pushed the play button and put the tape at regular speed. "I ain't sure who this is," he said of the first rider as a big black bull with a speckled front end erupted from the chute, looked as if he was going to spin to the left and then swooped back around to the right.

"That's a pretty nice ride," Paz commented at the conclusion of the ride.

The next bull out was a tall brindle with high horns. He did not spin, but bucked high and hard and shed his rider handily.

"How far into this are you and Bennett?" Wiley asked restlessly.

"I think I'm just a couple more trips away, if I remember right," said T.J.

"Well, fast-forward, man, unless there's somethin' really wild comin' up."

"I can't remember if there are any great rides or wild wrecks comin' up or not," T.J. said as he hit the advance button. "Must not be. If there were, I'd remember 'em." He let the tape spin forward until he recognized Bennett, up in the chute, pulling his bullrope. "Here's me, on one called Wildfire." A Charolais bull with no horns bailed into the arena, and spun both directions. T.J. stayed squarely in the middle of the bull for over six seconds. Then he loosened up and got slammed down.

"Wow," critiqued Wiley. "You never shoulda' bucked off that bull."

"I know it," concurred T.J. "A bull like that'd never throw me off today."

"Fast-forward to Bennett's ride."

T.J. sped past five bullrides and pushed the play button, "O.K., here it is."

Wiley leaned forward on the couch as Bennett slid to his rope and nodded his head. As the gate swung wide, a short-legged cowboy burst onto the screen atop a wide horned dark gray ball of fire. The cowboy's arm was cocked, his chin was tucked, his back straight, toes out, spurs in, and his upper body out over the bull's shoulders. His bull kicked high and dropped hard. He spun to the right so tight that Bennett nearly ended up between his horns. Wiley cheered and nearly jumped from the sofa as Bennett thrust his chest out, pushed forward with his riding hand, and threw his outside leg at the bull's shoulder. After two dizzying revolutions the bull changed his pattern from a tight, hard-dropping spin, to a wild lunging mayhem. Instinctively Bennett switched riding styles as quick as the bull had changed bucking styles. Instead of pushing away from the bull's head, he was suddenly lifting on his rope, reaching forward with his free hand, squeezing with his legs and clawing at the bull's ribs with the rowels of his spurs. The bull leapt along the front of the bucking chutes, sending the gateman and chute boss scrambling up the fence for safety. Then with no warning whatsoever, the bull spun around to the left this time, just as tight as he had before. The momentum sent Bennett to the outside of the spin, but he cocked his head to the eye of the hurricane, looked over the bull's inside shoulder, and pumped his free arm savagely over his head. At the sound of the buzzer, he looked to the outside, let go, and was ejected completely out of the television screen. When the camera caught up with him, he was trotting across the arena, appreciatively tipping his cowboy hat to the crowd, and the bull.

"Man!" Paz exclaimed genuinely. "That guy was sticky! Just like you said he was! Do I really ride like that?"

T.J. stopped the tape. "That coulda' been you," he insisted as he rewound to the start of the ride. "Let's watch it again in slow motion."

As frame-by-frame the bull coiled up and unraveled beneath Bennett McKinney, Wiley paid closer attention, this time to Bennett's moves, instead of the bull's action. "Everything this bull does," he thought aloud, "Bennett has a move to match it." As the bull's front hooves slowly collided with the arena dirt, he sucked back to the right. Even in slow motion, his head seemed instantly where his tail had just been. "He tipped him forward, there, right away, but all Bennett does is compensate by pushin' off and comin' across with his free arm...He makes it look so easy...How's he do that?"

T.J.'s eyes never left the set as he said, "You oughta know. You been ridin' like that all year."

Wiley momentarily glanced over at T.J. Was he serious? Wiley knew he was riding tough. Real tough, as a matter of fact, but until now, he'd had no idea that he had been making this type of ride, with this sharp of moves, these kind of recoveries, with virtually *no* reaction time. It was like his body was a machine, and he was actually a part of every bull he got on.

"Watch, when the bull goes to lungin'," T.J. commented, "Bennett don't miss a beat. Now he's liftin' insteada pushin', and chargin' the front end..."

"Like a whole 'nother rider," Wiley concluded.

"Here's somethin' you didn't see the first time, Wiley;" T.J. pointed out, "this bull'll stutter-step and kinda skip before he goes back into his spin. He sets most cowboys up, that way."

Sure enough, Wiley watched as the bull made a short buck, with very little kick, then skipped forward, before planting and pivoting back to the left.

"Bennett use'ta study them bulls," T.J. remembered. "He'd find little quirks and movements about 'em that I'd a' never caught."

As Bennett finished his ride and slowly sailed away from his mount, T.J. concluded, "That's ol' Cat Scratch Fever. First time he ever got rode."

"No kiddin'," Wiley asserted. "How many points did he go?"

"Ninety-one. He won the round on him."

"That was a heckuva ride," Wiley's demeanor went from envy and appreciation to wonderment. "Did Bennett ever make it to the National Finals?"

"Nope," T.J. shook his head solemnly, "never did."

"How come?"

T.J. paused, and thought carefully about his answer. "When me and Bennett were goin'...basically, we were just in it for the party. I mean, we both rode purty tough, s'pecially Bennett, but we were more interested in what was goin' on after the rodeo than the rodeo itself. We were just in it for fun. The money we won was just icing on the cake, just a means to go have more fun. I guess we were afraid to get serious and go hard, afraid that that'd take all the fun out of it...I dunno...maybe I held him back. He sure had more talent than me. I don't regret them years. We sure did have a good time. Sometimes I just wonder what we coulda' done if we'd a' really set our minds to it."

The action on the TV screen clicked away in slow motion, unmindful of the two as Wiley gazed into T.J.'s reflection.

"Aintcha still havin' fun?" the younger cowboy inquired.

"Oh, yeah," T.J. immediately responded, "I'm havin' a great time. Hell, I'm makin' more money than I know what to do with. But there's more pressure on me than there ever was before. For one thing, you been on my tail every step a' the way...Y'know, sometimes when I'm drivin' down the road or tryin' to go to sleep, I'll ask myself how long can this ride last?...Am I really this good, or have I just been real lucky this year?"

"You really have them kinda doubts?" Wiley asked.

" I have 'em a lot, when I'm thinkin' alone," admitted T.J. "How do you keep such a positive outlook?"

"I just don't think about it," said Wiley. "I just do my very best. What happens, happens."

"C'mon, Wiley...Yer twenty years old, the Finals is two months away...don't you even think about winnin' the world?"

Wiley's dark brown eyes lit up. "I *dream* about winnin' the world. But all I can do about it is enter as many big rodeos as I can, and when it comes down to it, ride as best I can."

"Well, you got the right attitude, buddy," endorsed T.J.

"So do you, T.J., in a way. You're full a' doubts when yer thinkin' all alone, but when you get to a rodeo, anybody can see that all them doubts are gone from yer head. When you nod yer face, you *know* yer gonna ride!"

T.J. smiled as a few doubts disappeared. "You know, yer right, Wiley. But how do I keep them doubts from comin' back?"

Wiley thought for a moment and suggested, "I'd just quit thinkin' when yer all alone."

Chapter 23: November 1990

The Cow Palace in San Francisco. They call it the Grand National Rodeo–the last 'big' rodeo before the National Finals. There are other big rodeos coming up, but not as big as this one. The Cow Palace is an extremely important rodeo for the cowboys who are in the top fifteen in the world standings and perhaps even more important for those who are not in the top fifteen, but who are close. As the National Finals Rodeo, next month in Las Vegas, draws near, this is the rodeo that can move a cowboy up into the top fifteen and secure him a spot in the most prestigious rodeo in the world, or, just as easily, it can knock a cowboy out of the standings, reduced to sitting on the sidelines, watching the rodeo that every rodeo cowboy dreams of winning.

As for T.J. Jergenson, his trip to the National Finals was secure. Still ranked number one in the world, he had increased his lead over Wiley Paz by nearly thirty-five hundred dollars. Thirty-five is not much, in comparison to go-round pay-off at the Finals. That is why T.J. had come to the big San Francisco rodeo – to try and protect his lead by even more money. At this point in the game, the money won by T.J. and Wiley did not mean money to spend or money to put in the bank, it didn't really even mean money. It was point-standings. Each dollar represented one point, and each point was just as, if not more important to Wiley Paz as it was to T.J., since Wiley was coming from behind.

So, the two of them had driven down from Pasco, Washington the night before. They arrived in town shortly after midnight, and got a room at the Holiday Inn. T.J. talked to Randy Corey on the phone at about ten in the morning. Randy and Dave Whitney had just arrived at the airport from Bismark, North Dakota. He said he had placed in the steer wresting, Dave had won the bronc riding, and it was damn cold up there. He also said that they had a ride lined up into town, so T.J. had told them to leave their gear off at his room, get their swimming trunks on, and meet him at the hot tub, which is where he was sitting right then.

He groaned with pleasure as a warm jet stream massaged the week-old bruise on the back of his right shoulder where he had been thrown from the back of a bull into a fencepost at Del Rio, Texas. His weary bones and tense muscles were totally relaxed as thoughts of rodeo escaped his mind and he watched the splashing, squealing children playing keep-away with an oversized beach ball at the shallow end of the swimming pool. One little kid in particular had a very shrill, very loud screech that echoed off the walls and plastic dome ceiling all too often. That alone, T.J. concluded, was reason enough not to take a chance on having any kids of his own. Although he did not admit it to himself, he did enjoy watching the game, and grew restless after their parents rousted them from the pool and up to their rooms. He glanced all around the room, wondering what the time was and what was taking the boys so long to get there, when he heard a familiar war whoop from the hallway door.

It was Dave Whitney, clad in a pair of oversized green swimming trunks, and he was running toward T.J. and the hot tub at full speed. With a final "Wooooo-hoooo!" he leapt into the air, grabbed his knees and cannonballed into the middle of the tub. T.J. just shook his head when Dave's face bobbed up and down in the water, arms flailing wildly as he melodramatically cried, "Help me!...Help me!...Somebody...Please!..." When he realized that T.J. was not going play the game and come to his rescue, he rolled over and floated face-down for awhile, then stood up and greeted with a friendly "Howdy!"

"I was *so* relaxed until you got here," said T.J.

"You thought I was drownin', didn't ya!" Whitney boasted.

"I *hoped* you was drownin'," T.J. replied.

Randy Corey walked to the edge of the tub wearing his blue running shorts and a white motel towel draped over his shoulders.

"Corey, ain't you got him trained yet?" asked T.J.

"I'm still tryin'," said Randy, as he stepped down into the hot bubbles and sunk to his chest. "There's some wild mustangs that you just never can get the wild clear out of 'em."

"Where's the girls?" Dave asked.

"What girls?" T.J. asked back.

"The girls!" demanded Dave. "Where are they?"

"There ain't no girls!" responded T.J.

"No girls?" whined Dave. "What's the use of bein' in a hot tub if there ain't no girls?"

"Then go find some girls!" urged T.J. "And bring 'em back here. Make sure there's three of 'em. Six'd be better."

"So you did O.K. up at Rosco, huh?" Randy injected.

"Not too bad," reported T.J. "Took third. I increased my lead over Wiley. Was he up in the room?"

"Can't believe you didn't bring no girls," grumbled Dave.

"Yeah, he was just layin' around and relaxin'. I asked him if he wanted to come down, but he didn't."

"Prob'ly knew there wasn't no girls here," complained Dave.

"He didn't seem like his old self," said Randy.

"I think the pressure's finally gittin' to him," T.J. maintained. "He's bucked off his last two bulls. It's finally hit him – how close he is to winnin' the world – and it's startin' to mess with his head."

"I'll tell ya what messes with *my* head," Dave retorted, "a big ol' hot tub and no girls."

"Well," said Randy, ignoring Dave's comment, "bad for him – good for you."

T.J. sighed. "I wanna win the world, bad," he said, "but I sure don't wish no bad luck on Wiley. He's a great guy and a helluva bullrider."

"...No girls..."

"He'll have other years," said Randy.

"Hell," T.J. replied, "so will I. I ain't retirin' any time soon."

Dave stood up and pointed at the door. "Girls!"

There were two of them, both appearing to be in their mid-twenties. The one with the long dark hair wore a black one-piece bathing suit and had a towel wrapped around her waist. The other one had light brown shoulder-length hair. Her suit was concealed by a pink t-shirt.

"Hi, girls!" Dave waved.

The one in the t-shirt made a slight attempt to wave back.

Dave gave a thumbs up to Randy and T.J. "I'm in there! Damn, she's got nice legs!"

Randy and T.J. studied the newcomers for a moment, and went back to their conversation.

"Ol' Wiley might just be on a bad run a' luck, too," suggested T.J. "He might not be fightin' his head at all. He might jump out there tonight and go ninety points."

"Do you guys know what you've drawn?"

"Wiley's got a good little bull they call Zambu Express. I've seen 'em go ninety on him before. I got a big ol' juice-hog called Black Cadillac. I oughta get to the short-round on him."

The woman in the black one-piece unwrapped the towel from her waist and lay it across the back of a chair on the very farthest side of the pool.

"Not fer me," Dave surveyed. "Legs are too fat, tits are too small."

The other one peeled her pink t-shirt off, exhibiting a very smooth, shapely form covered by a very revealing white bikini with vertical green stripes.

"Oh, yeah!" Dave whispered loudly to the boys. "I got mine picked out. You guys are gonna hafta fight over the ugly one."

"Wiley's a good rider, all right," Corey confided, "but he ain't got near the experience that you do."

"But he rides like he's been doin' it for years," T.J. returned. "It's unreal how far he's come along."

As the ladies stepped into the pool and slowly submerged their bodies in water, Whitney rose from the hot tub proclaiming, "I'm goin' swimmin'."

"Go swimmin', Dave," agreed T.J.

Dave climbed out of the tub and walked along the pool, greeting the girls again, with little response.

"Are you worried that Wiley's gonna catch ya?" Randy asked T.J.

Jergenson pondered the question. "It's a concern," he responded, "but not a worry. Wiley gave me the best advice. He said I was thinkin' too much. He said just enter the big rodeos and ride the best I can. He makes it so simple. Here, he's givin' me advice. Ain't it s'poseta be the other way around? He helped me get here, and now he's my biggest threat."

Midway along the edge of the pool, Whitney was showing some good old cowboy try. "How's the water, girls?" he asked, receiving no response. Reaching his foot over the pool's ledge, he slowly lowered his toe until it came in contact with the water. "Daaahhh!!! It's too cold!!!" he shrieked as he scampered back and, once again, cannonballed into the hot tub. The second his head emerged from the water he asked, "Are they laughin'?"

"Dave, will you get the hell outta here?" griped T.J.

"Are they laughin', Randy?"

"No," Corey answered, "they ain't laughin'. You better try again."

Once again, Dave rose from the security of the hot tub, and bravely trod to the edge of the deep water.

"Y'know," Randy reminded T.J., "Wiley ain't your only threat. There's thirteen other guys that want that Gold Buckle as bad as you do."

"That's true," agreed T.J., "but I'm twelve thousand bucks ahead of the guy in third place, seventeen over the guy in fifth. I ain't too worried about them. The real competition is the bulls. All these numbers and figures sometimes makes us forget what it's really all about. I'm just gonna try my hardest to ride 'em all."

Dave Whitney stood at the edge of the pool. His short-term goal was to accomplish something he had never mastered before – a dive. His long-term goal was to win over the pretty blonde in the green and white striped bikini. This dive would be only a stepping stone – a means to impress her. He pressed his hands against each other, fingers together, in diving fashion. With legs slightly bent, he leaned over the rim of the pool, and jumped in feet first. He came up for air and dog-paddled to the side. "Almost did it," he said.

"Do ya think Wiley can catch ya?" Corey asked.

"He's gonna do his damnedest," said T.J.

"But can he do it?"

"Hell, I don't know. What do you wanna hear from me, Randy? He's gonna do his best – I'm gonna do my best. There's ten rounds, he's less than four thousand behind me. Hell, a go-round'll pay more'n that. Sure, it could happen – but it ain't goin' to."

"What can you do about it?" Randy questioned. "You said yourself that when it comes right down to it, it's just between you and the bull."

"It is," agreed T.J., "and I'm just gonna ride every bull I get on." He leaned forward to Randy and pointed to nowhere in particular. "I've watched and studied every bull that'll be at the Finals. There ain't a bull in this country that can throw me off."

"If yer on yer game," added Randy.

"Oh, I'm on my game," T.J. attested. "Have been all year."

"Hey, guys, watch this!" Whitney announced from the diving board. "I'm gonna do a back flip!" After checking to make sure the girls were watching, he turned his back to the pool. "Ready?" he bounced a couple of times, and launched himself backwards off of the board. His body stiffened in midair, causing the girls in the pool and the cowboys in the hot tub to cringe as Dave's back slapped the water like a beaver's tail. When he slowly swam to the surface, he summed up his feelings in one word – "Ow."

Ignoring Dave, Randy reminded, "Y'know, T.J., Big Mac'll be there."

When T.J. looked Randy in the eye, Randy saw a deep confidence. A confidence that he had been carrying with him all year long. One that seemed to 'click on' the moment he showed up at a rodeo and looked at the draw sheet to see which opponent he would be conquering that night.

"I know he will," said T.J., "and I'm gonna draw him."

"Big Mac's never been twisted," Corey warned.

"I know the stats on Big Mac," stated T.J. "I also know his moves, his habits, his buckin' style. I know everything he can possibly throw at me, and I've got a move for every one of 'em. I've got the advantage – he ain't been studyin' *me*. I want him to have his best, rankest trip ever, and together, me and Bennett are going to break the record for the highest point ride at the National Finals Rodeo."

The seriousness of T.J.'s convictions made Randy's mouth go dry. "T.J.," he said with an outstretched hand, "if you say you can do it, then, by God, you can do it."

"Cannon-ball!"

Randy blinked, ducked and braced himself for Dave to come bounding into the tub like a surprise bonsai attacker. He heard the splash at the shallow end of the swimming pool and turned his head in time to see the girls catch the full force of Dave's splash from four feet away. As they scrambled to get away from what they saw as either a madman or a moron, he came to the surface doing his drowning routine again, kicking about, slapping the water and pleading, "Help me!...Help!...somebody!..." in three feet of water. He finally went under and slowly floated to the top again, facedown, as dead as he could act. Unimpressed, the girls gently swam to the other end of the pool.

Dave lifted his head and looked around. "Thought I was dead, didn't ya!"

The girls said nothing.

"Goin' to the rodeo tonight?" he asked.

Still nothing.

"Stuck-up bitches..." he said under his breath as he got out of the pool. Directly in front of him was a door with a sign reading 'Pool Storage'. "Hmm," he mumbled. "This must be where they store the pool." He twisted the door handle to see if it was unlocked. It was.

T.J. never even noticed Dave carrying on. "I'll tell ya somethin' else, Randy," he ascertained, "I'm gonna ride him in the tenth round."

"The tenth round?" repeated Corey.

"I'm sure of it."

"Whattaya been on, the psychic hotline or somethin'?"

"I just feel like that's the way it's gonna happen," T.J. explained. "Maybe that's just the way I want it to happen. It'd be so perfect that way."

"T.J., yer countin' yer chickens before they're hatched," cautioned Randy, "I hope it don't get you in trouble."

"O.K.," T.J. conceded, "it might not be the tenth round, but I know I'm gonna draw him. I can feel it in my bones, I just know it. There's no doubt in my mind, that I'm gonna draw him and ride him...and I bet it'll be in the tenth round."

"What if you don't draw him at all?" asked Randy.

"Ain't gonna happen."

"T.J.," Randy emphasized, "you have absolutely no control over the draw. You're worryin' about shit that you can't do nothin' about."

"I ain't worryin' about nothin'," stressed T.J., "I'm just tellin' ya what's gonna happen. It's meant to be. It's *fate*."

"Look, I don't wanna argue with ya. If you think you can ride every bull at the Finals, I think you've got the power to do it. You've got the physical ability, the mental ability, and the opportunity. But this stuff about knowin' what yer gonna draw and in what round, I just can't buy. Fate ain't predetermined. Fate ain't even real."

"You don't believe in fate?"

"I believe in coincidence. I believe in determination. I believe in goals. Hell, I even believe in luck."

"You don't believe that Bennett is Big Mac," T.J. alleged, "do ya?"

Randy stumbled over the question. "...No...No, I really don't, T.J."

"Even with all the proof?"

"T.J., I can't explain any of that," Randy responded. "I just don't believe it. Look, I don't wantcha to think I'm goin' against you in any way. Even though I don't believe everything that you believe, there's one thing I believe in real strong – and that's *you*. If you say yer gonna git it done, then yer gonna git it done.

"Jesus. Will ya look at that?"

Dave Whitney appeared from the pool storage room looking like the frogman of Alcatraz. Big black flippers slapped the floor with each step he took. A yellow and blue inflatable duck was wrapped around his mid-section. An underwater facemask covered his eyes and nose, and a snorkel curved from his mouth, around his face, past the back of his shower-capped head. On his wrists were children's flotation devices and in his arms he carried an assortment of beach balls, inner-tubes, Frisbees, floating air mattresses, a football, soccer ball, water gun, toy fire truck, and a lawn chair.

"Whitney, what the hell are you doin'?" laughed Randy.

Dave tried to speak through his snorkel, "Mfrhmgrph-mnifhugra." He traipsed around the edge of the pool, stepped onto the diving board, and announced, "Mhfrguirwia!" and waddled to the end of the board and jumped in. When he hit the water, toys rippled in every direction. His shower cap, snorkel and goggles floated on the water without him. He returned to the surface hacking, coughing and spitting all the way to the side of the pool.

Randy and T.J. were now standing in the hot tub, watching with great amusement.

"What's the matter, Dave?" T.J. shouted.

When Whitney finished coughing, he explained, "I lost my snorkel." As he climbed out of the pool, the duck smiled just below his chin. Still clad in the flotation devices on his wrists, the flippers and the duck, he walked over to the hot tub, leaned over and whispered, "I think them gals are startin' to like me, though."

"Oh, I'm sure they are," Randy agreed sarcastically. "So much that they figured they better just get outta here before they lose control."

Dave turned around just in time to see the door close behind the green and white vertical stripes of the brown-haired girl's bikini-covered butt.

"Oh, well," sighed Dave as he slid into the hot tub, "she was ugly, anyway."

Chapter 24: December 1990

The crowd cheered as Miss Rodeo America blazed into the arena, her pearly white teeth sparkling like the sequins on her sapphire-blue blouse, her blonde hair waving behind, along with the fringe of her purple chaps, the red, white and blue of the American flag she so proudly carried, and the cream-colored swishing tail of the Palomino stallion that carried her among the feather-clad Las Vegas showgirls prancing and strutting in unison beneath the music, smoke and fireworks kicking off the first of ten rounds at the 1990 National Finals Rodeo!

The crowd was young and old, western, eastern and far eastern, northern, southern, from north of the border, south of the border, and south of the equator. Families, groups and couples arrived in Las Vegas via cars, vans, pickups, airplanes, and tour bus package specials. Some had a favorite cowboy in their preferred event. Some were only there for the thrills and spills, but every one of the seventeen thousand eager fans crammed into the Thomas and Mack Center was there to witness just a little piece of cowboy history at the biggest, toughest, richest, and most prestigious rodeo in the entire world.

To say that the building was full of energy would be an understatement. The crowd was pumped up, the announcer was pumped up, the producers, technicians, coordinators, commentators, and contractors – pumped up. The men and women working in the concessions – not pumped up. The competitors who worked all year just to make it to the National Finals Rodeo – extremely pumped up. Even the top-rated bucking stock from all over the U.S. seemed to sense and possess the enthusiasm that spread throughout the superstructure.

Behind the bucking chutes, T.J. Jergenson and Wiley Paz tried unsuccessfully to relax, as the entire stadium around them disappeared into darkness except for the two spotlights that shone on Old Glory, the giant American Flag that hung from the dome's ceiling. They placed their black Stetsons over their hearts. Lumps grew in their throats, as, side by side, they watched and listened to Reba McEntire singing the national anthem.

As the lights glared and the music blared, T.J. felt overwhelmed as he gazed at the symbol of the freedom that meant so much to him. "She's beautiful, ain't she?" he asked Wiley.

Wiley wiped away the moisture that blurred his vision, and sighed, "She sure is, T.J....She damn-sure is."

The arena cleared of all but the chute boss, gatemen, judges, pickup men and their mounts, and the announcer began to babble on at an auctioneer's pace.

"Well..." said Wiley, looking like a lost child, "here we are...now, whatta we do?"

"Same thing we do at all rodeos, I guess," T.J. replied. "Watch the bareback ridin."

The night's pen of bucking stock would feature the 'nice' bulls and broncs. This is not to say that they were easy to ride, but they were generally good, hard, honest buckers. The horses would kick high and buck straight away and the bulls would spin consistently and showy, without 'dirty' moves and tricks to throw their riders.

T.J. and Wiley were both pretty pleased with the bulls they had drawn for the night.

T.J.'s bull – number 53, Mister Bill – was one of the bigger bulls in the pen, suitable for T.J.'s long legs. He was a handsome multi-brown and white bull, with classic rodeo-looking horns. He generally spun to the left – into T.J.'s riding hand.

Wiley's bull suited him as well. Not so big or good-looking, a little black bull named Rocky Top, number 4, and he, too, spun right into Wiley's fist.

By the time the bronc riding was over and the calf roping had begun, Wiley and T.J.'s chute help had arrived: Randy Corey and Dave Whitney.

"You boys ready?" was Dave's greeting.

"You know it!" replied T.J. as he clenched Dave's extended hand, and then Randy's.

Wiley sat on a folding chair against the wall and never looked up.

"What's wrong with Wiley?" asked Randy.

"First-time jitters, I guess," T.J. answered. "He was the same way in the locker room."

"Heck, yes, he's nervous," stated Whitney. "He ain't never been to a rodeo that has locker rooms before." He studied Wiley from afar. "Man, he sure looks pale. 'Specially for a Mexican. He's as white as...me! It suits him. I think he should go with it."

Disgusted by Dave's tasteless jokes at a critical moment like this, Corey walked over and lightly touched Wiley's shoulder and asked, "You alright?"

Wiley swallowed hard and returned, "Yeah." Then he looked up at Randy and admitted, "I got butterflies in my guts...bad!"

Randy squatted beside Wiley and inquired, "How come?" When Wiley failed to answer, Randy said, "O.K. – stupid question. Listen, Wiley, you've got the bull you wanted, just loosen up and ride him. Have fun. Think of it as just another rodeo. You get this first one out of the way, and the rest of it'll be a breeze." Suddenly Randy felt as if he might be speaking out of place. Having never competed at the Finals before, he had never experienced what Wiley was going through. Yet, in a lot of situations, it seemed that a person could see a lot clearer when he was looking in from the outside. He patted Wiley on the back and assured, "You'll be alright."

Shortly after the back pen workers loaded the bulls into the bucking chutes, Wiley walked down the hallway to the locker rooms and puked into a trash barrel. It seemed to help.

With the top fifteen bullriders there and only ten available chutes, T.J. and Wiley's bulls were still in the narrow alley leading to the chutes. With the help of Dave and Randy, they snugged their ropes up around their bulls' bellies and waited and watched. One by one the bullriders nodded their heads and were released into the whirlwind of glory or defeat.

Dave nudged T.J. in the ribs after a good bullrider got tipped to the outside of the spin and bit the dust. "You'd a' rode the shit outta that bull," he confirmed.

T.J. looked over at Wiley, who was breathing deeply and glaring down at Rocky Top.

"Wiley!" he hollered.

When Wiley turned his way, he smiled determinedly, winked, and gave him the thumbs-up sign. Wiley echoed the thumbs-up back to T.J.

Mister Bill was directly behind Wiley's bull as they ambled into the chutes and awaited their turns.

As the time grew nearer, Wiley, already in his chaps and spurs, worked his tight leather glove onto his riding hand. He straddled over Rocky Top on the chute rails and cautiously made his way down until he was sitting on the bull's back. He yanked the tail of his bullrope from where it was tucked under his handhold, and handed it to Randy, who was leaning over the gate.

"Just another rodeo," Randy reminded him.

Wiley repeated the words in his mind, "Just another rodeo. Just another rodeo..." when another thought interrupted. "Just another rodeo, my ass! This is the National Finals Rodeo and I'm gonna ride like a National Finals cowboy!" When he worked the rosin on his glove into the rosin on his bullrope, he nearly jerked the tail of the rope from Randy's hand. "Pull 'er up, Randy," he ordered. The rosin chunks crunched against the rope and granulated in the palm of his glove. He heard another bullrider's buzzer and knew his time was near.

He felt a hand on his back and heard the familiar voice of Sonny Joe Barker. "We know yer a Champ, son. Now, show the rest of the world!"

"That's my plan, Sonny," he replied. "Is the last bull outta the arena yet?"

"He's headin' for the catch pen, Wiley," Randy answered. "Let's git it on!"

"Slack." He thrust his hand into the handhold. "Pull...more...that's good." He laid the tail end of the rope across his open palm, wrapped it around his hand and wedged it into his precisely closing fist. "They ready?"

"It's time!" yelled Randy.

"Get 'em, Wiley!" T.J. yelled from the back of his own bull.

As Wiley smacked his fist closed, tucked his chin and slid to his rope, the voices of encouragement slid past the back of his mind and disappeared, along with the buzz of the crowd and the ramblings of the announcer. As Wiley zoned in on the bull, everything else faded into nonexistence. The building that surrounded him was gone. The ground below him – gone. It was as if even Wiley himself ceased to exist. The only thing real was the bull, and Wiley had become a part of that bull. He subconsciously nodded his head, and the bull blasted from the chute into oblivion. Unlike countless past rides, where the buzzer seems an eternity away, this one came almost the instant that the ride began. So quick, in fact, that it surprised his conscious mind. Suddenly, the world existed again. The rumble of the cheering crowd rattled at his eardrums. The ground appeared below him. He grabbed his wrap, bailed off and landed at a full run, not stopping until he was on the fence. He remembered absolutely nothing of the ride, and yet he knew that he had just done something great.

"Eighty-seven points and we have a new leader!"

Straddling the fence, he threw his arms in the air and embraced the exuberant crowd. He then tipped his hat to the bull that carried him to this emotional high as Rocky Top exited the arena.

As Wiley jumped off of the fence and strutted back toward the bucking chutes, the bullfighter picked up his rope and handed it to him with a pat on the back. "Nice ride," he complimented.

"Thanks," smiled Wiley.

Randy Corey and Dave Whitney reached their open hands into the arena as Whitney came by and he high-fived them enthusiastically.

"Does it feel good, Wiley?" Dave grinned.

"Feels great!" Wiley beamed.

Sonny Jo Barker also offered his hand to Wiley. Instead of slapping it as with the others, Wiley embraced it.

"You made it look easy, son," congratulated Sonny.

Still in awe of the moment, Wiley honestly admitted, "It *was* easy!"

"And now, ladies and gentlemen, we are down to the last bullrider in this evening's performance. This man is the traveling partner of Wiley Paz and is ranked as the number one bullrider in the world. I have just been informed by our rodeo secretary that in order to hold on to his lead over Wiley Paz, this man has got to at least place in this round, and I believe with your help, he can do it. He has drawn the good bull, number fifty-three – Mister Bill; let's hear it for T.J. Jergenson of Enid, Oklahoma."

Wiley reached through the chute slats and squeezed T.J.'s leg. "O.K., T.J., your turn! Be there, now!"

"Pull!" T.J. said to Dave, at the tail of his rope. Then he looked over at Wiley, winked, and said, "Watch this!"

Wiley backed up along the chutes and then jumped up and perched on an empty gate just as T.J. and Mister Bill surged to freedom. Instantly, Wiley's face cringed as he witnessed what was taking place before him. The bull had not even made his descent and T.J. had already lost his hold with his legs and feet, as his spurs wavered a good two feet from Mister Bill's calico hide. Then, as the bull's hooves collided with the ground, T.J.'s dull spurs thumped him in the ribs. And when the bull bailed in the air and around to the left, T.J. let his spurs fly, and did it again. Wiley's eyes widened and his jaw dropped as he realized – T.J. hadn't blown his feet, he'd come out spurring from the first jump! And again! And again! Suddenly Wiley was on his feet with the rest of the crowd, roaring fervidly as T.J. spurred his way past Wiley's eighty-seven points, "Yeah! Yeah! Go, T.J.! Go with 'im!" As Mister Bill switched directions, T.J. rode into the spin as if he knew it was coming, and never missed a beat. At the sound of the buzzer, T.J. jerked his wrap from his hand, threw his long leg over his bull's head and was launched nearly ten feet into the air. Like Wiley Paz before him, he landed squarely on his feet and skittered to the safety of the fence.

Again, the coliseum thundered with ovation. So much so, that it was difficult to hear the announcement, "Ninety championship points! And T.J. Jergenson retains his lead in the race to be the Bullriding Champion of the World!"

T.J. stepped down into the arena, took off his new black Stetson and flung it high into the air. Before T.J.'s hat ever hit the ground, Wiley dropped his own bullrope and ran to him at a full sprint. With his face against T.J.'s chest, Wiley embraced him around the ribs. T.J. hugged him back before letting out a triumphant victory yell.

Wiley looked up to T.J. "That was awesome!" he exclaimed. "Yer my hero!"

Still holding on to Wiley, T.J. replied, "I couldn't have done it withoutcha, Wiley. Yer *my* hero!"

Their testimonials were interrupted by the arena director's orders. "Git on this horse and follow that rodeo queen for your victory lap!"

T.J. grabbed his hat, took the reins and swung aboard the man's paint mare. He realized immediately that the stirrups on the saddle were over a foot too short for his dangling legs. As Miss Rodeo America pranced her Palomino mount by and broke into a full gallop, T.J. kicked the stirrups loose and gave the mare her head. She responded by following the lead horse, just as she was supposed to. Everything was going fine until they neared the far end of the arena. As they came upon the left curve of the fence, T.J.'s reactions were a bullrider's natural instincts; he leaned into the turn and squeezed with his legs and feet, drawing his spurs against the belly of his ride. The mare's ears pinned back against her head as she snorted and kicked behind her. T.J. felt her slight buck and again squeezed even tighter, causing her to buck a bit harder, causing him to squeeze even tighter, as so on, until he was scratching for a solid spur-hold like it was the second-round bullriding at the National Finals Rodeo and she was bucking beneath him like it was the second-round bronc riding. A stirrup-less T.J. was grabbing leather for all he was worth when his feisty showhorse-turned-outlaw popped him from the saddle and he landed in a heap by the fence as she exited the arena with her tail sashaying high behind her.

T.J. tried to hide his blushing face by pulling his cowboy hat down, all the way to his eyebrows. What once were cheers and applause were now hoots and laughter. He looked back toward the bucking chutes. Although Wiley was trying to hold back, Randy and Dave were laughing heartily along with the rest of the cowboys. Even Sonny Joe Barker was laughing! Sonny Joe never laughed at anything! As T.J. picked himself up from the arena dirt, a thought suddenly occurred; was this televised? Please, Lord, let America be watching a Dodge truck commercial – or a different channel.

A cowboy loped his horse across the arena and skidded to a stop. "You O.K., T.J.?"

Realizing that it was no use trying to hide his embarrassment, T.J. conceded, "I just got bucked off some girl's pony at my first round of my first N.F.R....Ain't nothin' hurt but my pride."

"Then ya better git up on the fence," the cowboy warned as he rode away, "I'd hate to see ya git run over by yer first stagecoach!"

No sooner came the warning when a red stagecoach rumbled full-speed into the arena, drawn by a team of six perfectly matched, coal black Quarterhorses. T.J. leaped for the fence and turned around just in time to read the inscription of 'Binions Horseshoe Hotel and Casino' as the coach blazed by.

By the time T.J. and Wiley got their gear packed up, talked to reporters, signed a few autographs, talked to more reporters, and made it to the rodeo office to collect their checks and to see which bulls they had drawn for the following night, nearly three hours had passed. At last they made it out the back of the coliseum and crawled into T.J.'s van.

"With all the excitement earlier, Wiley, I never got a chance to tell ya," said T.J. as he held out an upright fist for Wiley to punch, "Way to go!"

"You know it, buddy!" exclaimed Wiley as he commemorated the moment by greeting T.J.'s fist with his own, "We had a good night, didn't we?"

"We had a *great* night," T.J. corrected as he fired up the van and headed through the mostly-empty parking lot toward the road. "Every night it's gonna be like this. Every night."

"I sure hope so," said Wiley.

"They are!" assured T.J. "Every night is gonna be just like this one. I can *feel* it!"

"Well, I hope they ain't just *exactly* like tonight," Wiley joked. "I hope ya let *me* win once in awhile."

T.J. laughed and reached over and squeezed Wiley's shoulder. And said nothing.

He pulled onto the highway and headed toward the Strip.

"Hey, where's Dave and Randy?" asked Wiley.

"They're prob'ly shootin' craps down at the Horseshoe by now," T.J. reckoned.

"I'll bet Dave just goes crazy at them tables, doesn't he?" guessed Wiley.

"Nah, Dave's most likely tryin' to hold Randy back," said TJ. "Randy's the one that goes crazy at the tables."

"Really? He don't seem like that kinda guy."

"Gamblin' is Randy's one vice," stated T.J. "Y'know, he don't drink or chew or smoke, but when he hunkers down over that table, you better look out."

"No kiddin'?"

"He gets this wild-ass look in his eye and starts to talkin' and hollerin' at them dice, you'd think he was crazy. He played for thirty-nine hours straight one time. I seen part of it. He never left the table, except to piss. Same table, the whole time. Put up a helluva fight, but he lost everything he had. That's the only reason he quit. At one time he was sixty thousand ahead."

"Why didn't he quit when he was sixty thousand ahead?" asked Wiley.

"Thought he could win more," T.J. answered. "There's always more out there, and Randy wanted it."

"Jeez," said Wiley, "I'm glad I don't gamble."

T.J. laughed, "Whattaya mean 'you don't gamble'?"

"I don't," Wiley affirmed. "The only time I ever gambled was that night we played poker at yer folks'. I didn't even like it."

"Buddy, you gamble every time you sit down and nod your head," T.J. corrected. "In fact, you not only gamble with yer money, but with yer health as well. And maybe even yer life."

"Well...yeah..."

"Randy ain't that much different than me or you or everybody else that's competin' out here this week. There's more out there and we want it. Whether it's gold or glory. And most of us ain't gonna stop 'til we're busted, one way or another."

After a pause, Wiley admitted, "I guess I never looked at it that way before."

As they neared the center of town, the flashing lights and signs got brighter, and the traffic – pedestrians and vehicles – became much thicker. Neither of the bullriders seemed to be impressed much with the sights and sounds of the city.

"Hey, yer folks' comin' out?" T.J. asked as they waited behind a long line before a red traffic light.

"No," replied Wiley, as he concealed his disappointment. "They're both workin'. Dad still thinks this bullridin' is just a kid phase I'm goin' through. I swear if I win the world, he'll say 'Good. Now you can get a job and go to work.' Yers?"

"Yeah, my folks are comin' out on Friday and stayin' 'til it's over. Got an aunt and uncle comin' with 'em. So, what bull are you gittin' on tomorrow night?"

"Oh, I got a good one. Double Deuces. I placed on him up in Calgary, remember? What do you got?"

"I don't know him," said T.J. as he swerved his van through the crowd and around the corner. "Number six-thirty. They call him Supper Time. He came from the Webster and Laird string outta Louisiana. I think I'll go out to the stockyards tonight to look at him. You wanna go?"

"I'll pass, T.J. Think I'll just go to the room and go to bed. Maybe get somethin' to eat first. You can just let me off in front of the hotel, if ya want."

"You ain't gonna go try yer luck at the casino?"

"Couldn't if I wanted to," Wiley responded. "I ain't old enough yet."

"Oh, yeah, that's right," said T.J. "I keep forgettin' that I'm travelin' with a juvenile." He pulled up to the front of the hotel, and stopped to let Wiley out. "We'll see ya in the mornin'," he said. Then he winked and added, "Let's keep this hot streak burnin', now."

As Wiley opened the door and stepped out of the van, he agreed, "You know we will!" He stopped and looked at T.J., stretched his hand across the van and solemnly continued, "And thank you, T.J., for everything."

Although T.J. was not quite certain just what he was being thanked for, he took Wiley's hand and squeezed as he shook it. "Yer more than welcome, partner...anytime."

After T.J. had pulled back into the traffic and was down the road a ways, he got to thinking about that thank you and the handshake. They felt good. Suddenly, what had had him confused back at the hotel, became so clear in his mind; when a friend shakes your hand and thanks you and you don't know why, he is simply thanking you for being a friend. That alone meant as much to T.J. as winning the rodeo that night. Almost.

As he drove to the far end of town, his mind possessed a satisfied feeling shared with a resolute determination to make a repeat, the following night of this night's ride – except for the victory lap buck-off. That memory – fresh in his mind – forced his lips into a sheepish grin and he wagged his head from side to side. He was glad he was alone right then. Away from the noise and the hype and the celebration. There would be no celebration, he vowed to himself, until the final buzzer excused him, and he was the Champion of the World.

When he got to the stockyards, the livestock haulers had already unloaded the animals from the night's performance and were shutting down their semis for the night. Stock contractors filled their athletes' feed bunks with crushed corn, sprinkled generously over loose hay and made for certain that every water trough was full.

T.J. showed his admission pass to the security guard and eased his van on in. He cruised along the east side of the corrals until he spotted the Webster and Laird pen. He turned off his lights and ignition, stepped out of the van and ambled toward the pens. As he stepped up on the first rail of the pen and peered over the fence at the bulls gathered around the feed bunk, the yard lights were bright enough that he could clearly see the brands on their rumps. Of the eight bulls in the pen, number six-thirty was easy to pick out. As black as the Nevada sky, he had thick wide gravel-colored horns that converged to a dirty dark blue towards the tip. He was a meaty creature with plenty of loose hide left over, long drooping ears and a solid mass of hump riding high over his shoulders. T.J. guessed him to be a Brahma, with some Watusi blood in him. He should be no problem. Just another good bull, T.J. figured.

As he turned to leave, T.J. inadvertently noticed that the next pen over was empty except for one bull, leisurely feasting from his private trough. The dark red of the bull's ugly hide and the wide, splintered horns immediately brought T.J.'s blood to a boil. His chest felt tight and his heart thumped faster as he glared at the detestable brute that had murdered his best friend and partner. It was Triple Zeros, Genghis Khan. Genghis momentarily glanced over at T.J. and continued eating.

After more than three years, T.J. still despised the bull for doing what came naturally in a world that was forced upon him. He hated the fact that Genghis was allowed to live and breathe. He hated the fact that he did not have a pistol or rifle with him, to do the world a favor and put a bullet between the savage's evil eyes. Suddenly, T.J. even hated Sonny Joe Barker for owning and caring for such a putrid, loathsome monster.

He walked away, got in his van and left the yard. As he drove back toward the hotel, he tried to leave his hard feelings and thoughts of Genghis Khan behind him. If only he could drive away from his memories and emotions the way he drove away from the bull...He tried to concentrate on Supper Time, his opponent for tomorrow night, black in color, and not quite as big, but built a lot like the big dirt-red killer that refused to leave T.J.'s mind. He tried to feel the joy again of making the winning ride that night. It had to be somewhere inside, but where? He tried to laugh at himself, for his blundering victory lap, but the laughter was deadened by the stinging thought of his worst enemy standing there at his feed bunk, munching on clover hay and oats. What bothered T.J. the most was, Genghis seemed so peaceful and harmless alone in his pen. He never snorted or pawed the ground or waved his horns around. When he had looked at T.J. there was no animosity in his eyes, no staring him down, no daring him to come closer. No emotions. Suddenly, it was hard to truly hate the animal for doing what came naturally.

So, he went to the motel, ordered room service, ate, and went to bed.

The next night, T.J. and Wiley Paz were primed up and ready to ride–which they did. Although neither of them won first in the round – Supper Time only bucked hard enough to get T.J. to a fifth place and Wiley won another second on Double Deuces – they both came away satisfied that they did their level best, and they were steadily increasing their leads on the rest of the pack.

Even Randy Corey had a good night at the tables. He had promised Dave that he would limit himself to no more than three hours a night on the tables, and he obeyed his vows. After two nights of gambling, he was nearly seven thousand dollars to the good.

The third round again proved to be successful – a three-way tie for third place along with the cowboy who had come into the Finals in the fifteenth position.

The boys were hot – brimming with confidence as they picked up their third consecutive checks.

On the way to the secretary's office, T.J. asked Wiley, "You wanna hang around and see what we drew for tomorrow night?"

"Hell, it don't matter what we draw," bragged Wiley, "we're just gonna ride the shit out of 'em anyway!"

"I'm with you, buddy," agreed T.J. "We'll find out soon enough."

The fourth night of competition featured the 'eliminator' pen. Those bulls were considered the 'baddest' of the bad. They sported the highest percentage of buck-offs of all of the bulls there. The feared bull Genghis Khan was in the draw tonight. The known cowboy-killer had been ridden only once in his six-year career. At a regular-season rodeo, many bullriders would pay a steep turn-out fine rather than risk possible death and probable injury tangling with rodeo's most dangerous bull.

The only bucking bull in the nation that could boast a one hundred percent buck-off rate was also performing at the Finals that night – the big gray Brahma, Big Mac. Although he was unridden, every bullrider here would like to have a shot at Big Mac. The high kicks, powerful drop and tight spins were every bullrider's dream. To ride this bull at the National Finals would guarantee a go-round win and secure a place in rodeo history. This night, the lucky dreamer that would get to try his hand on the back of the rankest bull in the world was none other than Wiley Paz.

When Wiley Paz saw Big Mac's name next to his on the draw-sheet, he closed his eyes and thanked the Lord for another opportunity to conquer his toughest and most respected rival.

As if Wiley needed a pep talk, T.J. Jergenson squeezed his shoulder blade and reassured, "You can ride this bull, Wiley. You've been on him twice before and this time you got his number. Just bear down and do it!"

"Damn right I will!" announced Wiley as he trounced off toward the locker room.

T.J. stood there alone, remarking, "He didn't even want to see what bull I drew."

And that bull was number thirty-nine – Beefcake. If T.J.'s memory served correctly, a big black and white bull that fades across the arena when he spins. He had seen a guy almost ride him in Clovis, New Mexico. Should be no problem.

Feeling like old hands, now, at this National Finals thing, T.J. and Wiley didn't even hang their ropes on the back pen fence until the saddle bronc riding was completed, and when they did, they were joking and cutting up with the other cowboys behind the chutes. As bullriding time grew nearer, however, a faraway look grew in their eyes, and their lighthearted banter and laughter subsided. Their heartbeats rose in unison as they strapped on their spurs and donned their chaps. Being numbers one and two in the standings, T.J. and Wiley's bulls were, again, held back to the last of the pen, so that the rodeo performance would climax with the top-seated cowboy.

The first bullrider on the list had drawn the worst bull in the pen. If the bull did not knock him unconscious in the chute with his wide horns or smash his leg against the chute gate, he would unquestionably try to kill or maim him in the arena. He was the loathsome monstrosity who bore the brand that all bullriders feared; Triple Zeros, Genghis Khan.

T.J. did not even climb up on the platform behind the chutes to watch the upcoming match, but Wiley did.

As the rider attempted to ease down on Genghis' back, Sonny Joe Barker warned him from the flank, "Be as quick as you can in the box, son. This bull has hurt more cowboys in the chute than in the arena."

Genghis was already wallowing back and forth and slinging his horns above his shoulders, as if it was his first time in the chutes. As soon as the rider slid his palm into the handhold of his bullrope, Genghis leapt high in the air and dropped hard to the ground, jerking the rope from his opponent, leaving him standing on the rails above.

"Stand still, you ornery sonuvabitch!" Sonny Joe scolded.

The bullrider's helper, at the tail of his rope, offered some tactical advice; "He's just messin' with yer mind, Cory. He's just tryin' to psych you out!"

Wiley peered at Cory. From the empty look on his face, Wiley feared that the bull's plan may have worked.

As soon as Genghis stopped moving about, Cory tried it again. He got his hand in the rope and his helper pulled it tight without incident. Genghis continued to bang from side to side in the chute as the bullrider wrapped the tail of his rope around his hand. Knowing that if he sat down on the bull's back before he called for the chute, the bull might not give him a fair shot – he might not anyway – Cory nodded his head and dropped down to Genghis' back as the chute gate swung wide.

Genghis bailed high and snapped back to the ground, turning back to the right and slinging his horns like knives at the intruder upon his back.

Cory stayed solid on the bull for the first two full wraps, before he began to loosen up and flop back and forth between his bullrope and the flankrope. Both of his feet were popped from Genghis' belly and his riding arm was stretched to the max when he was jerked back toward Genghis' head. He tried to get his hand between his own face and the bull's head but it was too late.

T.J. heard the 'thud!' from behind the chutes and saw the crowd rise to its feet.

The unconscious cowboy had barely hit the ground before Genghis was upon him, scooting him around in the dirt and stomping him deeper into the ground, paying no attention to the bullfighter.

"Genghis!" the bullfighter yelled as he grabbed the bull's right horn.

With a flick of his mighty neck, Genghis clubbed the bullfighter in the chest and sent him sailing backward through the air.

Landing on his back, and rolling to his feet, the bullfighter did his best to ignore the pain of his newly broken ribs, and charged again back to the bull and his victim. This time, he offered himself as bait as he crouched low behind Cory's limp body and slapped Genghis across the nose. Genghis looked up from his helpless prey, snorted and bolted over the top of Cory in pursuit of his new offering. Barely one step ahead of death, the bullfighter high-tailed it straight for the open catch pen, and barely made it over the panel fence with the help of the bull's big right horn to the seat of his baggy pants. He landed on his back, directly in front of T.J. Jergenson.

"Did he hurtcha bad?" asked T.J. as he helped the cowboy lifesaver to his feet.

"I dunno," the bullfighter whispered hoarsely. He pressed on his own broken ribs with both hands. "Yeah, he hurt me," he added as he made his way back to the arena, "But not bad."

By the time he made it back into the arena, the paramedics were kneeling next to Genghis' latest conquest, strapping a brace to his neck and stuffing cotton up his nose.

As they carried him from the arena on a stretcher, there was a soft silence in a room of seventeen thousand souls.

That silence only lasted until the next bull and rider burst into the arena and fought over the next eight seconds.

The butterflies from the first round returned to Wiley's guts. He was confident that he could ride Big Mac, *if* he did not make a mistake, *if* he was not overpowered by the bull, *if* his reactions were quick enough to move with the bull, *if* he was not out-smarted, *if* he could shuffle his feet and get new holds...*if* he could quit thinking of all of the ifs, and *just ride*. He jumped from the platform to the ground and began to pace and whisper to himself, "Charge! Hustle!"

As, one by one, four more bulls were bucked, the chutes emptied and were refilled with more bulls. Big Mac strode into his starting spot and peered through the horizontal iron bars at the familiar dark-complexioned cowboy who was walking his way with a bullrope in his hand and a victory on his mind.

With Wiley was Randy Corey, eager to help set Wiley's bullrope, offer heartfelt encouragement and send him on his way to the high point ride of the night. As they put the rope on Big Mac, Randy looked up at Wiley. He saw a calm determination in his eyes. Randy felt as though he should offer some words of assurance, but what could he say? Wiley had all of the bases covered. Sometimes – and this was one of them – it was better to just be there and be quiet than to interrupt a man's thoughts and convictions, so Randy said nothing.

Wiley sat down on Big Mac, focused his eyes on the bull's brawny neck – the spot he watched when he rode, and he rode Big Mac in his mind. Every twist and turn, every kick and spin brought forth a counter-reaction and Wiley visualized the perfect ride. He stored it in his mind. He replayed it, graded it, and again it was the perfect ride. In a few short moments, his visualization would become a realization.

He crawled off of Big Mac's back, and left the bull standing alone in the chute. He inattentively watched the next four rides as he pictured his flawless, impeccable trip to the glory of eight seconds and first place.

He felt a supportive hand on his shoulder. It was T.J. Jergenson.

"Give it to 'im with both barrels, Wiley," encouraged T.J. "I know you can do it, and there ain't no better place to do it than here."

Wiley looked up at T.J. The words were encouraging, but the look on T.J.'s face was not.

T.J. gave Wiley a thumbs-up sign and quickly walked away, feeling unbridled guilt for having to hide his true feelings from his compadre. For the truth was, he didn't believe that Wiley could ride Big Mac. He thought he could come close, but he didn't think he could get it done. With all the faith T.J. had in Wiley's ability to ride bulls, he had just a little bit more faith in Big Mac. So, he lied to Wiley. What other choice did he have? If he would only have admitted it, T.J. did not believe that there was another cowboy, and did not want there to be another cowboy, who could ride Big Mac, except for himself.

As he set his own rope on Double Deuces with the help of Dave Whitney, he caught himself thinking more about Wiley and Big Mac than of his own project at hand.

He watched Wiley's head swivel on his shoulders as he remained loose and cool while he slid his leather glove onto his riding hand. He saw Sonny Joe Barker pat him on the back with more false words of encouragement. His own heart began to race as Wiley crawled over the rail and sat down on the big gray Brahma.

Everyone in the building knew of Big Mac's record and reputation. Everyone there, and those all across America watching on television, knew that Wiley Paz was considered the underdog. And everyone knew that maybe – just maybe – the little cowboy could pull it off; reach down deep inside and do something that nobody had ever done before; ride the unrideable, beat the unbeatable.

T.J.'s emotions swayed toward those of the rest of the country – those who believed that with enough hope and determination, anything was possible.

"Ride 'im, Wiley!" T.J. hollered just before their chute gate opened.

The pair exploded into view in unison. Big Mac leapt high and far, his back hooves kicking even higher behind him as his front hooves pounded the arena floor. Wiley's chin was tucked, his spurs set, and his crotch against the back of his riding hand. Big Mac tossed his head to the right and whirled left. Wiley threw his right arm over his head and chunked his foot at the bull's outside shoulder. Big Mac planted hard and sucked back underneath Wiley. Wiley automatically pushed on the bullrope and thrust his chest at the bull. Big Mac made another tremendous leap into the air, came down hard and steep, blew forward and came around the other direction. Wiley slashed his free hand through the air, shoved his hips to his rope, got a hold with his feet and never lost sight of the bull's head.

The crowd rose to their feet with a deafening cheer.

T.J. clenched his fists, and like every other spectator, leaned into the action. He murmured, "Come on...come on..." and then he yelled, "*Come on*, BENNETT!"

Again, the bull bailed toward the sky and slammed back to the earth, jerking Wiley away from the bullrope and sending him sailing over his right shoulder.

T.J. heard the buzzer, saw Wiley slam onto the ground, and saw Big Mac go back for the kill.

"Get him outta there!" screamed T.J.

Wiley got to his feet just in time to take a hard shot to the hip. The impact knocked him fifteen feet away just before the bullfighter distracted the bull and led him from the arena.

When Wiley got up, T.J. could see that he was holding his right arm at the elbow where his shirt was ripped and bloody. He was wide-eyed, looking hopefully at one of the judges.

"Did I ride him?"

Looking up from his stopwatch, the judge's face revealed true regret as he shook his head and pointed his thumb at the ground.

T.J. read Wiley's face and lips as his eyes cast down and he cursed himself.

The older cowboy did not know if he felt regret or comfort in the situation – possibly both – but he had no time to sort it out now; T.J. had a bull to ride.

With a slap on the back, Dave Whitney asserted, "Savin' the best for last! Do it to it, T.J.!"

Beefcake stood solid and straight in the chute while Dave pulled T.J.'s rope. T.J. wasted no time taking his wrap, sliding to his rope and nodding for the gate. As predicted, the big black and white bull moved across the arena while he spun, like a rolling tornado heading across a Kansas cornfield. T.J. never missed a trick. He rode with such confidence and agility that his opponent, who threw off a lot more riders than not, really did not have a chance.

When the buzzer announced the end of the ride, T.J. grabbed his wrap and bailed off. The bull's momentum sending him into a mid-air cartwheel, he landed on his feet and trotted to the edge of the arena as Beefcake found the catch pen gate. He tipped his hat to the cheering crowd and listened for his score.

The announcer relayed the news that T.J Jergenson rode Beefcake to the score of eighty-four points and on this particular night, that was enough to win the round!

In a flutter of glory, T.J. swung aboard the paint mare that was led into the ring and paraded around the arena behind Miss Rodeo America for a flawless victory lap, again tipping his black Stetson to the thundering approval.

It wasn't until the next afternoon, on the way to the Thomas and Mack Center, that T.J. and Wiley really got a chance to talk about the previous night's performance. Wiley, having bucked off, had had no check to pick up, avoided reporters, and hailed a taxicab back to his hotel room. He was obviously still bummed out about it, and T.J. felt the guilt of not being behind his partner and friend one hundred percent.

The elbow on Wiley's free arm was swollen, bruised, and scabbed over, but not busted, and his hip was bruised and sore, but not enough to affect his riding. T.J. just hoped that his buddy wasn't injured emotionally. He shouldn't be; the best of them buck down every now and then.

Just in case he was, T.J. wanted to help. As he navigated his van through the thick Vegas traffic, he advised, "Better put last night outta yer mind, and start thinkin' 'bout what ya gotta do tonight."

"I know," admitted Wiley. "I just wish I knew what I did wrong."

"Wiley, I seen that whole ride," coached T.J. "Yer feet were in him, you were on yer rope, you were movin', hustlin'...You didn't do nothin' wrong. He just flat bucked you off."

That was not the answer that Wiley wanted. When a bull bucks a cowboy off, there has got to be a reason. "Big Mac is not better than me." He punched the dash, declaring, "No bull is!"

"Don't dwell on it, man," T.J. warned. "It's gonna eat atcha and it's gonna affect yer ridin', if ya let it. Now, listen to me! Yer gonna turn into yer own worst enemy, and this ain't the place to do that! Just get over it and get on with it."

Wiley thought about it for a while. "You're right," he confessed. Then he thought some more. "T.J....before I got on Big Mac, last night, did you think I could ride him?"

"I *knew* you could," lied T.J. "I still know you can. Last night just wasn't yer night, that's all. You'll get 'im next time."

T.J.'s pep talk must have done some good, because Wiley took the victory lap that night, and T.J. was genuinely proud of and happy for his little buddy. T.J. rode his own bull as well, but, as bulls sometimes do, he had an off night and didn't even get T.J. to the pay window.

The sixth round again proved to be productive for the boys. Wiley, riding in winning fashion with his old winning attitude, won fourth place money, while T.J. increased his lead over Wiley by winning a second, losing the round to last year's champion by a single point.

Randy Corey's luck was not so consistent at the craps table. Nearly eleven thousand ahead, and three hours into the game, he began to lose. Dave Whitney got drunk and neglected to pull Randy from the table after his allotted time. In fact, excited by Randy's five-night winning streak, Dave was encouraging Randy to keep going and to bet bigger. Randy lost everything except his plane ticket home. He flew out that morning.

In his mind, T.J. Jergenson was truly unstoppable, and in a lot of other people's minds, also. At this point, the only cowboy who had a chance to beat him for the title was Wiley Paz, and that in itself was a long shot. As he learned from the press, if he rode his bull that night, he would have the record for the most consecutive bulls ridden at one National Finals. This record was set, back in '79 by then World Champion, Scotty Redwood. T.J. also learned that if he rode all ten bulls at the Finals, he would be the first ever to do so.

He saw Scotty that day at a restaurant. Their eyes met, but Scotty looked away, immediately. It made T.J. wonder if Scotty would ever shake his hand and congratulate him after he won the Gold Buckle.

T.J. broke the record that night for riding the most consecutive. He only won a fourth, but breaking a world record was a major personal triumph for T.J. – an achievement that was so far beyond his goals that he had never even thought about it until this day. The media hounded him for hours after the rodeo and he enjoyed it. He was growing to be very comfortable with the cameras and microphones, memorizing the best answers, typifying the modest yet determined cowboy from Enid, Oklahoma. And, for the first time in his life, some of the girls didn't just kind of like him, but *all* of the girls *really* liked him.

Wiley, while riding excellently, was riding in T.J.'s shadow. He had won a fifth that night, a mere two points below T.J.'s score. Satisfied that he had done all that he could do, and determined to keep doing the same, he went to his room and went to bed.

It was two in the morning when T.J. finished talking to fans and reporters. He had sorted through all the girls, and culled out the best looking buckle-bunny in the herd. As the two of them strolled down the hallway past the secretary's office, he stopped and looked over the draw sheet, just to see which bull he would be riding tomorrow night. He wished he hadn't, for he cringed when he saw #000, Genghis Khan, next to his name.

T.J. telephoned Randy Corey at home at about ten o'clock that morning, to tell him the news and solicit some advice. Randy advised him not to get on. He tried to call Shot Palmer, but could not reach him anywhere. He met with Wiley and Dave for lunch in the cafe downstairs at noon. The two were already seated when T.J. joined them. Wiley already knew.

"Hey, guys," greeted T.J.

"Sit down, T.J.," welcomed Dave. "Saved ya a seat."

"How ya doin'?" asked Wiley.

"Oh, pretty good," T.J. returned, "I guess."

"Did ya see who ya drew?" Wiley inquired.

"Yeah, I did."

"Who'd ya draw?" asked Dave.

The boys were interrupted by the waitress. "May I take your orders?"

Dave looked up at her. She looked like a seasoned veteran, with a sense of humor. He figured her to have been a showgirl, or a stripper, in her younger days. "You work here?" he asked.

"No, honey," she replied sarcastically. "This apron and nametag are the latest fashion. I wear them everywhere."

He read her nametag. "Well, Liz, they look very nice on you," he complimented. "Yer *stylin'*, girl!"

"Thank you," she said politely, but not sincerely, before she got on with the business at hand. "Our special today is the chicken-fried steak, and we have the buffet for only four-ninety-five."

"What's special about it?" asked Dave.

She looked at him quizzically.

"What's so special about the special?" he repeated.

"It's just the special of the day," she explained.

"But why is it special? I mean, is it cheaper than usual today?"

"Well, no...It's just...special."

The boys looked at her, saying nothing.

"Every day," she expounded, "we have a different special...today, it's chicken-fried steak."

"Sold," announced Wiley as he slapped the table. "Bring me a special!...and a Coke!"

"You're a sweetheart," Liz commented as she wrote down his order. "Next?"

"You serve breakfast?" asked Dave.

"Twenty-four hours a day," obliged Liz.

"Bring me...eggs!"

Her pen stopped and she looked up from her pad. When he neglected to expand on that order she reiterated, "Eggs?"

"Eggs!"

Not knowing whether her customer was a backwoods country hick who seldom gets to town or a genuine smart ass, she asked, "How would you like your eggs cooked?"

"Boy, that'd be great!" Dave replied jovially, much to the amusement of his friends. "Nah, just funnin' with ya! Over easy, side a' ham, white toast, coffee."

She scribbled it onto her pad and commented dryly, "Very funny...And you, hon."

"Just coffee fer me," requested T.J. "I ain't very hungry today."

"O.K.," she said cheerfully, as she swiped up the menus, "I'll have that for you in just a few minutes."

"We'll be timin' ya!" Dave warned, just as cheerfully as she hurried away. "She's a good ol' girl."

"So." Wiley took a sip of his water and asked T.J., "Whatcha gonna do?"

"Do about what?" T.J. came back.

"You gonna git on him?"

"I'm plannin' on it," T.J. answered weakly.

"Git on who?" Dave wanted to know.

T.J. sighed, and looked at the table.

"Huh?" urged Dave as he nudged T.J. in the chest.

T.J. reluctantly answered, "Genghis Khan."

"Oh, no!" Dave exclaimed. "You ain't gittin' on *that* bull!"

"Yes," T.J. calmly stated, "I am."

"The hell you are," argued Dave. "He's already killed one best friend – he ain't gonna kill another!"

"I ain't gonna argue with ya, Dave," contested T.J.

"Good!" agreed Dave. "I'm glad we settled that...You ain't really gonna git on him, are ya?"

"Dave, I don't have a choice," explained T.J.

"You do too have a choice," challenged Dave. "You can choose to *live!*"

"Listen," T.J. calmly established, "if ya turn out a bull at the N.F.R., they won't let ya get on yer remaining bulls. That's the *rules!*"

Dave pounded his fist on the table. "Screw the rules!...Is that really a rule?"

"Yes!" T.J. assured him. "To get on my last three bulls, I *gotta* get on Genghis."

Dave sat back in his chair and folded his arms, thinking hard. "You can get a doctor's release!"

"I'm perfectly healthy!" T.J. disputed. "Everybody knows it!"

Dave searched for a counterpoint.

Wiley offered a suggestion. "I know whatcha could do..."

By the manner in which Wiley spoke, and from the look on his face, T.J. sensed that his buddy had been thinking about his dilemma for quite some time.

"You could sit down on him – you don't even hafta take a wrap – nod yer head and hang on to the chute."

"Yeah!" beamed Dave. "Good thinkin', Wiley!"

"I ain't real sure that'd be legal," considered T.J.

"I already looked in the rule book," Wiley reported, "and there ain't nothin' in there says ya can't. And you wouldn't be turnin' him out."

"Then it's settled," proclaimed Dave. "You'll just sit on 'im, call for 'im, and step off on the chute."

"Now, wait a minute!" T.J. stopped him. "*I'm* the one who decides this stuff. I'm the one who drew 'im."

"I know," Dave said apologetically. "I just wanna help ya make the right decision. I just wanna keep ya alive...so ya gonna do it?"

T.J. thought for a moment. "I dunno."

"How can there even be a question about it?" Dave asked dumbfounded. "You know what that bull can do. You've seen it!"

T.J. leaned forward and rested his elbows on the table. "Guys," he explained, "I thought about this all night long. And I thought about it both ways. I've considered not gittin' on. But, to tell you the truth, I wanna spur holes in his sides. I wanna ride 'im...for Bennett...for me...and I know I can."

Wiley had nothing to add to that statement, and Dave could not find the words to argue the point, so he didn't.

After lunch, T.J. said goodbye to the boys and drove out to the airport to pick up his parents and his aunt and uncle. The afternoon flew by as he showed them the sights of the town, played some slot machines, got them checked into their rooms, and then went down to the hotel lounge. T.J. never revealed to them that he had drawn up on the bull that killed Bennett McKinney, but it stayed on his mind all day. His mother noticed that he seemed a little quiet and distracted, which, when she thought about it, was the normal way to act, given the pressures of riding bulls at the National Finals.

He excused himself early and drove out to the coliseum a good two hours before the night's opening ceremonies. He walked around the back pens. The bucking horses and bulls rested peacefully in their pens, but he saw no sign of Genghis Khan. Maybe the bull had been injured or was sick, T.J. thought. If so, he could instead get on the first re-ride bull. His heart felt hopeful relief as he hurried to the drawsheet on the office wall. Genghis' name had not been crossed off of the list. T.J. tried to act nonchalant when he asked the secretary if she knew of any change in the draw. As far as she knew, and she would be the first to know, there were no changes. Perhaps he had just overlooked the bull – no way. He went back to the pens and rechecked anyway. Genghis Khan was definitely not here.

A stock handler entered through the outside door. T.J. stopped him and asked where Genghis was.

"Right here," said the man as he opened up the door and pointed at a semi-truck and trailer.

T.J. went outside, and through the slats of the trailer, he saw Genghis' evil eye already staring him down.

A chill ran down T.J.'s spine as the man explained, "They gotta keep him alone at all times. He likes to fight with the other bulls, and he's a bad..."

"I know," interrupted T.J.

Of course. How could he have forgotten about that?

He walked over to the locker room, where he sat alone, and thought. He thought about the old days, when bullriding had been just fun, plain and simple. Back when the pressures of riding bulls hadn't started until the bulls were in the chutes, and had ended at the end of the ride, win or lose. These days, the pressure was a constant companion – when he ate, went to sleep, when he woke up. It was always with him, and it was a far greater pressure. He thought about Bennett and the days when the two of them had ridden solely for the love of riding bulls. When he hadn't minded riding with a hangover, and the rodeo dance had been just as important as the rodeo. A wistful smile spread across T.J.'s face as he remembered the laughter. He did not remember what the laughter had been about, but it had been there. It had always been there.

Four hours later T.J.'s bullrope hung on the fence as he heated the rosin between his handhold and his glove. Wiley Paz stood beside him, doing the same. Wiley had drawn a tall black bull named Cobra, with upturned horns and a reputation for being hard to ride. The load on Wiley's shoulders seemed small compared to what T.J. must be going through.

Dave Whitney snuck up and jabbed Wiley in the ribs with a thumb. "You ready to rumble?"

"Damn right I am!" proclaimed Wiley.

"That's what I like to hear!" Dave celebrated. His demeanor sobered when he looked at T.J. and quietly asked, "How you doin', T.J.?"

T.J. looked up from his bullrope and answered, "Doin' alright."

"You gonna git on?"

Nodding his head, T.J. replied, "Yeah."

"Well, I know yer gonna git on," conceded Dave, "but are ya gonna hang on to the chute, like we talked about this mornin'?"

T.J. looked Dave in the eye and clarified, "No."

That was the answer that Dave was dreading. "You sure that's what you wanna do?" he checked.

Again T.J. nodded his head.

"Well, if that's the way it's gotta be," said Dave as he reached up and squeezed T.J. at the collar, "then I'm behind ya all the way... You sure you wouldn't rather..."

"No, I wouldn't!" T.J. interrupted.

"O.K.," agreed Dave, as he backed up a step. "I'm gonna go get a beer. I'll be back before the bullridin' to pull yer ropes."

He had time for a couple of beers before the start of the barrel racing signaled that he had better get back to the boys. When he returned to the chutes, the bulls were being loaded and T.J. and Wiley were stretching, warming up and staying loose.

Genghis Khan, being the last bull to be bucked tonight, would not even be unloaded from the truck until all of the other bulls were up the alley and secure in their chutes.

There was a flurry of activity behind the bucking chutes as the stock handlers loaded the chutes, flankmen hung the flankropes around their bulls and the bullriders, along with their helpers, set their bullropes.

As T.J. buckled his spurs snugly to his boots, Dave approached him. "Good luck, T.J.," he said.

T.J. looked up. "Thank you, Dave," he said as he reached up to shake his hand. "Hey... when this is all over tonight, let's drink some beer together."

Dave smiled as he shook T.J.'s hand. "That sure sounds good to me, ol' buddy."

The last barrel racer whisked through the out gate and the clown rolled his big red padded barrel into the arena, as thousands of excited fans anxiously awaited the climax of the night's performance.

As the announcer babbled melodramatically, T.J. tucked his chin and clenched his arm and fist and spun in a circle as he threw his free hand over his head, riding Genghis Khan in his mind, through ducks and dives, twists and spins, and every dirty trick imaginable. As he did so, he told himself out loud, "Lift! Charge! Hustle! Feet! Feet!" Then he slowed his system down and began to take long relaxing breaths. He reminded himself not to tilt too far out over Genghis' head, and invite a horn to the face. With that, he hopped up on the platform behind the chutes to watch some of the bullrides.

Wiley came over and gave him a supportive pat on the back. "Show 'em who the Champ is," he encouraged.

T.J. echoed the sentiment back to Wiley with a single determined nod.

Five bullriders, one by one, mustered up the expanse of their courage and determination, and for eight long seconds, each of them put forth as much effort as physically and mentally possible to stay aboard the beasts who were expending as much effort to throw them off. Two of the five were successful.

"My bull's in," Wiley announced. He hurried to the fence where he gathered up his bullrope and, with T.J. and Dave following closely, met Cobra at the last bucking chute. He climbed up and over the bull and lowered the loop of his rope, with his bells fastened to it, down the right side of the bull. Dave was already on the other side with his hook. He reached it under the bull's belly and pulled the loop to himself, then handed it through the rails back up to Wiley. Wiley fed the tail of his rope through the loop, and let the loop slide back down below Cobra's black belly. He then snugged up the rope, and tied it off.

As Wiley hopped to the ground, T.J. heard the rattle of the overhead door of a cattle trailer being slid open. He looked to the outside door in time to see his abhorrent opponent amble down the unloading chute, into the building. Snorting and waving his horns at any human that neared the fence, Genghis Khan appeared alert and ready for a fight. He held his vile head high, and scanned the surroundings as he trod down the alley way. When the red tint within the darkness of his eyes spied the tall cowboy with the lump in his throat, he stopped, and focused on the prey.

T.J. felt uneasy, and Wiley and Dave felt uneasy for him. They said nothing as Genghis took his place in the narrow alley leading to the chutes, never taking his wicked eyes off of T.J.

"Shall we put your rope on him?" asked Wiley.

"Not yet," said T.J. "Let's wait 'til he's in the chute."

Again, Dave appealed to T.J.'s better senses, "You don't hafta do this, ya know."

T.J. said nothing.

Dave searched for words of expression in the dirt at his feet. He wanted to be able to support T.J. on this ride, but he really, really did not want him to go through with it. He pushed the dirt from the toe of one boot to the other. Nothing was there but more dirt. "Whatever you decide," he said as he walked away.

T.J.'s throat became rough and dry as fear and hate filled the goosebumps on his arms and lit a fire in his soul. His face grew pale and his eyes became bloodshot as he glared back at the blood-red murderous brute that had haunted his sleep ever since that mind-chilling night in Houston. He walked up to the fence separating himself from the bull and proclaimed, "Yer ass is mine, tonight, you son of..."

Genghis lashed a horn at T.J.'s midsection but was stopped by the iron fence. T.J. backed up.

A hand touched the back of his shoulder and startled him. He jumped slightly and whirled around.

Sonny Joe Barker pardoned, "I didn't mean to scare ya, T.J."

T.J. looked relieved, but said nothing.

"I just wanted to tell ya," continued Sonny, "I know what you must be goin' through, and I feel responsible," and stopping just short of an apology, added, "But that's rodeo."

That's rodeo. The man who owned the animal who killed T.J.'s best friend was still making money on the very animal. Still taking chances on other people's lives. But he was right. That was rodeo. T.J. embraced Sonny Joe's right hand with his own. He never uttered a word, but his eyes responded: it's a rough life, and that's rodeo.

A slide gate was pulled open in front of Genghis Khan, and he barged through, into his own chute.

As Sonny Joe set out to hang the soft cotton rope around Genghis' hips and snug it to his flanks, T.J. gathered his bullrope from the fence. Dave Whitney walked with T.J., saying nothing. T.J. climbed up the outside of the chute and dangled his bells down the right side of the bull. Genghis had already started his psyching out process of rocking from side to side as he bellowed forth a low intimidating growl.

Dave climbed over the chute, and hopped down to the arena floor. Reaching under Genghis' belly with his hook, he pulled the loop of T.J.'s rope to himself before the bull had a chance to rake it from his hands with his back hooves. He then handed the hook up to T.J., who extended it down along the left side of the bull, seizing the loop and lifting it up to himself. He straddled above and back a ways, away from Genghis' horns, careful not to let the bull snag his rope from his hands, like he had the last time, as he snugged the bullrope around his belly. Even though Genghis was rattling both the slide-gate and the chute gate, so far, everything had gone well.

From the next chute ahead, Wiley Paz yelled back, "Dave, there's one more, before me!"

"I'm there!" reported Dave, and he jumped up on Wiley's chute gate.

As Wiley warmed up his rope, T.J. attempted to put his own upcoming battle out of his mind, for the moment, and support his friend and partner.

"Ride, Wiley!" was all he could think of saying.

The bullrider before Wiley called for his bull, went about three seconds, and was catapulted off the back end of the bull.

Dave pulled Wiley's rope tight and got out of the way. T.J. watched as Wiley slid to his rope, nodded and rode the trashy Cobra bull with skillful ease.

When Wiley bailed off and tipped his hat to the thunderous applause, T.J. had neither the time nor the inclination to be happy for his friend, for the moment was there. It was win or lose, life or death time.

T.J. pulled his glove onto his riding hand, made a fist and growled at Genghis Khan as he bared his teeth and punched himself one time in the chest. For a split second the image of Bennett McKinney lying dead on the arena floor flashed through T.J.'s mind. He blinked, shook his head and took two deep breaths.

This was the time when Sonny Joe, at the flank, usually told the bullriders to be as quick as possible in the chute with this bull, but he knew that T.J. needed no warning. "Ride smart," was his advice, "and get off runnin'."

T.J. crawled over the chute and looked down on Genghis.

Dave carefully climbed up the outside of the gate to pull his rope. He whispered, "Don't touch him with yer spurs 'til ya nod yer head."

As T.J. lowered his body toward the bull and grabbed the tail of his rope to hand to Dave, again he saw Bennett dead on the floor.

Suddenly Genghis leapt into the air and tossed his head back, waving his horns inches in front of T.J.'s face. He felt a steadying hand against his chest, and another on his back. He looked to his side. Scotty Redwood held him firmly. "Ride, Champ!" he urged.

He handed the tail of his bullrope to Dave, and stuck his gloved hand into the handhold. "Pull." Dave swiftly but smoothly pulled the rope snugly around the bull's belly, until T.J. indicated, "That's good." As T.J., still straddling the wallowing bull with support of the chute rails, laid the rope across the palm of his hand and handhold, he again saw Bennett, his lifeless body lying out flat in the dirt, eyes open, blood trickling from his nose and mouth. T.J. wrapped the rope around the back of his hand and lay it across his palm again. He squeezed the rope and quickly cocked his thumb over his forefinger. He nodded his head and jumped to the bullrope.

As the gate latch tripped, Genghis thrust his mighty head against the gate, slinging it wide open, and sending the gateman behind it plowing into the dirt on his back, three bucking chutes away.

Genghis followed the end of the gate around and bore down on the gateman, the way he had borne down on Bennett McKinney nearly four years ago. The gateman rolled to his knees and clambered up the chute gate, making it just in time with the help of Genghis' right horn to the seat of his blue jeans. With no more distractions in the arena, the bull focused his attention to his rider. Waving his horns inches from T.J.'s face, Genghis bucked along the fence line, attempting to scrape him off against the steel panels. With his right knee banging against the panels, T.J. grunted as he furiously began spurring the bull in the ribs with his left foot. Trying to hook T.J.'s leg with his horn, Genghis tossed his head to the left, and, fervently leaping and twisting, followed around with his back end. As T.J. hoisted his leg to slam a spur back into the bull's rib cage, he felt a horn crack against the bone just below his kneecap. He left his spur against Genghis' left ribs and chopped at him from the right side, provoking the bull to sling his horns and spin to the other direction.

The crowd began to rise as the long tall cowboy sat in the middle and stuck like glue to the infamous and treacherous Genghis Khan.

Suddenly Genghis planted his front hooves firmly in the ground and shoved back as he chucked his head in the air. T.J. found himself being bowed over the bull's head. He dug in with his spurs and pushed away with his riding arm. He heard the dull thud of his own cheekbone as it collided with Genghis' horn directly below the right eye. T.J. bounced back to the middle of the bull's back, and continued riding as his blood flew freely and splattered where it might.

The dull buzz in T.J.'s throbbing head was interrupted by the loud buzz of the eight second buzzer. Not seeing the bullfighter, he assumed that he was behind them somewhere. T.J. knew that if he just bailed off, that the bull would swap ends and mow him over. He plucked his cowboy hat from his head and tossed it in front of Genghis' face. As the bull chased down the hat and mauled it into the ground, T.J. swung a long leg over and hit the ground running. When he was safely perched on top of the fence, he exclaimed "Yes!" and pointed at the bull defiantly with both hands.

When T.J. awoke the next morning, he was unable to open his right eye. He lay there for a time, thinking about the night before. He felt a shallow pride in riding a bull that had only been ridden once before, but he expected so much more. He 'got even' with the bull that had killed his best friend. Got even? Not even close. Bennett was just as dead, and T.J. had won a third in the round. Genghis Khan hadn't even seemed that hard to ride. Miserable, yes. Definitely no fun. Weighed against the degree of nervousness and anxiety he had had to weather ever since he'd discovered that Genghis would be his opponent, the whole thing had turned out to be dismally anticlimactic.

Coming into the finals, T.J. had told himself that he would not drink or party until he had actually strapped on his World Championship Gold Buckle, but last night he'd gone out and had a few beers with Dave. It hadn't been quite like old times, but, after all, what was? They'd played blackjack for a while, and then gone to the rodeo dance. Every shiny little buckle-bunny who would walk up and introduce herself to T.J., T.J. would introduce to Dave, until Dave had hooked up with one to his liking, and while Dave had danced and romanced the night away, T.J. had come on back to the room.

He rolled to his side and sat up at the edge of the bed. His left leg was swollen and bruised from when Genghis had smacked him just below the kneecap. Just hanging it off the edge of the bed made it throb. He'd put ice on it a little later. That'd make it better. Or was it heat? One or the other. He stood up and limped into the bathroom. He flipped on the light and looked into the mirror at his swollen cheek, and he touched the stitches that the doctor had sewn his skin together with last night. He hoped that by the night's performance he would be able to open his eye. Maybe some ice would bring the swelling down. Or heat.

He would find out which this afternoon. He had an appointment at two with his sports-medicine doctor. T.J. trusted these guys. A regular doctor would just tell him not to ride. A sports-medicine doctor looked at it more from the athlete's point of view. He would work with T.J. and help him to where he could be as physically able to ride as possible, under the circumstances.

Before that, he was scheduled for lunch with his parents, aunt and uncle, and Dave and Wiley.

After that, he had an autograph session at four-thirty, and other than that, his only plans were to ride another bull that night.

By the time the bullriding came around, T.J.'s limp in his left knee was much less noticeable and the swelling in his right eye had gone down enough that he could see rather well. He drew a good bull that he had ridden the spring before at Cherokee, Iowa. He rode well, despite his injuries, and won a second place and could not have been happier, for it was his little buddy and traveling partner, Wiley Paz, who won top honors for the second time.

When Wiley completed his victory lap for the crowd, T.J. was waiting at the out gate. Wiley pulled the paint mare to a whoa and, throwing his leg over her neck, hopped off in bullrider fashion. T.J. grabbed his hand to shake and then threw his arm across the little guy's shoulder.

"Beautiful ride!" he acclaimed.

"Thanks, T.J.," Wiley hailed back. "You too!"

Before the reporters reached them, T.J. had time to add, "One more time, Buddy! Tenth round is tomorrow night!"

Suddenly, the boys were looking at the ends of a half-dozen or so microphones.

"Wiley Paz," began one reporter, "Though unofficial, our figures tell us that you can win the World Championship Buckle if you ride and place tomorrow night and if T.J. Jergenson bucks off. Any comment?"

Wiley looked at the mikes as if they were eyes gathered around to stare at him. He cleared his throat and said, "Uh, I dunno. I never tried to figure it out. I just ride the best I can every time. The rest of it is outta my control."

"Knowing what this World Championship would mean to you, Wiley, and knowing that you are indeed this close, do you wish any bad luck on T.J.?"

Wiley looked up at T.J. "No way," he answered automatically. "I been haulin' with T.J. all year. He took me under his wing and helped me ride tough and taught me how to rodeo. I prob'ly wouldn't even be here if it wasn't for T.J. He's ridin' awesome and I look up to T.J. and he deserves to be the Champ, 'cause he's the best."

The lump in T.J.'s throat swelled with gratitude.

One of them held a mike up to his face. "For you, T.J., it's practically in the bag. Tell us how you feel."

"I uh...I don't know what to say," he stammered, "it's been a long time comin'...a damn long time."

"Is there an added pressure, knowing that all you have to do is ride your bull to win?"

"I s'pose normally there is," T.J. theorized, "but I can ride under pressure. I proved that, all week. That's somethin' that Wiley taught me; just ride, and the outcome'll take care of itself."

"The two of you traveled together all year. Now you are each other's biggest threat. Tell the truth; is there an animosity between you?"

"None at all," T.J. asserted. "We're here because of each other. If I wasn't gonna win this, I'd want Wiley to."

After a few more minutes of needling, T.J. was finally able to break off from the reporters. All their questions about the rivalry between him and Wiley had made him feel uncomfortable, especially with Wiley present.

As he brushed the arena sand off of his gear before putting it away in his gear bag, he began to think about the next night. In an hour or so, the next night's draw would be posted. He was almost certain that fate would allow him to be matched with the bull that was meant for him to ride. The initials for Big Mac, the bull who has never been ridden, are sure to be next to T.J.'s name, for it was meant to be. It was to be the destiny for the two of them, just like they'd decided on that trip north, nearly four years previously.

Bennett reached over and squeezed T.J.'s shoulder, and with a shake that sent T.J.'s head teetering from side to side, said, "Yeah, and it'll be you and me to the end...I got plans for you and me, Buddy. We're goin' to the National Finals and one of us is gonna win it. It may not be this year and it may not be next year, but before we're through – we're goin'..." Bennett smiled and held out his fist to T.J., and proclaimed, "To the National Finals" and taking his cue, T.J. gave Bennett's fist a brotherly punch and repeated, "To the National Finals."

Avoiding the reporters, T.J. carried his gear bag outside and threw it in the van. He climbed in and played the radio for a while, but didn't listen to the songs. After ten minutes or so, his restless feet took him back to the building. As he approached the door, Wiley was just coming out with his gear bag slung over his shoulder.

"What's goin' on?" smiled T.J.

"Thought they'd never git off my back," said Wiley of the reporters.

T.J. chuckled, "It's hell when ya get famous. You gonna hang around and look at the draw?"

With a confident grin, Wiley responded, "Hell, no. Whatever we draw, we're just gonna ride the shit out of 'em. Right?"

T.J. cocked his head slightly. "Yeah," he agreed, "but I think I'll hang around, anyway."

"You think yer gonna draw Big Mac?" asked Wiley.

"I can feel it in my bones," T.J. asserted.

"Well," Wiley didn't want to call 'bullshit', and wasn't sure if 'good luck' was in order, so he simply said, "See ya tomorrow!"

T.J. went inside and strolled up the corridor toward the rodeo office, stopping and visiting with several friends, fellow contestants and well wishers. By the time he got to the office, nearly an hour had passed. There was no line at the payoff desk, so he approached the secretary. "Howdy, I guess you got a check for me."

"T.J.," she smiled, "I sure do. I hear you made another real nice ride." She ripped his already filled-out and signed check from the large bank book on her desk and handed it to him. "Second place – ninth round – congratulations. And good luck."

"Thanks," T.J. returned. "Have they drawed bulls yet?"

"Should be anytime now, T.J.," she said. "I'll post it on the wall just as soon as it's available to me."

He thanked her again, and went out in the hall.

There were plenty of people out there, talking about today and tomorrow, but T.J. strayed away from any conversation. He just leaned against the wall, and thought about Bennett, and Big Mac.

When she brought out the draw sheet and tacked it to the wall, T.J. was the first to look it over. His forefinger slid down the names of the other bullriders and stopped at his name. On the right side of the sheet, directly across from his name, T.J. was caught by surprise to see exactly what he expected to see – BM – *Big Mac*. He jumped back on his heels. He had the urge to burst out with elation, so, after double-checking the list, that's what he did. His "Woooooo-hooo!" echoed off walls and ceilings all the way around the coliseum. "Yeah! Yeah! Yeah!" People stood back and cautiously smiled and he let go with another cry for joy and hopped around in a circle. "I got 'im, boys! I got 'im!" He ran down the hallway, jumping and swinging his fists, still yelling at the top of his lungs. He burst through the door and let the Thomas and Mack parking lot hear his joyous exhilaration. He jumped in the van, cranked it up, shut off the radio, slapped the dash, turned on the lights, stuck it in gear, dropped the clutch, and killed the engine, trying to burn rubber.

"I gotta tell somebody!" he exclaimed aloud, as he re-started the van and headed for the highway. Darting into the traffic like an irate taxi driver, he headed for the center of town. Wiley was his first thought. He might be sleeping, but that's alright. Or Dave, but there's no telling where he could be. Maw and Paw – they'll be glad to hear the news. Maw and Paw it is, he decided, and headed for the hotel. Cutting in and out of the busy Las Vegas traffic both right and left, he slowed and stopped only when the backed-up traffic left him with no other choice. The driver of a green sedan that T.J. had cut off in traffic a half block back, pulled up beside, yelled "Idiot!" and flipped him off. T.J. gave the driver a neighborly wave and yelled back, "Thank you, sir, and you have yourself a good evening!" before he tailgated off in the fast lane. When he got to his parents' hotel, he passed it up and sped on by.

They can find out in the morning. That night he wanted to be with the only one that really mattered.

He drove to the stockyards on the west end of town, pulled in and showed the night guard his pass. The stock had all been fed and most of the animals were already bedded down for the night. He crept the van in slowly, so as not to disturb them. He stopped when he arrived at the pens that held Sonny Joe Barker's Stingin' B rodeo stock, and turned off his lights and ignition. Standing in this end of the pen next to the fence, T.J. had found who he was looking for.

Big Mac stood like a living statue in the gleam of the stockyard lights, his striking figure partially erased by the shadow of his own hump, deep smooth wrinkles furrowed vertically through the loose thick hide that draped over a broad neck and shoulders. His dark eyes, not much more than slits beneath a crown of spiked ivory. His only movements were his jaw, slowly filing back and forth on his cud, and an occasional bat of the ear and swat of the tail.

For a moment T.J. just had to stare. Feelings of pride, bravery, respect, loyalty, honor, and even patriotism swept over him. He was staring at a symbol. The Brahma bull, although not indigenous to the U.S., represented to T.J. what the American bald eagle represented to the United States of America.

He grabbed his jacket from the passenger seat, stepped out of the van and put it on. Then he quietly moved toward the pen, where the bull stood in hushed repose. When he got to the fence, he stopped and whispered loudly, "Hey!"

Big Mac opened his eyes slightly and looked at T.J. but did not move.

"It's me...T.J....Guess who I drew for tomorrow night...That's right – you!" He put his hand on the fence and leaned toward the bull. "You heard me, I'm gittin' on you!...Isn't that great?" His voice broke from a whisper, "It's me an' you at the Finals, Ol' Buddy, just like we talked about."

The bull slowly swung his head T.J.'s way.

"We're goin' down in history together, Bennett. It couldn't a' turned out any better! I guess everything happens for a reason, huh?" T.J.'s face beamed and his eyes gleamed as he went on, "They'll close the show with us – the Champ against the Unridden! It's gonna be like nothin' anybody's ever seen before! They'll be showin' films of us at the Hall of Fame forever! Nothin'll compare to this, not even Freckles and Tornado!"

With a slow grunt, Big Mac lowered himself to a knee, then the other and reclined in the straw bedding below him.

T.J. also dropped to his knee. "You had it planned all along, didn't ya, Bennett? You knew!...Somehow, you knew, that night when you said we were goin' to the National Finals together...I thought you were nuts, 'til I seen you at the Bakersfield rodeo. Now everybody thinks *I'm* nuts. We'll show 'em!...Tomorrow night, Pardner, me an' you!" He sat down in the short growth of weeds by the pen. "'Member when you said I needed to quit relyin' on you so much? Ya said you might not always be there for me? I believed it when you died. I thought you'd left me for good...And, now, here you are – takin' care of yer ol' buddy again...just like the old days!...That's what tomorrow night's gonna be like – just like the old days! Only better!" He rested his weight on an elbow, and looked the big bull in the eye as he continued, "I wish Randy and Shot could be here for this...they never believed me. I told 'em aboutcha, I showed 'em yer brand...hell, they were there that night in the motel in Rapid City and seen yer tattoo!...What more proof do they need? They still don't believe that it's you!" He lay his face down on his arm and tipped his Stetson over one eye. "We're gonna show 'em all, Bennett, the whole world's gonna see this ride...

"Hey, 'member that time we were comin' back from that rodeo in Alberta and we got drunk and rolled yer pickup down that bank? You broke yer nose and I didn't even get a scratch outta that deal..."

"T.J....hey...wake up."

T.J. opened his eyes to the morning light.

"Wha'd you do, go out an' get drunk last night?"

It was Sonny Joe Barker, grinning in amusement as he nudged T.J. in the ribs with the toe of his boot.

T.J. sat up and looked around. He scratched his head, and then covered it up with his beat-up Stetson. He looked for the friend that he had fallen asleep talking to last night.

BM was at the breakfast bunk with his teammates.

"Shit," T.J. commented hoarsely as he reached up for a helping hand from Sonny Joe. "Naw, I didn't get drunk," he said as Sonny clasped his hand and pulled him up from the weeds. "Just came down to see my bull...guess I fell asleep."

Sonny looked around the ground. No empty bottles, so he must be telling the truth. "You drew Big Mac?" he asked.

"Yeah," T.J. yawned, "I did."

"I had a feelin' you might," said Sonny, as he lightly punched him on the arm. "You better cock yer hammer for this bull, son."

"My hammer's always cocked," returned T.J. "What time is it?"

"Eight-fourteen. Damn, didn't you git a little cold out here? Why didn't ya at least go sleep in the van?"

Ignoring Sonny's questions, T.J. rubbed his swollen eyes and smacked his lips. "Tastes like a buffalo shit in my mouth, and I didn't even have nothin' to drink. You want breakfast? I'm buyin'."

"I got all the stock fed," Sonny said. "Hell yeah, let's go."

Sonny took his pickup and followed T.J. to a busy little restaurant down on the strip. At breakfast, he again halfheartedly inquired as to why the hell anyone would sleep outside in the weeds when he had a perfectly good hotel room paid for. That was when, for the first time, he heard T.J.'s version of the correlation between Bennett McKinney and Big Mac. As T.J. told the whole story, Sonny tried to remain open-minded, but eventually began to wonder if T.J.'s boat had taken on too much water. He said nothing to agree or disagree, just a matter of fact "Huh," every now and then, and a "Well, I'll be damned," at the end of the story. T.J. also told him that he would rather he kept this news to himself, and Sonny agreed that this would be a good idea.

Wiley Paz lowered himself down on the coal-black back of his final bull of the National Finals Rodeo. Number 204 – Rumble Seat – was a tall, wiry Angus-Brahma cross, who boasted a seventy-eight percent buck-off rate. Wiley had seen the bull perform twice before and was very pleased to have the opportunity to tangle with him.

As Dave Whitney pulled his rope and T.J. Jergenson and the rest of the rodeo world looked on, the announcer's voice blared through the P.A. system and speakers, "Now, folks, as you probably know, Wiley Paz is currently setting second in the world standings. Two bulls stand between this young cowboy and the Championship of the World – Rumble Seat, the famous bucking bull, who, so far has thrown nearly eighty percent of his riders, and who Wiley Paz is getting ready to nod his head on any second, now, and the other bull, known as Big Mac, of the Stingin' B Rodeo Company. In order for young Wiley to win the World Championship, not only must Wiley ride Rumble Seat to the full eight seconds, but Big Mac must also throw his rider off. Keep in mind that Big Mac has got a one hundred percent buck-off record. That's right – the bull has never been ridden. But also bear in mind that his rider tonight is none other than T.J. Jergenson, ranked number one in the world standings, and has not been thrown off in the previous nine rounds here at the National Finals in Las Vegas!"

"Ride 'im, Wiley," T.J. genuinely coaxed, "You know you can do it!"

Wiley wasted no time sliding to his rope and determinedly nodding his head. Rumble Seat exploded into the arena, kicking high and whirling around to the right. Wiley bailed into the storm in perfect form, his free arm slashing through the air from front to side with each jump, his outside foot releasing and spurring, again and again, while his body never moved back off of his rope. When the bull changed directions and went into a left spin, it was as if Wiley had predicted it. He pumped over his head and began to spur with his other foot.

T.J., Dave and nearly everyone in the place were cheering so loudly that Wiley could not hear the buzzer. When he saw the bullfighter come in to the bull's head and pull him out of the spin, he jerked his wrap and bailed off, waving his hat to the crowd, as he ran to the sidelines.

"Yes! Ladies and gentlemen, this young cowboy makes it look easy! Almost *too* easy! Now, I don't want to second-guess our judges, here, but I predict that there will be a change on our leader board. An eighty-five score holds the number one spot so far. I see that one of our officials has finished tallying up his score, a forty-three on that side and our other official turns in a forty-five for a total of eighty-eight championship points and we have a new leader!

"Now, folks, one man and one bull can shatter the Gold Buckle dreams of Wiley Paz. Do you think T.J. Jergenson can ride the unridden bull, Big Mac?"

The noise level throughout the coliseum was so great that a distorted hum buzzed in Sonny Joe Barker's ears as he snugged and tied off Big Mac's flankrope. Up front, T.J. sat down on the bull's back and Sonny stroked his shoulder. "Be the first!" he yelled above the crowd. "Be the Champ!"

A look of pure exuberance glowed from deep within T.J.'s swollen dark eyes, the same look that emanated from the face of the bull that was about to carry him to his spot in rodeo history.

"Pull, Dave!" he ordered as Dave Whitney tugged on his rope, "that's good...just a little more...O.K.!"

As he took his wrap, Wiley peered up at him through the slats and touched his knee. "Stick it on him. T.J.! If yer the Champ, I'm proud to be the runner-up!"

T.J. pounded his fist around the rope. "We're gonna do it," he said as he rubbed the bull's big gray hump, "Me and Bennett, we're goin' all the way!" He slid to his rope and said to the bull as well as the gateman, "Let's go!"

The second the gate crashed open, Big Mac turned his head toward the arena and bailed high in the air. When he touched down he was in a tight left spin. Like Wiley before him, T.J. stuck like glue to this whirling flurry of unleashed energy. He pumped vigorously over his head, charged his rope and shuffled his feet, legs and hips, every time the bull snapped back to earth and fervently leapt into the air again, throwing his head high, then cocking it to the left and chasing his tail as it slung back and forth over his rump like a stock whip. With bound-less violent agility, the two danced to the music of seventeen thousand screaming rodeo fans. He could feel the glory, as it hovered above his head. He could nearly smell the roses and taste the champagne of success. He could see the Gold Buckle. Big Mac switched directions. T.J. stumbled. His hips swiveled from the rope. His right foot slid back to the flankrope. His chest bounced off of Big Mac's hump and his free hand hit a horn as he was spun like a defective boomerang and slammed into the arena dirt. The thunderous cheer became a song of chagrin as the eight second buzzer chastised his unbelieving ears.

T.J. rolled to his back. Big Mac spun around and faced him. The bullfighter was directly behind the bull, out of his sight and mind.

Big Mac charged at T.J. as he lay looking up at him, and stopped short. He snorted and waved his horns. His eyes were wide and intense as he waited for T.J. to make his move.

T.J. stared in open-mouthed incredulity. His instincts were to scramble, but he did not act upon them.

Big Mac stared back, poised as though ready to pounce on the slightest movement.

T.J.'s lips trembled. A look of shock flooded his face and hurtful astonishment filled his eyes.

Big Mac lowered his nose, tilted his head forward, and backed up a step.

T.J. continued to stare in disbelief. "It wasn't s'posed to happen this way," he whispered to himself, and then repeated to Big Mac, "It wasn't s'posed to happen this way...You fucked up, Bennett. What the hell was you thinkin'?...You...you blew it!...We were s'posed to win the world together! You son of a bitch!"

Big Mac's eyes narrowed. The fires that burned from within them suddenly died. He lifted his head nonchalantly.

"We had a deal, Bennett. We had a goal! Why did you do this to me?...Why?" Tears moistened the folds underneath T.J.'s puffy eyes. "All those miles...all those rides...everything we worked for – gone!...Well, go ahead, ya son of a bitch, run me over! Stomp on me!...Ya might as well, ya took the only thing that mattered!" His voice began to crack and his chest heaved as he closed his eyes and sobbed, "We were so close..."

Big Mac turned his head and slowly walked to the catch pen gate. "...so close..."

Chapter 25: January 1991

An eight-by-ten photograph lay next to a dirty ashtray and a few empty beer cans on the bunkhouse table. It was a picture of Bennett McKinney aboard the famous bucking bull Rapid Fire at the Cheyenne Frontier Days Rodeo several years before. Also scattered about the table were various action photos of Shot Palmer fighting bulls, an old picture of Shot, Bennett, Randy Corey, Dave Whitney, and T.J. Jergenson standing in front of Shot's old red pickup, and a studio portrait of Shot's latest ex-wife, Rachel.

Thumb-tacked to the wall by the table was a small photograph of Bennett and T.J. standing in front of a western-wear store in a snow-covered Roundup, Montana. Below that photograph, a pair of wooden crutches leaned against the wall.

An old, dirty carpet covered the creaky wooden floor of the bunkhouse. Strewn about the carpet were some rodeo magazines, some men's magazines, an outdated newspaper, some dirty paper plates and plastic silverware, and a miniature steer-head roping dummy.

In the corner by the unkempt bunk was a large open gear bag. In it and on it were a pair of hip pads, baggy jeans, a knee brace, and a pair of football cleats.

The midday winter winds whistled through the stovepipe and fanned the coals in the old pot-bellied stove on the far side of the room and the tainted windowpanes tipped back and forth in their frames.

Through the front door an enclosed porch sheltered an old roping saddle that straddled a wooden sawhorse. A pair of chaps, a cap, a straw cowboy hat, coat, and a rain slicker hung on nails above an old pair of cowboy boots and mud-caked overboots.

Outside, a dirty white flatbed pickup rumbled past the barn and came to a squeaky halt at the front of the shack. Slowly climbing out of the rig with the aid of a wooden walking cane was Shot Palmer. His old gray Stetson was as weather-worn as his face. His unkempt red hair poked out from beneath the hat. He limped into the house, where he bypassed the nails in the wall and tossed his hat and heavy work-coat on his bunk. He had been fixing fence a couple of miles west, and came in for a sandwich and a hot cup of coffee. Before he went to the refrigerator, he stopped at the table, and looked with fond memories at the picture of himself and the old gang in front of his red pickup. That picture must have been nearly ten years old. He went to the fridge and grabbed a loaf of bread, a packet of lunchmeat and some cheese. He tossed them onto the table, rinsed out a coffee cup from the sink and had filled it with steaming hot coffee when he heard the engine of another vehicle approaching. He glanced out the side window just in time to see the tail end of a white sedan but could not see who was driving. By the time Shot had hobbled to the front door, he could see his old friend Randy Corey, already out of the car and walking up to the house.

"Hey!" greeted Shot with a crooked smile. "What the hell are you doin' clear out here?"

"I came out to see ya," Randy returned with a handshake. "You ain't easy to find."

"Well, come on in outta the wind," invited Shot as he motioned Randy inside. "I'll gitcha a cup a' coffee."

Randy stepped inside and looked around. The place was a mess, just the way he'd expected it to be. "What day does your maid come in?"

"Smart ass," Shot chuckled as he punched him in the shoulder, "I missed you too."

Shot led the way, past the bunk and table, to the coffee maker and Randy noticed, "Yer walkin' purty good considerin' ya broke yer back in two places. How long ya been workin'?"

"'Bout six weeks now," Shot answered as he picked the cleanest dirty cup from the counter. "I can't ride a horse yet, but I oughta be able to by calvin' time." He handed Randy his coffee. " If I'd a' knowed I was gonna have company, I'd a' cleaned this place up."

"Yeah, sure ya would."

"How'd ya find me, Randy?" Shot asked as he pulled out a chair and sat at the table.

Randy did the same. "Called Rachel. She didn't have much good to say about you. You must a' really made her mad!"

"Aw, she's been mad ever since I married her. It's like, listen to this; I come home drunk – she gets pissed off. I come home drunk – she gets pissed off. I come home drunk – she gets pissed off! I mean, what do I have to do to *please* that woman?"

Randy sensed that Shot was not seeking advice, just someone to listen to his problems and see it his way. He listened thoughtfully.

"Here's what really did me in – this was the last straw; I go downtown for some cigarettes – by the way, I smoke now – anyway, I run into some friends, we get to drinkin', I don't make it home for three days. You would think that after three whole days, she'd be glad to see me, but no, she starts to bitchin' and raisin' hell, that's when I left her. Screw her, I tried to make it work."

Randy shook his head. "Yer never gonna change, are ya? So other than that, how are ya?"

Shot sighed and gave Randy a mournful look. "I ain't healin' near as fast as I used to. Sometimes I can't hardly stand the pain. If I ever git to where I can fight bulls again, it'll be a long time down the road. And if I can, I don't know if I'll be able to get any jobs. There's so many young hotshots comin' up. I might just stay here on this ranch." He gazed out the window. "Damn, it's been dry and windy. We don't git some snow, there ain't gonna be nothin' left in these pastures but sand...How the boys doin'?"

"Dave's takin' some time off," said Randy. "T.J. quit. I'm goin' at it alone, right now. Headin' for Rapid City."

"Rapid City," Shot smiled. "We've had some fun up there, ain't we?"

"Came to see if ya wanted to go with me."

"Aw...I better not," declined Shot. "Got too many critters to feed. Too much fence to fix."

"Yer welcome to come along if ya want to," Randy repeated.

"Thanks, but I'll pass. How'd T.J. do at the Finals?"

"Runner-up. Damn near won it. You know that BM bull that crippled ya? He almost rode him in the tenth round. I wasn't there, but Dave told me 'bout it. He said it was kinda weird. Said he slammed him down and lined him out, but wouldn't charge. Just stood there and looked at him. T.J. laid there and cussed him fer throwin' him off, and he just turned around and walked off."

"Huh," Shot responded. "That is weird."

"Yeah. That little Mexican kid, Wiley Paz, won it," said Randy as he set his cup on the table. "Well, Shot, I hate to cut this visit short, but I gotta be in Rapid this afternoon." He stood up and shook Shot's hand.

"You didn't even drink yer coffee," protested Shot.

Randy looked at the dirty, brown-stained cup and the little chunks of something floating in the coffee. "Never been much of a coffee drinker. Good to see ya again."

"You too, man," Shot said without getting up. "Come back when you can stay longer."

Randy closed the door behind him.

Shot listened as he started the car and headed down the dirt wheel-rut driveway until the noise of the engine faded away and nothing was left but the wind in the stovepipe. He sipped his coffee and stared out the window at the sparse grass laid over by the cold north-easter. If they didn't get some moisture, soon, there'd be nothing left in those pastures but sand.

Order Form

YES, I want ___ copies of *The Reincarnation of Bennett McKinney* at US $12.95 each plus US $5.00 shipping and handling per book. Canadian orders must be accompanied by a postal money order in U.S. funds. Please allow up to 15 days for delivery.

❑ My check or money order for $_____ is enclosed.

❑ Please charge my: _ Visa _ Master Card _ Discover

Name: _____

Address _____

City/State/ZIP _____

Phone _____ Fax _____

E-Mail _____

Credit Card # _____

Expiration Date _____

Signature _____

Please make checks payable to **Nonetheless Press**.
Send orders to: Nonetheless Press
20332 W. 98th St.
Lenexa, KS 66220-2650 USA
Or fax your credit card order to: (913) 393-3245

Order Form

YES, I want ___ copies of *The Reincarnation of Bennett McKinney* at US $12.95 each plus US $5.00 shipping and handling per book. Canadian orders must be accompanied by a postal money order in U.S. funds. Please allow up to 15 days for delivery.

❏ My check or money order for $_____ is enclosed.

❏ Please charge my: _ Visa _ Master Card _ Discover

Name: _____

Address _____

City/State/ZIP _____

Phone _____ Fax _____

E-Mail _____

Credit Card # _____

Expiration Date _____

Signature _____

NONE THE LESS PRESS

Please make checks payable to **Nonetheless Press**.
Send orders to: Nonetheless Press
20332 W. 98th St.
Lenexa, KS 66220-2650 USA
Or fax your credit card order to: (913) 393-3245